HOMEPORT JOURNALS

JOURNALS

A PROVINCETOWN FANTASIA

A.C. BURCH

THE
HOMEPORT
JOURNALS

A PROVINCETOWN FANTASIA

A.C. BURCH

WILDE CITY PRESS

WILDE CITY PRESS

www.wildecity.com

The Homeport Journals © 2015 A.C. Burch
Published in the US and Australia by Wilde City Press 2015

Published by Wilde City Press

ISBN: 978-1-925313-03-1

Cover Art © 2015 Wilde City Press
Map by Madeline Sorel

For Alex

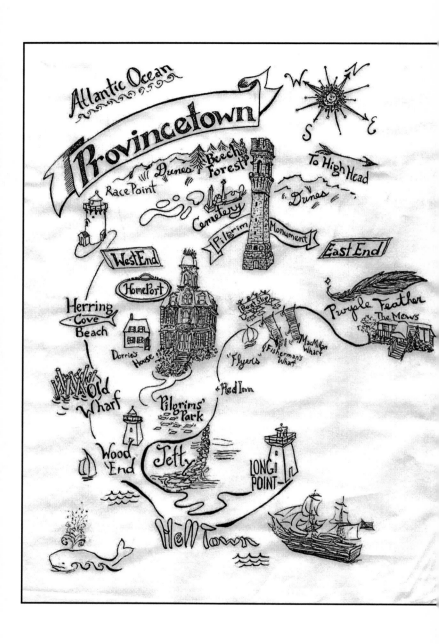

Provincetown People have always resisted change. They fear the threat of the unknown lest their town become something else. Yet it has remained uniquely itself in the midst of perpetual modification.

Mary Heaton Vorse, Time and the Town

CHAPTER 1
KISMET

November 13ᵗʰ, 2008 – Provincetown

You never really know a place unless you live there. Until last night, Provincetown was a state of mind—a place that spoke to my heart. Now I'm actually here, I'm not so sure....

Setting down his pen, the young man cradles a cup of hot chocolate, then scans the near-empty café. His light blue eyes reveal exhaustion and disillusion. When the theme from *Mission: Impossible* shatters the midmorning stillness, he snaps shut a leather-bound journal and rejects the call.

Right on schedule. Brandon's never up before eleven after a night of party'n play. What could he think we have to say to each other?

Offshore, a nor'easter closes in on the back beach. Ominous clouds darken the dunes of East Harbor, then the East End. Raw, heavy mist bathes trees and buildings in a prelude to the pelting rain to come. As the storm moves ashore, Long Point recedes into a murky, gray infinity.

When the phone rings a second time, the young man mutes it, eyes the screen until the name fades, then stares out at Commercial Street in search of distraction. There isn't much to be found. Provincetown has entered its dormant phase. Worn, tawdry, and forlorn, the scene before him shows no trace of the vibrant mecca that captured his imagination just weeks before. It had been Carnival then; thousands of revelers, raucous laughter, outrageous costumes, and general goodwill had crowded Commercial Street in a euphoric celebration of summer, sun, and sex.

In the muted November light, the bleak streetscape retains few traces of those frenetic days. Cockeyed, scruffy buildings with peeling paint, faded fliers tacked to telephone poles—their events long forgotten—boarded windows with hastily scrawled thanks for "another great season," all contribute to a petulant air, as if the town begrudged those who decamped at summer's end.

The only person in sight, a stooped old woman with a large paper bag in each arm, shuffles along the sidewalk. She's tiny, even elfin. Her face is furrowed; her back hunched under a thick wool coat laden with damp. When the downpour starts, she seeks refuge in the café. As she tugs the door open, a gust of wind rips it from her grasp. Before the young man can come to her aid, the bags give way. Cans, bottles, and packages roll down the steps and into the street.

"Goddamn son's a bitches," she mutters, hands on hips.

When he sprints past her to save a large can of beef stew from an oncoming car, she yells into the quickening gale, her shrill voice rising high above the wind.

"Thanks, dahlin'. You're my knight in shinin' ahmah."

While her knight scavenges the flooding gutter, she seats herself at his table. Her dark, penetrating eyes never leave him, watching his every move with amusement and subtle assessment. By the time he's salvaged everything in a pile by the door, she's ensconced like royalty, greedily downing his hot chocolate.

"Hey kid, your phone's lightin' up. Oops, you missed the call—some Brandon fellow. "

Incredulous, the young man stares at her, his blond hair plastered to his head, his sopping clothes glued to his pale skin. Her eyes twinkle, and the corner of her mouth starts to curl as if she's losing the battle to suppress a smile.

"I didn't answer, in case he was a trick. Didn't want him thinkin' your grandmother was nosin' 'round your love life."

She chuckles lasciviously, then extends a gnarled hand.

"He'll call back, no doubt. Dorrie Machado."

"Marcus Nugent," he responds, dazed by a dose of frigid rainwater, the loss of his hot chocolate, and a strong sense of déjà vu.

"Well, Marcus Nugent, thank you for savin' those goddamn groceries. Most folks wouldn't do such a good turn for an old lady they didn't know from Eve. Somebody brung you up right, that's for damn sure."

Marc studies her wrinkled face. She's eighty if a day, with close-cropped white hair, a little flap of skin under the chin, and leathery, wind-burned skin. There's something mischievous in this woman's bearing—a smug sense of knowing—as if she's watching an opening act with full awareness of the final outcome.

"You're new here, Marcus. I ain't seen you 'round."

"Just got here early this morning. Please call me Marc. I've never liked Marcus. It sounds too much like a character from ancient Rome."

"If that's what you want, that's what you'll get. Now tell me, Marc. Are you running from somethin', or did you come here to find love?"

"Excuse me?"

"You heard me. Don't go gettin' all bitchy-queenie with me. I'm askin' are you runnin' or searchin'? There's only two things that bring you boys to town this time of year. I know that much after more than eighty years of livin'."

"I'm not sure that's any of your business."

"Ha. Ha. Ha."

Dorrie's brittle cackle fills the room, coaxing a grin from the man behind the counter as well as two men at an adjacent table who've been surreptitiously studying Marc's physique, his sodden clothing having left little to the imagination.

"If you're gonna live in this town, dahlin', everybody's gonna know your business whether you want them to or not. There are busybodies at every corner, just waitin' to get the goods on you, and not all of them are old bags like me."

Dorrie glares at the two interlopers to drive her point home.

"Better get used to that sorta bullshit from the get-go!"

As the two men rapidly split a newspaper between them and dive for cover behind its pages, the counterman produces a large cardboard box for the groceries. A wide, self-satisfied smile softens Dorrie's rough-hewn features, showing decades of cigarette stain. Marc smiles back despite himself.

"You got a cah?" she asks, looking up at him with a slight tilt of her head, like an inquisitive fowl.

"Yes."

"A place to live?"

"Not yet."

"Tell you what. You get me anotha one of these here," Dorrie says, holding up his empty cup, "and a ride home, and I'll do somethin' 'bout that."

His phone vibrates. Dorrie nods in satisfaction.

"Ah! Brandon! Him again. I figured as much. You're a runnah!"

Marc shrugs, orders two hot chocolates, and throws in two pieces of chocolate cake for good measure.

The rain stops as suddenly as it had begun.

Come on-a My House

"Just a sec, dahlin'. I gotta have me a smoke."

Dorrie turns her back to the wind, lighting up with all the skill of a fisherman in a squall.

"Those are lousy for you."

"Oh, I don't pay no never mind. I already know how I'm gonna die, and it ain't from this shit."

When she finishes, she tosses the butt on the sidewalk, then crushes it with her foot.

"Where to?" Marc asks.

Dorrie points a crooked finger toward the center of town.

"The West End. Follow Commercial Street all the way to Pilgrims' Park."

Marc drives the deserted street past the Town Hall, the "meat rack's" empty benches puddled with rainwater, then the Boatslip, nearly as lifeless and forlorn as the gray harbor it surveys, and finally the West End parking lot, where the only car in residence is an ancient Cadillac convertible pockmarked with rust. Descending a slight hill to the Red Inn, he spies the cluster of trees bounding Pilgrims' Park.

At first, the park seems nothing more than a few benches, granite pavers, and some rustic plantings in the middle of a roundabout. When they reach the Provincetown Inn, the expanse of the moors and its granite breakwater come into view, providing one of the best vistas in town.

Dorrie points toward two large wrought iron gates supported by massive granite columns. On the right-hand column, a bronze plaque announces One Commercial Street. The left bears a matching plaque with a single word: HomePort. Someone has spray-painted an *o* over the *e*.

"Stop the goddamn car."

Dorrie's ferocious scowl is more than a match for her tone. She gets out to wipe the still-wet paint with a handkerchief.

"Idiots," she grumbles when Marc offers help. "They think they're so smart. Every year, all across town, it's the same damn thing. The *f* in Whorf's Court becomes an *e;* the second *o* in Cook Street becomes a *c*. It ain't funny to begin with, never mind when you've seen it over and over again for years."

Dorrie gets into the car with more difficulty than she'd exited it.

"Good thing we got that cleaned off before Lola saw it. She'd have a conniption fit."

There are two houses beyond the gate. The first, halfway up a steep hill, is built in a traditional Provincetown style. Modest in scale, it's clad in weather-beaten shingles and white fascia boards. A mottled green door sports a sheer curtain behind its etched glass. On each floor, two windows with delicate lace curtains face the drive. A back door and an adjacent half-window are just visible at the far right of the house. Farther up the hill, the chimneys, gables, and tower of an ornate Victorian mansion soar above the treetops like a castle at the edge of a forest.

Dorrie points to a gravel parking space beside the smaller house.

"Park here. Move quick once I open the door, in case Lola's snoopin'."

Before Marc can respond, Dorrie is walking briskly toward the front door. He races to the trunk and grabs the box of groceries.

"No! No! Leave those be," she yells from the steps. "They go to the big house. Bring the steak, though. I'll need to wash it and wrap it in somethin' different. The paper's shot."

Marc retrieves the soggy steak and dashes into an immaculate parlor whose highly polished furniture is draped with aged lace and antimacassars. Sepia photographs adorn two end tables and all four walls of the low-ceilinged room. Most are of schooners under sail, with a miniature of the ship's captain inset in the upper-left corner. The furniture, photographs, and dim light cast a muted glow—the color of freshly brewed tea in a delicate cup.

Dorrie ushers him through to a spotless kitchen, then plops down at a Formica-topped table.

"Okay, now," she says, catching her breath. "It's nearly eleven. I gotta get you primed to deliver the order to Her Majesty. Here's what you do. Walk up to the house, don't drive. Lola won't answer the door if she sees a strange car pull up, 'specially if it's a man she don't know. Go 'round to the kitchen. It's the red door. Knock real loud. She could be anywhere in the joint, but don't worry, she'll hear ya. She's got ears like a huntin' dog. It may take some time for her to get to the door, though."

Dorrie sounds as though she's planning a military incursion.

"When she asks who you is, tell her you give me a ride home from gettin' her groceries, and that I told you 'bout the gardener's job. Be sure to tell her first thing so she don't throw you out on your ass. She don't trust nobody, that one, but mentionin' the job might get you in. She ain't had a gardener since the Brazilian left, and she'll be wantin' one before the snow flies."

"Gardener? For the winter? That doesn't make any sense. Besides, I'm not a gardener."

"Perfect. She don't have a garden."

"That makes even less sense."

Dorrie lights a cigarette and takes a long drag.

"That's it in a nutshell, dahlin'. Don't expect nothin' to make no sense over there. Lord knows after all these years, I don't. Just roll with it. You need a roof over your head if you're plannin' to stay in this town, and there ain't a place cheaper than Lola's where you get paid to stay 'stead of the other way round."

"Huh?"

"It's all kinda backwards. She pays for company and calls it employment. The work is piddlin'. Run some errands, drive to the doctor now and then, and shovel a bit of snow. Nothing a city slicka like you can't handle. And for that you get paid and a place to live."

"I'm not a city slicker. I grew up in the country."

Dorrie dark eyes brighten with amusement.

"All the bettah." She hands him the steak, freshly wrapped in butcher's paper. "Get on with you, then, before it starts to rain again. They give rain for all day."

CHAPTER 2
WHATEVER LOLA WANTS

One Commercial Street had been built to impress, and the Italianate mansion has lost none of its grandeur in more than a century. Freshly painted, with its bright work still intact, the house dominates the lesser of two dunes on its extensive grounds. Its three-story façade, capped by elaborate cornices, faces a circular, clamshell drive. A bronze statue of a whaler in a longboat commands the circle's center. Captured just as he is to let fly his harpoon, the whaler's face contorts with purpose. There's something graceful yet malevolent in the tensile strength of his upraised arm.

At the sight of it, Marc feels his stomach clench. He shakes off the sensation, then strides purposefully past the front of the house where massive granite steps lead to an ornate porch with a blue, bead-board ceiling. A brass ship's lantern hangs above a mahogany double door with etched glass panels embellished with frolicking sea nymphs. Like their elaborate surroundings, they seem frozen in time.

Rounding the side of the building, Marc spies two staircases at either end of a narrow, second-floor balcony—more like a catwalk—that encompasses a squat, two-story ell. Four vestibules open onto the balcony, two on each side.

In contrast to the Victorian ebullience of the main house, the rear wing has all the appeal of a third-rate motel.

At the crest of a lesser dune overlooking the harbor, he spies a small cemetery enclosed by a wrought iron fence. Inside are two granite obelisks boldly engraved with the name *Staunton*. A scattering of older headstones stands behind them.

Marc finds the red door at the far end of the ell, knocks, waits, then tries again.

A distant voice yammers, "Hold your horses. I'll be there presently, you silly old cow. You're three minutes late. You can't possibly expect me to wait around for you all day long."

The dead weight of the groceries is taking its toll. Marc chafes at the delay, appalled Dorrie attempted to carry them from the other side of town. At last, the door is opened by an elderly woman in a purple silk kimono. Just under six feet, with a slight stoop, she's neither thin nor overweight. Her figure is full for her height and at odds with her aged features, as if her body has had more success resisting the ravages of time.

Her face, sans makeup, has few wrinkles in its parchment-like skin. A mane of white hair cascades over both her shoulders. Her old-fashioned cataract glasses curve upward to a point, with thick lenses that make her watery blue eyes appear oversized and intimidating. She recoils at the sight of Marc, her eyes brimming with suspicion and the slightest trace of terror.

"Who are you? Where's Andoria?"

The lilt in the old woman's voice would sound comic if not for her imperious glare and palpable anxiety.

"Marc Nugent. With your groceries. Do you mean Dorrie?" he asks, sounding calmer than he feels, given the gold-handled cane brandished just inches from his nose.

"Her name, young man, is Andoria. That lazy good-for-nothing."

The cane slowly descends, but the woman's large eyes remain wary, her body tense.

"She was named for my father's flagship, so I should know. If I'd thought she'd hand off the job to some man I've never met, I'd have done without. Pesters me to death, the foolish old witch. I suppose she made a martyr of herself and has you delivering some paltry excuse for her tardiness. You can tell her for me it won't get her anywhere."

"Not exactly. She was walking back from the East End when the grocery bags broke in the rain. I picked them up and gave her a ride home. She's too old to be—"

"Did you take anything?"

Lola dismisses his observation with a wave of her hand. For a moment, her face registers concern, then the scowl quickly returns. "Come in here this instant, so I can make sure nothing is missing. I wasn't born yesterday, you know." She backs away from the door certain Marc will follow, but he stands his ground.

"Now, wait just a minute. If I hadn't helped, your groceries would be flattened on Commercial Street."

"Be that as it may, I simply refuse to take anyone's word without checking facts for myself. You'd better come in, young man, unless you want to stand there holding that heavy box all day. I'm Lola Staunton, by the way. Call me Miss Staunton, *not* Ms., and mind you, wipe your feet."

Marc surrenders and enters what had once been a servant's kitchen. A vintage wood-burning range, covered with trailing philodendron, stands against one wall. Nearby is its replacement, a large gas stove with a heating attachment vented into the same chimney. The room's spartan accommodation and massive size remind him of the kitchen of an English country house. Marc can practically see the ghosts of kitchen staff bustling about.

"You may place them there."

Lola indicates a large, copper-topped table in the center of the room. He sets down the heavy box, his relief tempered by notions of modern-day servitude.

She points to a rounded kitchen chair beside a square oak table. "Sit over there. And keep your distance."

Lola remains behind the larger table, painstakingly checking off each item on a handwritten list. As he waits, Marc stares out the window past pots of red geraniums whose petals press against the glass as if trying to escape.

At last, she finishes.

"Well, you're no thief. I'll give you that much. Why did Andoria send you instead of coming herself? She usually tries to see me whenever she can fabricate an excuse."

"She thought I might be a good candidate for the gardener's position."

A frown worthy of Queen Victoria darkens Lola's features.

"She did, did she? She ought to mind her own business."

Marc's heart sinks. Lola surveys him with a critical eye, much as if choosing a horse.

"But seeing as you are here," she says at last, her frown fading slightly, "take off your coat, and we shall discuss it. Don't get your hopes up."

Despite Marc's pique, the quaint, outdated surroundings and their Gorgon of a mistress intrigue him. He places his chin in his hand and stares around the room. His eyes light on one old artifact after another: cast-iron frying pans, metal muffin tins, and multicolored bowls stacked on open shelves. He smiles to himself at Lola's tone.

It's as severe as her surroundings. I wonder if she's this way from living in such isolation for so long. Or was she just born a bitch?

Lola crosses the room and sits in the chair beside him.

"Okay, young man, let's get down to brass tacks. How old are you?"

"Twenty-five."

"Whatever made you move to Provincetown at this time of year?"

"Well, I had to leave New York City and—"

"Why?"

As she stares intently into his eyes, Marc scrambles for an answer.

"I got tired of the Chelsea scene."

"Oh, come now, don't gaslight me. That wasn't all, was it?"

"No, not really."

He pauses to study the vast room and its outmoded furnishings. Its quiet dignity and near-spiritual simplicity draw him in like a novitiate seeking sanctuary at a monastery gate. He ponders whether to say this, then quickly thinks better of it.

"So what was it? Did he run off with someone else?"

Although Lola's tone has moderated, she presses on, jarring Marc from his internal monologue.

"No, not that. It's sort of hard to explain. I want to be a writer," he adds hastily, "and I couldn't get any work done living with my ex, Brandon. All he wanted to do was party and stay out all night."

Though recognizing his answer sounds vague and slightly petulant, Marc is certain further detail will cost him the job.

"No way to live. You did the right thing. If you don't answer the Muse when she calls, she may not call again."

Lola stares into the distance and begins to recite, as if an ancient Sibyl:

"Then, rising with Aurora's light,
The Muse invoked, sit down to write;
Blot out, correct, insert, refine,
Enlarge, diminish, interline;
Be mindful, when invention fails,
To scratch your head, and bite your nails."

"That's Jonathan Swift," Marc says, stunned.

Lola's blue eyes light up.

"Yes, it is. You may not think it to look at it now, but HomePort was once *the* bastion of culture in this town. My grandmother was a highly regarded artist. Her son, my father—the third Captain Staunton—was an author and lover of poetry. He used to declaim that quote each morning before going upstairs to write. I can still hear his voice.

"Father and Grandmother kept journals of their travels around the world. The Historical Society already has Grandmother's. They've been trying to wrest Father's from me for years. I've been resisting for reasons I can't quite fathom. They'll get them when I'm gone, I guess. That's certainly time enough."

A wistful expression clouds Lola's face, followed by disappointment, then consternation as she absentmindedly tugs a loose strand of her snow-white hair. Marc studies her closely, maintaining a respectful silence. He's getting used to the way her glasses magnify her blue eyes, and amplify the myriad emotions they convey.

It's like staring into a well. You can estimate the width, but not the depth.

When Lola resumes her interrogation, her tone is less wary.

"Where did you grow up?"

"Swan River, Manitoba."

"Does your family still live there?"

"No. I was an only child. My father died when I was two and my mother five years ago."

"I'm sorry to hear that. Is that why you came to the states?"

As Lola's tone softens, Marc takes heart.

"In part. Once my mother died, there was no point in staying. Swan River is the kind of place where everything is pat and predictable. I always felt I'd never be happy there. As I grew older and understood why, I knew instinctively I had to be somewhere where there were people like me."

Lola's quavering voice contains the slightest trace of empathy.

"Good. Good for you. People should never stay where they don't fit in. That's for darn sure."

Marc considers how much of an outsider he's been for most of his life.

Even in New York City, I lived in isolation. Dorrie was right. I am a "runnah."

"And if you could have anything you wanted right now, what would it be?"

Lola's tone has grown pensive.

"Hmm, that's an odd question, almost like rubbing a lamp and conjuring a genie."

Marc grins to show he's not being sarcastic. Somewhere in the course of this bizarre interview, his consternation has turned to admiration. Lola's dour defensiveness is replaced for just an instant by an arched eyebrow and the slightest hint of a smile.

"Well, this *is* Provincetown, my dear. One never knows. Tell me what comes to mind, and we'll see what gets conjured up, as you so quaintly put it."

"To be honest, I'd like a room with a lock on the door and a good night's sleep in a nice, warm bed. Tomorrow I'd like to wake up refreshed, have breakfast, and then just sit down and write."

"That's all? That's not much."

Lola hesitates, tugging her loose strand as Marc struggles to maintain the appearance of nonchalance. After a while, she nods twice. After yet another pause, she assumes the regal tone of a monarch addressing a courtier.

"You're on a two week trial, young man, subject to Helena's approval. Your duties are as follows. Drive me if necessary. I don't go out often, except for medical appointments. Go to the post office every day for my mail. Do the grocery shopping on Thursday. I buy everything I can from Angel Foods. We Stauntons have patronized local businesses for nearly two hundred years. I'll expect you to mow the lawn in summer and shovel snow in winter. Do you cook?"

"A bit. I did some catering work in New York," Marc replies tentatively.

"Well, if you want, you can cook your meals in here. A woman comes every day to prepare my dinner, so that's not your responsibility. If you use the kitchen, though, you must wait to eat until she's done. And, of course, clean up after yourself."

Delighted his meager culinary skills won't be put to the test, Marc hesitates then asks, "What does the job pay?"

Lola answers as if the subject were irrelevant.

"Three hundred fifty a week. Free room and bath with food, heat, and electric. Tuesdays off."

"May I see the room?"

"Of course. I shan't go with you, though. I seldom climb stairs these days. Take this, go up that stairway, and unlock the door to the left of the first landing."

Handing him a tarnished, brass skeleton key, Lola gestures toward the far end of the kitchen where an oak baluster protrudes from a shadow laden corner.

The theme from *Mission: Impossible* reverberates through the room. Lola starts, then points as Marc mutes his phone.

"Leave that infernal thing here for security, in case you get the notion to steal something."

"Now look," he says, matching her cantankerous tone, "I'm no thief."

"Good for you. You're a straight shooter like me. We may just get along."

As Lola beams, Marc feels something quicken between them. Holding out the phone, he can't help but smile.

"Here."

"Forget it, kid. I'll send Helena up to interview you when she gets back from the library. Unless she has strenuous objections, you're in."

Room with a View

The narrow stairway is only two feet wide. After a few twists and turns, it arrives at the second floor landing. Unlocking the door to the left, Marc steps back in astonishment. A long corridor paneled in lustrous mahogany, contains three more doorways, two of which stand open. Through the first, he sees a lavish bedroom with a four-poster bed, two chairs, a silk-covered chaise, and two antique highboys. The second opens into an enormous bathroom with an elaborate, claw-foot tub as well as a separate shower tiled in tiny, black and white tiles. The bathroom's antique porcelain fixtures gleam as if new. Marc tries the third door, which must lead to the front of the house. His key won't turn the lock.

The lavish bedroom has been dusted within the week. A lace-trimmed canopy festooned with allegorical figures presides over a bed with white silk sheets and a beautifully crocheted bedspread. Steam hisses from a massive radiator beneath a large window whose upper panel is a stained glass depiction of a whaling ship under full sail. The colored glass filters the outside light in shifting hues of gray, blue, white, and brown that play against the canopy, imparting subtle movement to the mythical characters encircling the bed.

As Marc stares out the window, a heavy, older man in a hooded raincoat exits the apartment nearest the drive. He hastens across the balcony, down the stairs, and into the woods that slope to Commercial Street. There's something furtive about him. His hood obscures most of his face even though it's not raining, making him look like a woodchuck scuttling to its den.

Marc watches until the man vanishes from sight, then gazes past Long Point to the shimmering bay, a painting in silver, white, and gray. Nearer to shore, sunlight pours through a gap in the clouds, illuminating the harbor with a radiant shaft of light.

It's the way God speaks in the movies, Marc jokes to himself, though, in truth, the scene captivates him.

Beyond the shelter of Wood End, a lone sloop, seemingly fragile and ill-suited, steadfastly maintains its course against a barrage of incoming whitecaps. A whale breaches off the boat's port side, sending spray high into the air. Swimming rapidly along the surface, it soon leaves the toiling yacht in its wake.

Marc ponders the view from the tower. Surrendering to a powerful impulse, he climbs the stairs to the third floor. Passing what he assumes is an attic door, he reaches a brass ladder. He climbs it, pushes open a glass and wire hatch, then gasps in awe.

The town, East Harbor, the dunes with their weathered shacks facing the Atlantic, all lie before him. To his left, a Cape Air flight descends toward the dark strip of the airport. Like the sloop, it seems insignificant against the vast expanse of sea and sky. At Race Point, the surf rolls inevitably to shore, coming to rest near a wrack line that meanders as far as the eye can see. The occasional breaker whose spume reaches the line merely creates an indentation in the dark, undulating threshold between land and sea. From Marc's vantage point, that boundary seems tenuous at best, for from this height it's obvious Provincetown is built on nothing but sand.

Perhaps it takes a special type of person to live in a place more water than land.

Marc scans the horizon for solid earth. Nearby Beach Point, the eroding cliffs of Truro, and the sandy length of Jeremy's Point in Wellfleet seem nearly as fragile. In contrast, the distant shores of Manomet and Plymouth look substantial and verdant, despite being composed of little more than gravel and scrub pine.

It seems that HomePort has surrendered none of its original grounds to the passing years. Behind the mansion, acres of silver beech trees undulate within the bounds of a rusted wrought iron fence—another wrack line that seems to delineate past and present. Marc studies the taller dune within the far confines of the estate.

What an amazing place for a house. The view from there would surpass even this.

Marc notices an old foundation at the top of the hill and wonders about its purpose.

"Staunton's Lookout."

The name comes without warning, accompanied by a subtle tingling at the back of his neck. Marc waits for something more. At last, stunned by how much time has passed, he races back to the kitchen where Lola waits anxiously by the stairs.

"Is the room to your liking?"

Her voice has a hopeful lilt.

"It's fantastic. A beautiful room. I'm so very grateful."

Marc is more enthused by the tower with its magnificent views than the overly ostentatious bedroom, but he's more than satisfied.

"You'll sign on?"

"Yes. Yes, I will. And thank you so much."

Lola replies with a tentative touch of warmth that seems oddly out of character.

"It's *I* who should be thanking *you,* my dear. It will be nice to have another man to help around the house. I rely too much on Cole, though he'd never say so. Here's a key to the kitchen door. You can keep the one to the bedroom. Helena has a spare for the cleaning up. Bring your car from Andoria's to the side drive. It'll be fine there."

For her age, Lola doesn't seem to miss much.

"Now get out of those damp clothes before you catch your death. I'll see you again at tea. Four, sharp. Don't forget now, kid."

Marc ponders how Lola's tone alternates between compassionate interest and outmoded formality.

Her autocratic bearing seems as much a defensive mechanism as a character trait. Much like the fence that bounds her property, what is outside differs dramatically from what is inside. Perhaps she lives in two worlds, too.

On impulse, he leans down and kisses her cheek. Her body trembles at the touch of his lips.

Maid in the Mist

It takes Marc little time to move into what he hopes will be his winter quarters. Chilled to the marrow, he strips off his damp clothing, locks the landing door, and heads to the shower. The pipes sputter at first, then slowly the water pressure and temperature stabilize. He steps in, lathers up, and begins to sing.

After several moments of bad Verdi, an ominous silhouette darkens the shower curtain. The shadow of a long, curved implement rises slowly and deliberately upward, above the waist, the shoulder, and—after what seems an eternity—the head of the sinister figure.

Certain he's hallucinating, Marc remains rooted in place until the curtain flies open and the weapon arcs downward. Then he yells, cowers in the far corner, and covers himself with both hands.

Through steam and spray, he sees a pale face, bright red lips, eyes weighted with mascara, and a mane of black hair pinned up in an enormous bun. The intruder, wearing a drab, black, high-collared blouse with matching floor-length skirt, has a large beauty mark on her right cheek. She holds a towel in her left hand, secreting whatever weapon is in her right hand behind the ample folds of her skirt.

She surveys him from head to foot without a trace of embarrassment. "Not bad. Not bad at all," she says at last in a low, sultry voice that makes it clear he'd not covered himself in time. "I just *adore* tall men who actually live up to my expectations. So many *will* deceive a girl and turn out to be *such* a disappointment when push comes to shove. You'll do well in this town, darling. Very well, indeed. I bet I could bounce a quarter off that butt, and that six-pack? Simply *fabulous!*"

With a salacious grin, she fans herself, then slowly retrieves a wooden back scrubber from its hiding place.

"Need your back scrubbed, hon?"

Marc stands, though his hands remain firmly in place, making it impossible to command much in the way of authority—or dignity, for that matter.

"Who are you? What do you want?"

"I'm Mrs. Danvers, the housekeeper. Welcome to Manderley."

"Cut the crap. What are you doing in here? Are you Helena?"

"Not He-*layhn*-a, darling. *Hel*-eh-*nah,* as in Bonham Carter or Rubenstein, take your pick. *Hel*-eh-*nah* Handbasket, part-time maid, full-time impersonator. I put the '*H O*' in HomePort."

She shimmies suggestively, her lithe frame gyrating beneath the folds of the voluminous dress.

"As for what I'm doing, Lola sent me to interview you. I also wanted to give you this so you don't drip on my freshly waxed floor."

Helena holds out a plush towel. Marc continues to cover himself. A standoff ensues.

"Here, take it," Helena sighs. "You don't have to hide your junk from little old me. I've got me one of those too, you know, and it's even bigger than yours, honeybun. Besides, when you've seen as many up close and personal as I have, they all start to look like turkey necks."

Despite two Janet Leigh moments in the last hour, Marc is charmed by Helena's madcap antics. He reaches for the towel with his right hand while maintaining an inadequate attempt at modesty with his left.

Helena holds on to her end just as he knew she would. Her dark brown eyes shine with glee.

"Okay hon, this is supposed to be an interview, remember? Now that you know who I am, who are you?"

"Marc Nugent, aspiring writer and candidate for gardener-chauffeur. Just arrived in town today," he says, suddenly feeling like a recruit at an induction station.

"Oh, a writer!"

In an instant, a new character stares back at him through wide, penetrating eyes.

"How long is a movie script these days?" she whispers in a throaty, yet instantly familiar voice. "I mean, how many pages?"

"Depends on what it is, a *Donald Duck* or *Joan of Arc*."

"This is to be a very important picture. I have written it myself. Took me years," she says in the same ethereal tone.

Marc drops his end of the towel. Sauntering across the expansive tile floor, he tugs at a roll of toilet paper, turns, and speaks the next line from *Sunset Boulevard*:

"Looks like enough for six important pictures."

"It's the story of Salome. I think I'll have DeMille direct it."

Against strong odds, Helena has become Norma Desmond, in a tiled bathroom with a naked man as her foil. Marc leans against the sink, enchanted.

"I'm really impressed," he says, meaning every word.

"Full-time, twenty-four seven, living the dream!"

Helena beams with delight, then executes a little pirouette.

"I can see we're going to be great friends," she says, her dark, lustful eyes scanning his dripping body.

Marc wrests the towel from her grasp.

Turkey necks, my ass!

Getting to Know You

Taking great care not to drip on the floor, Marc returns to his bedroom.

Helena follows uninvited and flounces onto the chaise.

"So. You rate. Whatever did you do to impress Her Ladyship? I've been here four years. No one has ever stayed in this room in all that time. We've all had to stay out in the Bates Motel."

She points toward the nondescript rear wing.

Marc shrugs.

"To be honest, I haven't a clue. Lola asked a million probing questions, then gave me the job and this room."

He walks to the dresser, pulls out a pair of boxer shorts, turns his back, drops the towel from around his waist, and steps into them.

"Lordy me!" Helena shrieks. "Don't you be showin' such secrets to a poah maiden lady! Ah's not used to such sights. Mah world is very sheltered, he-ah at Homo-Port."

Marc sits in lotus pose on the bed.

"Somehow I doubt you're *that* out of practice, Helena. So, tell me, what's the deal here? I'm grateful for such a nice setup, but I can't figure for the life of me what I've done to deserve it."

Helena replies in a breathless whisper.

"Well, Lola—actually Aloisa Davis Staunton, last of the illustrious Stauntons of Provincetown—has spent her entire life in this house being waited on hand and foot. By the way, don't you love the way she talks? A cross between Julia Child and Queen Elizabeth. 'My de-ah, how very amusing!'"

Helena's pasquinade is perfect. Even her features take on Lola's patrician mien.

"I've always said she was born with a silver shovel in her mouth. In any case, she's had a *staaahff* all her life, and she's not about to give them up at this late date. Who would want to if they had the means to keep it going? And, trust me, she *does* have the means. Where her ancestors hired locals, she surrounds herself with gay men who need a helping hand and are willing to play her game to get it. She has a real knack for finding them. I consider it one of the perks of my housekeeper's position, 'homo-delivery.'"

"Guys like my predecessor, the Brazilian?"

"Shhh! Lola can hear us downstairs. Enrique? How'd you find out about him?"

"Dorrie told me."

"Oh. So you've met Dorrie already? How'd that happen?"

"Her, or should I say Lola's grocery bags ripped in the rain. When I rescued them and drove her home, Dorrie recommended me for the job."

"Well, well, well."

Helena pauses, clearly weighing what and what not to say.

"A word to the wise in dealing with Lola? Don't make a big deal out of Dorrie. She's perfectly fine—a real old darling, in fact—but there's something odd between her and Lola. They're both wonderful people once you get to know them, but they get along like oil and water.

"This place was so isolated when they were young, all they had was each other. Maybe things were too intense. Maybe something happened. I don't know the details. What I do know is that Lola can't stand the sight of Dorrie these days. In fact, I'm stunned Lola hired you on Dorrie's recommendation."

"Okay, but what about the gardener, Enrique?"

Lola is clearly tough to please, and Marc is anxious to learn his predecessor's fate.

"He came to town a few years ago and fell into every pitfall: drugs, booze, all that shit. Nice guy. Kinda hot in a way, not that *I* sampled his wares. I was probably the only queen in town who didn't. They say he worked a while as an escort, but I didn't get the memo in time. When he moved in, he was allegedly battling sex addiction, so I backed off. Given that legions of men have told me I'm habit forming, it just didn't seem fair to tempt the poor child."

Helena bats her eyelashes before continuing. The contrast between her flirtatious gestures and drab costume is more than absurd, it's unnerving.

"Anyways, when he hit rock bottom, someone from the Soup Kitchen told Lola, and she had me interview him. That was a no-brainer. He was *gorgeous*! How *could* I disapprove? So she took him in and gave him the rooms next to mine in the Bates Motel. He didn't do much around the place other than keep her company and drive her wherever she wanted to go. Still, she saw he ate, paid him tons of attention, and helped him get his act together.

"Three months ago, doesn't he land a part in an Off-Broadway revival of *Love! Valor! Compassion!* It seems no one knew he had any talent, except Lola. She paid for the airfare and hotel for his audition and even gave him money to get settled in an apartment when he left."

"So she's loaded?"

"From what I understand, it's an inherited whaling fortune from the days when Provincetown was one of the richest towns in the state. The money is in some big WASP investment company in New York. Lola lives off the interest on the interest on the interest, with money to spare."

"Must be nice."

"Yeah, I'll say. Though she seems to give most of it away, as if she feels guilty about something."

"Does she spend that much time with all her tenants?"

"Don't ever use *that* word in front of her, Marc. We're *not* tenants. We're 'members of the household.'"

Helena's singsong imitation is perfect.

"She grew up with servants, but is more comfortable with that term. Working for Lola is like a big game we never discuss. There's a gardener, but no garden, a driver, but no place to go. The only thing she expects is that you spend time with her at tea every few days. Then she talks over your 'duties' for the week and reminisces about her family history. It's all really just her way of making sure she isn't alone all day long."

"She sure is crotchety."

"Yes and no. She's a real sweetheart when you get to know her, but she's got some issues. Something must have happened when she was a child. She's never said, but I've never seen a straight man in the house save Dolores's son, Jimmy, whom Lola's known from birth. It's always gay guys or women. I think that's why she likes me so much. In a way, I'm both."

Helena spreads her arms as if modeling a new ensemble.

"Even after a guy has passed her tests, she's still tough to get to know. Take a hint from me, don't try to get too close to her. If anything comes up, tell me. Lola uses me to keep the world at bay.

"I almost forgot. She told me to fill you in about tea this afternoon. It's the last step in her interview process. If you make it past my inquisition, which you certainly have—I've never seen a candidate with less to hide—you've got to demonstrate enough breeding to be what she calls front parlor company. She figured you wouldn't know the drill, so she told me to explain things.

"Listen carefully. Tea's at four o'clock, sharp, in the front parlor. Be prepared. It's a trip. Very staid and old-fashioned, like something from *The Bostonians*. Lola does most of her living through books, and to hear her tell it, she taught herself nearly everything she knows. I've always thought she sounds more like a Victorian novel than an everyday person, especially when she's telling one of her tales. Perhaps it's because she's so old and people used to talk that way. I'm not quite sure. In any case, I wouldn't believe all you hear from her, especially if other people are present. Not that she's lying, the poor old thing. I'm just not sure she can distinguish between fact and fiction once she gets caught up in the past."

Marc heaves a sigh.

"Well after all this, I'm sure you're looking forward to tea," Helena says with a sympathetic grin, then snaps her fingers as if she's forgotten something. "Oh, and come by the front door, like real company. She'll love that. Dress is casual, but impeccably clean and pressed."

"Guess a summons to tea comes with the job, then?"

"It *is* the job, hon," Helena says, smiling patiently. "Lola's a bit of a card in her own way, tough as she may seem. We're all somewhat dependent on her, though at her age who knows how long that's going to last. But for now, it's not a bad way to earn a week's pay. The trick is to give the old girl whatever she wants. Trust me, it's the best way. And she wants high tea at four as she's had it all her life. As I said, it's all rather formal and old-fashioned, though. Propriety and good conversation are a must if you want to make the right impression. The only place more formal than HomePort is Buckingham Palace, even though there are more queens in residence here than there."

Matt struggles to redirect his thoughts from what is looming as a major ordeal.

"Who else lives in the Bates Motel?"

"Well, there's Cole. He left this morning to rescue some dolphins. Doesn't that sound butch? Well, it fits. He's sort of our general repairman. More like a walking wet dream, if you ask me. I wish he'd repair my plumbing. Very handy, very cute. Drop dead gorgeous, in fact, but not open for business, if you get my drift. He lives in the end apartment on the woods side of the house. He doesn't say much to me, though. I think I scare him."

"If you stalk him in the shower the way you did me, I wouldn't be surprised if he were scared to death. How many rooms are up there anyway?"

"There are four suites, bedroom, sitting room, and bath. They used to be servants' quarters. They still are, if you really think about it. I live in the one closest to the main house facing the drive, in case you're interested."

"Who's the guy beside you?"

"Oh, you saw him?" Helena's tone grows grave. "Boy, for someone who just came to town, you don't miss much. What are you, some sort of detective?"

"I want to be a writer, so I observe things. At least I try to."

"Well, don't try digging too deep into my past," Helena replies sarcastically. "I love a good mystery as much as the next gal. In fact I'm a big Miss Marple fan, but my secrets are strictly off limits. I consider any kind of personal question an invasion of privacy."

"I don't think a simple question about your next-door neighbor is an invasion of privacy."

"Well, Sherlock, since you're so insistent, that's Marvin the Terrible, as I call him. I think he was Enrique's pimp or something. In any case, Enrique convinced Lola to have Marvin take his place when I wasn't around to veto the idea. Having him here turned out to be a big mistake."

"Why? What's wrong with him?"

"Do me a big favor? Don't mention Marvin to anyone, especially Lola. I don't want her to find out what he's up to. She'd be appalled. What's more, it will feed every suspicion she's ever had about men, gay or straight. I've worked hard to get her to be less of a recluse, but if anyone could set Lola back, it's Marvin. She may be close to tossing him out, though I doubt she will without provocation. He needs a place to live for the winter, and lately he's been hiding from her in hopes she'll forget about him for a few months.

"Listen to me carefully, Marc. Lola's more than ninety years old, an age where her fears and anxieties can do her real harm. She's got a weak heart. She doesn't think I know, but I found the medicine in her bathroom. She's prone to fits of nerves and needs her routines to stay calm. She thinks she's got three men here to protect her, and that provides some degree of security. I don't want anything to change until next spring when more people are around, and I can find a replacement for Marvin. So until then, mum's the word. Okay?"

Marc nods. "That leaves one more suite, the one closest to the main house on the woods side."

"That's Charlotte Grubb's. She uses it when she's here in the summer. She manages most everything from New York the rest of the time."

"I assume she's a lesbian."

"The way she dresses would lead you to think otherwise."

"Oh, come on. She has to be a lesbian. What would a straight woman be doing in Provincetown? What does she do?"

"You are so perceptive, Marc. Are you sure you're not a detective? I guess you'd say she's sort of a business manager. She pays the bills and manages the money, properties, dividends, investments, and so forth. Lola doesn't give a fig for that stuff."

"Are we talking about *that* much money?"

"You better believe it. According to Charlotte, the principal hasn't been touched since Lola's grandfather, the second captain, died. Not even during the Great Depression. And Charlotte would know, the Grubs have managed the Staunton fortune for more than a century."

Marc feels more than a trace of envy.

"It's amazing that a place like this still exists."

"It's like *Upstairs Downstairs*, just a hundred years later and a bit more twisted."

"Well, a place this size must keep Rose, the parlor maid, pretty busy."

"To be honest, I do it to stop Lola from making more of a fuss than she already does," Helena says, turning serious. "She's a tough old bird and can be incredibly demanding. She doesn't often climb the stairs because of her heart, but I know she expects things to be exactly as they were in the old days. All the rooms up here except this one are kept as if in a museum. The place is chock full of memories, as you'll hear this afternoon."

Helena stands and pirouettes.

"I just flit around and keep the dust down, which makes Lola happy. Or as happy as she can be, the poor old dear. It's the least I can do after all she's done for me."

"She's been that good to you?"

"Yes. She and Dorrie both, but that's a story for another day. It's way past time to walk Frida, Cole's dog. I said I'd watch her while he was in Wellfleet. I'd love to trade places with that bitch. She's the only one around this joint he seems to care about."

Helena glides out of the room before Marc can say good-bye. He hears the sound of a key in a lock, then the door to the Bates Motel clicks shut.

* * * *

November 13ᵗʰ, 2008 – Homeport. My new home, God willing.

Just a day after leaving the city, and I'm in out of the cold. What a lucky break. Of course, it's all rather tenuous. Lola, the old gal who owns this place, is in pretty tough shape. Older than dirt with a bad heart to boot. I could be out on the street if she dies, or she could throw me out for no good reason. Helena says she's quite the demanding old coot. Well, we'll see how I do at teatime—part three of the interview process.

Note to self: Schedule HIV test in a month. And write out what Brandon did just in case he tracks me down. For now, if anyone is reading this, and I've gone missing, Brandon Hanson did it.

Tea for Three

Helena pulls open both massive front doors just as a portentous grandfather's clock strikes four. She's changed from her long housekeeper's dress to a short, black skirt with a white blouse whose fabric strains across an enormous bosom. A purple lace handkerchief fans out over her right breast, and a black and white maid's cap perches jauntily on her head.

"Good afternoon, sir," she intones, Mrs. Danvers once more.

"Is Miss Aloisa Staunton at home?"

Marc feels sudden gratitude for the old British movies he and Brandon watched during their sedentary days in New York.

"Yes, sir. And expecting you."

Helena's voice seems louder than necessary. She signals with a toss of her head that Lola is listening. As he enters the vast front hall for the first time, Marc hears a shuffling noise to his right and pictures the dowager scuttling to her seat.

Helena waits a moment, then with a flourish, slides open two enormous pocket doors and announces, "Mr. Marcus Nugent, ma'am."

Marc's hostess, her white hair in a French twist, sits behind a lavish tea table piled high with pastries. She's wearing a purple, floor-length, satin dress. The legs and arms of her curved wingback chair are shaped like a swan.

"Mr. Nugent."

Lola's voice is forthright yet drawn out, more regal statement of fact than greeting.

"Miss Staunton."

Marc bows long and low over her blue-veined hand.

"Thank you so much for your kind invitation. I received it with delight. As a newcomer to Provincetown, I know few people."

Helena, who has moved to a position behind Lola's chair, gives his performance a discreet two thumbs up. Lola fingers an enormous, pear-shaped diamond pendant as she inclines her head in patrician fashion.

"Why thank you, Mr. Nugent. I try to uphold the common courtesies."

"If I might say, Miss Staunton, some of the less common as well. That is the loveliest tea I have ever seen."

Marc feels like he's performing on *Masterpiece Theatre*.

"Well, by all means," Lola says grandly, "do sit down and partake."

He sits in a swan chair opposite Lola and takes a moment to survey the room. A trove of antique furniture is placed in strategic clusters: gentlemens' chairs, an S-shaped love seat, and a luxurious sofa set all carved in the same swan motif. The plaster ceiling, with its ornate carved moldings, is at least fifteen feet high. A sculpted medallion graced with four hovering putti marks the center of the room. From it hangs an enormous crystal chandelier.

A marble fireplace with a mahogany over-mantel dominates the rear wall. Polished oak floors glisten through the fringe of a plush oriental carpet. Chinese-red wallpaper festooned with peacocks and lush foliage offsets dozens of gilt-framed paintings hanging from picture rails. The riotous colors of contemporary works are in contrast with the staid blues and grays of several masterful seascapes.

An impressive painting of a whaling ship under full sail dominates the north wall. Its black hull glistens with spray while its brightly-colored figurehead confronts a towering wave. A flag flying from the topmast identifies the ship as the *Andoria*.

Framed by the formal parlor, Lola seems an aged Lady Dedlock. As Marc rummages his thoughts for yet another pleasantry, Helena, an implausible domestic at best, pours pale, golden liquid from an ornate silver teapot into delicate china cups. She hands one to Lola, then serves him. As he raises his cup, Lola reaches across the table and clicks hers against it.

"Bottom's up, kid!"

Lola drains her cup in a single gulp, then smacks her lips in satisfaction. Marc takes a cautious sip, recognizes fine whiskey and, forsaking his affectations, shakes his head in genuine bewilderment. When Helena avoids his questioning gaze, Lola bursts into hearty laughter.

"Forgive me, Marc. I must have my fun," she says between guffaws. "When Helena told me how she'd surprised you in the shower and convinced you everything was so stodgy around here, I simply couldn't resist. I found it all so very amusing. I simply *had* to get in on the joke."

Marc stares at her, slack-jawed.

"Let me explain so you don't think I'm totally insane," Lola says, catching her breath. "High tea was an ordeal when I was a girl. My mother ruled this place like the Queen of Hearts, and teatime was the worst of it. For years I sat here all dressed up in uncomfortable clothes, only speaking when spoken to. I promised myself when I grew up, I'd do things differently. I love the sweets but hate the formality, so I came up with a compromise that keeps the tradition intact. Drink up, kid. Drink up."

Marc takes a dutiful sip and eases into the moment, his frenzied search for pleasantries forgotten. Recalling his recent thoughts of HomePort as a monastery and himself a novitiate, he's dismayed at his naiveté.

"We went over your duties this morning," Lola continues. "Here are a few more details: I'd appreciate having the mail back at the house by eleven thirty. Helena will give you the post office box combination. I have an eye doctor's appointment a week from today. Other than that, you have no duties unless it snows. Would you kindly leave your phone number so I can reach you?"

"Thank you, Miss Staunton. I shall make sure these things are done to your satisfaction."

Catching himself sounding like Jeeves, Marc blushes slightly, then hands her his business card.

"Forget that Miss Staunton nonsense, kid. Call me Lola. Helena says you'll fit in well here, and her insights are more than enough for me. Let's have a nice chat."

Lola studies the card for a moment.

"Helena, Marc's a writer. He was telling me about it this morning."

Marc intervenes.

"Well, I'm really just getting started. I have little formal training other than a few classes in New York. I want to write a novel. I'm hoping I can finally get to work on it."

Lola takes another impressive, yet ladylike, sip.

"It makes all the difference to have a passion for something, Marc. Something your very own. Not what someone else foists upon you. Find whatever makes your heart race, then do all you can to pursue it on your own terms. My passion is my family history. I come from a long line of seafarers. Unlike many families in this town, we Stauntons have kept things intact."

"Yes. I admire that."

"You do? Well, I'll be. I'd have thought someone your age would find all this fusty and passé, even if they were too polite to say so."

"I lived in a loft in New York. That was great, but there's something to be said for continuity and family tradition. Once it's gone, it's gone forever."

"Why thank you, young man. You seem to understand. And, oh yes, New York. We must talk about that in a bit. I think I have some real estate holdings there. You may know them. Helena, please pour our guest some more tea? You were saying, Marc?"

"It's probably because I know nothing of my family history, but I'm impressed by a place that has been lived in over generations. Every object seems to have a story to tell."

"And if these walls could talk? Eh, Helena, dear? Especially out in the servant's wing."

Lola lets forth a hearty chuckle and holds out her cup for more tea.

Comfort Food

When the dinner gong sounds, Helena brusquely herds Marc to the front porch. Without a word, she races away to prevent Lola from toppling over as she weaves her way toward the dining room.

As the heavy doors slam behind him, Marc reviews his day: A chance meeting with a tiny old woman led to a job interview with an ancient recluse, which led to a nude encounter with a female impersonator, which led to a four-hour tea party where he got tanked drinking old whiskey from a hundred-year-old teacup. Now, he's barely standing in the dark outside the mansion he calls home.

Regaining some focus, Marc notices a light shining from Dorrie's kitchen window. He's inexplicably drawn to it and is at her kitchen door within moments.

She greets him as if she'd been expecting him.

"Booze," she sniffs. "I suppose she's had you to one of her goddamn tea parties?"

"As a matter of fact, yes. It wasn't quite what I expected."

"I'll bet. Sit down before you fall down."

"C'mon now, I'm not that bad," Marc mumbles, just making it to the kitchen chair.

"Don't give me none of your bullshit."

Dorrie sounds harsh, though her wide, cigarette-stained grin undermines the effect.

"Bigger drinkers than you had to be carried out of her goddamn teas. You know what they say about Provincetown—a drinking town with a fishing problem. Wait a sec, I'll get you somethin' to soak up the booze."

Marc notices two place settings at the kitchen table.

"I had food at Lola's."

"Yeah. All that goddamn sugar. I'll bet between that and her 'tea,' you're as high as a kite. I take it this means you're a 'member of the household?'"

Dorrie's imitation of Lola is devastatingly accurate. Marc briefly wonders if having one is a residency requirement at HomePort.

"I came to thank you for all you've done for me. The job is perfect. I should be able to get a lot of writing done."

Dorrie's smile begins to fade, and her dark eyes grow pensive.

"I'm glad to hear it. Now, a couple of words to the wise. Lola's been looking for another gay guy to help Cole out around the place for a couple of months now, ever since that Brazilian gigolo left for New York. You're in, but she'll be watching you like a hawk, at least for the first month or two."

Dorrie's face furrows, and the little flap under her chin seems to vibrate in indignation.

"And another thing. Marvin, the other guy over there, is no damn good. Keep your distance from that one, or Lola will sour on you real quick. He sleeps all day and does devil knows what all night. I guess she thinks the men she picks are good men, whether they're worth two cents or not, 'cause she's the one that picked 'em. She's always been like that, doin' as she damn pleases while livin' like a hermit 'fraid of the world. Nobody can tell her a damn thing. She's got the money, so she gets her way every time.

"And one last thing, don't make a big deal out of me over there. Talk me up, and you'll be out on your ass. Lola and I were like sisters as girls, but the last sixty years or so, we ain't seen eye to eye. She don't like to hear a word spoken about me, good, bad, or indifferent.

"She's a piece of work, that one. You gotta keep watch on her to be sure you know where you stand. If you have any questions, ask me. I'm on to all her stupid tricks, even if she don't let me near her anymore, the silly old coot."

Marc leans forward, hands cupped under his chin, vaguely aware he's tilted to one side but unable to figure how to come back to center. "Helena said as much. What happened?"

Dorrie's face hardens. "Never you mind. That was ages ago, and it don't matter at this late date. How 'bout you tellin' me what you're runnin' from, instead?"

"Well, I'll tell you mine if you tell me yours," he says with a laugh.

Dorrie's half-smile has a trace of sadness. "Depends on how good yours is, 'cause mine's a lulu. Now, eat."

Marc blushes, realizing he's been intrusive. Seeming not to notice, Dorrie fills a bowl from a simmering pot and sets it in front of him.

As the pungent smell of spices, garlic, and tomato beguiles his nostrils, Marc is suddenly ravenous. Dorrie's squid stew is worthy of a Michelin star. She spoons a bit into her bowl, then places a Portuguese sweet bread on the table. Sitting beside him like a doting grandmother, she watches with satisfaction, repeatedly offering extra helpings.

"Tell me, Dorrie," he asks between greedy mouthfuls, "why were you carrying those heavy groceries all that way when Lola can certainly afford to have them delivered?"

"Bruce never come back for me. He was probably out in the Beech Forest doing the-devil-knows-what in his cab. Today was mighty strange. I never shop way over there, but Lola insists. Folks from Coastal Studies called Cole about a dolphin strandin' in Wellfleet. It was a big one, and they needed everyone they could find, so he had me cover for him at the very last minute. Poor kid hated to ask, but Dolores draws the line at doing the groceries, and Helena's been cranky lately. Just scared off another boyfriend, I suspect. And of course, goddamn Marvin's good for nothin'. Cole didn't have any other choice 'cept me, it bein' November with no neighbors around and the summer help gone back wherever the hell they came from this year. Lola's so damn fearful, she'd rather have even me before takin' chances on a stranger. Truth told, I was surprised she even invited you in."

Dorrie rattles on in an agitated tone, taking short breaths between her drawn-out descriptions of what has clearly been an extraordinary day. "Lola won't change a goddamn thing over at that place. Everything happens the way it did in her grandmother's day: washday on Monday, ironin' on Tuesday, shoppin' on Thursday, as if written on a tablet from the mountaintop. Her Ladyship has to have her order by eleven on Thursday morning or it's 'off with their heads.' That's pretty much the long and short of it."

Marc begins to wonder what he's signed up for. *HomePort seems like some feudal society complete with a lady of the manor, servants, and even a court jester. What does that make me?*

"That stew was fabulous Dorrie, but you hardly touched yours."

"Oh, I don't eat much at all these days. Does my heart good to see you put it away, though."

"Why did you have all this food prepared if you don't eat?"

Dorrie lowers her gaze in a meek, schoolgirl manner. "I had a feelin' you might stop by. Thought it would be nice to have somethin' ready in case you did. Don't see many folks other than the girls on Friday. It's pretty isolated out here."

"With food this good, I'm surprised there isn't a line out the door."

"My mother was the cook at the big house, so they tell me. I never knew her, but folks used to say I cooked just like her."

"Did she die during childbirth?"

"Disappeared."

"Disappeared?"

"So they tell me. The day after I was born."

"I'm sorry."

"Well, it's water over the dam at this late date." The look on Dorrie's face tells another story. She seems to shrink within herself. "I don't want to talk about it, Sherlock. I want to hear what brings my knight in shinin' ahmah to Provincetown in the middle of Novembah."

Marc, fascinated by the speed at which his new nickname has made its rounds, sits back, sated. It may be the alcohol, the warm glow in his stomach, or simply the letdown from the most astounding day of his life, but suddenly he wants to tell her.

At least some of it.

Bird in a Gilded Cage

Marc describes what it was like to be an only child with no father and a working mother. He speaks of the boredom, isolation, and sameness of his hometown. From there he progresses to his mother's slow death his first year in college, recalling the moment when he was finally free to live his own life. He still feels guilty about the sense of relief that washed over him when he realized he could go wherever he wanted. Finally, he explains how he traveled to New York to find work when the scholarships ran out.

"Long way for a country kid," Dorrie says.

"Yes, in more ways than one."

"Hang on a sec. You ought to have a cup of tea." She fusses over the stove and returns with a steaming mug. "So you moved to New York…."

"Yes. I did what a million wannabes do. I worked for a catering company at night and took my writing classes during the day."

"When did you realize your nature?"

Marc can't help but smile at the archaic phrase. "I think I've always known. My first opportunity to explore was when I came to the States."

Laughing to himself, Marc thinks how anthropological his answer sounds. *Stalking the wild homosexual—one farm boy's journey across a continent in a futile search for love.*

His drunken state is not all that contributes to his giddiness. He's euphoric to be hiding out in this strange little world that Dorrie, Lola, and Helena inhabit. For the first time in months, he's safe.

"So when did Brandon come into the picture?"

"You don't forget anything, do you?"

"An old lady alone has plenty of time to remember. Too much, sometimes." Dorrie's tone conveys deep sorrow.

Marc presses on to create a distraction, describing in detail how he first met Brandon at a catering job at his parents' beachfront estate. He'd sought Marc out at the end of the evening with a large tip and an offer to drive him back to the city. Theatre and dinner dates followed in rapid succession. When Marc lost his job just three months later, Brandon had invited him to move in.

It had been good for the first year or so. They'd traveled and shared many good times. Brandon had been so kind and generous, Marc thought he'd found love. Over time, everything changed. It was more than the loss of novelty, it was as if Brandon desperately needed something Marc could no longer provide.

Marc struggles to describe the soulless comfort of the loft, and the way endless funds made every temptation too readily available. Brandon alternated from bored petulance to near-manic intensity, obsessively collecting art, ancient weapons, and pottery. Marc shares how each project came to a rapid and indifferent halt in favor of another, freshly-minted distraction.

"I think, for all he had, his life was terribly empty." Marc hesitates, unsure how much more to say. "I tried to make a difference, but I don't think I knew enough to help with his problems."

"What kind of problems?"

"Drugs. Crystal Meth."

"Tina?" Dorrie leans forward in her chair, horrified. "That shit's bad news."

"You know about tina?"

"Hell, yes. Dolores' son, Jimmy, is on the rescue squad. They have to race someone to Cape Cod Hospital nearly every week in the summertime. It pulls 'em right down the drain and fast."

Marc silently recalls Brandon's childish petulance and towering rages; the shattered furniture, replaced the next day by something more expensive; the pathetic appeals for forgiveness; the heartfelt promises that unraveled within a week. In his drunken state, Marc can hardly distinguish past from present. He grasps the table to ground himself, then realizes Dorrie is expecting him to say more.

"Tina can change a person so you no longer recognize them. I got tired of wondering where he was and what he was doing, so I left."

"Sounds like a damn good thing you did."

Marc sighs and folds his hands, working them slowly against each other.

"I don't feel great about doing it."

"There's very little a body can do in such a case, try as they might. Best to leave it to the professionals before it's too late."

"It was incredibly hard to leave him. Brandon had been good to me, at least in the beginning. He paid for everything and was so generous it often embarrassed me. All he ever seemed to want in return was for me to love him. I struggled not to take advantage even though I felt trapped by his kindness. Part of me wanted to go out and get a job to even the score, but every time I tried, he came up with some reason why I should wait: a vacation, a party to plan—another distraction.

"Even though we were in the middle of New York City, I think we were too isolated and dependent on each other. When he started to change, I immediately suspected drugs.

I don't want to go into all the details, but it turned out to be far more than casual use. When I make a commitment, I keep it, so I tried to do whatever I could to get him to quit. But he refused my help, denied he had a problem, and the situation became intolerable. I don't want to get into that, though."

"No need. I get the picture clear enough. I've heard what that goddamn stuff does to people. When did you realize you had to get out of there?"

"Last night. It just became too much. I drove all night and slept in the car at Herring Cove. Then I met you at the Purple Feather. I tried hard to stand by him, Dorrie. I really did. He'd showed me the kind of life I never knew existed. But it got so bad."

"I know what goes on," Dorrie says quietly. "Guys that can't handle that shit lose all reason, forget what's important, and take all sorts of risks. He's lucky if he's not been infected with goddamn AIDS."

Marc feels the color drain from his face.

Dorrie stares at him, her eyes wide and troubled. "You don't think you're…?"

An oppressive silence invades the room.

"I don't know. I just don't know." As Marc fights to control his tears, Dorrie takes his hand in hers. When he finally speaks again, it's in a halting whisper. "I just found out he's been cheating almost from the beginning, and he forced me…." Marc stops and stares at the floor.

"Sweet Jesus." Dorrie says, looking up at a faded print on the wall where a halo of white light radiates from Christ's oversized, blood-red heart. She makes the sign of the cross, then squeezes Marc's hand with surprising strength. "Don't think the worst, dahlin'. Everything's gonna be all right."

The young man and the tiny old woman sit in silence until the parlor clock strikes ten.

Empty Bed Blues

As the chimes fade, Marc struggles to his feet.

At the kitchen door, Dorrie, stooped and scraggy, touches his elbow, her dark eyes studying him closely. "Just you remember, Marc, you're young, with your whole life ahead of you. You've shown more courage than you realize breakin' free and comin' here. All things happen for a reason, never forget that. I'm always here if you need somebody to listen. God knows I have plenty of time for a friend."

Marc smiles distractedly, nods, and steps into the darkness.

At the top of the dune, HomePort looms against the starlit night like a darkened vessel. The autumn sky displays more constellations than he's ever seen in the States. One light is brighter than the moon, a small round circle that shines from the vestibule of Marvin's apartment. As a shadowy figure crosses the balcony of the Bates Motel and tiptoes down the stairs, the light goes out.

Marc lets himself in the back door and fumbles his way across the darkened kitchen. A ray of moonlight illuminates the oak stairway. He follows its golden trail to the ship's ladder, then climbs to the tower. He clutches a handle near the hatch to steady himself, then stares, spellbound.

The beacon of Cape Cod Light shears the sky. Beyond Race Point, the navigation lights of a lone tanker shimmer on the dark waters of the Atlantic. Across the bay, three cellphone towers signal their warnings in brief flashes of red. Wood End and Long Point Lights respond in alternating red and green. A swath of moonlight extends across the harbor to the Truro shore. Rippling waves impart gentle movement to the golden trail, as if it were alive. On either side of its span is darkness.

Inside, there's just enough moonlight to see the niches in the oak wainscoting. A framed map of the Cape dominates the south wall. A tarnished barometer hangs opposite, while on the west wall, two rectangular slabs of oak hang from ornate brass hinges. Marc lifts one slab, and a pair of table legs unfolds. As he raises the smaller plank, two short legs drop to form a bench, exposing an electrical outlet.

Marc feels the same presence as earlier in the day, sensing it has waited anxiously for his return. The signs are subtle: the same tingling sensation, greater acuity, and a powerful sense of longing, though no words come. Restoring the bench and table to their original position, Marc takes in the view one last time before climbing cautiously down the ladder.

When he returns to his room, the bedside lamp is on, the covers turned down, and a wrapped piece of chocolate rests on his pillow. A note in a quaint, florid hand, contains Lola's post office box number and combination and closes with *Sweet dreams, stud. If anything comes up in the night, you know who can take care of it for you.*

A key is taped to the bottom of the page. Marc smiles, shakes his head, and strips for bed. Once under the covers, he replays his talk with Dorrie in his mind.

Despite all that went so right on this incredible day, the bed feels vast and empty. Sleep eludes him. As if attuned to his loneliness, his cell phone flashes. Marc doesn't even check to see who it is. Instead, he removes the key from Helena's note and jiggles it in his hand, recalling what was once good about the elegant and contained world he and Brandon had created in New York.

"I sound like Sarah Bernhardt in *Camille,*" Marc says to the empty room, then shuts off the phone, tosses the key on the nightstand, and waits for sleep.

Within moments, a dark figure creeps silently up the stairs outside Marc's window, then crosses the balcony to Marvin's vestibule. There's a soft knock, and the circle of light reappears.

CHAPTER 3
DAWN OF A NEW DAY

November 14th, 2008 - HomePort

Provincetown has always been a place of beginnings. Pilgrims escaping religious persecution; slaves following the Underground Railway; sailors from the Azores—smuggled onboard whaling ships in the dark of night; artists in search of perfect light; writers, romantics, Bohemians, misfits, and geniuses. They all came here, to Land's End, to begin again. Some stayed the rest of their lives, some moved on, but their new life began here.

Now it's my turn... Marc stares at the page as minutes pass. *...and I can't write another fucking word. Maybe a change of scene....*

He showers without interruption, then dresses to go out. Opening the inner door to the Bates Motel, he sees a short stairway leading from the landing to a central corridor. Four doors open onto it, two on each side. Fighting the urge to knock on Helena's, he descends the stairs to his car instead, reminding himself to avoid all entanglements and focus on his work.

Despite the minor literary setback, the second morning of his new life feels great. Dorrie's delicious stew has somehow spared him a massive hangover and allowed him to appreciate a magnificent Provincetown morning.

On a whim, Marc returns to Herring Cove and parks facing the bay. As if to welcome him, the ocean reflects a spectacular sunrise in shimmering patches of color, like jewels in a gray velvet box. As sea and sky merge to seamless silver-gray, the colors fade. Off Race Point, growing swells counter the rush of incoming tide, marking the conflict between ocean and bay with a static wall of whitecaps.

The morning is unseasonably mild. A fog bank rolls in from the Atlantic. First just a wall of grey in the far distance, soon it has blanketed ocean and shore in an endless void. What had been radiant and beautiful is soon obliterated. Waves appear mere seconds before they crash on the beach, sound, not sight, announcing their arrival. It's as if he's peering over the edge of the world.

Security is mortals' chiefest enemy. Even Marc's favorite quote loses some of its power in this vast nothingness. While the ocean's ways are new to him, they invoke the same impressions as when he'd climbed the Duck Mountains as a boy. *A person could feel isolated and adrift in a fog like this or they could study whatever is right in front of them and find their way from one point to the next. A lot like trying to write—you can spend an eternity worrying about what you can't see, or get down to detail and focus on what you can.*

As he considers this newfound sentiment, the fog lifts enough to let in a trace of dim, morning light. An impatient bark alerts Marc he is no longer alone. Just yards down the beach, a golden retriever prances with excitement. In the pale mist, the dog and its owner appear then disappear from view, immersed in play, running and dodging across the sand. The dark-haired man's natural grace is impressive. He runs barefoot, displaying confidence in his body and perfect accord with his surroundings. Marc, confined behind the wheel of his car, feels pangs of envy.

The wind picks up from onshore, and the fog bank retreats. The man tosses the stick. On command, the dog bounds into the surf, surmounts the powerful waves, retrieves the stick, rides a large wave to land, and joyously drops its prize at its master's feet. As Marc watches spellbound, the dog begs for another toss. Her tail wags rapidly, and she leaps high in the air when the stick is held beyond her reach.

Man and dog lope toward Marc's car. When they are within twenty feet, the man stops, sheds his clothing, tosses the stick into the frigid surf, and dives in after it. The dog plunges in, valiantly paddling to get there first.

Marc slouches in the seat, sensing he's violating a private moment. For an instant, he considers joining the race, but soon thinks better of it. Even if he could tolerate the cold water, such a move would only be misinterpreted as a sexual advance.

At one with the waves, the man bodysurfs to shore. His faithful companion paddles in his wake with the stick in her mouth, then rolls victoriously in the sand. Making eye contact with Marc for the first time, the man pauses, then smiles mischievously.

Marc feels the tug of sexual tension. After a moment's hesitation, the man turns his back, then steps into his shorts. Certain he's misread the signal, Marc averts his eyes in embarrassment. When he looks up at last, man and dog have disappeared over a dune.

Marc stares out at the waves, chastising himself for timidity and neediness. Eventually, hunger triumphs over self-pity, and he decides to return to the Purple Feather. Partway to town, he sees Dorrie shuffling down Bradford Street. Her crooked, wooden walking stick seems to be the only thing preventing her from folding onto herself. He stops, lowers the passenger window, and eagerly calls out.

"Hi there."

Dorrie removes a half-smoked cigarette from her mouth and smiles broadly. "Hi, yourself. Glad to see you're up and at 'em this mornin'. I wasn't so sure you would be."

"That was a wonderful dinner last night. Thank you again."

"Nothin' to it. I got plenty of leftovers if you want more."

"Where are you going, Dorrie?"

"I usually go for a walk after breakfast. Where you headed, Marc?"

"For coffee."

"Where at?"

Marc shrugs, suddenly wishing she'd join him. "The Purple Feather, I guess."

"Can I come too? I got a hankerin' for one of their apple tahts."

Again, Dorrie has that heads-down, schoolgirl look. As Marc ponders the needless barriers that youth and sexual preference can erect, the spontaneity and joy of the man at the beach speaks to him. He steps gallantly out of the car to open the passenger door. "I'd love nothing more."

"Get your ass back in there this minute. I don't want no Queen of England treatment. The day I can't open a car door for myself is the day I hang it up."

"As you wish, Your Majesty." Marc jumps back behind the wheel, saluting as Dorrie slides onto the seat. She responds with a playful slap to his cheek.

When they enter the cafe, the only other customer is a young black man intently typing on his computer. Dorrie nods at him, and he responds with a grin.

"What will you have?"

"Apple taht and hot chocolate—my treat," Dorrie says reaching for her jacket pocket.

"No way. Not after your help finding me a place and a job, to say nothing of that great stew last night." Marc's at the counter before she can protest. When he returns with their order, he says, "Dorrie, I feel I imposed on you last night, pouring my heart out like that when we'd just met."

"Bullshit. I knew we'd be pals when I first laid eyes on you and that something good was gonna happen. When I get an instinct like that, I follow it come hell or high water. Despite what Lola might say to the contrary, I'm damn good in the friendship department. So, no more apologizin'. If friends can't tell each other their troubles, we're all just a bit more alone in the world.

Dorrie hesitates, toys with her fork, then continues.

"I knew someone a lot like you, once. His name was Daryl. He rented a room from me one summer and stayed on for five years. We became damned good friends. Did we ever have us some wonderful times. Laughs? No one had as much laughter in him as Daryl. He'd make fun of folks in town and have me in stitches every day. I was getting close to sixty-five back then and wasn't dealing with it so good. He teased me all the time about it, sayin' things like 'Hey, Dorrie, I've dug a big hole in the backyard. Why don't you try it on for size? Might as well be sure you'll be comfortable.' Or he'd ask me what it felt like to greet Myles Standish when the Mayflower first landed here. Daryl was silly and fun, with a heart of gold. And flowers—did that boy ever love his flowers. He kept a beautiful garden behind my house. It's all gone to weeds now."

Marc is touched by the lonely look in the old woman's eyes. "What happened to him? Did he leave town?"

"No. He's here… in St. Peter's Cemetery. He died just before they started havin' all the lifesavin' medicines. He's buried in the family plot—my mother's spot, as a matter of fact. Given she disappeared, and I never knew my father, there was plenty of room for a good friend. God knows it tore me apart to be the one to put him in the ground 'stead of the other way round."

"I'm so sorry."

"You know, it was the damnedest thing how lonely I felt once he was gone. I'd never had anybody I could talk to the way I talked to Daryl. He just got it."

As Dorrie's eyes grow moist, Marc stares at his cup. "Got what?"

"Hard to say, in a way. Somehow, he knew what it was like to be me. Never having no family, always bein' an outsider, never fittin' in. Even though he'd lived in all these highfalutin' places, Los Angeles, Montreal, San Francisco, and the like, he still knew what it was to live from day to day as a person just tryin' to make the best of things. I was at the Best Western back then, doing chambermaid work to fill my days. Daryl waited tables at the Mayflower Cafe. When he took sick, I quit my job and helped nurse him. The last thing he said to me before he died was, 'Thanks for being the best friend I've ever had.'"

Dorrie shudders. Her lower lip quivers. All at once, she looks centuries old. Feeling awkward and incapable, Marc waits for the moment to pass. Eventually, she looks up and smiles. "Weepy old women—nothing worse on God's green earth."

"Far from it."

"Well, I got a joke for ya," she says with a mischievous gleam in her eyes. "It was one of Daryl's favorites. What are the only geese that don't fly?"

"I give up."

"Portu-Geese."

Cast On My Grave a Flower

Dorrie and Marc stroll to his car in easy conversation. "Where to next?" he asks.

"Go up by Napi's and cross Bradford, then go straight. At the end, cut left over to Alden Street. I want to stop by and see Daryl." Dorrie points to a side street, making it clear she'll navigate a neighborhood he's never seen before.

"Is that where you go every day?"

"Every day that's fittin' for nearly twenty years now."

"Wow."

"What the hell else do I have to do? Cut the interrogatin,' Sherlock, and drop me off at the goddamn cemetery. Make it a round trip, though. It ain't my time just yet." She grins before continuing, "And, if you don't mind, I got some grocery shoppin' of my own I wanna do afterwards."

It's just nine as they drive up Freeman Street. A large delivery truck is parked by Napi's Restaurant, and Marc can barely squeeze past it. Dorrie coaxes him with cryptic hand signals he can barely interpret, making him feel both amused and slightly annoyed. Finally squeezing past and crossing Bradford Street, Marc parks at the Provincetown Florist.

Dorrie turns to him with a quizzical glance. "What the hell are we doing here? Don't tell me you fell in love overnight? You boys. Honest to God."

Marc laughs, runs into the shop, and buys a small bouquet of Paperwhites. When he returns, he places the flowers on the console and follows Dorrie's convoluted directions toward Alden Street.

"Now to the left. Now right. And up this drive."

Marc sees a crucifix outlined against the fog-shrouded sky, and behind it, a tiny, domed chapel. All else is a sea of gravestones, some with artificial bouquets that look garish and rigid in the gray half-light. The names carved on the stones are a roll call of Azorean families: Silva, Costa, Travers, Cabral.

Dorrie points to a large stone inscribed with the name Machado. "There it is. Over there."

Marc hands her the flowers. "These are for Daryl, with my compliments. Now get out of the car before they wilt at your touch."

She smiles, then fumbles with the door to no avail. When he jumps out to assist, she scowls. "What did I tell you about that bullshit? I'm not helpless."

Marc waits beside the car as she extricates herself and climbs a slight incline to the Machado plot. She places the flowers in front of a small, square marker, then lowers her head, crosses herself, and begins to pray.

When she wipes away a tear, Marc leans on the open car door and averts his eyes. Suddenly, everything hits far too close to home.

Taxi Driver

Dorrie's shopping doesn't take long. Even so, Marc chafes at the delay, anxious to return to his writing. Once her groceries are loaded in the car, she says, "Stop by Adams."

Fighting a frown, Marc drives Commercial Street until he spies a sign that reads *Adams, est. 1875*. He parks, expecting Dorrie to get out. Instead, she issues another command.

"Go in and tell the girls I'm gonna head on home and put my groceries away. I've taken enough of your time."

"What girls?" Marc sighs.

"The only goddamn girls in there. It's past nine-thirty. Our time is nine on Fridays. They won't be hard to find. There's only four tables in the joint, for God's sake."

He makes his way into the shop where three elderly women sit at a corner table.

"Dorrie's not coming today."

The combined ages of "the girls" must approach two hundred and fifty years. The nearest one surveys him from head to foot in a deliberate manner.

"You're new. I ain't seen you around before."

"Yes, I am," Marc says with resignation.

"Where you headed?"

"I'm taking Dorrie home. She's got groceries to put away."

"Sorry. Forgot my manners. Name's Dolores, by the way. Dolores Delgado. This here's Bea Silva and Lydia Butler."

The other women wave as Dolores stands. Clearly, she's the leader of this geriatric pack. She reaches for a clear plastic rain hat and puts it on. "Say. You can drop us home, too. This wind will ruin my hair."

Marc, wide-eyed, doubts any force of nature would even make a dent. *It's got to be the last beehive on the planet. A throwback to another time. Indestructible, like the coelacanth. Still alive and swimming when everyone said it was extinct.*

Without waiting for his response, the three women waddle toward his car. He follows, his annoyance building. *I've been in town for twenty-four hours, and I'm already a walker. If this is how my life is going to be living here, maybe I should just get out while I still can.*

The odd assemblage tours the West End via Conant, Brown, and Pleasant streets. At each stop, Marc's routine is the same: rush out, open the door, hoist an elderly woman out of the car by her fragile arm, escort her to her front door, wait for a key to be found in a voluminous purse and the door unlocked, then smile sweetly as each one says, "Thanks, dahlin', see you next Friday."

He has the strangest feeling they will.

We Are Family

Returning to HomePort, Marc studies the house. Far above, its rectangular tower flaunts ornate arched windows set into a shingled mansard roof. At the peak, within the bounds of an ornate cast-iron railing, a weathervane in the shape of a whaling ship points north, a spouting whale just off its bow. Once again, he feels drawn to the tower. He ignores the call this time, partially as a matter of principle, mostly out of spite.

When he reaches his room, he's hardly surprised to find Helena stretched out on the chaise. Her right arm hangs languidly over its back as her svelte legs extend beyond its length. A slingback pump dangles from each foot. She's dressed in white capri pants, a purple halter top, and a short, red wig. Marc estimates her true age to be in the early thirties. It had been impossible to tell when she wore the Mrs. Danvers getup.

A large pitcher, two croissants, and two champagne flutes rest on the table beside her. The scene looks like a brunch shot from *Better Homes and Gardens* circa 1958.

"Hair of the dog, hon?" Helena pours a mimosa without waiting for his answer. "You're an early riser, I see. Or is this a walk of shame?"

"Just getting in from breakfast," Marc replies, silently bidding farewell to his muse for the day. *There's simply no escaping the denizens of HomePort; it's futile to resist.*

Helena's penciled eyebrows arch. "He wanted you to stay for breakfast? How marrrrrvelous! Tell me is it *L-O-V-E...* love?"

"I'm not sure yet, but both parties are definitely intrigued."

When Helena hands him his drink, Marc raises his glass. "Here's to romance in all its infinite possibilities."

Her forced smile fades. "Oh sure, story of my life. I provide the turndown service, and then get turned down."

Marc flushes slightly. "Not quite."

There's something about Helena's wide-eyed vulnerability and ready emotion that moves him. Her passion is refreshing and somewhat endearing, to say nothing of the fact that her blatant interest is flattering. He quickly dismisses any notions of romance. *Life, liberty, and the pursuit of literature. No emotional entanglements. Not for a long, long while.*

"I ran some errands for Dorrie and then drove her girlfriends home from Adams," he says with a slight trace of sarcasm. "After that, I helped her put away her groceries. Not exactly a night of unbridled passion, was it?"

Helena searches his face, then smirks. "Oh. I should have guessed there'd be another Provincetown marriage in the making."

"What the hell is a Provincetown marriage?"

"I made it up, darling. It's what sometimes happens between an old Portuguese woman and a young gay guy. It's not a fag hag thing, and it's not a grandmother thing. It's something totally different."

"I've never heard of it."

"You don't see it that much these days. There aren't many of the old gals left—or their gay 'husbands' for that matter. Years ago, you'd see them all over the place. A Portuguese landlady feeding a starving artist from her husband's catch and getting a portrait in return or 'gentleman boarders,' who cut hair to pay the rent."

Helena raises her glass with her little finger extended.

"Before I moved to Homo-Port, there was an old gal on Franklin Street who was as poor as a church mouse. All she did was watch television and smoke cigarettes. When her TV died, the guys in the neighborhood chipped in and bought her a new one the very next day. Later on, I found out they'd paid her oil bill for years. I've never seen anything like it except here in P'Town. These Portuguese ladies are something else. The gay guys just love them, and they sure love their gay guys."

Marc takes a sip of his Mimosa. "I met some ladies this morning with Dorrie, including one with a beehive that defied gravity."

"Dolores Delgado? She's the cook here."

"That's the one."

"Isn't that hairdo of hers something else? I've tried to copy it, but the hair on my wig must be too thin. It topples over like the Leaning Tower of Pisa."

"I bet you don't have industrial-strength hair spray."

"Don't be so sure, hon. I've tried stuff you could lay brick with. It wilts after two feet, like seaweed out of water."

"Dolores doesn't live here. I dropped her off at her house."

"No, she comes in, makes dinner, and serves it. I usually eat with Lola to keep her company."

"Speaking of Provincetown marriages, did Dorrie ever talk to you about a gay friend who died?"

"Daryl Rousseau?"

"Yes."

"Well, from what I know, that was one beautiful example of what I'm talking about. She saw him through to the end and spent most of her savings on his care. Without her, he would have died broke and alone."

"You knew Daryl?"

"No. He was before my time. Some older friends told me how she took care of him. I've had a soft spot for her because of that, amongst other things. She's such a survivor. I feel better just hearing the raspy sound of her voice. She props me up in the romance department when my love life craps out, which is about every three months like clockwork, should you be interested in taking a turn."

Marc blushes. "By the way, thanks for the turndown and the chocolate. That was really sweet of you."

Helena sets her drink on the table, rests her chin in her right hand and stares into his eyes. For an instant, she looks like a silent film actress, though there's hurt in her veiled gaze that seems totally at odds with her flawless makeup and pert wig.

"You could have thanked me last night, you know. I left you a key. Most men would kill for the opportunity. But you, *foolish boy*, let it slip right through your fingers." She drapes her legs back over the chaise in what seems a forced show of indifference. Only the slight downward turn of her ruby-red lips gives her away.

"Look, Helena—"

"Don't look Helena, me," she interrupts, her eyes flashing. "I know what you're going to say: Thanks, but no thanks. Not my type. Good for a laugh, but not exactly someone you'd bring home to mother. Spare me. I've heard 'em all." She throws up her hands in disgust.

"You don't know what I was going to say, and unless you shut up and really listen, you never will."

Helena neck snaps backwards. She lowers her legs to the floor. Placing her hands on her knees, she sits quietly like a toddler made to take a time-out.

Marc struggles to keep the morning's accumulated frustrations from boiling over. "That's better. Now I want to be sure you understand something. I'm not interested in you." He pauses to allow her temper to ignite for a second time. "Nor am I interested in anyone else right now. I left my lover yesterday. As much as I had no choice, I'm not about to take up with someone new right away. Surely, you can understand that. When the time comes, I won't care what he wears, or what he does for a living. But until then—"

Helena stands, throws her hands in the air like a gospel singer, and yells, "I's shakin' hands with the unemployed."

Though her joke helps ease the tension in the room, Marc is unwilling to let her off so easily. "Great line, Helena, but let's stick to the topic at hand, if you'll forgive my poor choice of words. I like you a lot. But right now, what I need is a friend. I've left my entire life behind…."

Helena takes his hands in hers.

Mission: Impossible. Brandon.

Marc crosses the room, sighs, and shuts off the phone. When he returns, Helena adopts the manner of a streetwise reporter, clasping an imaginary pen and pad.

"Was that your ex? Lola told me he's calling all the time. You should change your phone number. I hope your cell plan doesn't charge for all those calls from that jerk." Helena's tone is admonishing, almost maternal.

Marc remains standing, unnerved by the feelings welling up inside. *There will be no attachments for at least a year. None.* He stares out at the harbor, choosing his words carefully.

"Don't worry about it, Helena. After what happened with Brandon, I'm just not ready for someone in my life right now. It's not you. It's me."

"Well, there's a man out there somewhere for *me* and *him*," Helena says, pointing to herself twice, "even if it isn't you. And, when *we* find him, he's going to be one lucky fella. Imagine, a three way every night! Keep *that* in mind, darling, in case you have a change of heart."

Marc can't help but admire her persistence.

"I simply have to get going," Helena says with a tight smile. "Places to go, people to see, clothes to iron, dust to raise. One last thing about that ex of yours. Take some advice from someone who's been around a lot more than you or I. The Lady Chablis has a great saying, 'Two tears in a bucket. Motherfuckit.'"

Helena stands, brushes her hand seductively across Marc's face, slaps his butt, and runs from the room.

Sparks Fly

Still digesting the exchange, Marc makes his way to the kitchen only to find Lola seated at the table by the window, a teacup in her hand.

She motions him to sit. "Do have some tea."

"It's a bit early for me, thanks."

"This is the genuine article. Fortnum and Mason. Imported from London."

"Well then, why not?"

Lola retrieves an ancient Brown Betty and a second cup. "Might I ask what brings you to see me? Is anything wrong?"

"No, everything's great. I did have something to ask you, though. Would you mind if I used the tower for a place to write? There's a sort of folding bench and table up there that would do nicely."

Lola seems astonished. "You want to write way up there? That's quite the coincidence."

"Why?"

"Well, that's where Father wrote, most every day, in all kinds of weather. Before the house was electrified, he used a kerosene heater to keep warm. He'd always say, 'I'm off to climb Staunton's Lookout,' which meant he was going up to write and should not be disturbed." She fills Marc's cup. "Lemon?"

"Yes, thanks. Please tell me more about Staunton's Lookout. I've heard that name somewhere."

"HomePort is the second house on these grounds," Lola says, unbending slightly. "Before that, there was a house built in the early 1700s. It was added to over the years and burnt to the ground in the 1860s. The original Staunton parcel goes back to the time when Provincetown was known as the Province Lands. Commercial Street ended at our bounds, and our property ran to the low water mark. Father sold some frontage to the Provincetown Inn, but the town took the rest to extend Commercial Street. He always said they had no right to take away our harbor access and claimed the street as our property for as long as he lived."

Lola's voice takes on an ethereal quality, as if she were telling a fairy tale to a child. "Before this house, there was a tower on the large hill behind us. It was just a scaffold, really. You can still see the foundation. They called it Staunton's lookout. My grandfather, and his father, and perhaps even his father before him, used it to identify ships rounding Race Point. When a Staunton ship was spotted, they'd hightail it into town to make preparations at Staunton's Wharf. When this house was finished, the old scaffold wasn't needed. It fell into disrepair and eventually was torn down. Everyone called the new tower by the same name.

Suddenly, she seems to return to the present. "You're certain you want to work way up there? It gets quite cold when it's windy."

"I was thinking I could use an electric heater. There's an outlet."

"Well, I don't see any reason why not. In fact, I think there's a heater in that closet over there. Father used it after we got electricity. I'm a real old Yankee. 'Waste not, want not.' I'm quite sure it's still there, unless Helena snuck it out during one of her cleaning binges. Why not see if it still works?"

Lola directs him to a closet under the stairs. Behind an assortment of mops and buckets, Marc uncovers something that looks like a satellite dish. Lola smiles in recognition. "That's it. Give it a try. Might be a good idea to dust it off first, but go ahead and test it out before you get the mail. It would be lovely to have someone writing up there again."

"Thanks Lola. You're the best." This time, she's ready for his kiss.

Marc sprints to the tower, opens the table, and lowers the bench. He's about to plug in the heater when a tall, dark, shadow appears on the balcony below. It's the man from the beach. Seeking distraction, Marc plugs in the heater. There's a pop, a spark, then the smell of burning rubber.

"Power's out," Helena yells from her apartment door. "Cole, sweetie, be a love and go check the fuse box?"

Marc reaches the second floor landing just as Cole, still dressed in the clothes he'd shed earlier, enters from the Bates Motel. Cole registers a trace of discomfort when Marc extends his hand.

"I'm Marc Nugent, the new gardener. I think it was my fault. Lola gave me this heater. When I plugged it in up in the tower, all hell broke loose."

Discreetly surveying Cole's broad chest and arms, Marc decides he must be a couple of years older. Up close, Cole's body seems so different from the chiseled types back in New York. His muscles are not emphasized, they are so well integrated his entire body radiates strength and balance. Marc imagines him running wooded trails for hours, more satyr than man, his adoring retriever loping beside him.

"Cole Hanson," the satyr says after gazing at Marc's outstretched hand for a tense moment. "I'll go reset the fuse. I should take a look at the outlet upstairs as well, by the look of that mess."

Cole touches the scorched rubber plug. "You can't use that old thing."

The sullen demigod whose deep green eyes take in everything yet reveal little in return captivates Marc. "Apparently not. May I help in some way?"

"No thanks. If need be, I'll replace the outlet, but you'll need another heater. We should monitor the circuit when you try it." Cole points to the second apartment. "I live over there. Come and get me when you get one."

Marc tries not to stare too long at Cole's rich, thick lips. "Okay, I'll pick something up when I do the mail run."

Cole strides down the stairs and out of sight.

In a few minutes Helena yells, "Lights are on. Thanks Cole, honey."

Marc grins. *He's certainly knocked mine out.*

Mail Call

Marc has underestimated the time it takes to walk to the Post Office. He gives up on the hardware store. Beginning the trek back to HomePort, he hears Ellie, P'Town's timeless showgirl, singing Gershwin in front of Town Hall. Her deep voice fills the empty streets with the lyrics to "The Man I Love," which causes Marc to revisit his tense conversation with Cole. *He did come on to me at the beach. What an idiot I am.*

Marc pauses at the Boatslip and stares out at the deserted harbor. He's surprised to see a whale-watch boat pass Long Point until he realizes it's heading south for the winter, part of a steady migration that has nearly emptied the harbor. He strides past the general store, now stripped of all its goods, and reaches Flyer's Boatyard where the pungent smell of low tide assaults his nostrils. Where Commercial Street turns left at an ungainly white house, a bust of Shakespeare stares down from a second-story window, startling Marc with its incongruous presence.

"Okay, Will," Marc yells up to the statue, "don't begrudge me a little security. I figured I'd be the starving artist when I came here, but I doubt even you'd have turned down this setup."

A tall, spindly woman with a cane and large rectangular glasses rounds the corner. She studies him closely. Marc jogs past her, certain news will rapidly spread of the new guy in town who talks to statues. He passes a small red house at the water's edge with a gilded sign that reads "A Home at Last," then the West End Beach, and finally, on the lower side of the hill, the Red Inn. Checking his watch, he sprints up the path to HomePort.

When he enters the kitchen, Lola is nowhere to be found. As he stands panting by the stairs, the cellar door opens, and Cole appears with a pair of wire cutters in his hand.

"Hi Cole! Where's Lola?" Marc asks, immediately regretting how perky and effete his voice sounds.

Cole stares at the floor, obviously still uncomfortable. "The mistress's parlor. She'll be waiting for her mail. I'd get in there quick if I were you. It's gone half past eleven, and she likes her routines."

Marc finds Cole's brooding intensity both sexy and disconcerting. "Where's the mistress's parlor?"

Cole points to a large oak door. "Through there, last door on the right, diagonally across from the big parlor. By the way, the wire up in the tower burned right through. You were lucky you didn't burn the house down. I'll have to run a new line from the fuse box. Drive me to the hardware store after you finish with Lola, and I'll get what we need."

Marc, delighted there hadn't been time to buy a heater, laughs to himself. *One minute's conversation with a handsome man has rallied every domestic thought I've ever had. Looks like nothing gets my nesting instincts in high gear like home improvement.*

Marc lowers his voice an octave in a lame attempt at nonchalance. "Great. I'll look forward to it. See you at noon. Right here."

He jogs down the hall to an open door. The mistress's parlor, papered with pale white silk, is filled with delicate, varnished furniture. Lola sits at a beautifully carved desk made of inlaid mahogany. In front of her are three rectangular oak boxes, one labeled "Social," one labeled "Charity," and one labeled "Charlotte." Charlotte's is overflowing with mail.

Lola looks up when he arrives. Her white hair is tied in a ponytail, exposing more of her translucent skin as well as thin wrinkles around her throat. "Come in, young man, come in. I see you found the room all right. You know, in the old days, this was the heart of HomePort. My mother saw to everything from this very desk, plotting her moves like a general. There wasn't a goings-on in the house or the town she didn't know about from her command post at this desk. Of course back then, it was quite a different operation. The cooks lived in the house next door, sometimes with a handyman/chauffeur husband, too. We seemed to go through them like water. Cooks, I mean. Not husbands. The parlor and kitchen maids were housed out back on the second floor, two to a room. All those young women at the end of nowhere. You've never seen such catfights. Sometimes, it would take two or three hours to sort through the doings of the day. But don't worry; we won't be that long. Better sit down and take a load off, though."

Overwhelmed by Lola's prattle and unsure of her expectations, Marc sits on the edge of a tub chair. She replaces her pointed glasses with a pair of oversized round white ones that, with her long white hair and parchment skin, make her look like an aged film star. Reaching for the stack of mail, she takes a quick look, then passes it back to Marc. "Read me the sender, then hand it to me, and I'll put it in the right box."

"Citicorp."

"That's Charlotte."

"Seaman's Savings."

"Charlotte."

"Provincetown Art Center."

"Charity."

"Bernard L. Madoff Investment Securities LLC."

"Charlotte."

Most of the mail is for Charlotte. When they reach the last envelope, Lola issues her orders. "Tomorrow, put everything that's been set aside for Charlotte in a priority mail envelope and send it to this address. She insists I send her this stuff once a week." Lola hands him Charlotte's business card. "Now go on with you. It's a beautiful day out there. Enjoy it, kid."

Real Man's Work

Cole is eerily silent during the short drive to the hardware store. Once there, he prowls the aisles with focus and efficiency. Marc tags behind, enjoying the diverse glimpses of humanity at every turn. He sees a grandmotherly woman with orange hair, a girl with two prominent nose rings, and a stately queen transfixed by a daunting choice of dishwashing liquid. These cameos all present themselves to the sounds of a vintage pop radio station. While Marc drinks in the scene, Cole seems oblivious. Their purchases take little time and even less discussion.

Once back in the car, Marc makes another effort. "Do you need to stop anywhere else while we're out?"

"Nope."

"It must be difficult trying to maintain a place like HomePort."

"Not really."

Before Marc can come up with anything more meaningful to say, they're back at the house.

"I'm going to trace the old wire back to the fuse box," Cole says, seeming more at ease once out of the car. "Then I'll need some help running a new wire down from the tower."

"That's fine with me. I'm happy to help since I get the benefit. You don't have to do this right now if you have other things to do, though."

"Might as well. Everything else is okay for the moment. You'd better get into old clothes. It could be messy. I'll see you up in the tower in ten minutes."

Cole races up the stairs leaving Marc to his thoughts. *He tells me when and where to meet him just like Brandon. There's a sign, for sure. It feels so damn familiar, I could slip right into the same routine. Thank God I've got the willpower to stick to my resolutions. Yeah, right. If that guy stuck out his finger, I'd perch on it in a second. Who am I trying to kid?*

By the time Marc climbs to the tower dressed in his oldest jeans, Cole has a plan. "Okay, so we're in luck. The wire runs through a couple of studs, then drops down a dumbwaiter shaft. We can attach the new wire right beside the old one. I never knew this thing was here," he says, pointing to a partially opened door in the oak paneling.

Cole opens the panel, and Marc notices a large rectangular box suspended from a pulley by a thick, braided cable. The box is large enough to contain a person, though he'd have to hunch over.

"That dumbwaiter must have brought Captain Staunton's food to the tower," Marc says. "Lola told me he wrote up here."

"Makes sense," Cole says. "Hold this spool. I'll check the cable." He oils the pulley, which begins to turn after a few tugs. "The pulley at the base probably needs to be done as well, but I think this will work to get us started. Once we run the new electric line, I'll check the whole cable, since it's been in one place for so long."

"Where does it go?" Marc asks.

"All the way to the basement, I suspect. Probably stops on every floor."

"Do you think they used it much?"

"Don't know. I wasn't here then, you know."

The project seems to have made Cole more comfortable. Marc smiles to himself. *Man stuff, obviously. Wish I'd practiced it more as a kid.*

"For now, string this wire down there, will you, Sherlock?"

Marc can no longer suppress a grin, though Cole seems not to notice. Once they descend to the third floor, Cole opens the attic door with a rusted skeleton key. "I've never been in here. I had to get the key from Lola. Until now, this place has been as off limits as the first floor study," he says in the same businesslike tone.

Dim bands of light filter through shuttered skylights placed high up on the north roof. The enormous space is filled with furniture, picture frames, and canvases all under a century of dust. A harp stands in one corner, its strings unbroken. Even though the detritus of generations, little seems damaged or unserviceable. It's all preserved—better said conserved—in the incurable Yankee expectation that no matter how outmoded, it might prove useful one day.

Marc feels the same tingling sensation as before, but the source seems softer, gentler, and more feminine. There's the same strong yearning and yet another welcome to what is clearly a sanctuary.

Cole points to a wall that divides part of the room. "The dumbwaiter should open about here. Probably behind this picture."

The base of a large gilt frame peeks out from beneath a dusty sheet. The men move the heavy painting out of the way and lean it against a long, mahogany table. Before they turn back to their work, the sheet slips to the floor unveiling a masterful portrait of a woman in a red evening dress who is playing the very instrument before them.

The painter has captured her at the apex of youthful, extraordinary beauty. Her figure is trim, yet sensual and provocative despite the dated clothing. She's no longer a child, but not quite a woman. Her features suggest a trace of uncertainty, yet her eyes betray hauteur that makes them seem cold and condescending. The painting seems to place her at a crossroads, eager to please while slightly resentful of the need to do so. She wears the same diamond pendant that Lola wore to tea, along with matching earrings. Marc recognizes the front parlor in the background. It's hardly changed.

Whatever has engaged Marc's senses suddenly expresses a violent reaction to the portrait. Venom, vengeance, and rage pour through him. His knees start to shake, and he nearly reaches out to Cole for support. The emotions fade as quickly as they'd arrived.

Cole's eyes grow bright. "Wow. That's fantastic. It looks like a Morrison."

"How can you tell?"

"Well, he painted women in that kind of languid pose, with lush hues. The signature should be about here." Cole takes a corner of the sheet and brushes dust from the painting with delicate, almost reverent, strokes. The work seems to respond to his touch. Its colors become more vivid, the woman's face more beautiful. "Yeah. Here it is. This thing is worth a fortune."

"How do you know so much about art?"

"I studied painting at RISD. A few years later, I did a residency here at the Art Center."

"May I see your work sometime?"

"No. Sorry." Cole replies as his face grows taut.

Marc surveys the room, blushing slightly. A ray of sun illuminates a complex set of ropes and pulleys attached to shutters on the north ceiling.

Cole's enthusiasm seems to return against his will. "Someone used to work up here. There's paint on the floor and those easels. The skylights are right where they should be to catch the north light. It's a damn fine studio." As his eyes grow wide and his voice more resonant, he points to a far wall. "There are signatures and dates on those canvasses. Let's see if we can find out whose studio this was."

Marc flips a light switch.

"Laetitia Staunton," Cole says, picking up a dusty painting and cleaning it. "That's Lola's grandmother. This was *her* studio. These paintings aren't bad." Cole looks around in awe, seeming to forget Marc who is lost in his own experience. The essence has returned. The sensations are gentler this time, but still convey loathing mixed with concern. Marc slowly recovers his equilibrium, watching in fascination as Cole paces the floor, points to the skylights, and calculates trajectories.

"This would be one kick-ass place to paint," Cole says at last. "I bet it hasn't been touched in a hundred years, but whoever designed it knew exactly how to get the best light." The impassioned radiance in Cole's green eyes and the energy in his voice quicken Marc's pulse. Afraid of giving himself away, he turns to study the ancient harp.

Cole relapses into sullen silence as they string the wire to the basement. Once he oils the second pulley, the dumbwaiter moves with ease. He checks the cable, wires the outlet, then ties the wire into the fuse box.

Marc is greatly impressed with Cole's diligence, which he considers a great quality in a husband. The notion is banished with the usual admonitions.

The two men return to the tower. Marc plugs in the newly purchased heater, which glows without smoke or sparks. "Fantastic," he says, trying mightily to keep the simper out of his voice. "Thanks so much, Cole. Where did you learn how to do wiring? I can barely operate a light switch, never mind do something like this."

"My uncle was a building contractor. I worked for him every summer until I came here." Cole's tone is slightly wary.

"Where is he now?"

"A nursing home in Quincy. He had a stroke two years ago. It's too much for my aunt to care for him at home."

"And your parents?"

Cole traces a pattern in the dust with his right foot. "Dead, if you must know."

"I am *so* sorry. I didn't mean to pry."

Cole's jaw tightens. "Yeah, whatever."

Marc feels as though he's been slapped. With a quick, apologetic glance, Cole wipes his hands on his jeans, opens the hatch, and disappears from sight.

CHAPTER 4
THE TEAPOT DAME
CONSPIRACY

November 14th, 2008 - The Tower, HomePort

First entry from my new writing space. I can see for miles in every direction. The only thing in the whole town taller than this tower is the Pilgrim Monument.

I should be working, but I can't take my mind off that fiasco with Cole. I really blew it asking all those questions. I should have left well enough alone. He's not all perfection, though, despite how gorgeous he is. I may not be a writer yet, but at least I haven't given up. Why did he abandon his art? I could tell in the old studio he still loves painting, whether he knows it or not. Maybe he needs a little push.

Now wait a minute. You saw how he reacted to you. You'll just end up in front of Town Hall like Ellie, singing "The Man I Love." Remember, no matter what that song says to the contrary, Tuesday is ironing day around this joint....

* * * *

At four thirty that same day, dressed in freshly pressed chinos and a blue Oxford shirt, Marc passes through the kitchen into HomePort's grand front hall. Crossing its parquetry floor, he peers into a vast dining room whose gracious mahogany table could easily seat thirty. A closed door is across from the dining room, and beside that, an oak-paneled library with pristine, bound-leather volumes in leaded-glass bookcases.

He pauses for a moment at the ornate staircase. A bronze statue of a draped woman stands atop the newel post, an ornate gas lamp cradled in her upraised hands. Marc imagines the woman in the portrait descending the staircase. He can almost see the soft light reflecting in her diamond necklace.

Marc rouses himself from his reverie, passes the mistress's parlor, then the ornate grandfather clock with its golden, celestial face. When he reaches the double doors of the front parlor, he takes a deep breath and knocks.

Helena slides the doors open dramatically, then smiles in surprise. She looks stunning in an off-white dress with a low cowl that flows partway down her pale shoulders. The dress complements her height and lean physique. Her makeup is subdued, with none of the exaggerated palette that characterized her Mrs. Danvers outfit, though the beauty mark is still in place. Today, she's an elegant, statuesque, society debutante wearing a pearl choker with matching bracelet.

Helena blinks coquettishly as Lola looks up expectantly.

"I'm terribly sorry," Marc says. "It must be Helena's day for tea. Am I intruding, or might I have a word with both of you?"

"Oh, please, do come in, my dear. We're just about out of girl talk, aren't we, Helena?"

Lola is comfortably dressed in a flowered housedress, her white hair flowing over her shoulders. She looks relaxed, but her large eyes have dark circles under them that, when magnified by her cat-glasses, remind Marc of a raccoon.

"Nothing that can't wait, which is all I seem to be doing these days," Helena replies, her eyelashes fluttering rapidly.

Marc sits next to Lola, who seems to be trying to decipher the exchange. When he explains the power outage, Lola dismisses the topic with a wave of her hand.

"Yes, Cole came to me for the attic key. I hadn't even noticed. But you didn't come here to discuss such mundane matters. What is it you want, my dear?"

"Well, I'm not certain where to begin. I don't want to meddle."

Helena laughs and hands him a teacup. "Don't be coy, Marc. Meddling is a winter sport in Provincetown. How else does a girl survive the bad weather?"

"C'mon, kid. Out with it," Lola adds.

"Do either of you know Cole was, or rather is, an artist?"

Helena replies after a puzzled glance at Lola. "Yes. I do."

Marc studies Helena, still impressed with her ensemble. One would swear she was a New York heiress come to visit an elderly aunt and about as far away from Mrs. Danvers as a drag queen could ever get.

Lola chuckles. "At long last I have one on you in the gossip department, Helena. And I'm going to make the most of it. Most people don't know I'm a patron of the Provincetown Art Center. I tire easily in crowds, and the Center is kind enough to let me see the fellows' work in a private showing. About three years ago, an old friend told me there was a show in the East End by a promising young artist, and that I should be sure to see his work. As you can readily guess, it was Cole. His paintings were impressive— transcendent, in fact. Some were tranquil, almost celestial, while others were incredibly violent, with images so real you wondered if the canvas itself was on fire. There were two pieces in particular that spoke to me, for reasons that aren't relevant to this conversation."

When Helena starts to speak, Lola seems to come to a decision. "A picture's worth a thousand words. Come with me, my dears. Both of you." She rises with effort, leads them down the hall to the room beside the library, takes a key on a long silver chain from around her neck, and unlocks the door.

"Marc, this was my father's study. I use it as my bedroom and keep it locked for reasons that shall become clear in a moment. Helena is the only other person who has a key."

The large room is spacious and dimly lit. Rich wood paneling, marble statues, and sculpted plaster moldings give the feel of a New York townhouse from *The Age of Innocence*. Scores of paintings hang on the four walls, a few readily identifiable as Staunton whaling ships, though the works run the gamut from Chinese art to French Impressionism. Lola's single bed, covered with a worn, yellow spread, seems incongruous in such a lavish setting.

Lola parts thick brocade drapes. As waning daylight illuminates the room, two large paintings, hung above a massive, carved oak desk, glow in the light. One is of a young boy of seven or so seated with his mother and father on the rocky shore of a lake. A second, younger child stands at the water's edge, looking at the others with intense concentration, as if trying to make a memory last. In the companion piece, the same boy is staring at a wall of fire. The family is barely visible behind the flames, in exactly the same pose, as if the memory were incinerating as he watched.

Marc is overwhelmed by the paintings' power and astonished to learn Cole painted them.

"I thought I recognized them when you described them, Lola. How in the name of God did you get them?" Helena asks eagerly. "Everyone said he destroyed all his work."

Lola smiles knowingly and flips a switch. Two picture lights increase the intensity of color to the point where the flames seem to radiate heat. "The moment I saw these two, I simply had to have them. There was a part of me that resonated with the child's loss of his family. Cole's parents and brother died in an automobile accident, you know. Cole was thrown from the car and watched them burn to death, the poor boy."

Marc hardly listens as Lola continues her story. He's too busy chastising himself for pressing Cole about his parents.

"I'd forgotten my checkbook, so I arranged for my friend to buy them at the opening that night. When he arrived, he found two men savaging Cole's work in an attempt to knock down the prices. My friend warned the manager, who marked these paintings as sold to encourage others to buy. Just then, Cole threw everyone out, closed the show, told the manager to take down all the paintings, and ran off. I understand it was quite the scene."

Marc studies Helena closely. She seems intensely interested.

Lola continues her tale with a trace of drama in her voice. "My friend roused me, and we hatched a plot right in this very room. As he described what happened, I had a powerful intuition that Cole's work was in danger. I swear I heard my grandmother's voice telling me to send the poor man up to the attic to retrieve two unfinished canvases. At my insistence, he drove me to the gallery where I grabbed my two purchases and, with the manager's help, substituted the ones from the attic in the pile on the floor.

"I swore both men to secrecy, telling them of my premonition and convincing them we had a moral obligation to protect at least some of the work, even from the artist who created it. They agreed as long as they could deny involvement were Cole to find out." Lola's eyes sparkle, and she seems to stand a bit taller as she explains how she enlisted Enrique to help her search the town for Cole the next morning.

"Once we spotted him on MacMillan Wharf, I engineered a chance encounter, then brazenly chatted him up. He didn't know how to handle the old bat talking his ear off, but he was polite enough to listen, the poor thing. And with an atrocious hangover to boot. His mood frightened me, but I used his innate courtesy to win him over and spirit him safely to HomePort. Once he found how far from town I lived, he came willingly enough. I don't think he cared what he did as long as he got away from the Art Center and anyone who knew him as an artist. When I showed Cole his quarters, and we settled on a salary, I grew confident he wouldn't harm himself. While he retrieved his things, I phoned the fire and police chiefs and saw to it no one bothered him. One of the benefits of being brought up in this town is you know the people in charge. Sometimes, it makes all the difference.

Marc grins at Helena who is clearly impressed by Lola's machinations.

"I've never found a way to tell Cole I have his paintings, or to pay him for them," Lola says, her face clouding with sadness. "You can't do one without the other, don't you know. They're hidden in here until I'm sure he won't destroy them. I may have saved them from his fury, but I'll feel like a thief until he's been paid what he's owed. I've tried everything to reach him. I've showed him part of Grandmother's collection and her art books. He's polite, but gets to a certain point and just goes quiet. When that happens, it's as if a steel wall drops between us. I'm so afraid he'll be destructive if I confess what I've done. Cole has to be ready to move past that night, and I'm not sure he is yet. Until then, he and his work won't be safe."

Lola sighs and shakes her head. "The money is in Seaman's Bank—nearly twenty thousand dollars—just sitting there in both our names, collecting interest. I'm totally at a loss, my dears, totally at a loss."

Marc walks closer to the fire painting and studies it in detail. "Well, I've got an idea."

Lola stifles a yawn. Marc starts, then looks out the window in embarrassment, unsure if he's been rebuked. "Forgive me, my dears," she says sheepishly, "I don't mean to seem rude or disinterested. It's just that I tire so easily. May we continue this discussion over dinner, the three of us? I usually take a nap from five to seven, and after yesterday's protracted tea, I need my beauty rest more than ever. I want to be at my best for you, Marc. I hope you understand."

He smiles and nods, all umbrage forgotten.

Lola pushes a button on a vintage intercom and brings a round earpiece to her ear. "Dolores, dear, can you do one more for dinner? Oh, that's wonderful. Yes, the usual time. Sorry about the short notice." Lola puts down the earpiece and smiles. "You two cogitate for a while, and we'll regroup at dinner. Marc, I'm *thrilled* you brought the subject up. I've struggled to find a way to fix this for years."

Lola's head is on the pillow before Helena closes the door.

Dinner at Eight

At the appointed hour, the three conspirators gather at one end of the long dining table. As a fire crackles in the fireplace, Dolores announces four courses: onion soup, salad, roast beef, and chocolate cream pie for dessert. Then she winks at Marc and dodders back into the kitchen.

Lola tilts her head and rolls her eyes, signaling that Dolores is eavesdropping behind the kitchen door. "We'll save your thoughts until brandy, dear boy. We should talk in a more intimate setting where I can be certain to hear every word. In the meantime, what shall we discuss?"

"When Cole and I were rewiring today there was a—"

Mission: Impossible. Brandon.

Marc mutes the phone.

"Let me guess?" Helena says. "The beastly Brandon? Again?"

Marc nods, feeling his color rise.

"You'll have to deal with him some time or other, hon. He's not going to give up." As Helena wags her finger in mocking reproach, Lola comes to Marc's rescue.

"Now, now, Helena, don't lecture the poor boy. All things in time, my dear. All things in time. Some people need time before moving on. Do let Marc have a *bit* of privacy. He's entitled to a few days amnesty before we worm all the details out of him."

They've finished all but dessert when Marc returns to the topic derailed by Brandon's untimely call. "Up in the attic, there was this beautiful portrait of a woman with a harp. Cole said it's a Morrison. It's so lovely; I'm curious why you don't have it hanging downstairs."

Lola slumps in her chair, her wineglass partway to her lips. "Gardenias! That thing. I almost forgot it was up there. Well, why not? I'm not going to be here forever, and I'm darn tired of being the only one alive who saw what happened."

As Helena and Marc exchange puzzled glances, Lola drains her glass, then takes a deep breath. "It *is* a Morrison. The woman in the portrait is my mother, Prudence Staunton. May she rot in hell."

Helena and Marc stare in astonishment while Lola reaches for more wine, then describes how the painting was commissioned by her grandmother, Laetitia, as a gift for Lola's father when he returned from a three-year voyage.

"Cole is right," Lola says, looking embarrassed. "It *is* a masterful work, and it hung in the front parlor between the two porch windows, until the day after my mother was buried. Then Father carried it to the attic himself and never spoke of it—or my mother—again. It's been up there ever since. Even after he died, I couldn't bring myself to hang it downstairs. He loathed it so, and truth told, I don't want any more reminders of that woman than there are already. I'll leave it to the Art Center when I die, I guess, but I refuse to dredge up scandal in my lifetime, so it will stay in the attic until I'm well past caring."

"Why do you think he hid it?" Marc asks.

"I don't think. I know. He hated my mother, and I'm pretty certain he had good reason. I know I did."

A chill invades the room. As the kitchen door creaks, Lola signals for silence. Helena and Marc sit quietly while Dolores serves her pie. When she finally leaves, reluctantly it seems, Lola speaks again. "My, what delicious pie! That Dolores is such a wonderful cook." Then she winks and begins to eat.

"In the old days," Lola says at last in a cheerful voice, signaling with her eyes that Dolores is still at her listening post, "the ladies would withdraw to the parlor and leave the gentlemen to their port. Shall we do away with that custom for this evening, my dears, and all of us regroup in the library?"

Helena stands. "Absolutely. I have enough of an identity crisis as it is, without trying to figure out whether to go or stay."

Through the Eyes of a Child

In the library, firelight reflects in the glass-fronted bookcases, casting multicolored hues on the oak-paneled walls. A bottle of brandy and three snifters warm by the hearth. Marc sits next to Helena on an antique sofa while Lola makes herself comfortable in a vintage Morris chair. She presses a button, and the sound of Maria Callas singing "Vissi d'Arte" fills the room.

Lola takes a large gulp of brandy. "Alright, my dears. Now that I've topped off my liquid courage, I shall tell you what I know. It all happened a long time ago. I may not remember the words exactly, but the events are seared in my brain.

"I was ten. The day began like any other, not too long after the New Year, as I recall. I heard raised voices in the kitchen and snuck downstairs to listen. I hid on the back stairs, at the turn before the last three steps. I often laid low around the house, spying on my mother and father. Neither of them had much time for me. Later in life, I came to understand my father's gruff, distant love, but at that age I seldom saw much of him without a certain degree of espionage.

"Excuse me, I digress. Where was I? Oh yes, I was hiding on the back stairs. Andoria, our young cook, was trying to see Father, who was up in the tower. We called her Annie, and she was a favorite of mine. I had not seen her for some time and was distressed by what I saw. Her hair had come out of its bun, her face was red and drenched with tears, but it was her eyes that I remember most. They were wild, like a wounded animal's. I heard her scream 'I must, I must see him. I must go up to him.' I loved Annie, and I had never seen her in such a state. Her voice struck terror in my young heart.

"When I stuck my head around the corner, I could see into the kitchen. Agnes, the housekeeper at that time, stood barring Annie's way. My mother, who had been in the mistress's parlor, came in but didn't see me. She told Annie my father had left that morning for an extended trip. I knew he was upstairs in the tower, so this confused me. What she said after that made even less sense until years later. She told Annie she'd backed the wrong horse, and that my father lacked the gumption to stand by her once he'd gotten what he wanted.

"'He's abandoned you to the consequences of his lust,' my mother said. 'Don't come looking for sympathy from me. I told you to move out yesterday. I meant it then, and I mean it even more after this disgraceful scene.' Then she told Annie if she didn't leave immediately, she'd see to it she never worked another day in her life.

"I couldn't believe my mother could be so mean and spiteful. With that, Agnes took Annie by the arm. She tried to break free, but Agnes bent her arm behind her back and dragged her toward the door. Annie kept pulling, trying to reach the stairs. I was so upset I leaned too far, slipped off the step, and gave myself away.

"Everyone stopped in their tracks until Annie pointed at my mother and spoke a curse that raised the hair on the back of my neck. It went something like this: 'Your lust has corrupted your heart and shall soon destroy your beauty. Within five winters, you shall be food for the worms, and your own flesh and blood shall loathe the very memory of you.'

"There was a stunned silence. My mother clasped her hands to her face and tottered as if she might faint, before ordering Annie to leave at once. Again, Annie refused. Agnes cried 'witch,' picked up a broom, and began to swing it wildly until Annie ran from the house. The last I saw of the poor girl, she was running down the hill toward the moors. I can still hear that curse after all these years."

Lola shudders despite the fire's warmth. "My mother stood clutching the banister. Suddenly, Father came running down the stairs so fast I barely had time to get out of his way. He stared at her with hatred such as I have never seen.

"'What have you done?' he said, his voice cold as steel. 'You should have let me deal with her. You'll be the ruin of me yet.' My mother glared back with defiance and loathing, but said nothing. He began to speak, seemed to think better of it, then raced out the door after Annie. Then my mother ordered me to my room."

As firelight reflects in the lenses of her pointed glasses, Lola seems to choose her next words with care. "Father was gone for three days. The next morning, I overheard the servants talking. One of them said that Annie had drowned herself out at Herring Cove, another that someone had seen her leaving town in an ambulance. Then Agnes said Father had killed Annie and buried her in the dunes.

"I fled to my room. All I could think of that night was the look on Father's face. Why was he so angry? And what did that have to do with Annie? I struggled to understand. I didn't want to believe what I had heard, but the more I relived the moment, the harder it was to ignore.

"When Father finally returned, he wouldn't say a word to my mother, nor did she speak to me. It was as if she couldn't bear the sight of her own child. She left for months at a time after that, leaving me in Father's care, not that I saw all that much of him. And three years later, she left for good.

"Father was never the same from that day on. Whenever I asked after her, he told me to mind my own business in a voice so filled with anger I soon knew better than to ask again. He hired a new cook immediately, and before long, all the gossiping servants, including Agnes, were dismissed. Nothing was left but emptiness once Annie ran down the path to the sea.

"So now you know."

The silence is laden with discomfort until Lola speaks with false heartiness, "Marc, you poor thing, you certainly got more than you bargained when you came for a word at teatime. It's ten at night, and you still haven't had it. Out with it, kid."

Marc grapples for the right phrase, then finally says, "Cole needs our help."

CHAPTER 5
MONEY TALKS

By the time November gives way to December, the daily mail runs have become routine. Marc finds Helena was right; Lola's language and temperament do vary depending on the audience and the nature of the tale. Noticing how much mail she blindly sends to Charlotte in New York, Marc begins to worry if Lola is capable of looking out for herself. She seems to focus on the past despite an enormous fortune to manage in the present. He considers discussing this with Helena, but decides to broach the subject directly during a mail-sorting sessions.

"I don't mean to interfere Lola, but do you think you should be relying so heavily on one individual to manage your money? There's a lot going on in the market these days. I assume you realize that, but you don't even look at the things you send to Charlotte."

"Why, I never! No one has ever said something like that to me. What brings this up, young man?"

Marc is rattled by her tone. "I just thought you might not know there's been a major stock market crash."

"To be honest, Marc, you're right. I haven't a clue what's going on in the market these days. I have implicit faith in

Charlotte and don't bother to follow Wall Street or any of my other investments for that matter."

"Faith is all well and good, but it can leave a person vulnerable." The words are out before he's had a chance to consider them. He suddenly feels awkward saying this to a woman nearly four times his age, even more so when he sees her astonished look.

"Let's talk this through for a moment, Marc," Lola says as she tugs a strand of her snow-white hair. "At my time of life, I'm looking back over close to one hundred years. While you might think I'm unaware, I made something of myself way out here all on my own. I've studied, read, and met lots of different people. Human nature is what I know best. I can spot a fabricator at fifty paces. My father used to say it was a gift from his mother, my grandmother."

Marc struggles to recover. "I'm sure you have experienced the less appealing side of humanity, everyone asking for handouts and such."

Lola nods. "That's for sure. Social responsibility was drilled into me as a girl. My grandmother Lettie, in particular, was always talking about my *Position in Society.* As if you could call the rich ship-owners who lived in town back then 'Society.' They might have had tons of money, but they still smelled of fish. My grandmother was an amazing influence on me, by the way. She traveled everywhere and was a voracious reader. When things got… oh, well, it doesn't matter what they got." Lola scowls as if she's caught herself about to give something away. "What I mean to say is that Grandmother taught me more about life than any school ever could. She showed me how to educate myself when others were too distracted to care, making me who I am today, even if I may be out of place in the modern world you seem to worry so much about."

Lola stares absentmindedly at a silver inkwell. This happens often during the conversation, as if she's struggling to remain in the present. "Getting back to your concerns, young man, I grew up with money and saw the best and the worst of having it. I can afford to be generous—very generous—to people who deserve my assistance, but I also know the risks. We Stauntons have made a difference around here for nearly two hundred years. I take that legacy and the responsibilities that go with it very seriously."

Marc studies Lola, trying to tell if he's made his point. Suddenly he realizes she's studying him in return. Recalling Dorrie's warning that he'd be under strict observation, he quickly looks away.

"I can't help wondering at the reason you asked, Marc. But I'll give you the benefit of the doubt and assume you have my best interests at heart. In any case, don't you worry yourself about *my* money. I don't. If I lose it, I lose it. Grandmother Lettie used to say it all the time: 'I, John Jones, being of sound mind, have spent all my money.'"

Hush… Hush, Sweet Charlotte

The first Thursday in December, as Marc writes in the tower, his cell phone rings.

"Marc, it's Lola. I need you to meet Charlotte. She's on the Cape Air flight that arrives at ten fifteen."

"Of course. How will I recognize her?"

"Just look for the most petite, lovely, stylish, energetic young woman getting off the plane. That will be her. And Marc, you can take *that* to the bank."

* * * *

Marc waits in the terminal, worried his conversation with Lola has precipitated Charlotte's sudden visit. As he ponders unemployment, two of Brandon's crowd, Chuck Thetford and Alan Connor, stroll languidly through the gate. Marc scans the remaining passengers in case Brandon is with them. He's not.

Convinced his days at HomePort are at an end, Marc considers running to his car, but Chuck and Alan have already spotted him.

"Well I'll be damned," Chuck says in a loud, effeminate voice. "Look what I've found!"

Dressed in tight jeans and leather jackets, each man has an earring shaped like a small spoon in his right earlobe. So thin they appear malnourished, they constantly scan the room as if in search of an audience.

"Hi guys," he says, noticing how reptilian and predatory they appear. "So this is where you ran off to," Alan crows. His shrill voice draws everyone's notice, including a woman with the most piercing eyes Marc has ever seen.

"What are you doing here?" Chuck asks. "Meeting some new trick? Brandon was devastated when you ran out like that. He's still hasn't gotten over it. He doesn't go out, just hangs around all day waiting for you to return his calls."

Marc stands mute, praying they'll leave before Charlotte overhears anything more.

Alan raises the volume. "So, tell us. Where are you living these days? In your car?"

As Marc colors, an arm links in his. The woman with the piercing eyes speaks to the two men in a voice that brooks no nonsense.

"Sorry to break this up, girls, but Marc and I have some important business to discuss. It can't wait." She starts to walk, and Marc has no choice but to tag along.

As they reach the door, he hears the two men exclaim to each other, "Him? With Charlotte Grubb? It can't be. He can't possibly have enough money for someone like *her* to be bothered."

Charlotte doesn't break her stride. "Friggin' idiots! They cornered me at JFK, and then again at Logan. Couldn't stop talking about how they were wiped out, and did I have any advice for them. Then they start in on you like a couple of fishwives. What a pair of dopes. They deserve every loss they got and more."

"Charlotte Grubb," she says, holding out her hand. "Lola's told me a lot about you. I've never seen her so high on a 'member of the household' before. Has she heard the bad news?"

"You mean about the market? I don't think so. She seems pretty vulnerable though, based on the mail she's been sending you—all that stuff from Madoff. I thought her money was socked away in a conservative WASP investment company."

Marc studies the attractive woman at his side. Her brown bangs flatter her wide brown eyes and long eyelashes. She wears tailored beige slacks with a matching jacket that sports a gold pin comprised of three interlocking triangles. Two gold chains drape over her white silk blouse. Her shoes appear to be Italian leather, as does the bag she carries over her left shoulder. He feels a surge of energy and efficiency from her, and much to his surprise, extraordinary warmth.

"Oh, you think she's vulnerable, do you? Like those two assholes?" Charlotte grins, pointing toward Chuck and Alan who are just hailing a cab. "Not with Charlotte Grubb on the job. Let me tell you something, Marc. Lola's made a friggin' killing in this market. She's not *invested* in a conservative WASP investment company. She's the majority shareholder in a conservative WASP investment company—C. Grubb & Company. In case you're wondering, that's a huge difference. There's so much money in that trust the big guys have been chasing after her, trying to pry a bit loose to cover their fat butts."

Marc doesn't know what to think. He's been convinced all along that Lola's faith was misplaced.

Charlotte continues with a triumphant smirk. "All funds come directly to me in New York. Lola gets solicitations all the time from people trying to work around me. She's smart enough to send them to my office without even bothering to look. That's what you saw. Last ditch pitches from greedy fools with one foot on the ledge. When she told me you were concerned, I figured I should come and show her how she's positioned. Given all the turmoil in the market, I'd hate for her to be worried at her age. Besides, I need to do some Christmas shopping."

When they reach Marc's car, Charlotte clutches his arm. "Is that your Volvo? I love that model! I cried for days when mine died after three-hundred thousand miles. May I drive it? I haven't driven one in years."

Charlotte gets behind the wheel and holds out her hand for the keys. Racing from the parking lot, she drives through the Beech Forest, regaling Marc with nonstop tales of how she sold short months before the crash. As she tells it, each early tremor in the market foreshadowed a calamitous result that no one else anticipated but her.

Far from being mismanaged, the Staunton fortune is intact. Despite this reassuring news, Charlotte's monologue from the outside world and questionable driving skills leave

Marc slightly frazzled. He's forgotten what high-powered New Yorkers are like, both in conversation and behind the wheel. His thoughts wander back to Chuck and Alan, two of Brandon's drug buddies. Obviously, they are still in touch with him. They certainly owe Marc no allegiance. It's likely they'd have phoned Brandon as soon as they could. Marc recalls their inane chatter and constant sexual innuendos. *There's no sense even trying to persuade them to remain silent. They couldn't resist the drama of having found me. The news will race through Brandon's circle of friends in less than a day even if Chuck and Alan don't tell him themselves.*

Then Marc thinks of his HIV test results, due in four days. He doesn't even notice when Charlotte pulls into HomePort and parks the car. She tries to hand him the keys. When he doesn't take them, she taps him on the shoulder and stares in concern.

"C'mon in and see Lola with me. You need to get past your suspicious nature, Sherlock, and I've got a thing or two up my sleeve that ought to help. Better yet, find Cole and meet me in the mistress's parlor. I need a couple of witnesses for some routine paperwork."

Charlotte's Web

When Cole and Marc arrive, Charlotte and Lola are reviewing papers spread all over the desk. Standing beside her diminutive trustee, Lola seems a giant.

Charlotte holds up a balance sheet, making sure Marc can see it. "So, you not only didn't lose, you *gained* a little ground in all of this, Lola sweetie. Not a bad showing, if I do say so myself." Charlotte waves at Cole, winks at Marc, then looks up at Lola with undisguised affection.

"Well, thank you, my dear," Lola says, returning her loving gaze. "As I told you on the phone, Marc was worried, but there's really no need to come all the way up here to reassure me. I have every confidence in you, Charlotte. I always have. Just like your father and grandfather before you."

Charlotte's tone holds a trace of embarrassment. "To tell the truth, everyone in New York is ready to jump out a window. I needed a break and figured this was the one place in the world where things would still be the same."

"Amen to that," Helena says, entering the room dressed like a fashionable woman of the post-Civil War era, complete with parasol. "Are you giving away money today, darling? Where do I sign? Make it quick, please? I've got a mudpack heating up with my name on it, and no time to spare."

Charlotte throws her arms around her. "Hi honey. Maybe next visit. *If* you will just behave for once. I'll go upstairs with you, though. I've missed our girl talk."

An hour later, Charlotte, in black jeans, a black leather jacket, and a cowboy hat with a black leather band, knocks on Marc's door to propose a walk at Race Point. As they drive through the National Seashore, she seems to have lost some of her intensity, as if HomePort has restored her in some way. "Like I told you before, Marc, I've heard great things about you from Lola. She's got a tremendous amount of confidence in you."

"I'm surprised to hear it. I thought I really pissed her off when I asked about her investments. I was afraid she'd throw me out on my ear."

"Don't dwell on it. You'll probably never know for sure, but something about your concern clicked with her. I've never seen her so pleased. Lola's a tough nut to crack. For years, I thought she didn't like me, then when I got my Master's, she turned the Staunton Trust over to me as a graduation present. I suspect Dad had something to do with it since he was getting old, but she's never questioned my judgment. There's nothing I wouldn't do for Lola. The income from that trust set me up in business and made me what I am today."

"And according to Chuck and Alan, you're a goddess of Wall Street."

"Damn right. But if those two twits think I'm given' it away for free, they got another thought coming." Charlotte grins, then pokes him in the chest. "Now you, on the other hand, given how good you've been to Lola, if you ever need anything—anything at all—you just let me know."

"Well, there might be something…."

As they stroll by the water's edge, Marc speaks of Lola's fear her father had committed murder, as well as her estrangement from Dorrie. "I have a hunch that there's much more to it," he says, stepping back quickly when a large wave rolls too close. "I think it likely Lola and Dorrie are half-sisters, but I don't believe the murder angle. I have this powerful feeling someone has gotten it all wrong. It's as if some psychic force wants me to set things right. I know it sounds crazy, but I can't describe it any other way. Do you know anything that might help sort out this mess?"

Charlotte seems to be deciding whether to trust him. "I'll go through my father and grandfather's files," she offers at last. "They're both dead, so there's no one I can ask. I don't have the same hotline to the afterlife as you do."

Marc colors with embarrassment. When Charlotte grins, he realizes she was teasing. "Would you mind doing that? If we can clear up this whole mess before it's too late…."

"Alright. I'll check the electronic files while I'm here and review the rest back in the office. Let's see if we can make it all the way to the lighthouse and back while the tide is still out. I haven't had my power walk today, and if I don't get one in, bad things happen."

* * * *

The following Monday, Marc is up in the tower confronting yet another blank page when his cell phone rings. It's a New York area code but not Brandon's number. Marc takes a chance and answers.

"Hi. It's Charlotte. I've been through Lola's records. There is one strange thing, but it's not telling me much."

"What's that?"

"Well, for years, from February of '26 until three weeks before he died in '52, there were weekly cash withdrawals from the captain's personal account at Seaman's Bank. The money is significant for those days. Much more than pocket change. The amount goes up by five, ten, or twenty dollars a week in January, but stays the same for the rest of the year. Always on a Wednesday, with a cash withdrawal from the teller's window."

"Your records are that specific?"

"Absolutely. I had all the old handwritten ledgers and statements digitized when I took over. What strikes me is these are the only expenditures I've ever seen where Captain Staunton noted the withdrawal but didn't document its purpose. Hope it helps."

"It might. Hey, Charlotte?"

"Yes, Marc?"

"I'm glad you're in on this."

"Wouldn't miss it for the world, Marc. Lola's all the family I've got left."

A House is not a Home

The next afternoon, Marc is on Bradford Street when a Jeep Wrangler passes, then slams on its brakes. Before Marc can escape down a side street, Alan has hold of his arm.

"There you are! We've been looking all over town for you!" Alan's shrieks, his voice taut with false, unnerving heartiness. "Let's head back to the house and catch up on old times."

"Thanks, but I have some errands to run."

Alan tightens his grip. "Marc, we should talk about Brandon. There are a few things you ought to know."

Marc considers his plight. These two are Brandon's closest friends, and while he loathes them, perhaps he might be able to enlist their silence after all. He jumps in the back seat.

Chuck and Alan's house, an oversized, misguided attempt at a Cape Cod shingle style, sits at the crest of Telegraph Hill. Once inside, Marc is surprised to find there's hardly any furniture.

"We're sort of in-between," Chuck says with a trace of awkwardness. "Renovations are about done, but we haven't sold our place on Bayberry yet. Let's sit on the sun porch. I've got some folding chairs out there. What do you want? Wine, beer, hard stuff, some blow?"

"Nothing, thanks. I can't stay long." Marc studies the view, which, while lovely, doesn't come close to that of the tower at HomePort. Of all of Brandon's entitled, pushy friends, these two are the worst. The blatant pretension of their house makes him feel superior.

Alan's voice gains intensity. "Well, let's cut to the chase then, since you're so rushed. We want in with Charlotte Grubb."

"What are you talking about?"

"Don't give me that innocent crap. All New York knows she's a goddamn dyke investment genius and about the only one to come out of this mess unscathed. What do you have to do with her?"

"That's none of your business."

Alan reddens with anger. "Well, then let's talk about something that is. You walked out on Brandon. He's a fuckin' mess. All he talks about is how he can't find you. He doesn't call it a party without you anymore. As dear friends, Chuck and I feel we have to tell him where you are. Unless you get us set up with Charlotte baby—and fast." Alan grins at Chuck as though he's scored a victory.

Marc bristles.

"Look. I left Brandon because he was *already* a mess. He didn't become that way because I left. The best thing for him would be for his folks to get him into rehab."

Memories of Brandon overtake Marc's thoughts, the optimism of their early days, the gradual dawn of disappointment, and the brutal finality when there were no more excuses to be made.

"I don't think that's gonna happen," Chuck replies sarcastically.

"Well, that's their problem, not mine."

Alan seems incredulous. "You really don't know, do you? Brandon's convinced you found out."

"Found out what?"

"His parents are broke. Just about everything they own, including Brandon's loft, is up for sale.'

"No. Brandon never said a word, and neither did anyone else. I'm sorry to hear it, but that's no concern of mine anymore."

Alan's lips contort into a sneer, accentuating his predatory appearance. "It will be when we tell him where you are. He'll be in town the very next day. He went wild when you left. He tells anyone who will listen you bailed when the money ran out. He says he's going to kill you. If I were you, I'd be at least a trifle concerned."

Marc stands, flush with anger. "Oh, come on. Get real."

"Wait a minute. Don't leave. Try to understand," Chuck pleads. "We're fucked, too. We built this house with a one-year bridge loan. Now the market's dead, and our stocks aren't worth a cup of piss. The real estate market is shit, and we can't sell our other place. We need to reposition fast, or we're going to lose our shirts."

"Sorry to hear it, but I don't know Charlotte as well as you might think."

"You know her better than we do, and she seems to like you well enough," Alan says, looking directly into Marc's eyes while speaking in a low, malevolent tone. "I'd suggest you hook us up with her or Brandon will make your last hospital stay look like a week at the Ritz."

Marc scans the room for a quick exit. "I don't like being threatened."

"Marc, don't mind him. He's freaked out." Chuck silences Alan with a glance. "C'mon, we're desperate. Give us a break, huh? At least think it over. Here's our number."

"I'll think about it, but no promises." Marc takes the number and walks out.

* * * *

Once back at HomePort, Marc retreats to the tower to consider his options. With reluctance, he calls Charlotte in New York. When she answers, he skips the pleasantries.

"Charlotte, I can't believe I'm asking a favor when we've only just met, but I really need your help. Those two guys from the airport are threatening to tell my ex where I am unless you help them. They say he's even more violent, and there's good reason to believe them. If Brandon comes after me, I'll have to leave HomePort to protect Lola. I don't want things to come to that."

Charlotte hesitates. "Listen, Marc, I gotta get some more perspective on all this. Why are you so convinced he'd harm you?"

Marc takes a deep breath. "He was addicted to crystal meth and grew extremely dependent toward the end of our relationship. He became obsessed with the idea I was going to leave. The more strung out he got, the more he tried to force me to stay. I didn't realize just how far he'd go until it was almost too late. I barely got out alive."

"And you're certain he'd try to find you if he knew you were in P'Town?"

"Positive." Marc winces at the double meaning of his answer and the memories it invokes.

Entering their bedroom, he'd found Brandon with two men. One, a tall Latino, was stroking himself while the other was penetrating Brandon from behind. A video camera sat on a tripod in the corner, its red light flashing. Brandon had grinned and beckoned Marc to the bed.

"C'mon baby, take a hit. It's fuckin' fantastic. You're gonna need all the help you can get to handle Ramon and Luis, here. They'll keep you occupied for a long, long time," Brandon had said, his eyes dilated, his voice eager.

Marc had stepped back as the two other men leered at him, their tweaked out faces reminding him of two death heads. "I don't want to do this."

Brandon had disengaged himself and jumped up from the bed. "For Christ sake, Marc, don't be such a jerk. I'm tired of all your Pollyanna shit. Let's get into some new territory. This isn't Kansas, anymore—this is fuckin' New York."

"No way. I'm leaving."

"Ramon. Grab him!"

Ramon had raced after Marc, caught him, pinioned him to the bed, grabbed his head and forced him to look up at Brandon who, by now, held an ancient katana in his hand. "Who the fuck are you to say no to me after all I've done for you, Marc? I want to see how you handle them both at once. Just shut up and get out of your clothes before I cut them off you."

"Put that knife down, Brandon. C'mon now. I'll leave and come back later, and we can talk about this. Don't do anything you'll regret."

Instead, Brandon had brought the katana to Marc's throat. "Ramon, hold his mouth open. Louis, take a hit, and then shotgun him, good. Don't let him exhale. If that doesn't work, rip his clothes off and put a shard up the other end...."

"Marc? Marc? Are you all right?" The anxiety in Charlotte's voice restores him to the present.

"No, Charlotte, I can't really say I am."

"I'm sorry. It's just that I needed to know what we're up against. Helena told me you had a rough time in New York, but nothing more. Don't worry. I'll take care of everything."

Marc sets down the phone and rests his head in his hands.

If only you could, Charlotte. If only you could.

Friendship Put to the Test

The day his HIV test results are due, Marc wakes early and tiptoes downstairs to the kitchen. After making a cup of coffee, he sits at the table and stares distractedly through the frosty windowpanes. The geraniums, their brown stems weak and brittle, have only two small buds, which are as far from the cold glass as they can be.

He's about to go for a walk when Lola shuffles into the room wearing a tattered chenille robe, her white hair stuffed under a hairnet. With her translucent skin, pointed glasses, and oversized eyes, she seems extraterrestrial.

"Oh Marc, you surprised me. I'm not dressed."

Marc rises. "Sorry Lola. I was about to leave."

"Sit for a minute, won't you? I've not seen much of you these last few days. I was saying to Helena only yesterday you've seemed distracted all week. Is anything wrong?"

"Nothing I can talk about. I'm dealing with some personal stuff right now. Thanks for asking, but I've got to handle it on my own."

"We all have times like that, and I'm not one to intrude, but are you sure—"

"Damn it, Lola. I'm sure." Marc pushes back the chair and strides toward the door as Lola pales, then grabs the copper-topped table for support.

"Now listen here, young man. Don't take that tone with me! Sit back down!"

Fearful she'll have a heart attack, Marc returns to his seat. Lola, seeming to recover, sits beside him. "You need to get it into your thick head that friendship is a two-way street. You seem to feel perfectly comfortable telling me what I should and shouldn't do with my financial affairs, but you act like a brat when I inquire about your well-being. For God's sake, grow up."

Marc smiles. He's been caught out and can't really argue. "I'm sorry Lola. It's something I'd rather not discuss. I apologize for yelling."

"Just don't make a habit of it."

Annoyed with himself, Marc leaves as soon as he can. Deep in thought, he follows the path through the woods to Commercial Street. Crossing to Pilgrims' Park, he studies the memorial carvings for a moment. Then, on a whim, he strides to the breakwater and steps onto the first stone.

The wind is from the Northeast. Its bite numbs his skin. Large waves course the harbor as gale-force winds transport icy spray that stings his face and brings tears to his eyes. The stones are slick and treacherous. He treads carefully to a point halfway between both shores, then stops to survey the scene before him.

The harbor is more than inhospitable, it's threatening. Few boats other than a hulking derelict remain at their moorings. Even the flats seem hard and unyielding. Something about the howling wind and biting cold suits Marc's mood, as if the elements amplify his rage. A seagull hovers overhead, its stark white feathers brilliant against the seething gray of the clouds. A second joins it, seeming to master the fierce wind with ease.

Marc imagines captaining a sailing ship under such conditions. *The waves and cold would be much worse outside the harbor. You'd have to plan every move to conserve energy. How could anyone who had never experienced such moments ever truly understand what it must have been like? Isolation such as this must have affected those at sea for years, forcing them inward, separating them from the rest of the world. Could I have endured such a life, and, if so, what kind of man might*

I have become? Perhaps the solitude, the one-on-one combat against nature has its own rewards.

He's hardly surprised when the mysterious presence from the tower answers with an impassioned *Yes*. The essence departs as quickly as it arrived.

Looking toward shore, Marc spies someone in a hot pink jacket delicately stepping from stone to stone. He waits sullenly with hands clenched behind his back.

"Helena."

"Marc."

"What the hell brings you out here in the middle of a gale?"

"If you want the God's honest truth, I was coming down the back stairs and heard your fight with Lola."

"Great. I guess I fucked things up pretty badly, huh?"

"Well, I wouldn't recommend doing it again, but she seems to have cut you some slack. In fact, she was so worried I decided I'd better find out what's been eating at you."

"Damn it, Helena. Can't a guy keep his thoughts to himself in this goddamn town?"

"Now look, Marc. You haven't been acting right lately. Lola was worried. As for me, I've got plenty of good reasons to be concerned why you're out here."

"What do you mean?"

"For Christ's sake. You're standing in the middle of the jetty in December during a nor'easter. No one in their right mind does that unless they plan to be washed out to sea."

"Helena, what are you saying? Did you think I was going to kill myself? It's low tide. There's not a drop of water within fifty feet of here."

"I didn't consult a tide chart before coming after you. I figured you'd gotten positive test results and was worried you shouldn't be alone."

"What? You know about the test? Jesus Christ. How'd you find out about that?"

"Well, I didn't know for sure, actually. But Dorrie told me AIDS had come up in conversation."

"Exactly my point. Too much damn gossip."

"It's not that simple, Marc. I know what it's like to be at the end of your rope and feel like there's no way out."

"Helena, stifle the therapy session. I'm fine. I just don't want people meddling in my life."

"Good grief, girl, get a grip!" Helena says, forcefully directing him back to shore. "You're so cranked up you can't even see how much people care for you. Especially me."

It Ain't Necessarily So

Marc and Helena leap gingerly from icy stone to icy stone, making their way back to Pilgrims' Park. Climbing the path to HomePort, they reach the Bates Motel.

"C'mon over to my place to warm up," Helena says, taking his arm.

Marc tenses but realizes he has little choice. He's never been in Helena's apartment before. The place is modest and clean, with only a few pieces of furniture. If not for the bolts of cloth, sheaves of feathers, and spools of beads hanging from the rafters, it would seem monastic.

"Sit and let me get you some tea. It won't take a sec." Helena says, bustling behind a counter with a built in gas top. "Then we gotta have us some girl talk."

Emotionally drained and embarrassed, Marc resigns himself to the inevitable inquisition, though traces of his earlier annoyance remain.

Helena hands him a cup. "So, talk to me, hon. I assume you know the results?"

"Haven't got them yet. The appointment is late this afternoon."

"Oh, *now* I get it. Anticipation driving you nuts, huh? *That's* what's behind the Dr. Jekyll and Mr. Hyde routine."

"Yeah, sort of. What did Dorrie tell you?"

"Not a lot. Just that you freaked when she said something about AIDS."

"It's true. Brandon had a serious addiction to tina and played around way too much."

"But *you* played safe?"

Marc stares down at the floor, takes a moment, then tells her of the night he left New York, the men in the bedroom, the camera, and the katana.

When he finishes, Helena's face is grim, a spark of outrage just visible in her dark brown eyes. "Oh, Marc. Why on earth didn't you tell me?"

"I don't want people feeling sorry for me. And I *don't* want to dwell on it, especially today."

"But you shouldn't go through something like that alone. I don't feel sorry for you, just the fact you don't seem to be able to trust anyone."

"It's not that," Marc says, coloring slightly. "I don't want people to treat me differently because something happened that was beyond my control. I've got my challenges just like everyone else. I don't want people meddling where they don't belong or looking at me with pity in their eyes."

"I hear you there, Marc. But you need to know something. While we folks at HomePort may meddle a bit, we don't tend to expend a lot of pity."

"That may be, but you've got to admit there's more than 'a bit' of meddling. You, Lola, and Dorrie are up to your eyeballs in everyone else's business. What was it you said when I first came here? Meddling is a winter sport? You can't blame me for keeping my mouth shut."

Helena looks into his eyes. "I know what you're saying. It took me a while to get used to it, too. You know for yourself now how gray and bleak it can get in the winter. A person needs some sort of distraction or they'll go mad. At first, I thought that why all the interest in everyone's business, but I've come to realize it's just the way this town works. Even the 'washashores,' as they call us, have concern for their neighbors once they've lived here for a while. Sometimes I think of P'Town like a big ship in the middle of the ocean. You may not like everyone on board, but at certain times, it's comforting they're in the same boat. I'm not ashamed to say I've been worried, Marc. Even though you can be the world's biggest asshole sometimes, there are things about you I really admire. You've told me a hundred times you're not ready for a relationship, but that doesn't mean I can't care for a friend.

"Now then, what time's our appointment?"

What a Little Moonlight Can Do

The second martini tastes even better than the first. It's early yet. The Mews is deserted save for the bartender, a fixture for decades, who gossips with the hostess on the far side of the room. Seated by the window, Marc and Helena watch an enormous full moon cast its light across the harbor.

"Well, there is still a chance I could be infected. Nothing's truly certain until six months have passed," Marc says.

Helena raises her glass with her little finger extended. "Look, hon. I always say take your joy where you can find it. Life sucks so you should celebrate whenever you can."

"I suppose you're right. I guess I have been a bit wrapped up in myself."

"Wrapped up? I've seen actors less self-absorbed. Even ones out of work."

Marc lets out a guffaw that fills his body with relief. He signals for yet another round. "I'll never get over the look on that four-square gal behind the desk at Outer Cape Health. I couldn't believe it when you started to sing "Everything's Coming Up Roses." I should have waited to tell you the good news. I thought she was going to have you hauled away in handcuffs."

"Oh, they need to stop taking themselves so seriously over there at Outer Space Health. It wouldn't do those folks any harm to have their feathers ruffled now and then. Besides, under the right circumstances, handcuffs can be fun. But back to you, darling. You really should have told me about Brandon. You gave Lola and me quite a scare these last few days."

"Okay, Helena, perhaps you're right, but why follow me out on the jetty?"

"Because I know what it's like to be really, really down. The bad stuff takes over and crowds out everything else until you can no longer tell what's real. Trust me, that's when the nasty shit happens. It was all a bad dream until my grandmother found me and called the ambulance."

"What?"

Helena seems flustered, as if having said something she wished she hadn't. "Don't worry, Marc. It was just bad teenage drama. I've been fine since I moved to HomePort. I'm more concerned about you. This is your first winter here. It's no picnic."

Marc studies her carefully. "Let's make a deal. I'll try to stay out of the pits this winter if you promise you will. We've got enough to be concerned about without worrying about each other. Worrying is different from caring after all."

"So you *do* care for me?"

Marc contemplates the bottom of his martini glass. "Yeah."

Helena points to the ruffles on her blouse. "Despite all this?"

"Because of it. It's who you are."

Helena sits back, her eyes shining, an impish grin on her face. "Darling, I don't know how to tell you this, but…."

"But what?" Marc asks, feeling a twinge of annoyance at the door he's re-opened.

"It's only six o'clock, but if you keep drinking those martinis as fast as you are, you could be a married man by midnight."

"C'mon Helena, knock it off. You know I'm not looking for anyone right now."

Her mortification shows readily. "Marc, I'm *really* sorry. Helena, 'the other me,' as I call her, always tries too hard. She takes over sometimes, if that makes any sense, and doesn't have a clue unless you rub her face in it. It's sort of like having Ethel Merman living in your head."

"Speaking of the 'other me,' do you mind if I ask you a few questions about all that?" Marc asks, hoping once again to shift focus away from his love life.

"No, not at all, Sherlock. Fire away. I'll trust you with my secrets, at least some of them. Just don't ask me what I really look like. There's only one way to find that out."

Though tired of Helena's constant innuendos, Marc recalls her concern out on the jetty and lets the remark pass. "What does all this impersonation do for you? What do you get out of it for all the hard work you put into it?"

Helena seems to be taking his questions seriously for once. "No one's ever asked before. I'm not certain I even know for sure, but I'll tell you what I can."

Her past emerges in fragments as she tells of her parent's bitter divorce and their indifference to their only child. She tells of finding solace in dressing up and becoming another person, eventually managing to appear old enough to get into gay clubs. During each pause, she scans Marc's face for a negative reaction. He senses she's constantly monitoring audience reaction, albeit an audience of one. The slightest frown could cause her to shut down.

"When I was a junior in high school, Mom had a boyfriend who swung both ways. He came on to me one night when she was out drinking with her girlfriends. Before I knew it, I was doing him nearly every day. Of course, he was still doing my mother, so it was pretty weird!"

Marc struggles to contain his reaction. *Not as weird as your lover putting a knife to your throat and forcing you to do porn, but certainly weird enough.* He's a bit appalled at the sense of competition he feels, as if he and Helena are vying to win an award for life's worst experience. *Clearly, we'd both make the finals.*

"Eventually she found out," Helena continues. "And was she pissed! But not in the way you might think. She was jealous, plain and simple." At first glance, Helena appears nonchalant, though the way she clutches her drink offers a subtle indication of her discomfort.

Marc loses himself in speculation. *If Helena is constantly acting, where are her genuine emotions? Do they come out as hers or surface through one of her personas? If expressed through a character, whose feelings are they? Did all this really happen as she describes it, or is it over exaggerated like so many other things at HomePort?* He comes to no clear conclusion.

Helena checks again to see if she's holding his interest before continuing her tale. "When things blew up, I ran away to my grandmother's. When she pried out of me what had happened, she gave my mom a real talking to. Mom's response was to leave town with her boyfriend without even saying good-bye. That really did a number on me, and after that, I guess you could say I couldn't stand the skin I was in. That's when I went off the deep end.

At Gandma's, which was my pet name for my grandmother, there wasn't much to do but sit with her and watch old movies on TV. There was something about the actresses: Bette Davis, Joan Crawford, Mae West, and the rest. Those broads were so strong, they always got what they wanted, inside or outside the bedroom. They could handle anything. After a while, I wanted to be just like them."

Helena sits poised on the edge of the chair, drink in hand, chatting as if at a nightclub. Every mannerism, though staged, is assured. She leans forward with a thin smile. Her neck is arched, her eyes bright, if slightly tentative. Even so, Marc senses potent emotion beneath her studied aplomb. She catches his probing glance and hurries on in obvious discomfort. "I'd make up personalities that were fun and easy to like, and I'd become that person in the bar. It wasn't drag. It was more like leaving myself behind. The new me was popular, and it also got me laid, which is a pretty good reward, dontcha think?" She abandons her Bette Davis imitation and resumes in earnest. "People seemed to like the fake me better than the real me. After a while, so did I."

Marc is genuinely intrigued. "Do you still become a different person or are you always Helena but just playing different roles?"

At once, she turns defensive and brittle. "You know something, Marc? I've never talked with anyone about this stuff before. Not even the queens I worked with. What is it about you and your twenty questions? You seem so darn wholesome and corn-fed, but sometimes I can't help wondering about your motives. You know how I feel about this sort of prying. I was asking Lola just yesterday if it's really being a writer that makes you so inquisitive. What do they feed folks way up there in Moon River?"

Marc's color rises. "It's Swan River."

As quickly as the change arrived, Helena returns to her former self. "We're supposed to be celebrating darling, and now I've pissed you off. If we're going to be best girlfriends, there's something you need to understand, Marc. There's a 'me' inside but also a 'her,' if that makes any sense. Sometimes I feel I'm running the show but most times, *she* is, and I'm part of the audience just like everyone else. They're both me, I guess, but listen, hon, you need to be prepared to deal with whichever one wins out at any given moment. I'm sorry if *she* came on too strong just now. Don't read too much into it. The 'real me' is pretty much of a recluse, like Lola. He never lets people see what he looks like, in case they don't like what they see. If they don't like the costume or the makeup, Helena can always change that, but if they don't like what's underneath, well...."

She winces, then hurries on.

"He'd probably be happiest married to a big strong man who'd make him feel safe and needed—a tall order, though as you can see, Helena never gives up trying. It's tough out there for folks like me. As Quentin Crisp said, 'Men get laid, women get screwed.' I've never quite figured out where that leaves the two of us...."

She lowers her gaze and smiles tentatively. "Please try and understand?"

When she looks up again, the lines of her mouth have fallen. Her cheeks have sunk. Her brash confidence has disappeared, and with it Helena's persona, as though she's retreated deep inside. For an instant, a frightened young man peers out through misty eyes.

"Don't give it a second thought," Marc says, smiling back at the man-child beneath the façade—whoever he may be.

CHAPTER 6
THERE IS A SEASON

January 4th 2009 – The Tower, HomePort

From every point on the compass, Nature offers a different display. Some days, the wind assaults the old house and makes the beech trees dance. Sometimes, the snow swirls around the tower so wildly I feel as if I'm alone in the middle of the ocean. Other times, the waves are so high I can almost imagine Helltown—the town that used to be on Long Point—being overwhelmed by the sea. No wonder they floated the houses back here.

Yesterday's snowstorm turned the beaches a brilliant white, but now its high tide. The harbor roils in whitecaps that flatten as they cross Long Point. There's not a trace of snow to be seen out there. Then there's the light. Many mornings, the sunrise makes me believe in some sort of divine plan. Right now, sun is setting. Red and purple color the sky. The gulls are returning from the ocean to roost, flying past me so close I can almost touch them.

Being up here, surveying all, has given me perspective. I've come to understand the impact of winter's desolation on the people who live here. The houses beyond the gate are empty, as are streets all across town. The isolation is intense. You have no one but your neighbors, if you're lucky to have any. I can almost picture what it was like when Lola and Dorrie were children and there weren't even empty houses nearby.

Sometimes when I walk downtown for the mail, the only sound I hear is the creak of signs blowing in the wind. Often, I don't see another soul. Even so, I'm less lonely than I was in New York. Go figure. Open mic at the Mews, dinner with Lola or Dorrie, a movie with Helena, and Outer Cape Chorale concerts are pretty much my social life. I've been to the A-House a few times, but wasn't comfortable enough to talk to anyone. It's too soon.

That place is fantastic if you study the decor instead of the patrons. All that history, the Mapplethorpe photograph, the nude picture of Tennessee Williams, and the roughhewn beams. I walked around just taking in the feel of the place but tensed whenever someone cruised me, so of course, no one came near. I'd end up just having a beer and heading home. A wild night, indeed, but right now that's okay. I have more important things to do.

I came up with the notion of a book about the Stauntons as an excuse to read the captain's journals. Lola loved the idea and gave me a key to the study, but I'm not to say anything to Cole because his paintings are still hidden there. The thick journals, nineteen in all, are elaborately bound and numbered with Roman numerals. It seems there was once a set of twenty, but the nineteenth is missing and the twentieth is blank. For the first time in more than fifty years, they're back in the tower. It's eerie to read them up here. I feel the captain's presence, as well as what it was like to live in this house a hundred years ago.

The journals are an intimate, firsthand account of the town's most prosperous era and a trove of information about how life was back then. There are fascinating depictions of the gale that devastated the coast in 1838. It sank the paddle *wheeler Portland, which was filled with passengers en route from Boston, all of whom perished. The captain's description of the wreckage and bodies on the back beach is heartbreaking. He also writes of the decline of whaling and its impact on Provincetown, chronicling the departure of the Yankees and the ascendance of the Portuguese. Unfortunately, there's nothing about the fate of Dorrie's mother. Nor is there any reference to the cash withdrawals Charlotte discovered. Even so, I'm still going to get to the bottom of things.*

Every Grain of Sand

During a spell of unseasonably warm weather in mid-February, Cole proposes an outing to see a colony of seals at High Head. Marc has extended several invitations to Cole for dinner, walks, and such, but all have been politely declined. Even an offer to drive to Wellfleet with Helena for a movie had been graciously, but firmly, refused.

Their shared obligations and HomePort's isolation bring Cole and Marc together often enough, but Cole says little. Once, when Lola invited both men to tea, Marc found himself straining to fill the silence. He must have done well enough, for Lola schedules them both for the same day from then on. During these conversations, Cole has become a bit less taciturn, but that seems mostly for Lola's benefit. He remains close-mouthed anywhere else. For all these reasons, Marc is stunned and slightly unnerved by the invitation.

As the two men walk from the parking spot, the warm sand and bright blue skies foreshadow summer. Frida forges excitedly ahead as if on the trail of an important discovery. Her winter coat is a soft fluffy gold, her ears are pert, her tail erect, her eyes alight with excitement. She lopes down the path to a hollow, stopping to sniff the animal runs and drink from icy puddles of rainwater that shelter the cranberry plants.

Low scrub pine, gnarled and twisted, bear witness to the wind's power. The evidence is everywhere in their gray twisted branches, the bowl-shaped cavities at the base of a dune, and most of all, the vast sand mountains that ring the far edge of East Harbor.

As the roaring surf grows louder, Cole seems to relax even more. When they arrive at the spot, the seals are riding swells near shore, their curious faces bobbing above the waves as they watch their visitors approach. Frida stares at the largest male with such intensity that Cole laughs aloud.

"She's saying, 'What's that dog doing, swimming way out there, like that?'"

"And the seal is saying, 'What's that dumb seal doing walking that way? And where are his flippers?'"

"Animals are more human than you might think," Cole says, pointing to a large bull whose whiskers make him look like a haughty major from a Victorian parlor play. "See how he stares at us with his nose in the air like that? It reminds me of the critics that panned my work."

Marc gives his next move much thought. "I've always wondered why you stopped painting."

Cole answers in a pensive tone, "I should have known telling you was inevitable, Sherlock. From what I've heard, you never give up. That's why I asked you out here—to explain. I know you've been wondering for a long time, and I figured I'd better tell you. C'mon and sit down."

Cole sits on a large, round piece of driftwood and pats a place beside him. Not for the first time, Marc savors his natural grace. Cole stares at the ocean for several minutes then finally speaks. "There aren't any paintings to show you because I burnt them all."

"You what?" As Marc wonders if his response sounds authentic, Cole stares out to sea.

"I burnt all my work. I always hated critiques at RISD, and once I graduated, the posturing, criticism, and snobbery of the art world got under my skin in a big way. I knew I should just overlook it, but somehow I couldn't. It seemed those who had no talent were collecting for investment or giving unsolicited critiques after a glass or two of champagne, and no one else gave a shit. I constantly doubted myself, even when I got the Art Center fellowship. Finally, I decided my solo show would prove I could handle the pressure, or I'd give it all up. If two or more paintings sold, and I could deal with the public side of things, I'd keep going. If they didn't—or I couldn't—I'd quit for good. I guess I was trying to orchestrate my future—stupid as that sounds when I say it now, and I figured the show was the best way to figure out where I was headed. Well, I found out and fast."

Cole words sound as though he's rehearsed them. "My work just wasn't good enough. They ripped it to shreds."

"Who did?"

"The whole art crowd. My opening was in mid-August, and a ton of New Yorkers came dressed in black, like a bunch of pallbearers. Two guys tore my work apart while the rest listened with smug, phony smiles. I think the men were dealers, at least they gave that impression. They said all sorts of things that made me feel like shit. 'He shows promise, but hasn't found his voice yet. It's a compendium of styles, all borrowed, very derivative....'"

Cole's voice has a mocking, effete tone that heightens the venom in these words. "No one said anything positive after that, except the gallery manager, and I'm sure he was just trying to make me feel better.

"Suddenly there were red dots on my two best paintings. Just when I had what I hoped for, one of the men said something like, 'That's a wasted investment. Whoever just threw twenty grand away would have been better off buying two paintings on velvet for ten bucks.' When a couple of people laughed, I freaked and threw everyone out, ordered the manager to take down the paintings, and told him not to sell anything to anyone, no matter what they offered.

"I went to the Old Colony and got stinking drunk. After that, I gathered all my work, piled it on the beach, and sprinkled the lot with turpentine. I can still see the lit match dropping onto the canvas and the flames rising up. Then I ran to MacMillan Wharf to watch. It was far enough away to escape notice, but close enough to be sure everything was destroyed. I just sat there reliving the evening, trying to burn painting out of my soul. By the time the firemen arrived, there was nothing but a pile of white ash.

"Other than to paint the house, I haven't touched a brush since. I know now I'm better suited to work with a tangible outcome, like fixing the wire in the tower. I just can't take value judgments and bullshit when it comes to my art."

Cole sounds as though he's trying to convince himself.

* * * *

Weeks pass. Marc and Cole see each other at tea and, during a late February blizzard, spend most of the morning shoveling the walks and driveway. Marc sometimes offers to help Cole with his chores and drives him to pick up supplies. On these jaunts, Cole never refers to his art, nor discusses his family. For the most part, the men discuss Lola's needs and Helena's antics. Even so, their friendship grows.

Double, Double, Toil and Trouble

One day in early March, when Marc stops to pick up Dorrie for her weekly "confab" with the girls, she greets him in her bathrobe.

"Not up to it today, dahlin'. Feelin' kinda down. Not in the mood for all the cluckin' and gossip the girls will be dishin' out this mornin'."

Marc studies her closely, searching for signs of illness. "Are you sure you're all right? You usually eat that stuff up."

"Yeah, fine—just not innerested today."

"Anything I can do?"

"Yeah, there is. Pick up the girls like usual? It's icy, and I don't want one of them to fall and break a hip or somethin'."

"Sure thing."

Having spent time with the girls and come to enjoy it, Marc knows that fear all too well. One fall could be the beginning of the end, with significant impact on the others. Their weekly ritual at Adams is more than friendship, it's a support network now that children have moved away and husbands passed on.

Dolores is waiting outside in a pair of stretch pants, fleece-lined boots, and a heavy wool coat. Her beehive seems more elaborate than he recalls, though just as indestructible. She scans the passenger seat.

"Where's Dorrie?"

"Not feeling well."

"Anything serious?"

"No. Just a bit under the weather."

"Good of you to come and get me. So far's I know, Bea and Lydia are still planning to go out. Do you mind picking 'em up as usual?"

When Marc and the three women reach Adams, he extricates his charges in the usual fashion.

"C'mon in, Marc," Lydia says in her rough, scratchy voice. "You've driven us so many times, least thing we can do is buy you a cup of coffee."

"You ladies have a lot of ground to cover. It's been a whole week, after all. I'll be back when I've finished my errands."

"Nah. C'mon in, dahlin'. It'll be nice to talk to someone different." Bea tugs his arm as Dolores and Lydia nod in agreement.

"If you ladies insist."

"We do," all three say at once.

When Bea retrieves the coffee, the women draw close like conspirators. Dolores grins at the other two woman, then turns to Marc.

"So how's the detective work comin', Sherlock?"

"You know about that?"

"Of course. I know everything that goes on in that loony bin. I heard you interrogatin' Lola about the captain, and I've seen you searchin' through his journals. It seems to me you might need more evidence than you can get from her. She was just a kid when it all happened, and she's got plenty to hide, don't you think she doesn't. You need the whole picture, Marc. Dorrie won't say nothin' about it, but she said she'd stay home today so we could."

"You knew she wasn't coming? Why ask about her, then?"

Dolores' eyes sparkle with excitement. "Didn't want to scare you off, dahlin'. We had to be sure that we had you as a captive audience before we gave you the goods."

Marc decides to play along. "OK. What's your evidence?"

"Not me, dahlin', but Lydia and Bea, here. Two other people saw parts of the story Lola told you, and it all seems to add up to murder. We decided to share what we know and see what you make of it."

"Go ahead, shoot."

The women lean forward expectantly. Eager smiles expand across their wizened faces. Lydia whispers as if the shop were filled with spies. "I heard this all secondhand from my older brother, Manny, years ago, God rest his soul. He was an apprentice at the Staunton Cold Storage Works back then. One night, he and Pa had a row, and Manny decided to hide out until things calmed down. He was settling in to spend the night in the plant office when, all of a sudden, old man Grubb comes rushing up the stairs. My brother barely had time to hide in a storage closet before Grubb did the damnedest thing. He took a set of truck keys from the rack and raced back downstairs.

"Manny got an eyeful once Grubb left. Captain Staunton was in the drive, standing beside his car, the engine still runnin'. No lights on, though, which made it strange. When old man Grubb come down, they opened the repair bay, drove the captain's car inside, and locked the door. Then they each grabbed a shovel, got into a truck, and drove off in a hurry.

"It was a blinding snowstorm. They were the two head honchos of a company with seven drivers, so them taking a truck out for a delivery didn't make no sense. No sense at all. Who wants fish in a blizzard? Early the next morning, my brother was woke up by Grubb opening the repair bay. The old guy took out the captain's car and parked the truck where it had been the night before. Manny had just enough time to hide before Grubb came upstairs to return the keys. Then the old man drove away in the captain's car."

Marc is intrigued. "What do you think it all means?"

"I got a pretty good idea," Lydia replies, her eyes sparkling. "Folks at the big house always said the captain had his way with Annie—that she'd had his child and blackmailed him to keep the story quiet. He killed her to put an end to all that, so they always said. But it didn't quite stop, as you'll see in a moment. Manny and I always figured they used the truck to get out to the dunes and bury her body. Remember, they took shovels with them." Lydia sits back in triumph.

"Now listen to Bea," Dolores says, her eyes insistent. Bea leans forward in similar fashion, clearly enjoying her moment in the limelight.

"My aunt Agnes was the housekeeper at HomePort back then. She was very fond of the captain's wife and had taught her the running of the place when she first come to town as a slip of a girl. Agnes heard what passed between her and Annie that day. I know what Lola told you about their argument, but there's more to it.

"After the captain ran out of the house, the Missus told Agnes to go up to Lola's room and check on her. From the bedroom window, Agnes could see Annie running across the moors with the captain chasing after her. Agnes climbed up to the tower, long skirt and all, to get a better look. It was snowing so hard she could barely see, but she became convinced he'd caught up with Annie and drownded her. Not too much later, Agnes saw the captain put Annie's body in his car and drive off into the storm, and she weren't never seen again. Agnes swore to her dying day the captain killed Annie. Saying so to his face got her fired. Even though she ended up living off the town, she never stopped telling anyone who would listen that Captain Staunton killed the poor girl."

"What does Dorrie say to all of this?" Marc asks, feeling odd she's not part of the conversation.

Dolores answers without a trace of discomfort. "She won't hear a single word said. As far as she's concerned, her mother disappeared, and after more than eighty years, there's no way of findin' out why. She says she don't see no point in talkin' 'bout it."

Marc ponders this. "Why do you ladies think the captain killed Annie? She could have harmed herself, and he could have been trying to save her life."

Lydia is insistent. "What woman, giving birth the day before, would harm herself? That's what I'd like to know. It goes against all nature that a mother, carrying a child to term and going through labor, would take her own life the next day. I just don't believe it."

Marc remains unconvinced. "Well, from what I understand, the captain's wife was pretty brutal to Annie. She could have become unhinged during their argument."

"But that would have happened once she was *in* the house. It didn't bring her *to* the house," Bea says emphatically. "That's the main point in this whole business. The captain's wife kept Annie from the captain and gave her a piece of her mind. That weren't no help for sure, but what brought Annie to see the man who'd had his way with her unless it was trying to make him pay the price for his philanderin'?"

"I see your point," Marc concedes. "I've always wondered why she went to see him less than a day after giving birth. That said, though, it doesn't make sense she'd hit him up for money right away unless the baby was sick, and she needed to get a doctor."

"Or she had to get out of town quick," Bea says with the surety of an ace detective. "Just think about it a bit: She'd lost her place at the big house. Her good name was all shot to hell. Word would have gotten out as soon as she started showin'. Annie would have known for months she could never stay 'round Provincetown once the child was born. She'd have had a reputation no matter what."

"Well, she went somewhere above ground or below," Dolores says in a tone reflecting years of speculation. "'Cause she was never heard from again, God rest her soul. And the captain paid blackmail for the rest of his life, which proves his guilt so far's I'm concerned."

Marc's jaw drops. "Blackmail? How'd you know about the money? Are you sure it was blackmail?"

"Agnes wouldn't let go of the idea that the captain raped and then murdered Annie," Bea answers. "And his wife as much as told Agnes, who knew a lot of people 'round town. Once he fired her at the big house, she made a point of telling anyone who would listen he was guilty as sin. Most wouldn't pay her no mind, 'cause the Stauntons were so rich and powerful. Lots of folks depended on them for their livelihood. What did they care if some Portagee cook got done in?

"There were a few in town that kept their eyes open, though. One of them was a neighbor of ours by the name of Ginnie T. Hall. That weren't her real name. Nobody knew that, given she was left on the steps of Town Hall as a newborn with a note that said 'My name is Virginia.' They called her Ginnie Town Hall. Or Ginnie T. for short, and the town brung her up.

"Well, anyways, Ginnie T. turned out to have a good head for figures. She worked at Seaman's Bank and moved up in the ranks until she was head teller. According to her, every Wednesday, near closing time, Captain Staunton would withdraw cash in an envelope. All the years she worked at the bank, Ginnie T. never saw the captain take cash any other way. There was just the one account. When that grew low, all of a sudden there'd be a big transfer from the Staunton Trust in Boston. Nothing ever came out of the Seaman's account except the withdrawal on Wednesdays. It went on like that each week 'til the captain died."

"But why pay a blackmailer every week?" Marc asks.

Dolores takes the lead. "The way I see it, the captain was providing the blackmailer with a weekly allowance. Small amounts not likely to be noticed, but enough to keep a person going nicely over a year's time."

"Who do you think he was paying?"

Dolores is triumphant. "I don't think. I know. The Grubbs, of course. Father *and* son."

"Why do you say that?"

"Well, old man Grubb was with him the night they took the truck. The payments continued after the old man died in '48, so the son must have been in on it, too."

"But the Grubbs have managed Staunton affairs for three generations. And even if they were blackmailing the captain, why would he pay cash when they had access to all his money?" Marc likes battling with Dolores. She's a force to contend with.

She raises a crooked index finger. "What better way to make sure you keep the business than to have somethin' on the man with the money? Can you imagine how much in fees the Grubb family has made off the Stauntons over the years? And as for the cash, any damn fool knows you pay blackmailers in cash so they don't have to pay taxes. For all we know, the granddaughter might still be blackmailing Lola. Annie's out in the dunes, that's what I think. In fact, I'm damn certain of it." Dolores sits back in her seat like an attorney resting a case. As Bea and Lydia rub their hands in glee, Marc feels sudden concern for Lola.

Security is mortals' chiefest enemy.

For an instant, he wonders why the quote came to mind. Then he remembers it's from *Macbeth*—the scene with the three witches.

CHAPTER 7
IN ART AS IN LOVE

In early April, Cole returns from an overnight visit to his aunt. Waiting by his apartment door, Frida jumps up to greet him. As he bends to pat her, Marc runs out onto the balcony.

"Thank God you're back! The storm poured buckets last night. The attic's flooded. The second floor ceilings could cave in. Come quick! We've got to get things mopped up right away!"

Cole races past him, stricken. Frida and Marc follow him up the stairs at a brisk trot. Cole throws open the attic door then charges into the room as if he were putting out a fire.

"What the fuck!" He grasps the open door to steady himself.

The attic is bright and airy. The old studio has been rebuilt with tall, white partitions for displaying art. New canvases of varied sizes line one corner of the room. A sink and refrigerator stand against the far wall. A new couch and chair face a sophisticated sound system. The shutters are clean, the skylights washed. A palette with mounds of freshly applied paint sits on a nearby stool. Eight brushes of different sizes rest beside it. In just the right spot under the largest skylight, a brand new easel with a blank canvas awaits the first stroke of a brush.

Lola stands in the center of the studio, bathed in a halo of pure north light. Dressed in a long white caftan, she's without jewelry or makeup. Her white hair cascades over her shoulders, making her look like an ancient priestess presiding over a solemn ritual. Only the involuntary workings of her right hand betray her discomfort.

Helena, dressed in a conservative blue pantsuit, smiles tentatively. Dolores, her face garishly made up, her hair achieving new heights, stands with her son, Jimmy, who has helped with the work. He wears a clean pair of white overalls and an immaculate blue shirt. The small group forms a semi-circle in front of two old, paint-spattered easels whose tops are just visible.

When Cole backs toward the door, Marc stretches out his arms and blocks his way.

"No, Lola. No. I can't," Cole says, near tears. "I don't… I can't… I'm no good…." He paces back and forth in front of the group, as if unable to stop moving. His eyes seem to covet the space one instant and recoil from it the next. At last, he comes to rest and stares down at the floor.

Lola walks slowly toward him and takes his hand. "Take some advice from an old biddy who's seen it all, Cole. You should never think you can't begin again." Her voice, rife with tension, is the only sound in the room. Her hands are shaking slightly, and her face is taut. Helena is watching her closely, as if ready to come to her aid. The others seem to be holding their collective breath. Even Frida is still, her head down, her tail lowered between her legs.

Rather than being disappointed, Lola seems emboldened by Cole's anguished silence. "Besides, you stopped for all the wrong reasons. The men at your opening were trying to talk down the price of your work to make money off it. They weren't dealers, they were con artists. Charlotte and I had them investigated a couple of months ago. They buy up paintings on the cheap, then tell their clients they've made a discovery that will change the art world, like Basquiat or Warhol. This sets off a bidding war, and the two of them make a fortune. Sometimes the artist never even knows about the scam until after he's sold them his last painting."

She draws closer to Cole, her eyes searching his every reaction, her frail body tense. Her words come out tentatively at first, but she grows more impassioned as she sees he's listening intently. "You should never listen to anyone but yourself, Cole. It's the only way I've gotten through life. You have to teach yourself as much as you can and follow your heart wherever it leads you. It's your life, after all. You're the one who should be running it. Whatever anyone else says you should or shouldn't do, you have no obligation to take it as gospel. To hell with snobs and critics. Those that can't do, teach, those that can't teach decide they're experts. I've never, ever, believed you should let anyone else tell you the 'right' way to do anything, whether it's writing, painting, or jumping rope. As my grandmother used to say, 'You're the captain of your vessel. You chart the course of your life. You can study the chart and set your sails or be surprised when you run aground. The choice is yours and no one else's.' You've got what it takes to stand on your own two feet and thumb your nose at all those people, Cole, and we have proof."

On cue, Marc flips a switch. A track light shines down on the old easels. Slowly the human barrier parts. "C'mon Cole. This is great work. Surely you can see that now," Lola says, pointing to the paintings she'd rescued from his rage, then gently placing her arm around his waist. At the sight of the two works, Cole begins to sob. He turns to look at Marc, who can only point back at them. Cole slowly walks to the easels and touches each canvas as if to be sure it's real.

Lola extracts two envelopes from her over-sized purse and totters to his side. "Cole, dear boy, here's the money for the paintings I bought that day, plus interest. I'll tell you the whole story later. In the other envelope is an artist's contract for the Cortile Gallery. I had Kerry Filiberto to tea last week to see these paintings. She wants to sign you up. That must tell you something."

Cole puts his arm around Lola's waist. Her body quivers as if in relief, and she draws closer to him. With that, his anger seems to burn out, though his features remain frightened and wary. It's as if he's listening to an inner voice, his eyes slightly closed, expression puzzled, his head turned to the right.

"I don't know what to say… how to thank you…. I appreciate what you tried to do…."

Lola takes a deep breath, extricates herself, and hands him a brush. "Don't say anything right now, Cole. Just paint. Just paint for now, my dear. That's all you need to do. We can talk about all this later. But if you have anyone to thank, don't thank me, thank Marc. When he told me the way you reacted to Grandmother's studio, I knew you were ready. It was the spark I'd been hoping for. He's worked like a dog to put this place together for you."

Lola points to the Morrison portrait, now hanging under a brass picture light, her red dress vibrant, the diamond necklace aglow. "Marc told me how you admired my mother's portrait. I have to say, it doesn't look the way I remember her. She seems so young and innocent, and trust me, she was anything but. I haven't seen that portrait in nearly fifty years, and it still gives me the creeps, but that's beside the point. You keep it here for inspiration. It's about time some good came from the infernal thing."

Cole looks from the Morrison to his paintings and back again. Marc stares at the floor, afraid he'll be unable to contain his emotion. Frida paws his leg in a charming offer of comfort, drawing Cole's attention.

"Thank you, Marc" Cole says extending his hand, eyes alight in a way Marc has never seen before.

Marc can't find the words to reply. After a moment of silence that allows Cole to compose himself, Helena breaks the spell.

"Oh, now you've done it. After all this weeping, I'll have to redo my makeup before you can start my portrait."

A pensive smile slowly settles across Cole's features. "Her first, while she's up here," he says, picking up a brush, daubing the pallet, and pointing to Lola. "Then you, Dolores, tomorrow. Then you, Helena, the day after that. I need to work up to someone as glamorous as you."

"Story of my life," Helena says tossing her head and languidly dragging a hand across her brow. "Never top billing."

Light and Shadow

April 14th, 2009 – The Tower, HomePort

The first subtle traces of spring can hardly be felt in these moist, fog-shrouded mornings. Yet, by noon, an hour or two of fleeting warmth offers the faintest hint of summer. Around town, signs of life are slowly emerging from winter's thrall. Crocuses sprout in the gardens. The bushes of East Harbor are casting off their winter gray in favor of a subtle burgundy. Contractors hammer and curse from the tops of their ladders, readying storefronts for the all-too-short season. On weekends, day-trippers clog the sidewalks in the largest numbers since Valentine's Day, the vanguard of legions to come. Recently arrived Jamaican workers stroll in search of a second and third job. They clench their teeth against the cold while locals shed coats at the first trace of warmth. We smile at each other's folly.

My routine here at HomePort is oddly comforting. As cheesy as it sounds, I enjoy driving the "girls" to Adams on Fridays. It's easy enough, and in return, I'm showered with pies, bread, and homemade linguica. It's like having four grandmothers, say nothing of the fodder for my writin', dahlin'.

With a second negative HIV test, I'm out of the woods. Though it was almost a non-event, it's funny how the news has made me so grateful. The world seems brighter. Life seems so wonderful here in this little microcosm at the end of all things: Lola holds court at tea; Helena prances, flirts, and dusts; I write up in the tower for hours; Dolores cooks and snoops; Charlotte makes money, hand over "friggin'" fist. Most mornings Cole heads to the beach with Frida. He never asks me to go with him. I think it must be his sacred time, and I suppose I've come to terms with that. When he returns, he heads right to the studio and paints for the rest of the day.

I wish I knew what that light is at Marvin's door, but nobody ever talks about it. Helena told me not to ask, and I've kept my mouth shut so far. No small feat in this joint, I'll be tellin' ya.

Oil and Vinegar

Passing Dorrie on Commercial Street that afternoon, Marc pulls to the curb. "Hey lady, need a ride?" he asks, forgetting his regal passenger.

"Thanks, don't mind if I do."

Then Dorrie spies Lola, sitting rigidly, her head turned in the opposite direction. "Oh, I forgot. I gotta make one more stop. You go on."

"C'mon, get in, Dorrie. It's pretty raw out."

"No thanks," Dorrie replies with uncharacteristic coldness, before charging up the street and disappearing into a shop.

"You two are as comfortable with each other as a cobra and a mongoose," Marc says to Lola once he's back behind the wheel.

"Shall we go out to Herring Cove, dear?" Lola inquires sweetly. "I hear the whales have returned. They feed so close to shore this time of year, one can get quite a good look. I try to go out when they arrive each year to offer amends for my family's assault on their ancestors."

"As you wish."

By now, Marc is familiar enough with Lola's WASP mannerisms to know she has something important to say. Her back is ramrod straight, but she rubs her thumb against the fingers of her right hand, a clear sign of anxiety. When they pass HomePort, she's so distracted she doesn't notice that the plaque has been defaced yet again. As they enter the National Seashore, a burst of sunlight illuminates her face, highlighting the determined glint in her eye.

At the beach, a squabble of seagulls huddle face to the wind. Farther offshore, a brace of mergansers dive for food. Beyond them, five whales glide majestically through the sparkling waves. Marc stops to watch a young calf swimming close to its mother's side, changing course as she does. Two of the largest whales sound, and then he sees the telltale circle of water that indicates they are feeding. The air fills with birds diving for prey pushed upward by a bubble net. There are no cars in sight as Marc traverses the length of the lot, yet he knows to await further instruction before choosing a parking place.

Lola stares out at the crashing surf. "Seems as good a spot as any," she sighs at last. "You remember I told you how Annie ran out onto the moors, and my father followed?"

He pulls into the space just as the largest whale raises its fluke and slaps the water.

"Yes, I remember that very well. Annie was Dorrie's mother, right?" The whale raises its fluke a second time, making Marc wonder if Lola's apology has actually been acknowledged.

"Yes. I knew Dorrie was certain to have told you by now that her mother disappeared."

"And Dorrie's father was?"

Lola's voice cracks as she stares out over the bay. "I don't know for sure. God knows, I wish I had proof. In fact, I sometimes even wonder who mine was. There's so much gossip and scandal about both our births, I shudder to think of it.

"I don't want to discuss that, Marc, I want to tell you what really happened between Dorrie and me. We used to play together all the time. I was ten years older, but we made do for company back then. You could say I was a big sister to her. We were fast friends well into adulthood. One day, nearly sixty years ago, Dorrie came to see me. She told me she was quite certain we were sisters and wanted confirmation. I was in my thirties, but Father was still very much alive. I wouldn't hear a word said against him and sent her away."

"How did she find out?"

"It's a long story. When Annie disappeared, Father immediately hired a new cook. Her name was Carrie, but everyone called her Cookie. Her other duty was to raise young Dorrie. Father kept them in the same house where Annie had lived, the one where Dorrie lives now. He gave Cookie the money for Dorrie's upbringing and never told anyone but me.

"I figured he'd felt sorry for the orphan and decided to help anonymously. That was the Staunton way. I never gave his support a second thought until Dorrie came to me that day. Cookie was in the hospital for an extended stay, and Dorrie had learned who actually paid for everything: clothes, medicine, household expenses; the whole lot. She was surprised and baffled to learn they were paid for by a man who never said a word to her.

"Dorrie's fiancé at that time was Agnes's son. He fought with Dorrie about something or other. I never knew what. A week later, he came back to her house to make up. When they argued again, he told her she was illegitimate, and that her father had repeatedly raped and finally murdered her mother. He told her the whole town knew Annie's body was out in the dunes behind Mount Gilboa, where Father and Charlotte's grandfather had buried her."

Lola's voice shakes with rage. "To her credit, Dorrie called him a liar and ditched him for good. Even so, she was smart enough to check her facts. First, she got proof Father paid the bills. Then she came to me, her best friend, to learn what I knew. I'm afraid I was simply horrible. I had to stop the questions somehow, and knowing Dorrie as you do, you'll understand that rudeness was the only thing that worked."

"Why wouldn't you have helped her?"

"I didn't tell you everything," Lola replies, in a voice brimming with remorse. "I told you my mother sent me upstairs, but there's more….

"My childhood bedroom overlooked the moors. At first, I saw Father chasing Annie. After a while, he disappeared into the blowing snow. I'm certain the housekeeper, Agnes, who came up to check on me, saw him as well. I don't remember why, most likely I was hiding from my mother's wrath, but I stayed seated in the window seat, writing in my diary. I *saw* Father return with Annie's body. She certainly looked dead to me. Her head hung down, and she didn't move. What's more, he carried her as if she were dead weight and left her on the ground behind a dune, instead of bringing her back to the house, something I've never understood. Once he put her in his car, I never saw Annie again.

"What Dorrie described that day was exactly what I'd seen as a child. It meant what my mother told me was true. My father was a monster who had abused his wife and my beloved Annie. Even so, I couldn't side against my father and disgrace the family, not even for my best friend. I told Dorrie to leave and never speak to me again. She pleaded and refused to go. Finally, I had to have her shown out.

"From then on, I couldn't bear to look at her. She reminded me of what my father had done to her mother. Then I'd remember how Annie had been treated by *my* mother, and recall how I'd treated Dorrie. The shame simply paralyzed me, as did the fear she'd ask Father herself, though that wasn't too likely. He avoided her like the plague."

"Why would your father have drowned Annie?"

"Because he'd abused her and fathered her child, and she was making him pay dearly. That's what everyone said, and I never saw proof to the contrary, though I seldom saw my father and Annie together even before she moved to the small house. What's more, from the day she told me the facts of life until the day she left, my mother repeatedly alluded to his misdeeds in the most vehement of terms. The only thing that ever made sense to me was that he disposed of Annie to cover up his crimes and end the blackmail. I've lived with the whispers and speculation ever since."

Lola's face contorts in embarrassment. She places her hand over her left breast.

"But that could be partly your mother's vindictiveness and the rest just small-town gossip," Marc says gently. "You know how a story gets twisted over time with repetition."

"That's very kind of you, Marc, but Agnes also saw him with the body. I wasn't the only one, you know. Folks gossiped for years based on what she said back then. They still do, as I suspect you've already learned."

Marc smiles to himself as he thinks of the girls at Adams and their ruthless speculation. "And you sent Dorrie away despite the fact she might be your half-sister?"

"You have to consider all I saw as child. When Father returned a few days later, he had a bruise on forehead and cuts on his face. It certainly appeared as though he'd killed Annie or at least fought with her. Later on, I heard from several sources that he'd raped her. Even when Dorrie was a child, it was clear he wanted nothing to do with her. There was simply too much evidence to think him innocent, much as I always wanted to." Lola says, staring out at the bay once more.

"Didn't you ever ask him his side of things? He might have been trying to save Annie from herself."

"If you had known him, you'd know better than to ask me that, Marc. From the time Annie vanished, he was always the captain, barking orders, laying down the law. One obeyed and never spoke out of turn. I loved him but was also afraid of him, so I never found the courage to ask. Sometimes, I wonder how my life would have turned out if he'd been just a little less rigid. Let's move on. There's no point speculating about what can never be known."

Lola seems pale and fragile. One hand rests in her lap while she clutches the car door with the other. A blue-gray vein throbs violently above her left ear. "When Father died, he left the cook's house to Dorrie along with an annuity. I was nearly forty by that time, didn't need for anything, and really didn't care. As long as she stayed out of my way, Dorrie was welcome to all of it, though in my mind, it confirmed the worst of what everyone said, that he was paying her off. I don't think she cared all that much for her fiancé, but those days there weren't many choices but to get married, and the pickings were slim. I think she used his accusations as an excuse to send him packing. Dorrie always went her own way and had the good sense to keep things to herself. I doubt she wanted to give up her freedom to some man any more than I did. So I was sort of glad when she got the house.

"I continued to ignore the talk and keep Dorrie at arm's length. I didn't want a reminder of Father's crimes staring me in the face. My mother's words never left me. It was enough to live with them each day without sharing them with someone else.

"Of course, Dorrie is my only neighbor, and she still fights to get back in my good graces. To be perfectly honest with you, I was dumbfounded when she walked back with those groceries the day you came here. She was trying to prove she was still watching out for me. She could have had a heart attack carrying all that stuff."

Lola seems to answer Marc's questions before he asks them. "I actually tried to dissuade her by placing a big order, hoping she'd realize what I was doing, get angry, and back out. I couldn't see any real risk. I figured the cab driver would do the heavy lifting, but I knew she'd chafe at every item she bought. Then, when he didn't show up to bring her home, she walked.

"It's so like Dorrie to turn my machinations back on me to prove her point. I still can't believe she took a chance like that at her age! It's not the first time by a long shot. How many years, during a blizzard or hurricane, have I felt her looking over to be sure I'm safe? But every time I see her, I see Father carrying her mother's body across the dunes. Then I think of the circumstances that brought her into this world. How can I be a friend and keep secrets like that? And how can I explain at this late date I've always known and never told her?"

Lola's jaw is set in a rigid line. She seems to be drawing on every ounce of strength to suppress even the slightest trace of emotion. Her eyes show just a hint of moisture, her back is upright, and she breathes as if trying to contain a sob. That's the extent of it. Her Yankee reserve forbids any further display of emotion.

When she finally speaks, again it's a whisper. "It's hopeless, Marc. Simply hopeless. I can't bear to think he did such awful things, so I just don't think about it at all."

"I see," Marc says softly, convinced she's thought of little else for more than half a century.

Turn Back the Hands of Time

Once at HomePort, Marc helps Lola into the house. When she's settled, he scrubs the plaque, then races up Commercial Street, where Dorrie has just reached the Provincetown Inn.

"What took you so long?" she asks. "I've been expectin' you to show up and chew me a new one for the last forty minutes."

"We need to talk. This business with Lola is a mess."

"No shit, Sherlock." Dorrie hobbles to Pilgrims' Park in silence, then sits on a bench and lights a cigarette. When she finally speaks, her tone is surprisingly gentle. "As big a fool as she's been, I don't blame Lola. She don't want to deal with the rumors, and I get that. But we were like sisters as kids, and now we've lived next door without really speakin' for sixty years. Life's too damn short for such bullshit. It's a goddamn, miserable crime. After the woman that raised me, Lola was the only real friend in my life 'til Daryl, and now you, come along. Besides, it's not like *she* killed my mother. She shouldn't be so hard on herself about somethin' her father might have done."

Marc stares out over the moors—the scene of the supposed crime—so tranquil and pristine in the clear spring light. "You said 'might have done.'"

"Yep. I ain't so sure as I once was, strange as that may seem."

"Why not?"

"Well, I keep havin' this weird dream. It started 'round the time I met you and repeats almost every night. The captain's in it."

"Say more."

"He's younger than I remember, but I still recognize him. There's a little girl of about four or so that I'm pretty sure that's me. And Cookie, the woman that raised me is in it, too."

"So what happens in the dream?"

"We get on board a train at the center of town—Cookie, Captain Staunton, and me. I play with the very doll that now sits in my parlor as trees and houses whiz past. We finally get off at a station. There's a buckboard waitin', and we drive to this old farmhouse out in the woods. It's big and ramblin', with a lot of chimneys and two big barns. There's a huge silo, too."

"Do you know what town the house was in?"

"No, but I'm pretty sure we crossed the Canal. I remember this bridge over water. On the other side of the bridge, there were large fields and many more boulders than you see on the Cape."

"So what happened once you got there?"

"Inside the farmhouse are two women. One is fat and jolly, the other pale and sickly. The jolly one takes me by the hand and brings me over to the sick one, whose eyes are veiled, like her mind is clouded, or she ain't thinkin' right. The fat lady says somethin', and the thin woman reaches down and takes my hand. All of a sudden, the veil drops. She looks at me, falls to her knees, hugs me, and starts weepin'. So does the captain and the fat woman. Everybody's cryin'. At this point, the dream ends. It's always the same, night after night."

Marc walks to the far right where a stone bears the inscription *Some Other Spring*. Suddenly he hears a voice in his head. *There may not be another spring for Dorrie and Lola. Time is short to right things between them.*

When Marc returns to the bench, Dorrie seems wizened and fragile. The toll the estrangement has taken is clearly visible. Her dark eyes seem to overflow with sadness, which she makes no effort to conceal. "So, what do you think?" she asks, staring up at him.

The essence that frequents Marc's thoughts cries out for him to help her. Anxious not to unnerve Dorrie, he takes refuge in sarcasm.

"For starters, I think we should get your boney ass off this cold, stone bench."

Just the Facts, Ma'am

"I shouldn't be here, Marc. Lola will skin you alive if she finds out," Dorrie whispers for the tenth time in as many minutes.

Overwhelmed by emotion and unearthly voices, Marc has grown increasingly frustrated since leaving the park.

"Quiet! Get up those stairs," he says, as Helena steps onto the second story landing.

She shrieks in mock alarm, "Oh my gawd! Burglars!"

"Very funny, Helena. Be quiet and help Dorrie up to the studio."

"I'm not so sure I should get involved," Helena says with a smirk. "In fact, I'm rather nervous about witnessing whatever is going on here. After all, that's the Bates Motel over there," she says pointing at the servant's wing. "What are you up to now, Norman? Putting Mother in the window?"

"Give her a hand, will you, please, wiseass, and no more bullshit? Okay?"

Helena steps back as if he's hit her.

"Don't pay no mind to him, Helena," Dorrie says. "He's in a nasty mood all of a sudden. It's all my doin'."

Without a word, Marc guides Dorrie up the next flight. Helena follows looking petulant. Marc knocks on the studio door. Cole answers, paintbrush in hand, and ushers them inside. He points toward the alcove and offers them a seat. Marc sits beside Dorrie on the sofa. Helena perches on its arm.

"Cole, we need your help."

"Sure, Marc. What's up? Hi, Dorrie."

"Hey Cole. Nice work. Damn nice."

"Thanks."

"Enough pleasantries. Let's get down to business, Dorrie."

"Whatever that is, Marc. Draggin' me up here on some fool's errand."

"Be quiet you. I've had about enough. Cole, I need a break from all this drama. Just ask Dorrie about her dream and sketch what she tells you. I'll be back once I've got my head together." Marc is part way to the door when the image of a grandmother reading to a child crowds his thoughts. The young girl so full of vitality, it takes some time before he recognizes the young Lola.

"I failed her and her mother. Don't give up as once I did." As Marc turns in search of the voice, Cole studies him with a curious expression.

Marc returns to the sofa. "I've changed my mind. Here's the deal, Cole. Dorrie has been having a recurring dream. I want you to listen while I ask questions, then draw what she describes."

"Oh my goodness," Helena says breathlessly, "how very *CSI*! Can I be the ex-stripper-turned-crime-scene-investigator?"

"You can be anyone you want after you get Dorrie a cup of tea and something to eat. We're here for as long as it takes."

Dreams Made Real

By the time Dorrie's cross-examination is complete, Cole has produced four small drawings: the young girl with the doll, the house with its barns and silo, the couple, and the woman with the veiled eyes. Dorrie seems barely able to contain herself.

"Yes, yes, that's it! That's what she looks like. That's what I see in my dream."

The mystery woman has dark eyes with a distant look that seems both wise and constrained. She's not beautiful in the traditional sense, though her tranquil features and spiritual simplicity are arresting. Her hair is tied in a bun. Her lips are thin, but with a slight trace of sensuality. Helena studies the portrait from a distance, then turns to Dorrie.

"Sweetie, do you have any pictures of yourself as a young girl?"

"Yeah. Sure. Over at the house."

"Well, let's take these over there and see how things match up."

Helena picks up the portrait of the woman, takes Dorrie's arm, and escorts her to the door. Cole and Marc grab the remaining sketches and follow. Minutes later, they are in Dorrie's kitchen turning the pages of a crumbling scrapbook.

Helena points to a picture in the center of the page. "Look! That picture looks a lot like the little girl in the sketch. Dorrie, look closely at the doll you're holding in that picture."

"It's the one in the living room. It was my favorite as a kid."

"Are you sure?" Marc asks.

"Honest to God, that's the doll! Go get it."

Marc does as he's told. In the corner, sitting on a miniature chair, is an old-fashioned doll wearing a blue dress, gold slippers, and a bonnet with a satin bow. Curled, red hair peeks out from either side of a round face with faded red lips and bright blue eyes. He returns to the kitchen.

"Here it is. No doubt about it. Who's that woman in the picture with you?"

"That's Cookie."

Marc places the drawing of the couple from the farm next to the photograph. "Do you see the similarity? These two women could be sisters."

"There is a resemblance," Cole says, "but Dorrie could be dreaming of familiar faces."

"That's certainly possible, though there might be another possibility. I need to do some research to be sure, though."

"Look, guys," Helena says, "it's as plain as the nose on Marc's face. Can't you see? What's wrong with you two? Maybe it's because I'm looking in the mirror all the time, but honestly...."

"What? What do you see?" Dorrie says, leaning across the table and staring intently into Helena's eyes.

Helena leads her to a mirror in the living room, then holds the portrait of the placid young woman beside her. As the friends scrutinize the reflected images, traces of the young woman's features slowly surface in Dorrie's withered face.

Excited and energized, Cole, Helena, and Marc return to the studio. Cole offers a bottle of wine and a snack.

"Yeah, Cole, honey. Don't mind if you do," Helena says settling on the sofa as he fills her glass. Then she proposes a toast. "Here's to Nancy Drew and the Hard-on Boys. You just can't beat 'em." Helena's tone quickly changes. "I wish Lola and Dorrie were as kind to each other as they've been to me. Dammit guys, we've just gotta fix things between those two before it's too late." Even Helena seems surprised by her tears.

The Forest for the Trees

By May, the friendship inaugurated at High Head has developed a distinct pattern. Marc writes and Cole paints through midafternoon. Then they meet to walk Frida. Over numerous expeditions, Cole has shown Marc several hidden, magical places—parts of the secret Provincetown that few know.

As if by unspoken agreement, the past, especially Brandon, is carefully avoided. Talk focuses on art, creativity, and inevitably, those who share the place they both call home. Marc and Cole gradually come to rely on each other's insights, both spoken and inferred, for the two men often walk empty beaches for miles without so much as a word. Through it all, a tenuous spark of attraction flickers, but as if by mutual understanding, never ignites.

This fine spring day, they're walking in the Beech Forest. Following the trail for some distance, they branch off onto a narrow path, discernible only by a thin line of grass stunted by infrequent foot traffic. Cole shows Marc a shady patch where lady slipper orchids grow in profusion. They are just in bloom, their veined orbs looking both perfectly in place and otherworldly. Marc is flattered that Cole has shared such a special spot.

Returning to the trail, they climb a log stairway up the slope of a tall dune. Frida bounds ahead, taking the steps two at a time. They pass trees buried in fifty feet of sand whose tops look like feeble saplings, belying height and strength sacrificed to the elements. Stepping out into the sunlight, Marc stares in awe at a vast expanse of dunes with the sparkling Atlantic as a vivid backdrop. Cole calls Frida to him, pats her head, and scratches her ears.

"She loves it out here. It brings out the hunter in her. Watch her point if she spots something."

Cole guides Marc down a slope to the edge of a large pond that shimmers like satin in the afternoon light. When a sute of mallards fly up in alarm, Frida raises her paw. As Cole smiles in pride, Marc studies him yet again. *There's still a trace of the loner about Cole, as if he's just come in from the wilderness. He's let his hair grow longer for the winter; black curls grace its edges, and he's cultivated two or three day's growth of beard that makes him seem even more of a satyr. Even so, there's been a subtle change in his mood these last few weeks. He smiles more, and his wide grin transforms his face from absorption to radiant engagement. Damn, he's gorgeous.*

When they do speak, Cole seldom looks directly at Marc, rather he watches him out of the corner of his eye. More often than not, his glance gives way to a slight grin as if Cole has discovered something new about his friend.

Marc thinks of the first time he saw him. *Not once has he displayed the abandon of that day at Herring Cove. I can't forget seeing him like that. It dredges up the same feelings of inadequacy every time I think of it.*

Cole's firm muscles, his athleticism, and graceful nakedness are not so much a carnal image as a vibrant indictment of Marc's tense inner life. In moments of self-awareness, Marc gets a compelling glimpse of the type of person he'd like to be.

With the onset of spring weather, Cole's skin is just beginning to darken. Marc suspects Cole has begun swimming at Herring Cove and yearns for an invitation. This has become a near obsession, diminishing the discoveries the two men have shared. Marc chastises himself for getting so worked up, but the question remains. *I bet Cole swims from April to November. He shares everything else with me these days. Why won't he share that?*

Cole sits on a log near the water's edge. Marc, wondering why they seem to have their best conversations sitting on logs, sits beside him, trying hard not to study the graceful curve of Cole's legs as well as the enticing bulge where his pants stretch tight. Clearly, this is part of the appeal of sitting on logs, but Marc merely castigates himself further for sexualizing the moment.

Cole looks out over the water, then speaks in a wistful voice. "I want to paint out here, but have been waiting until I feel ready. It's a special place. I want to be sure I do it justice."

Marc nods. "That's for sure. I can't believe a place like could be so close to the ocean. Look at the reeds just turning green, and the way the sand cuts right down to the water's edge over there. The shadows of the pine trees and the dunes behind them would make for a fabulous painting. Who would believe we're less than two miles from Commercial Street? Most people who come to Provincetown don't even know this place exists."

Marc relaxes in the warm sunshine. Cole's proximity is comforting, enticing, and with their growing friendship, only slightly nerve-wracking. His mood seems more at ease than usual, more accessible. Marc decides to take a chance. "You seem to have hit your stride with these last few paintings. How does it feel to have overcome the fear that made you quit?"

"I wouldn't say I've overcome it as much as made peace with it. What an idiot I was to let other people keep me from what I loved. Until I started painting again, I didn't completely realize how much I missed it."

"Tell me about it. I think you and I are a lot alike. I love to write, but hate the idea of anyone else reading it."

Cole grins. "Speaking of that, I've shown you mine, when are you gonna show me yours?"

"Huh? You mean my writing?"

"Well, yes, unless you had something else in mind."

As Marc's face reddens, Cole stares straight ahead with the same crooked grin. After a moment, he stretches sensuously. The two men remain silent as Marc fights the urge to stare.

Cole finally speaks. "As I said before, I'd really like to read something you've written. Why won't you let me?"

As Marc ponders a response, he smells the pungent scent of pitch pine. This conjures memories of his mother's housecleaning on Saturday morning when every kind of air freshener, and scented cleaner was enlisted to keep nature at bay.

Marc remembers how the woods were a sanctuary for his younger, misfit self. To escape Saturday's domestic onslaught and so many other things, Marc had sought comfort and solitude in the hills and mountains outside the town. He'd discovered hidden glens and deep pools for swimming, straying farther from home over the months, while returning with reluctance that increased over the years until he'd finally left for good. Then, nature had become abstract, something found only in parks and picture books. Without its liberating presence, he'd slowly grown cautious and less sure-footed until these daily walks with Cole gradually revived his love of the outdoors.

At last, Marc breaks the silence. "I don't quite know how to say this, Cole. Remember how you couldn't stand people passing judgment on your paintings? I wish I could even get to that point."

"Say more?"

"I just can't get past myself. Most times, I can't stand what I write. Now that I've finally gotten the time and space, I can't bear for anyone to read my work, especially me. I changed everything to become a writer, and I'm getting nowhere. Day by day, this critical voice has slowly grown in my head. I've tried to start a novel several times, and I can't even get beyond the first sentence."

"Because?"

"I worry so much I freeze up. I sit in the tower every day writing in my journals, putting down thoughts and fragments, but whenever I go to assemble them into something cohesive, I get so blocked, I give up."

"So let me see if I understand. You have all these things you want to say, but you can't say any of them until the first sentence is absolutely perfect?"

"That's sort of it. Pretty fucked up, isn't it?"

"No value judgments. Why does the first sentence mean so much?"

"It's the open door welcoming readers into the story. You can't start with crap and then promise it'll get better. You've got a minute at best to hook a reader, or an agent, or a publisher." Marc halts, afraid of sounding foolish.

Cole seems to wait intentionally before breaching the silence. "I get it. You think the opening sentence is your first, best, shot to corral them and make them want to keep reading, which means it has to be so good that everyone will like it."

"Exactly."

"I can hardly believe this is me asking, Sherlock, but don't you think you're attempting the impossible?"

"Huh?"

Cole stares down at the water as if channeling words from deep inside.

"Let me put it in terms of painting, because that's what I know best. You know my hang-up about criticism. To be honest, I still struggle with it, but I've been talking with the other artists at the gallery. I'm learning that my work is *my* statement, and that people *must* be free to take it or leave it. I can't afford to worry what others may think. I have to focus on what I want to say and simply do the very best I can."

Marc nods. "That makes sense, but you have to sell work to survive, so at least *some* people have to like what you have to say."

"In a strange way, that's where truth comes in." The intensity in Cole's voice is new, as is the look in his eyes. When Cole draws close to drive his point home, Marc tenses. Cole seems surprised, but continues on.

"Some people will resonate because it's an honest statement of *your* experience. Others won't, and there's nothing you can or should do about that. Thinking you have to please or engage everyone is self-deception doomed to failure. It ain't gonna happen, so why even put that kind of pressure on yourself?"

"So you're saying my job is simply to write what I want to say and let it go out into the world," Marc asks, wondering if he'd ever be capable of doing such a thing.

"Exactly. You should please yourself. The closer you are to your own truth, the more likely it will resonate with a reader."

Marc lowers his gaze. "That makes sense, but there's still another big issue."

"Which is?"

"You have to be pretty damn certain you have something worth saying in the first place."

Marc feels the words leap out from the corrosive spot in his gut where they've lurked for months. As he grapples with having said them, a great blue heron flies past, looking angular and prehistoric against the dark hues of the lake. It lands at the water's edge not more than ten feet from the two men.

Cole responds without a trace of awkwardness. "I'm not sure I agree. Let me try to show you what I mean. See that bird there?"

He points at the heron, now standing motionless on stilt-like legs. Clouds cast their shadows over the bird's reflection, making it appear and disappear in the rippling water at the dune's edge. The heron is completely at home in its environment, its colors offset by the sky-blue of the lake, a trace of white at the breast, metallic gray at its legs, a spark of yellow in its eye.

"If I did a painting of that bird, what would my job be?"

"To render an accurate image, I guess."

Cole leans even closer. "Maybe. But there's more to it than that. My job is to convey its essence as I see it to the very best of my ability. The rest is up to the people who view the result."

At the far end of the pond, two swans paddle idly, their elegance out of place in such a squat, windswept domain. The more passionate his words, the more Cole moves his hands as if painting the thoughts he's trying so hard to convey.

"If they don't like my work, it doesn't mean the painting's no good. What's my obligation if people just don't get my work? Or even if they hate it? Up to a point, you could say I have the obligation to treat them with respect, but should

I self-destruct or beat myself up for having nothing to say? Hell no.

"Van Gogh said, 'Painting is a faith, and it imposes the duty to disregard public opinion.' Now, you could say he was crazy. He certainly didn't sell many paintings. But can you actually say he was wrong to stand by his vision? He opened the door, and, at first, only one buyer came in. Look what happened afterwards, though. You're probably thinking I'm a hypocrite, given my little adventure in pyromania, but tell me, Marc, should he have given up? If you follow your beliefs to their logical conclusion, your answer would have to be yes."

When Marc hesitates yet again, Cole gives him another pass. "Maybe I should just do my job to the best of my ability. Show the heron's color, his patience, and the coiled energy that will explode when an unsuspecting fish swims into view. If I've done that, and I'm honestly satisfied with the results, what else matters? Why do I have to please others to be an artist? Or even be successful? And why do you have to please anyone but yourself with your own creations?"

Marc answers with difficulty. "That's a tough one for me. I was brought up to please people by putting them first and myself last. Good old Lutheran self-sacrifice. Sometimes I think every word I've ever written has been self-edited to please everyone but me."

Cole is just inches away, listening intently, his face alight with affinity. When he speaks, his voice crackles with excitement. "Which is the real reason you aren't satisfied with what you write. It's not for you. It's for them, so there's no way it can be *your* truth. On some level, I think you already know that. You know if they read it and don't like it, you'll just end up like Miss Havisham, feeling jilted and angry. So you keep the door shut and futz around with your first sentence. It's a great way to avoid getting hurt, don't you think?"

Marc raises his eyes only to realize Cole is intently scanning his face. It's all too much. Silence overtakes the two men, though neither lowers his eyes. When Cole finally speaks, his voice is powerful but controlled, with just the slightest trace of self-consciousness.

"Just be yourself, Marc. Don't sell yourself short. Tell your story the way you want and just plain leave it at that." Cole fidgets for a moment as an ungainly silence takes hold. He seems to want to wait for Marc to speak, but eventually can't hold back. "As to being yourself, the trick is to strike a balance between what you give to others and what you save for yourself. If you do it the other way 'round, and start with others first, most times you'll have given it all away before it's your turn. Why *do* you give so much, by the way?"

Marc replies as if hypnotized. "I feel I have to because if I didn't, people wouldn't see anything in me at all."

Cole places his hand on Marc's chin and draws his face toward him, then sits motionless, his massive hand remaining in place as if weighing a decision. After a moment, to Marc's dismay, the hand is removed.

"That is total bullshit," Cole says after a lengthy pause. "You're the most wonderful man I've ever met. Since we're talking truth, that's mine. You should write that in your journal and read it every time you sit down to write."

"I once told Brandon he was the most wonderful man I'd ever met," Marc blurts out, as his memories crush the moment. "Given what happened afterwards, my words weren't worth much."

Cole studies Marc closely, then stands up, takes his hand, and, with little effort, pulls him to his feet. "C'mon back to the house. I've got someone I want you to meet."

An Ideal Husband

The two men walk silently to Marc's car, then drive to HomePort. In short order, they're in the studio. Cole removes a cloth from one of his canvasses and places the painting on an easel. It's a portrait of Marc seated at his table up in the tower. Captured in a moment of contemplation, he gazes slightly upward, his right hand cupping his chin. His blond hair, deep blue eyes, and the tiny birthmark on his right cheek are flawlessly rendered. Beyond his left shoulder, the harbor and Long Point provide a fitting backdrop for the author's introspection.

To Marc, the portrait seems far too idealized, the subject too imbued with intelligence and confidence. Beyond that, he's about to enter a revelation in a journal. Recalling his struggle for the right words and how much of his journal is dedicated to thoughts of Cole, Marc feels violated.

"Christ, Cole. How'd you do this?"

"From memory and a sense of what I see in you."

"But I don't look like that."

Cole looks downward. "To me you do. That's my truth."

"I'm not that confident or that attractive."

"So you say."

Marc thoughts rage and without his realizing at first, find their own voice. "You've got me sitting there writing like a pro when I can't even spit out the first sentence of a novel. The person on that canvas has nothing to do with me."

Cole takes a step forward and Marc a step back. The portrait of Prudence Staunton stands between them, as if a referee. Cole's tone is patient, but his voice grows more despondent with each word. "Did you ever think I might see things you don't?"

Marc pauses, looks at the Morrison and then points at Cole's painting. "I don't know that person any more than I know her."

"Well perhaps you should get to know him instead of wallowing in self-pity all day long."

Marc, fists clenched, turns away as Cole flushes. "That's right. Just back down, Marc. Like you always do. Don't face the truth, just run up to your tower and bury yourself in frightened, half-baked words that will never amount to a goddamn thing."

"You bastard."

Marc shoves the easel. The painting lands on an open box of frames, tearing a large gash across its entire length.

Wild-eyed, Cole lunges at Marc. "You fucking asshole! Get the hell out of here before I throw you out."

CHAPTER 8
WHAT GOES UP MUST COME DOWN

May 23rd, 2009 - The Tower, HomePort

Cole and I have avoided each other since I destroyed the portrait. He's in his studio day and night. I hear his footsteps when I'm trying to sleep, which of course I can't because I know he's up there. He only speaks when others are around. If I see him alone, he walks away without a word, and I don't blame him. I think we both understand it's for the best, but still I miss him, or better said, us.

Sometimes as I've passed his studio on the way up here, I've wanted to beg his forgiveness, but I can't trust myself to be alone with him for fear of another fight. We almost got into it over that portrait, and I'm not going to chance a rematch. Ironic, isn't it? I'm like a fairytale princess in my tower. My prince is only a floor below, but this is no fairytale. This fairy is too fucked up to believe in a happy ending.

In the midst of all this drama, the captain's journals have proved more than a diversion. They've finally offered a clue. Among the stories of distant islands, spouting whales, and raging seas, the name Castleton constantly appears in tales of trustworthiness and loyalty. With a second reading, I now know where the captain would turn in his hour of need.

I started to dig, and for a while, I thought I was on to something. When town records yielded nothing, I searched the Registry of Deeds in Barnstable. Unfortunately, there's no trace of anyone named Castleton owning property in Provincetown or anywhere on the Cape. So I've hit a dead end in more ways than one. I've got to stop worrying about the past and deal with the present.

Sanctuary. Remember? Above all else, sanctuary.

Look Before You Leap

Several days later, Helena joins Marc on his mail run. They're walking on Commercial Street when Marc suddenly pales. Without a word, he pushes the mail into her hands, races across Bubala's parking lot, and jumps off the seawall.

Helena, calm and collected, looks around to see if anyone is watching, then slowly crosses the street. She finds Marc cowering on a two-foot strip of sand at the base of the wall, waves lapping within inches of his feet. She bends over to look at him as if studying a fish in an aquarium.

"A sudden urge for calamari?"

"I thought I saw Brandon."

"What's he look like? I'll see if I can spot him."

"The red-haired guy in the Panama hat and dark sunglasses."

"You are such a drama queen. That boy has worked at Front Street for the last two years. I do have to say though, if that's what Brandon looks like, you have exquisite taste. Don't you think you should get out of there while you can, darling? I think the tide is coming in."

Helena strolls to the corner as Marc sheepishly walks up the path by the old firehouse.

"It's quite obvious I *do* need to consult a tide chart before any of our outings, Marc. Should I be packing a set of water wings as well?"

"Very funny, Helena. I didn't want to take any chances."

"Of course not, darling, but remember you're perfectly safe as long as Momma's around." She pinches his cheek, then they resume their trek in silence.

The Purloined Letter

Nearly five weeks later, Marc is writing in the tower when Cole pops his head through the open hatchway.

"You've gotta see this. You're never gonna believe it."

"Believe what?"

Marc is stunned. Cole has never sought him out since that fateful day in the studio. There have been no conversations other than those essential to Lola's well-being. Now the man Marc thinks of constantly is fidgeting in front of him as excited as a boy at Christmas.

"Come and see."

Cole clambers up the ladder, crosses the room, opens the wide panel in the wainscoting, and raises the dumbwaiter. Frida jumps out, her tail wagging.

Marc reaches down to pat her. "So? She loves to ride in that thing. Since you're in the studio all the time, she barks, and I go down to the second floor and hoist her up. She's lonely. You should spend more time with her. She's been up here tons of times. There's nothing special about giving Frida a ride in the dumbwaiter."

"That's just my point," Cole says with the slightest trace of pique. "It's like *The Purloined Letter*. They searched for weeks while it was hidden in plain sight."

Marc's tone is testy, his eyes flash with impatience. "What *are* you talking about?"

Cole seems unable to contain his excitement. "I put art supplies in the dumbwaiter to save trips up the stairs. This time, as I was loading it, I saw something I hadn't seen before."

Something about Cole's enthusiasm tempers Marc's annoyance. *He's so cute. Like a kid waiting impatiently to open a present. What's brought this on?*

"And that was?" Marc asks, rising from his chair.

"See for yourself."

"I don't see anything but an empty box."

"Exactly. Describe the box."

Marc rolls his eyes. "Top, bottom, two sides, and a back."

"And what else?"

"Screws holding the inner panels to the frame."

Cole smiles broadly. "Very good, Sherlock. Anything strike you as unusual?"

"Well, there are screws everywhere but the front floorboards."

Cole points to a thin space between the boards. "Exactly. And what's this?"

"It looks like a seam."

"Absolutely. Why not use one board?" Cole pushes and the front board springs up.

"It's got a trigger hinge."

"So?"

"So…." Cole folds back the panel in triumph.

Marc picks up a leather-bound journal and points to the gilded letters on the spine. "It's the missing one!"

"It sure is! What better place to hide it than this? What's more, the captain could get it whenever he wanted just by lowering the dumbwaiter to whatever floor he was on."

"Holy shit, Cole, you're a genius." Marc throws his arms around Cole and kisses him. To his surprise, Cole holds him tight and eagerly returns the kiss. At first, Marc closes his eyes and leans forward. Then he tenses, and drops his arms. The two men step awkwardly apart, heads lowered, eyes downcast as if they've been caught doing something they shouldn't.

Cole points to the journal as if welcoming a distraction. "See what it says. I haven't opened it. I wanted you to be the first."

Cradling the book in his right hand, Marc begins to read aloud.

CHAPTER 9
THE NINETEENTH
JOURNAL

January 15ᵗʰ, 1925 - HomePort

My family has called Provincetown home for more than two hundred years. Suspect in the eyes of the town, and unable to redeem myself, I have chosen to document my disgrace for future generations to judge. I find myself hesitant to commit this sordid tale to paper but must, if only for posterity.

The seeds were sown by the greatest mistake of my life, my marriage to Prudence Grant, a great beauty from one of New Bedford's oldest, most distinguished families. I came to know Prudence in New Bedford while the Andoria underwent extensive refitting not possible in Provincetown. I first saw my wife-to-be at a cotillion in the company of her more affluent relations. Even though she was not yet eighteen, I found myself dazzled by her beauty, grace, and refinement of manner. A courtship ensued, conducted in haste before I was to depart on a three-year voyage.

Ours was a winter-spring romance. Pru was fourteen years younger though so attentive I soon grew certain the age difference meant nothing to her. I proposed on her eighteenth birthday, and she enthusiastically accepted. The Andoria was secretly outfitted at considerable expense as my wedding present, so my bride might accompany me as my mother had my father.

Prudence and I married less than a week before we were to set sail. To my astonishment, she announced on the day of our departure she feared being the sole female amidst so many men. Despite numerous assurances and entreaties, including a written pledge of respect from the entire crew, she would not yield. At last, I gave in and agreed she should make her way to HomePort and assume her rightful place as mistress of the house.

My mother, Laetitia, or Lettie as she was known to most, had assumed the full responsibilities of HomePort upon Father's death. She was rather eccentric, fond of travel, and a prodigious collector of art, something few women did back then. She was forever hobnobbing with the artist types who came to town in ever-greater numbers. How she loved to hold court for these men, the grand dowager with her salon of sensitive admirers. If she realized what abominations they performed upon each other in the dunes and back alleys, she seemed to overlook it. But I digress.

Suffice it to say, save that glaring but understandable omission, I trusted Mother's judgment implicitly and felt the education and acclimation of my young bride to be in most capable hands. Mother's sensitivity and patience were my sole consolation amid the profound disappointment of Pru's rebellion.

After such joyous anticipation, I set sail in a state of confusion and anxiety, only exacerbated by subsequent events. By the time the Andoria reached the Azores, Prudence had been at HomePort for six months. Reading mail from home, I learned not all was as it should have been. Rather than cast aspersions, I have included Mother's letters as evidence.

In fairness, I must say there were many entreating missives from my bride, contradicting much of what Mother had written, but I became so incensed by the accusations they contained I pitched the lot of them into the tryworks.

Three letters, written in a faded, flowing hand are clipped to the page.

Marc reads the first:

August 6th, '04

Dearest Son,

I hope this letter finds you well with a hold a-brim with oil.

It grieves me to write this, but I fear you may hear scandal from some other source and be taken by surprise. I shan't beat 'round the bush. Your young bride has taxed my patience beyond its limits.

I realize Prudence is a young girl far from home, and newly returned to position in Society. I accept that, given their dismal financial circumstances, she should want to share her good fortune with her family. However, I do think there should be limits on the amount she spends. There is no earthly reason we Stauntons should support them in the style to which they were once accustomed. This point has been the source of endless argument with your bride, and I have finally had my fill. I have reduced her contact with them to one week every three months and forbidden her to receive them here. Their visits were far too protracted and an unnecessary drain on the household budget. Indeed, I found her mother most tiresome.

Your wife has had none of the training essential to run a large household. She should be far more grateful for the hints and gentle suggestions I have offered than she is. I am prepared to make allowances for youth and inexperience, but I must say I find her extravagances and willfulness so unnerving I have had no choice but to countermand her instructions on a daily basis.

Today, your wife refused to take direction as to the menu for Sunday's luncheon with the vicar. Last week, she fired Machado and his wife. I suspect they have firsthand knowledge of her indiscretions. She's already installed a new housekeeper—Agnes Medeiros, a horrendous gossip—over my strenuous objections. The woman's sympathies are clearly not with me, and the servants are already feeling her wrath. Two maids have given notice and even the groom, Harris, is making noises of departure.

This is the least of it. Prudence appears to have taken up with a man named Morrison in what might be politely described as an intimate fashion. I had commissioned him to paint her portrait as a surprise for you. I noticed the sittings had fostered a friendship but thought little of it at the time. Now, a number of independent confirmations as well as Machado's sudden departure foster grave concerns. If your wife were indeed unfaithful, it would not surprise me in the least. It would be the culmination of a consistent pattern of greed, selfishness, and lack of concern for appearances that seems her true nature.

I am besieged in my own home and able to do little to influence the course of events. Prudence is now Mrs. Captain Staunton, that is true, and one might well argue within her rights as the mistress of the house. That said, I must warn you that her actions may not reflect well on our family name or standing in the community. You know as well as I the nature of our small town. There are many who would relish a scandal at our expense. From all I can gather, there is one very much in the making.

I say now, and most fervently, it is on your head for putting the Staunton name in jeopardy. I urge you to hurry back to Provincetown as soon as your circumstances permit, and until then, to take a stronger, guiding hand in the letters you send your Godless bride.

Your affectionate and forbearing mother,
Laetitia Staunton

P.S. I have given a stipend to Machado in hopes of sustaining his loyalty and asked him to wait out this unpleasantness until your return. I cannot say with any degree of certainty he will. Whatever it was he witnessed, he seemed so offended by your bride's behavior I could barely get him to accept the money.

Wrong or Right?

"What a bitch he married," Marc says to Cole, after perusing other letters offering additional, detailed description of a spoiled and combative young woman.

"Hold on, Marc. Laetitia sounds pretty tough. I wouldn't want to live way out here with a mother-in-law like that. Never mind as a young bride who wouldn't see her husband for at least three years."

"True enough. Prudence *was* only eighteen. But that's the way it was for women in Provincetown back then. Their men were at sea for days, weeks, or even years. Many brides were widows for months before even knowing it. Maybe she was trying to be sure she'd be in charge if he never came back."

"Could be. I doubt we'll ever know.

"Lola's expecting me. Why don't you read the rest and let me know the high points?"

"Sounds good. I'll be right here when you're done."

As Marc stares down at the pages in front of him, the written words seem to come to life. He hears them in deep, antiquated, masculine tones whose language is formal and constrained. Images race through his brain in sync with the text: Prudence, her haughty features and elaborate fashions, her strident voice, her conflicts with a stately woman who displays the same rigidity and bearing as Lola. Cole knows intuitively this is Laetitia.

The captain's life at sea and the refuge it provided all become real, as if Marc is watching a movie projected onto the page. The words he reads create actual sensations and brand new memories: tropical islands; towering waves; the chase; the bloody, shark-filled ocean surrounding the Andoria; the putrid smell of the tryworks; the joy of rounding Long Point and arriving home, and the dreadful state of affairs that awaited him. These impressions merge with Marc's consciousness. Looking up from the journal, he finds the tower surrounded by a dense fog bank. All sense of time and place has vanished.

When he finishes reading, Marc feels leaden and exhausted. He barely has time to close the journal before his head drops to his chest.

Past Imperfect

Marc wakes confused. According to his watch, three hours have passed. The sky is without a trace of fog. The ocean sparkles with dappled light. He feels rested and refreshed, yet aware of words and images within that make him feel he's lived a lifetime since Cole left. Though a voice in the back of Marc's head struggles to make sense of things, he is for the most part oddly at peace.

He sits staring out over the bay, so deep in thought he doesn't hear Cole until he speaks.

"What did you find out?"

Marc decides to keep his recent experiences to himself, at least for now. Things with Cole are far too tentative since their argument. There's no point in introducing the supernatural. Marc makes room for Cole on the bench.

"You can't begin to imagine all that happened back then. If you believe what the captain says, Annie recovered from her suicide attempt. She went to live with the first mate's family at least for the rest of the captain's life. Prudence lived five years after the scene Lola witnessed as a child. The captain never knew if Lola was his daughter or not but decided to split the estate between Lola and Dorrie in any case. That's the gist of it."

"Did he actually attack Annie? Was that the scandal he wrote about?"

"He says he didn't, but also says the townsfolk suspected him of her murder. You've got to hear this for yourself, Cole. I'm not sure I buy all of his claims. I want to see how credible he seems to you. Besides, if we're going to try to settle all this, you'll need to know everything there is to know. I'll pick up where we left off."

Marc begins to read.

Suffice it to say, with word of similar battles awaiting me in distant ports of call, I was no longer besotted with my new bride. If Prudence had any capacity for love, it was clearly for my fortune, not for me.

I returned from three years at sea to a hen fight of colossal proportions. Prudence immediately demanded I banish my mother from the house, while my mother insisted I file for divorce. Mindful of the scandal inherent in either choice, I refused to act, even though it meant arbitrating petty differences nearly every hour of every day.

In short order, my wife refused all conjugal affection, claiming I never took her side against my mother. In truth, I suspect this was simply an excuse. She did seem extraordinarily close to Morrison, whom I'd had investigated during my absence. He was one of the few undeniably masculine artists in my mother's circle, and by the time I returned, the town was abuzz with speculation about him and my incorrigible wife.

Whaling was no longer profitable. With great regret, I resigned myself to a life of discord on shore. Never again would I find respite at sea. As scandalous as it may sound, Pru's infidelity was not an overwhelming concern, for my marriage had not taken hold. I found my own release, as I had in earlier days, at reasonable expense on trips to Boston and New Bedford, where safe, well-run houses of accommodation could still be found. In that regard, my ill-starred union had not changed me. I threw myself into the growth of my new cold storage business and found much solace in it. I felt, at the time, I was missing nothing save a child and heir.

There was one period in the fall of '13 when my so-called wife suddenly changed course. She became most affectionate and, upon her own initiative, resumed her conjugal duties with all the enthusiasm of a Lahaina boat-girl. These actions stunned me, but I had hearty appetites back then and chose not to delve too deeply into things. I readily yielded to her enticements, and the result was a child, born several weeks premature in May of '14.

I've often questioned the motive for this sudden change in course. In charitable moments, I believed it was a woman's desire for a child before nature closed that door, or even some attempt at rapprochement. In less charitable and ever more frequent moods, I became convinced it was to legitimize the leavings of another man.

After the birth of Aloisa, or Lola as she came to be known, Pru had a major altercation with Mother over the child's care. From then on, my wife's amorous attentions were withdrawn for good. It is clear to me as I write this that her goal had been achieved, and she no longer had need of my services. Again, sustaining the pattern of a lifetime, I chose not to delve further.

I must say, here and now, that whatever the pedigree of my darling daughter Lola, she became mine from the moment I first held her in my arms. A true gift from God, she brought joy to my heart and a purpose to my labors.

Marc stops reading. "He underlined that last sentence twice. I wonder if he really felt that way, or this was just a PR pitch for posterity. What do you think?"

Cole seems to appreciate the question. "I think Prudence tried to mend fences, and the mother-in-law came between them as she always did. Keep reading. Let's see what else he says."

Marc resumes.

And so I returned to a lonely existence defined by hard work and nourished by purchased affection. Such was my despair over the loss of intimacy, I doubt I could have endured save for the child.

The Machados lived in desperate circumstances after leaving HomePort. For reasons she'd never explain, Prudence would not hear of their return, nor give them a reference. I, like Mother, felt certain they knew something to my wife's detriment, but neither would say what it might be.

I helped the family as discreetly as I could, so I knew something of their daughter, Annie. I saw little of her until, at the request of her ailing mother, I hired her to cook at HomePort. By that time, my wife was away so often the household staff was of no concern to her. She left all decisions to Agnes, who was smart enough to know where her salary came from and offer no resistance to my plan.

I doubt Pru realized who Annie was until much later. It certainly would not have been in Agnes's best interest to tell her. Besides, Machado was a common enough cognomen in town that one might hire twenty cooks with that name.

HomePort became a ghost ship. Mother, driven to distraction, eventually retreated full time to the second and third floors. Laetitia Staunton, once the leading light of our tiny community, became a virtual prisoner in her home of nearly fifty years, taking dinner on a tray in her rooms with her beloved Lola at her side.

As Pru was frequently traveling or out about town, I was often the only one to eat downstairs. Wishing company at day's end, particularly in the gloomy winter months when few souls were about, I took to eating in the kitchen with Annie, whose simplicity, quiet dignity, and grace offered a refreshing change.

In the beginning, ours was a comfortable friendship, nothing more. I felt loyalty to her parents. Then, in short succession, Annie's mother and then her father died of influenza during the winter of '23. Having cared deeply for them both, I increased my interest in their daughter's welfare.

At first, my concern was parental. Gradually, without initial notice, these feelings shifted to admiration, then at last, a profound and surprising love. After some time, I learned Annie's feelings were in concert with mine. Still, I withheld affection out of propriety and consideration for my standing in the community.

Nature has a way of whittling down the most stalwart of resolutions. Eventually, our love was joyously consummated. We made our assignations in a small cottage on the northeast slope of the grounds. Once, our unbridled passions beyond our control, we made use of my own bed. I believe it was here, my second daughter, Andoria, now just a week old, was conceived.

Annie withheld her news until concealment was no longer possible, finally informing me of her condition with great anxiety. Much to her surprise and, I must say, my own, I responded with joy, resolving to free myself and make an honest woman of her. With that, my love's happiness knew no bounds.

I decided to settle HomePort and a significant sum upon my wife in exchange for an uncontested divorce. My mother had recently passed, leaving Lola bereft. As much as I missed Mother's wise counsel and her positive impact on her grandchild, a part of me felt liberated. She would never have countenanced my scheme. The transfer of HomePort to her archenemy would have surely killed her, had old age not already staked its claim.

At first, Prudence was amenable, if not genuinely enthusiastic. Negotiations commenced, arbitrated by the venerable Aloysius Grubb, for whom my first daughter, Aloisa, was named. Deeds were drawn. My wife sought and received a significant amount of money in advance of the transfer of the property, and I set about selling the business.

In December, Prudence left for an extended trip to New York, ostensibly for shopping, but I do not believe we deceived each other as to its true intent. Like a bitch in heat, she followed a young Italian artist back to the city. Her betrayal did not trouble me, for my future was filled with hope. Even so, I took the liberty of having my wife followed by a private detective during her time in New York. Additional evidence might help to convince her to abandon her position as the lordly Mrs. Staunton when the time came. Little did I know.

With Pru's departure, Annie rested quietly in the small house partway down the drive. I spent as much time as I could with her. That final month passed in joyous anticipation and was the best of my miserable life. Freedom shone before us like the dawn of a grand new day. We planned our trip round the world when the child was old enough to make the journey and considered where we might begin a new life together.

Trust No One

Marc lays down the volume. "There's so much more, including a part at the end where he begs Lola and Dorrie to reconcile. It seems he tried to make amends through his will. His appeal to Lola is heartbreaking. She's got to hear it."

Cole stares at Marc, begins to speak, then lowers his gaze. After a moment of apparent indecision, he adopts an assertive tone. "But not before we've confirmed the facts. We have to proceed carefully. Lola's not in the best of health. She needs answers, not more anxiety."

The two men sit silently for a few minutes, watching the sun set from the very place where the captain had written his last journal entry. Intense feelings of joy and gut-wrenching apprehension surge through Marc's brain. His neck tingles, his body feels more expansive and his thoughts more focused as the mysterious entity has its say. The emotions are complex: joy at the journal's discovery, profound remorse, but most of all, a fervent desire for reconciliation between Lola and Dorrie. All this is characterized by an urgency Marc absorbs more than hears, leaving him dazed and emotionally depleted.

When the thoughts abate, Marc, hesitant to relate his experience to Cole, simply says, "We've *got* to tell Lola and Dorrie."

Cole seems to craft his words with great care. "Give me some time to read the whole thing. Then let's discuss next steps. Ok? It's not that I doubt what you're saying, it's just we have to be very, very careful. I'll read it from cover to cover, then call you."

"Fair enough."

Cole slaps Marc on the back, grabs the journal, opens the hatch, and jumps to the third floor, his feet never touching the ladder.

Time Will Reveal

An hour or so later, Cole asks Marc to meet him in front of the house. Marc arrives first. As he waits, he ponders the blue ceiling of the porch, the sea-nymphs on the door, and the weather vane atop the tower. The exterior of the mansion exudes near perfection, so much at odds with the tensions and anxieties that lie within.

He's never gotten used to the statue, particularly its brandished harpoon. *It's a sort of a totem, not for the source of the family fortune, but for the all too real conflict the house has seen for more than a century. I hope Cole doesn't take too much longer, I get chills just standing near the damn thing.*

Cole finally arrives and suggests a walk so they won't be overheard. The two men amble down the drive past Dorrie's house as if they'd never fought. Cole seems more relaxed than in the tower, but darkness makes it difficult for Marc to be certain. Marc turns left on Commercial Street, and Cole readily follows. Reaching the West End Boat Ramp, the two men sit on the seawall, their legs dangling over the side.

Cole speaks first. "So let's compare notes. The captain says he tried to prevent Annie from committing suicide, and that she lived at least into her sixties. He also says Prudence and her housekeeper planted the rumors he'd raped and killed Annie. He was never sure Lola was his daughter, so he decided to split the estate between Lola and Dorrie."

"That's it in a nutshell. There's more to this than how it impacts Dorrie, though. Lola's whole way of life could be on the line."

"I'm sorry, Marc. Dorrie is one thing, but I have to insist on better proof before we tell Lola. I've known her longer than you have. Her family reputation is sacred to her, and I'm still not completely sold on what I've read. The captain seems to put all the blame on her mother. It *can't* be that simple. No one could be that evil."

As Marc's newfound memories surface, justice makes its case from within. "Lola is under no illusions about her mother, Cole. Maybe we should run all of this past Charlotte first. She's the closest thing to family Lola's got, and Charlotte's father and grandfather are involved. As far as I'm concerned, that gives her a right to know."

Cole's broad smile is just visible in the dim light. "Good idea. I can live with that."

"We have to be careful with Charlotte, though," Marc says as an afterthought. "Her grandfather knew about Annie, but we don't know if her father did, or whether he acted on the captain's instructions. This whole business is full of landmines. If you listen to Dolores, the Grubbs have been blackmailing the Staunton's for nearly a century."

Cole shakes his head. "Oh, come on, Marc. That's just the Adams gossip mill working overtime."

"No, Cole. There are witnesses behind the speculation. I don't believe the accusations either, but we still have to tread lightly when it comes to the Grubbs' role in all of this. There are a lot of unanswered questions. Did Captain Staunton ever dictate the codicil? If so, was it ever executed? Did Grubb Junior even know about Annie? We have to have answers before we talk with Lola. If the captain said he'd change the will and never followed through, he was just trying to make himself look good. If he did change it, and Lola undermined his intentions, then it's a different story. If one of the Grubbs helped her, that's collusion. If it's made public she defrauded Dorrie, the scandal could kill Lola."

Cole sighs. "You're right. We don't know if Dorrie and Lola split because of the rumors or over control of the fortune. Lola may not be the legitimate heir. The captain certainly had his doubts. She may have known that and crowded Dorrie out. After all, if Lola's father were Morrison, she'd have no claim at all. I can't see her giving up HomePort no matter how strong her principles. She'd have done anything to stay where she felt safe."

"So we're in agreement? We'll start with Dorrie and then Charlotte?"

"Yes, but Lola's is to be kept in the dark until we know more. Agreed?"

"Agreed…. And Cole?"

"Yes?"

"There's something else," Marc says sighing deeply.

"The portrait? I *knew* you wouldn't let that rest."

"I'm so sorry. I don't know what got into me. Something about that day and the way I looked in that painting made me freak…."

At a loss how to continue, Marc waits for a response.

Cole rubs his hands through his hair, then speaks. "Well, you brought it up, and there *are* a couple of things I've wanted to say for a long time. If you recall, out at the pond you said you were afraid no one would ever see anything in you. I thought if you knew what I saw, it might make a difference. Your portrait was sitting there, just waiting to make my case, so I decided to show it to you. Perhaps that was a mistake, but it doesn't take you off the hook. You were a real shit, Marc. Not about my work. I can handle that now, I think. What really pissed me off was how you dismissed the risk I took in showing it to you. The painting may be idealized as far as you're concerned. You have every right to think so, but I have to tell you, it's what I see in you. I still do. And goddamn it, I was trying to show you what I felt for you."

Cole pauses. His hands clasp the cold cement, his right leg swings in slow motion. "Maybe it was a cop out or a lame way to do it. Emotion comes hard for me, but you can't say I didn't share my truth. You could have at least shown some respect for that."

Marc feels a burden lift. "You're absolutely right. I apologize."

Cole stands, then speaks in a tone that is strangely upbeat, though as awkward as a teenager's. "Well, I've gotten that shit off my chest. Could we hold off on any further discussion on this topic for a while? Right now, Lola and Dorrie are more important than fighting over what we may or may not see in a piece of canvas."

Marc jumps to his feet and extends his hand. "You've got a deal. Let's go see Dorrie."

A Gift In Kind

Seated at her kitchen table, Dorrie stares inquisitively at the closed journal. Her features are clouded as if she anticipates bad news.

Before speaking, Marc looks to Cole for encouragement. "Dorrie, we've got news of your mother. Captain Staunton kept this journal apart from the others. It explains what happened to her. Cole found it hidden in the dumbwaiter that runs up to the tower."

"What's it say?"

As Dorrie leans forward to open the book, Marc picks up the journal. "Lola doesn't know we have it, so I'd rather you not read the whole thing. There's a lot of personal stuff about *her* mother and grandmother. We want Charlotte to decide whether to share those parts with Lola."

"Fair enough. I trust you to tell me what I need to know. Start readin'."

Marc turns to bookmarked page, scans it, then begins.

Last week, I arrived at Annie's house to check on her as I did several times a day. Her delivery date was three days prior, and we were still anxiously awaiting God's gift. Opening the door, I was stunned to hear my wife call Annie a whore and demand she vacate the house by the following morning. Then I heard a door slam, and Prudence brushed past me without so much as a word. She had returned from New York the day before in foul temper. As I later learned from the detective, she had broken with her Italian over New Year's.

Before I could reprimand my wife, Annie let out a scream of agony. Her crisis had finally arrived. I raced to her, leaving Pru to go where she might, fully intending to deal with her later.

Once summoned, Dr. Rhinelander fought mightily to stem the hemorrhaging and calm Annie's hysterics. I have no doubt my wife's venom created an extreme agitation that hampered the natural progression of the birth. Annie struggled for twelve hours, bringing into the world at last a healthy, beautiful girl at great damage to her own physical and, as I later learned, mental well-being.

I had secured a nurse from Boston in anticipation of Annie's confinement. To my eternal regret, the woman proved disreputable and fond of drink, often sleeping off binges at her post. This was how Annie, weakened and panic-stricken, snuck out the morning after giving birth, found her way to HomePort, and sealed her fate. It was only for lack of a plan and fear for her emotional state that I had not already reached out to console her. I thought I had more time and felt confident that, with quiet and rest, she would soon regain her equilibrium.

I was in the tower revising my plans for our escape in light of Pru's sudden change of heart. Staring absentmindedly out the window, I saw Annie run from the house. I raced down the stairs and, after a fruitless query of my wife's actions, followed my love into a blustery, January blizzard.

Annie had too great a start. I trailed her across the moors screaming her name, but the howling wind was against me. Her path led through waist-deep water to the old menhaden factory on the outer beach, where she clambered to the end of a rotting wharf just moments before I caught up with her. I followed her onto the pier, praying she would see me before it was too late.

The bay was more like the mid-Atlantic than the tranquil bight I knew so well. Gusts of wind hit like body blows. Breakers reared, then thundered to shore, rocking the neglected wharf. Spume-covered water streamed beneath its splintered planks like raging rapids. A piling lurched, then toppled into the sea, followed by a second, then a third, leaving one side of the wharf submerged and even more vulnerable to the relentless surf.

Annie survived the collapse, clutching the furthest piling, staring out into the sea as if indifferent to all danger. I drew closer and yelled. At last, she turned toward me. I pleaded with her to stand still as I clambered across the upper side of the wharf, now tilted like a foundering ship. When she reached to embrace me, I screamed she should hold fast. She grabbed hold again just before a wave swept over her.

I looked up, and she was still there. Fearful my weight would prove too great for the boards beneath her, I drew as near as I dared, grasped a nearby piling, then reached out.

My fingers came within inches of hers. I moved forward, tried again, and at last we touched. I pleaded with her to let go. She tried, lost courage, and balked.

For what seemed an age, I coaxed and cajoled her. Waves washed over the rotted pier, raising and lowering it with their might, working boards loose and straining the already weakened structure past its limits. When it groaned like a sinking ship, I knew we had little time left.

At last, Annie conquered her fear and let go. Her hand tightly clasped in mine, I pulled her toward me, my other arm still wrapped around the piling for support. Looking past her, I saw a large breaker towering above the others. It was but a few seconds before the mountain of water hit the old wharf like a cannon shot, sweeping the wood from beneath her feet. She screamed, then toppled into the churning mass of foam.

Miraculously, her hand remained locked in mine. Another wave broke over us, then another and another. In the intervals between them, I pulled her high enough to catch a breath. Then the next wave crashed over her, tossing her in its fury. Twice I felt her body hit the piling beside me. She held tight, though I could tell she was rapidly weakening. Her clothing weighted her, abetting the fierce pull of the churning water. Gradually, I hoisted her back onto the wharf and lay her down flat until I might safely trundle her to shore.

Another enormous wave crested under the wharf, wracking it further. The few remaining pilings strained, and the platform tilted farther to port. With a snap, the portion beneath us gave way. We plunged to the bottom, scraping against stones, rolling in the undertow, smashing against the pilings. Even so, we held each other fast. When Annie and I finally surfaced, our arms entwined, her terrified eyes locked with mine until we submerged once more.

We were at the mercy of the ocean. Blessedly, winds were onshore, but even so, a powerful riptide drew us out to sea. I knew to ride this current out, but feared the impact of sustained immersion upon my beloved. There was good reason. After several minutes, Annie lost consciousness. Her lovely body, dragged down by the sodden weight of her clothing, tossed and turned beneath the waves, sometimes surfacing for an instant, then disappearing yet again.

All the while, I kept hold of her arm, kicking for shore. Then, just ten feet from my goal, a bollard hit my head, disorienting me. For a moment, I may have lost consciousness. I am not sure to this day whether I actually did or the shock of the blow caused me to release my grasp. It is of little consequence, for by the time I recovered my bearings, Annie was gone.

Everything seemed in slow motion as I swam the cresting waves in search of her. When she finally surfaced, some fifteen feet away from me, her pale face was tranquil, and her beautiful hair trailed out behind her. After what seemed an eternity, I reached her and began once again to tow her to land.

Coming close to shore, I struggled to gain a foothold on the sand, which was constantly pulled from under my feet by the powerful undertow. Out of the water at last, I lay Annie on the beach and tried to revive her, pressing my lips repeatedly to her cold, lifeless mouth. After an age, her eyes opened, and she seemed to stare as if seeing a ghost.

"She said you'd abandoned me," Annie whispered.

She shook with violent spasms, then her eyes closed, and her head fell back. I held her close. She did not regain consciousness, though a weak pulse offered a faint ray of hope.

Trembling with fright and numb with cold, I carried her across the windswept moors, wading through the incoming tide and slipping on frozen sand.

When Marc pauses to take a drink of water, Dorrie wipes her eyes.

"So he loved her after all. He didn't rape and abuse her. I'm so glad to know I was born of love, even at this late date. Go on, Marc."

I got the automobile, then drove Annie to Dr. Rhinelander who examined her and determined a specialist was urgently needed. I phoned Aloysius Grubb and had him meet me at the plant. We hid my vehicle in one of the repair bays, retrieved shovels should we get stuck, and drove a panel truck back to Rhinelander's house. Arranging for his wife to rescue the newborn child, we placed Annie on a mattress in the back of the truck and set out for Hyannis.

The laborious journey up Cape, climbing icy dunes in swirling snow, held more fear for me than the worst calamity at sea. Our headlights barely penetrated the dense, wet snowfall. The truck gained and lost traction, making for torturously slow progress. Several times, we had to shovel our way out of drifts. Never before had my beloved Provincetown seemed so far removed from humanity. Where once I blessed its isolation and sweeping dunes, now I cursed them. Though wracked with seizures, Annie lapsed in and out of consciousness. I could do little but murmur words of encouragement as the bouncing truck traversed the dunes with the loyal Grubb at the wheel.

We arrived at the hospital under cover of darkness and swirling snow. When the specialist had seen Annie, I learned it was unlikely she would live to see the sunrise. Between immersion in cold water, blunt trauma, and prior loss of blood, her chances for survival were less than one in ten. I fell asleep in the chair beside her bed, afraid to leave for the shortest instant lest she relinquish her grasp on life without me to comfort her passage.

When I awoke in the early hours of the next morning and found her still breathing, hope slowly re-entered my heart and with it, a plan. First, I would deal with Prudence in no uncertain terms. Should Annie die, I vowed my wife would pay with her own life. Second, but of greater import, I swore should Annie live, we would be together no matter what the cost.

Marc reads how the captain reached out to his former first mate, Castleton, who immediately came to Hyannis. He offered the services of his newly widowed sister-in-law to care for the child. Castleton never once gave up hope, loyally standing by and sustaining his former captain, and in time, offering his home for Annie to recuperate.

Marc sets down the journal and studies Dorrie carefully. "This next part is going to be hard to handle. Do you want a cup of tea or something?"

"No. I'll be fine. Just tell me what I need to know. I've spent a lifetime speculatin'. The truth won't hurt no more than what I've imagined for all these years."

Marc does as he's asked.

I prayed nonstop for three days that Annie would live, even offering God my own life in exchange. On the third day, her eyes fluttered, then she smiled at me. It seemed my prayers were answered. They had been, but only in part. Annie could no longer speak. She produced only unintelligible noise. The doctor spoke of brain damage, most likely from a series of strokes. If there were no improvement in short order, she might never regain the use of language. I swore to Annie that everything would be done to help her, and she seemed to understand.

I returned to HomePort with such rage I could not utter a single word to Prudence lest thousands filled with hatred and loathing follow in its wake. I wrote a note ordering her to leave the house and not return until sent for. To my surprise, she departed at once, leaving Lola in the care of Agnes and a surly assortment of servants who immediately made their loyalties clear.

I made a pretense of going to the office for the sake of appearances but slipped on the train to Hyannis nearly every day, leaving Aloysius Grubb in charge of day-to-day business. I focused all my energies on Annie's recovery, my plans to divorce my wife, and preparations for my new life. If that life was to be devoted to the care of my beloved, I was undaunted, approaching even that eventuality with joy and gratitude. Having nearly lost Annie, I found myself unable to imagine life without her.

After a month, Annie was well enough to move to Castleton's farm. And this is how things stand. She grows stronger under their care, though the physician has declared it unlikely she will regain more abilities than she already has.

Recently, I became aware that rumors as to Annie's fate were flying about town like gulls behind a trawler. I gave them no mind at first, though I fired the housekeeper, Agnes, when I learned she was behind them.

Today, an incident with a former business partner has convinced me of the need for action. I plan to approach Prudence to revive our contract, free myself from this dreadful marriage, and tend to my love. Once Annie is recovered, we'll leave this hellish town for once and for all. The greatest risk in life lies in not living it. This lesson I have learned at last.

Marc places the open journal on the table. "There's a lot more, but it's almost midnight, so let me summarize the rest. According to this journal, Annie never spoke again. Your father says she lived with the Castletons at least into the fifties, which is when he made his last entry in the journal. He visited almost every week, and the last time he saw her, she was over sixty. He truly regretted losing the years he might have shared with your mother and you. Those were practically his last written words."

Cole watches Dorrie intently even as he starts to speak. "I want you to be careful about what you make of all this, Dorrie. We only have the captain's take on things. Marc and I plan to withhold judgment until we get more facts. I suggest you do likewise. I've read the entire journal, and your father spent a lot of time justifying his actions. It could be he's written what he wanted us to hear, not what really happened."

Marc closes the journal and places both his hands over Dorrie's. "What do you have to say about all this? It has to be quite a shock."

She extricates one hand and slips it under the table to pat Frida. The other hand stays where it is. "Not so much as you might think. First, I'm glad to hear 'bout my mother. It's good to know she was cared for and not buried alone out in the dunes with the wild winds and poundin' waves as I've always feared. Even before folks told me to my face, I always had suspicions that captain was my father. I knew I reminded him of somethin', but never knew for certain 'til now what the hell it was."

Cole nods sympathetically. "When captain left you this house and the annuity, did you see his will?"

Marc smiles to himself at Cole's ever-present concern for Lola.

Dorrie shakes her head. "Never saw the will. That Grubb fellow, Charlotte's dad, come to see me one day and told me I was set for life. I didn't care about nothin' save makin' up with Lola. That's all that mattered then and all that matters now. We had such good times as girls, and then it all went to shit. I've lived all these years watchin' her in that big house, buying friendship, telling tall tales 'bout a life that never existed. I've always known she was kin and that she needed me. She and me are the only ones left who remember."

"But even the captain isn't sure whether she's his daughter," Marc says. "If she's not, you might be entitled to the entire fortune."

With that, Dorrie erupts. She removes her hand and clutches the table, hoisting herself up to her full height. Her voice grows strident. "I don't give a rat's ass about her money. I don't want it and wouldn't take it, neither. Whether Lola is my birth sister or not don't mean a tinker's damn to me. She's still my sister. I'm meant to be with her, watching out for her to the end of her days. That's all there is to it, plain and simple."

Dorrie, seeming to notice Cole's puzzled expression, assumes a less forceful tone. "Cole, honey, this ain't just about kin. It's about a reason for livin'. I don't know how to say it no other way. Sometimes your birth family ain't your true family, if that makes any sense. I just know in my bones I need to take care of Lola. I don't give a damn if she's my sister, my aunt, or my goddamn parakeet. I love her and gotta see she has some happiness before it's too damn late. We got unfinished business in this life, her and me. Bein' with her is what I gotta do right now. That's all that matters."

The spirit who haunts Marc's thoughts expresses profound admiration for Dorrie as well as increased anxiety for Lola. Marc ponders its concerns for a moment, then chooses his next words with care. "We have to be very careful, Dorrie. Lola's spent her life maintaining an image of her family that will collapse once she hears this."

"You're right, though she's a tougher old bird than you might think. We have to figure how to break the news, but there's one thing we gotta clear up before we do."

Marc smiles at Dorrie's insight. "I'm with you. We need proof of what happened to Annie."

"You got it, dahlin'. If we can prove beyond the captain's words that my mother survived that day, we'll get through to Lola. She won't take nothin' on speculation. She'll want it all tied up pretty with a bow. There's been so much gossip, anything but solid truth will wrack her to pieces."

As Marc rises to leave, Dorrie steps away from the table, rousing Frida. "Now enough about stuff that happened years ago. Haven't you two learned anything from all this? About life? About love? When are you goin' to face facts?"

Marc sees Cole squirming with embarrassment and feels a twinge of anxiety. "What do you mean?"

"You know damn well what I mean," Dorrie says, poking Marc's chest repeatedly with a boney index finger. "Anyone with a half a brain lookin' at the two of you can tell you're crazy about each other. Yet you act like oil and water whenever you're together. When in God's name are you gonna shape up? After all the captain wrote, you gotta know life's too goddamn short for such bullshit."

Dorrie's face is red, her eyes wide. The wattle under her neck seems to shake with indignation. Marc can think of no way to shut down her harangue.

"For God's sake, Marc, don't waste any more time. Just look at Lola and me, or better yet, my father and mother. What the hell does it take for you to get it?"

Marc starts to protest, but Dorrie will not be thwarted. "Don't give me none of your bullshit, Marcus Nugent. Do you know what Daryl said to me just before he died? I'm gonna tell you whether you do or not. He said his only regret 'bout leavin' this life was the days he spent without someone to love. He cried in my arms wishing it had been different. How many things have to hit you over the head before you two assholes get it? Learn from Daryl, if no one else, before it's too late. Goddamn it!"

The old woman's shrill voice echoes through the kitchen.

"Well, Dorrie, I'm not sure I...." At the sight of Cole's grin, Marc feels his temper rise. *What right does Cole have to mock me at a time like this?*

"You *are* sure, honey," Dorrie spouts. "Sure as shittin'. Get outta your head, open your eyes, and listen to your heart."

Dorrie jabs her finger into Marc's chest one last time so forcefully it hurts. The little flap of skin beneath her chin vibrates to near frenzy as she hauls herself to her full height, purses her lips and bellows, "Now get the hell outta my kitchen, you goddamn fools, and do somethin' about this mess before I knock the two of you 'side the head with this here fryin' pan."

CHAPTER 10
PILGRIMS' PARK
IN THE DARK

Cole and Marc slink down the driveway like chastened delinquents. Their demeanor is oddly similar: heads down, hands in pockets, deep in thought. An awkward chill settles between them. HomePort is a shadow at the top of the hill, a haunting, black mass in the gentle moonlight. Now that Marc knows its secrets, the old place seems ominous, barren, and forbidding. As so many times before, the circle of light appears, only to vanish when a solitary man skulks across the balcony into the night.

"What do you think goes on up there?" Marc asks, hoping to gain some emotional distance from Dorrie's tirade.

"I've got my ideas, Sherlock. Do you really think we should be discussing them right now? Dorrie's right. We've got to deal with us. There's been way too much bullshit for far too long. C'mon, let's head over to the park."

Cole strides toward the gate. Marc lags behind, surveying the balcony. After a moment, and against his better judgment, he catches up. They cross Commercial Street to Pilgrims' Park, Frida trailing quietly behind, attuned to their mood, her tail wagging in a low, tentative arc. When they reach the park, the moonlight is as bright as day. Its golden swath illuminates the breakwater's march to Long Point.

Cole voice is rife with tension. "Sit down."

As Frida sits immediately, Marc smiles at her atypical response. After a moment meant to assert his independence, he sits on the bench where Dorrie recounted her dream.

Cole paces, then speaks in a halting voice. "This is difficult enough knowing you don't want to hear it, so give me time to get it out, Ok?"

When Marc nods, Cole stares at the ground, seems to struggle for an opening sentence, then begins. "When you knocked over the easel, I knew why. I'd been jazzed by our conversation out in the woods and pushed too hard. I tried to give you time to come around, but something had begun. Even though it scares the shit out of you, I've gotta tell you Marc. I'm in love with you. Not the man in the portrait, but you. I have been for months."

Cole's voice cracks slightly. He takes a deep breath and waits. When he seems to realize Marc either can't or won't answer, Cole resumes, his tone even more subdued. "I've stood outside your bedroom door several nights since that day, trying to find the courage to knock. I figured if we took a chance on us, everything else would fall into place. But I knew you'd never let me in, not after all that happened with that bastard in New York."

Marc feels a sudden chill as Cole continues, sounding less sure-footed than before.

"But even so, I knew I'd regret it for the rest of my life if I didn't at least tell you. It's all about truth, remember? It has to be." With this, his voice cracks.

Still getting no response, Cole walks toward the jetty. Marc jumps up, strides ahead, and abruptly blocks his path. A brutal silence ensues as the two men lock eyes. Neither gives way, until at last, Cole returns to the bench.

Marc peruses the memorial stones in the bright moonlight, taking in their tales of love and loss. His thoughts run rampant. *Is there any other place where so much pain is concentrated in a single spot? Look at all these names, most dead before their time. Just the perfect place for this conversation.* When he reaches the stone that reads *Some Other Spring,* his question sounds as if someone else were asking. "Cole. On this stone, here… *Some Other Spring.* What does it mean?"

Cole, seeming baffled and more than slightly annoyed, waits some time before answering. "It's a Billie Holiday song about an abused woman who wonders if she'll ever love again."

Marc stares at the inscription. *How many springs, how many months, how many weeks make up a lifetime? Not nearly enough. Is there any point in waiting to be better, more certain, or less vulnerable?*

"I don't know why," Marc says aloud, his thoughts transitioning to words, "but of all the stones out here, that one speaks to me the most."

Cole's reply is a whisper. "God knows the lyrics fit."

"What are you saying?"

"I have a good idea what Brandon did to you."

Marc's temper flares as clouds pass in front of the moon, and a flinty darkness descends on the moors. "Dorrie again! Goddamn this town!"

"Marc, you're wrong. Dorrie didn't give away your secrets. You did. I started your portrait as a way to thank you for working on my studio. As it turned out, studying you and trying to understand the man beneath the façade helped me understand all you'd been through. Dorrie merely confirmed my suspicions, and that was only a week ago. I went to her because I'd fucked up everything and didn't know how to fix it. I'm more scared of all this than you are, if you'd just believe me. I had to talk to someone."

"So you orchestrated her tantrum just now?" An odd vibration passes through Marc, weakening his legs, stoking his discomfort, and undermining his self-righteousness.

"No. Of course not. Dorrie did that out of love for us, Marc. If you want to be angry, be angry with me for telling her what was in my heart. If I'd known she was going to pull that stunt just now, I'd have tried to talk her out of it. I didn't ask her to...." Cole slouches in embarrassment as Marc, fighting nausea, glares out at the darkened moors.

Shadows slowly coalesce in the dimming, mist-laden light, morphing into an image of Annie running through a raging snowstorm with the captain in frantic pursuit. Marc blinks and shakes his head, only to see the captain return, staggering under Annie's sodden weight. Suddenly Marc is overwhelmed by potent grief and longing. He directs his thoughts to the now-familiar essence whose emotions mirror his own.

Such a happy ending for you two. Even if you did love Annie and saved her life, what good did it do you? Treating someone the way you did isn't love, it's narcissism. I'm sure she'd rather been dead than sit around unable to speak, waiting for you to show up once a week for a couple of hours. What right did you have to ask that of her?

Now take Brandon and me. Maybe it wasn't a grand passion, but it was better than your sham of a marriage. Yet just like yours, everything went to shit. And it will again with Cole, if I don't shut this madness down somehow. He's so confused he can't tell which end is up. He's got to understand; love's just a bullshit notion that causes nothing but pain.

Shifting his gaze to the harbor, Marc spies a ghostly procession crossing the jetty from Helltown. As the cortege draws near, sensations of sorrow and regret escalate to the point he can hardly bear them. He senses the final thoughts of drowning fishermen, the hopelessness of submariners trapped on the ocean's floor, and the final, sodden breath of untold suicides. Their suffering and regret sears his heart.

The procession passes him, glides across the moors to Annie's body, and slowly encircles her. As Marc watches, the spirits urge her to join their ranks. Gradually, a wraithlike figure ascends from her prostate body, fending off the shadowy forms with a light that grows stronger until the moors are as bright as day. Annie's beacon reaches Marc, astounding him with the depth of her courage and devotion. Summoned by the light, intense feelings of love and certainty enter him from the memorial stones beneath his feet. As these vibrant emotions pass through him, Marc shares the passions, hopes, and joys of every commemorated soul.

Many of these people had far worse happen to them than I have, and they never gave up on love. Some died of a horrible illness, but they went to their graves having lived and loved, mourned by those who cared for them. Even the captain, for all his self-inflicted, fearful decades, even he was loved. To stay with him, Annie triumphed over Death itself. If that's what love is, why am I so afraid of Cole loving me?

As if in answer to that question, the captain's dying words resound from within. *"The greatest risk in life lies in not living it."*

The dark forces cower in the light, then slowly begin their retreat. When the last spirit reaches the breakwater,

Marc feels drained. The experience has been too much, the emotions too overwhelming. He sits on a bench. The light moves with him, passing through him yet again as the last of the ghostly phalanx disappears from sight. Out on the moors, the captain carries Annie toward the road. Then the two spirits vanish, the clouds part, and the mysterious luminescence merges with the returning moonlight.

Marc catches his breath. Deep inside, he finds a speck of courage that grows of its own accord, as if shepherded by some greater part of himself. The ghostly visions are supplanted by feelings of excitement, anticipation, and desire. Flush with newfound confidence, Marc can't help but smile at the optimism and joy permeating his thoughts. Emboldened, he reaches for Cole's hand. It feels damp and unyielding. When Cole struggles to disengage it, Marc grasps his arm and pulls him closer.

"Dorrie knew how I felt too, even though I never said a word. I didn't have to."

Cole stares back, his astonishment clearly tempered by distrust and emotional exhaustion.

Marc takes a deep breath and searches Cole's eyes, the pained eyes of the child in the fire painting. "It *is* all about truth. But certain truths are hard to accept. Brandon beat me, Cole. He had his friends dope and rape me while he filmed what they did. I thought it was because there was something lacking in me—that somehow I deserved it."

Cole drops his gaze to the stones beneath his feet. His eyes glisten in the moonlight.

At a loss for further words, Marc releases Cole's hand, cradles his face, and as if in a dream, kisses him. Cole responds tentatively at first until Frida, tail wagging rapidly, pushes her full weight against his leg. Then Marc feels him slowly relax into his arms. The two men hold each other in the gentle moonlight, even their breath in harmony. The world around them fades, save the intense, if slightly smug satisfaction Marc feels from his otherworldly companion.

Glancing over Cole's shoulder at the moonlight reflecting on the water, Marc hears the words of Elizabeth Barrett Browning in the same clear, unmistakably masculine tones:

"Guess now who holds thee?"
"Death," I said. But, there,
The silver answer rang,
"Not Death, but Love."

* * * *

"I've got a CD of Billie Holiday's up in the studio," Cole says after a prolonged but comfortable silence, "singing 'Some Other Spring.' I've also got a good bottle of red wine. The night sky is amazing through the skylights. Want to listen to Billie, have some wine, and just stare at the stars?"

"Take me home, Cole. Please? I'm not fighting us anymore." Marc's voice falters, then fails him altogether when Cole brings Marc's hand to his lips.

The lovers cross Commercial Street and stroll up the drive to HomePort. Frida leads them home, her tail wagging contentedly. Dorrie stands watch in the parlor window, as Marc knew she would. Slowing the pace, he places his arm around Cole to display the result of her efforts. She raises her hand in a blessing, then catches his eye, flashes two thumbs up, and blows an extravagant kiss.

At the sight of Dorrie, Frida wags her tail. Just as Cole turns to see the cause of her excitement, the curtain falls back, and the quaint little house goes dark.

Harpo's Blues

Cole unlocks the studio door. He looks quickly over his shoulder as if to make sure Marc hasn't bolted. Catching Cole in an oddly reassuring moment of insecurity, Marc grins.

The portrait of Prudence Staunton glows in the moonlight. Marc points to it. "How can you work with her watching you? Don't you think she'd be a jinx?" Marc asks, relieved he can speak for all his chills and trembling.

Cole's boyish grin reveals his anxiety. "It's kinda weird. I've anointed her the 'Queen of the Critics.' See the way she's holding her head? So haughty and egotistical? Well, I figure if I can paint in front of her snotty-assed self, I can show my work to anybody and not give a shit."

"What would work for a self-conscious, hypercritical writer?"

"I have a couple of good ideas, but first, have a glass of wine." Cole pours two glasses, then escorts Marc to the couch. "Let me work on that writer's block." Marc's mind flits between anxiety and sensation while Cole provides a gentle massage. Sensing his distraction, Cole strokes Marc's face. "Relax. We're not going anywhere you don't want to go."

Cole's touch unleashes a shiver of anticipation. His hands are massive, yet something in the lightness of their movement gently seeks permission. Gradually, Marc relaxes, though powerful forces course through him: the electricity of Cole's touch, tremors of anxiety, the potent yearning of arousal. Marc stretches out on the couch, his body tingling with each caress. When Cole undoes the button of Marc's shirt and runs his fingers lightly across a nipple, he tenses.

"Cole, you should know I've got some major league hang-ups after all that happened in New York."

"Sshh, honey. You don't have to tell me anything more. Besides, we're not going to have sex."

"What?" Marc's disappointment surprises him. He's not sure what makes him more nervous, doing it or not doing it.

"We're not going to have sex. If we do anything at all—and we don't have to do a damn thing—we're going to make love." Cole tugs at Marc's shirt until he removes it. "Now just lie down here, relax, and let me work a bit on your lower back."

Marc relives his recent vision on the moors, imprinting them on his memory. The experience seems no less real the second time around. After several moments of contemplation, he sits up and drains his glass.

"Would you mind if…." Seeing Cole tense, Marc takes his hand. "Can we go down to my room instead? I've imagined you in my big bed for so long, I'd like to experience the reality."

"Not a problem. In fact, it's a great idea. This is the start of something, not a quickie. Let me go get a few things."

"Sure."

Marc thinks of Brandon. *What does Cole need to get off?*

Cole seems to sense Marc's discord, but merely says, "See you downstairs in two minutes. And don't undress. That's been *my* fantasy… undressing you."

Then he hastens to the Bates Motel.

* * * *

Lying on his bed, Marc stares up at the mythical figures that parade across the canopy. It's only been a few minutes since he returned to his room, but time is weighing heavy on his thoughts.

"Well, you didn't lock me out. That's a good sign." Cole stands at the bedroom door, a candle in one hand, a leather case in the other. Marc starts at the sound of his voice, then waves him in.

Cole's tone betrays the slightest trace of anxiety. "Now, just a few things in the atmosphere department. You know how we visual types can be about mood." He places the candle on the nightstand. Once it's lit, the smell of patchouli wafts through the room. "I'm going to save Billie Holiday for another time. I've found something much more fitting." He extracts a portable sound system from the case and turns it on. Phoebe Snow begins to sing, "At Last."

Cole removes two vials and a small box from the bottom of the case and places them on the nightstand. "I'm not insisting, but just in case."

Marc winces as images of Brandon's poppers and pills hijack his thoughts.

"What's wrong?" Cole asks.

"Nothing. Nothing."

"I won't argue, but I know you're holding something back. On your stomach. If you won't tell me, your body will."

Cole turns out the light and reaches for a vial. Marc feels warm oil trickle down his back and starts to laugh. "How the hell did you come up with warm massage oil on such short notice?"

Cole smiles proudly. "I used to be a masseur in college. A legit one, before you get any big ideas. I learned you could heat oil real quick in a microwave. As for the rest, it's easy enough to pull things together when you're as motivated as I am right now. Just relax and let your body talk to me."

Cole's supple touch quells Marc's churning mind until his thoughts focus exclusively on the man massaging him. When Cole crosses the room to adjust the volume, Marc whispers, "Ok, folks. Everyone out. Private time." Just as Cole returns, the spirits fade away, taking the last of Marc's anxiety with them.

"My turn," Marc says as he unbuttons Cole's shirt and runs his fingers through a forest of dark, curly hair. Marc feels Cole's nipples harden as he shudders, then removes his shirt and kisses him. When their lips touch, Marc's vision fades to gray. Cole lies down beside him, breathing hard, his body warm. Marc is stunned by Cole's desire. *For me. Not some idealized portrait. For me.*

Cole searches Marc's face for a reaction. "This is fine for now. It's enough just to hold you. The rest can wait. "

Marc smiles to himself. *Just what I've always needed to hear, and when I finally do, it's the last thing I want.*

In Marc's own time, at his behest, in the manner of his choosing, the men reveal themselves. Reserved, but brimming with anticipation, they explore and caress each other's naked bodies—so similar, though so different— so masculine, powerful and strong, yet tender, loving, and surprisingly vulnerable. They touch with a knowing certainty, two souls reuniting after centuries of separation.

After months of wistful desire, Marc is insatiable. He tastes Cole, strokes, and caresses him, losing himself in the beautiful man by his side. Through all this, Cole stands watch, yielding gently, taking the lead at times, yet always concerned for Marc's comfort.

Marc feels, yet again, the growing confidence within. *For the first time in years, I feel safe, and I can't believe it's not enough.* When the playlist has cycled through, he raises Cole's chin and looks deeply into his eyes.

"Please?"

"Are you sure? You don't have to."

"Never so sure of anything in my life."

Cole's skill and patience prepare Marc for his size. After what seems a lifetime of expectation, Marc nods. Cole reaches for a tube of lubricant and removes a condom from his bag. There's a bit of fumbling and adjustment as he tugs open the wrapper and finally puts it on. "I've heard a good whore can put one on with her mouth. I'm afraid my technique isn't quite up to those standards. I can hardly get one on with two hands."

Marc laughs. "Don't look at me. I've been around a bit, but not that much."

"Glad to hear it."

Reaching between Marc's legs, Cole begins to tickle him. Marc lets out a yelp. Cole's touch turns to a squeeze and then, after time, a gentle probing. He searches Marc's face yet again. When Marc nods in encouragement, Cole positions himself, smiles, then enters.

Adjusting to the sensations, familiar, yet strangely new, Marc grins up at him. The men kiss hungrily, and Cole's rhythm increases. Marc holds fast, pulling Cole closer. The creak of the bedsprings and the slapping sound of Cole's thrusts can be heard over the music. Marc, suddenly recalling Lola's bedroom is directly below them, struggles to banish the thought she might be awake.

The sensations that ripple through Marc's body surprise him. Before this night, sex had been a choreographed series of steps in a predictable sequence. This is completely different. He gives himself up to the moment, abandoning any need to orchestrate. His body acts of its own accord. Urgency, pleasure, vulnerability, and satiety all course through him. Marc wraps his legs tightly around Cole, pulling him closer, then places his hands on his butt, kneading, pressing, coaxing him further inside.

Cole's passion is powerful—insistent but not violent— though he seems to be trying mightily to restrain himself. Touched by this consideration, Marc urges him on. Soon, friction and sweat erase all sense of separation. He can no longer tell where he ends and Cole begins. All is one, powerful yet tender, and beautifully male. A revelation.

When Phoebe Snow sings "Poetry Man," Marc chuckles. "*Now* I get that bit about making things rhyme. Go for it, Cole."

With that, Cole seems liberated. His breathing accelerates. His body seems to be everywhere at once. Even so, his focus remains on Marc. When a movement or stroke evokes a gasp or moan, Cole recapitulates, lingers, and expands upon it, as a talented musician might engage a fine instrument in a series of subtle variations.

"Let this be my gift to you. Tonight is for you," he whispers, as his heart pounds mightily against Marc's chest.

As wave after wave of pleasure consumes him, Marc seems to float outside his body. Eventually, he can no longer hold back. Sensing this, Cole increases his rhythm and covers Marc's face with urgent kisses.

Release comes for both as one. Cole lets loose a muffled wail. Marc, faint and gasping for breath, holds him tight until his cries subside. As his breathing gradually returns to normal, he begins to shake uncontrollably. Cole covers him with his body, holding him close, repeating, "I love you, Marc," until the trembling finally stops.

"Don't leave, Cole. Stay."

Marc contemplates the beautiful man whose eyes have the same spark of fire he first saw in the studio. Cole props himself up on one elbow. "I'm not going anywhere Marc—ever. This is home for me. We both know that, now."

* * * *

August 10ᵗʰ, 2009 - HomePort

Cole is asleep beside me. I still can't believe it. Last night was a miracle. Poor Brandon never understood. Cole and I have been in my room for twenty hours and still can't get enough of each other. No more writing for now, I think my man is waking up. The Man I Love—and it's Tuesday. Perhaps Ellie knew what she was doing when she sang Gershwin the day Cole and I met.

The Joke's on You

The next day, Marc calls Charlotte. Part way through his story of finding the journal, she interrupts. "Tell me face-to-face. I want to be sure I get all of this."

"I can't drop everything and go to New York, Charlotte."

"Oh, for God's sake, Marc. Don't be such an old fusspot. Just come over to Telegraph Hill. You know the address."

"Huh?"

"Alan and Chuck's old place. See you in ten minutes?" She laughs before hanging up.

Cole is just getting up from his side of the large four-poster. Marc grabs his hand.

"C'mon. Let's take a quick shower and see what's up with Ms. Grubb. Something really strange is going on."

The shower, though shared, is far too rushed. The men dress hurriedly, returning with regret to the outside world. When Marc and Cole step onto the landing, Helena hails them from the corridor of the Bates Motel. She bounds toward them in a lavender jogging suit with matching headband and sneakers.

"There you are! I haven't seen you for two days! Where are you off to on this fabulous Provincetown morning?"

Marc quickly avoids her inquiring gaze. "We've got to check some details with Charlotte. She's over at Telegraph Hill for some reason. She may have some information we need about the captain."

Helena's imitation of Della Street is flawless. "Paul Drake and Perry Mason hit the road again, huh? Need a sexy secretary to tag along? I'd sure like to play detective rather than type all day long."

Marc had been a big Perry Mason fan as a kid. He can't help but smile. "Thanks Della, we're good for now. Tell Gertie to hold my calls."

Helena wets her finger, taps her hips, and makes a sizzling sound. "Sure thing, Perry. Don't forget your booty call at four."

Cole squeezes Marc's butt. "Don't worry, Della. I won't let him forget. You can count on it."

Helena stands spellbound, staring at the two men with wide eyes, as if seeing something for the first time. Marc retreats to his thoughts. *Shit. That's gotta hurt. Well, Cole had no way of knowing, and I did tell her not to push.*

Helena continues to stare in mute astonishment. At last, she speaks. "You mean, you?"

"Yes," Marc mumbles, staring at his feet.

"Almost every hour on the hour, for the last twenty-four," Cole says with such pride that Marc starts to blush.

A wide, if taut, smile expands slowly across Helena's face. Then she starts to cry. "Well, dip me in honey and throw me to the lesbians! Goddamn, guys!"

"Helena," Marc says, I…." He moves toward her with open arms.

She takes a step back, then stops, facing him. "Oh, don't worry. I'm fine. I take after Gandma. A regular waterworks. I always cry at weddings and shack-ups. Get back on the case. Della's fine."

As the two men depart, Marc looks over his shoulder. Helena, motionless and staring off into the woods, has never seemed so alone.

Little House Upon the Hill

Viewed from the crest of Telegraph Hill, the harbor seems an enormous mirror, reflecting anchored boats with barely a ripple. One yacht, its white hull gleaming in the sunlight, drops its mooring and motors toward Long Point, its shallow wake the only movement on the vast, tranquil expanse. Charlotte waits at the front door of Alan and Chuck's house. At her side is a man only slightly taller than she is.

Marc waves from the bottom of the drive then yells, "Charlotte, what's going on? Where are Alan and Chuck?"

"Come on in, and I'll tell you." Charlotte has never seemed so happy as she smiles at the attractive man beside her. "Cole, this is Brad, my fiancé. Brad, this is the fellow you want to thank for making our new home possible."

Brad offers his hand. "I have to say, when Charlotte told me how this all came about, I was stunned. I've never been to Provincetown before. She didn't even tell me about this place until it we arrived. It's magnificent. Thanks for putting her on to the deal."

Marc raises his hand as if in class. "Okay, folks, rewind a bit? I think I'm missing a piece of the puzzle here."

"Come on in and sit down," Charlotte says. "I've been messing with you, Marc. We'll fill you in." She leads them to a bright, tastefully decorated living room. One of Cole's seascapes hangs in a place of honor over the fireplace. Through French doors that open onto a large deck, Marc sees HomePort standing watch in the distance.

Charlotte can't seem to suppress a smug grin. "So, Marc, I suspect you remember Chuck and Alan?"

"Of course, though I haven't seen them since I called you. All you ever shared with me was that you'd take care of them."

Brad smiles proudly at Charlotte. "She certainly did."

"I figured they were desperate," Charlotte says, her eyes sparkling with mischief. "But I didn't want to take them on as clients. I know high maintenance when I see it. So I looked into their position, then made them an offer for this place. It was enough to get them out from under, but still a good bargain for us. Now that Brad and I are getting married, we need more room than I have at HomePort. Besides, I've always regretted my dad sold our family home in the seventies."

Marc is stunned. "Chuck and Alan sold this place to you?"

"They had no choice. Their creditors were closing in for the kill. Those two fools took the money and gave up on any other business dealings with me. We closed a few months ago. I've been furnishing it on the QT as a surprise for Brad and you guys.

"By the way, one of the stipulations is they never tell Brandon where you are. Twenty percent of the sale price has been set aside for two years. If they tell him, they forfeit the money. I expect they'll keep their mouths shut long enough for Brandon to get over himself."

"Wow. Pretty amazing. I appreciate your going to such lengths to protect me." Marc pauses for a moment. "Forgive me, Charlotte. It doesn't quite seem real that you own their place or that my nightmare is over. I've lived so long in fear that Brandon would find me, it's going to take time to get used to the idea. I have one other question, but I'm not sure how to ask it." He feels his face turn red.

Charlotte looks at Brad, then convulses in laughter. "Let me see if I can figure it out on my own?"

She laughs again, and this time Brad joins in. "How should I say this," she says when her mirth has subsided enough so she can speak. "You had me pegged for a lipstick lesbian!"

"Helena said—"

"Now Marc, I know what Helena said about me the day you met. She said 'The way she dresses, you might think otherwise.' When you questioned what a straight woman would be doing in Provincetown, she felt you were making a rash assumption. She asked me to play along and teach you a little lesson. Who would ever guess her little prank would last all this time?"

Marc hangs his head. "And I've been looking for a good woman for you for months."

Cole joins the laughter. Marc turns scarlet, and Charlotte seems to take pity on him.

"You aren't the first, honey, not by a long shot. It must be the power suits. I let everyone in New York think that so men don't hit on me. But you didn't come here to delve into my sexual preference. You started quite a tale on the phone. I'm dying to hear the rest of it."

Marc opens the journal and thumbs its pages. "The best way is to let the captain explain in his own words."

June 26th, 1925 - HomePort

Annie is like a child. With little memory of some things, yet excellent memory of others, she understands simple sentences spoken slowly. She has no means of communication at her disposal save gestures. Her own words continue to elude her, and so it shall ever be.

I had gradually come to expect this outcome, though it did not deter my desire to escape my marriage. Yesterday I told Prudence of the evidence my detective had secured in New York. She listened patiently without so much as a grimace. When I finished, I found that she, too, had set a trap. Several months ago, she hired an artist friend to follow me to the Castleton farm on two separate occasions. He photographed Annie and me in a chaste embrace and gave the pictures to my wife as proof of my infidelity.

Just now, I tracked the bastard down at gunpoint. He told me that when Prudence saw the photographs, she flew into a rage the likes of which he'd never seen. It was then she struck her blow. She refused to let him speak of what he had witnessed, took all the copies and the negatives and made him swear he had never seen Annie alive. Then, threatening to make his proclivities public unless he complied with her demands, she told him to spread word in town that Annie was murdered. Like a whipped dog, he's done all this and more, fanning flames of suspicion that had nearly faded away. I can barely walk

Commercial Street without an accusatory glance directed at me, but it will be several weeks before he can walk at all.

Emboldened by a supposed eyewitness account from her accomplice Agnes, my vile wife has chosen to cast me in the role of murderer in the eyes of the town. Even though her espionage proved the accusations false, she is determined to ruin me. Despite her knowledge of Annie's diminished mental capacity, Prudence can't be made to see reason. She's railed constantly since our conversation this morning, stalking me even here in the tower to continue her assault.

Her anger is not with my transgression, as might be expected—though that is certainly shaky ground given her own behavior—but rather with Annie herself. The fixation is more than hurt pride or even bitterness. It is as vile a compulsion as I have ever seen. Perhaps events have robbed Pru of her reason. I cannot tell, though I can find no other suitable excuse for her action save a heart of pure, unadulterated evil.

Knowing I am a God-fearing man of my word, Prudence refuses to show the slightest charity toward Annie. Nor will my wife-in-name-only agree to the amicable divorce we'd previously arranged. She claims she holds all the cards now, and that the law will see the pictures as proof of a continuing and flagrant affair of the most opportunistic, disreputable kind.

The photographs, the child, and the fraudulent testimony Pru assures me she will deliver would be more than enough to gain sympathy from any judge. When combined with my financial arrangements for Annie's welfare, which would inevitably be uncovered, the ensuing scandal would undo all Grubb and I have done to hush things up.

My hellish wife means to destroy me if I leave her. Knowing me for a gentleman who would never besmirch Annie's reputation, Prudence will settle for nothing less than my entire fortune, house, *business, and all, to proceed as originally agreed. As she put it, she will be mistress of HomePort with or without me.*

The price of my escape from ignominy is financial ruin. To gain my freedom and restore my honor, I will lose even the funds to keep Annie safe. As for Lola, my wife says I can raise her in a dune shack for all she cares. It's a Mexican standoff. I'd have to forgo one child to protect the other, which I refuse to do. So it seems our mutual loathing and distrust will chain us together for the rest of our days.

When Marc stops to catch his breath, Charlotte smiles and says, "How's married life appealing to you now, Brad? Maybe you should think about getting out while the gettin's good." When their laughter has settled down, Marc reads the next entry.

July 15th, 1925 - HomePort

The deed is done. I've given my oath to perpetuate a lie and ensure my reputation will be tarnished forever. Our fate is sealed.

For the past month, Pru has insisted I disown Annie and the child. Through Grubb's continued intervention, we've struck a devil's bargain at last. Prudence will receive a substantial monthly allowance for herself and another for her family. I will fund four trips a year not to exceed six weeks each. She will make enough time for HomePort that the town gossips should be hard pressed to find any new scandal to discuss. As for Prudence's other concessions, I will be allowed to see to the baby's needs anonymously and visit Annie once a week, but Dorrie should never know I was her father, nor anyone the true whereabouts of her mother. I have agreed to all this in writing and signed it under oath.

Abandoned by her younger paramour and by no means in the first blush of youth, I think Prudence gains perverse pleasure from the torment her actions are causing Annie and me. Despite

Pru's own indiscretions, which were far more wanton and numerous, she bears venom toward Annie the likes of which I have never witnessed in the most primitive of savages. For reasons I've never fully understood, Pru's determination to keep mother and child apart was the cornerstone of her demands, and she would not yield on the point. What pains me most is that to reach a settlement, I have had to promise to sustain the charade that Annie is dead.

Agnes saw me put Annie in the car, and the town already considers me a murderer, so there was ample opportunity for Prudence to exploit the situation. Time may prove this to be her greatest act of revenge, for now that I have pledged my word, my ruined reputation will no doubt outlive me.

Defeated at most every turn, I drew the line at one final point. Prudence would not pollute the Staunton plot with her corrupt and blasphemous remains. I could not tolerate the thought of resting by her side for eternity, nor would I desecrate the sacred ground where my beloved mother lay.

Prudence seemed strangely resigned to this demand, and immediately agreed, with the stipulation I fund a plot and suitable monument to her in New Bedford, carved with her maiden name. I accepted and our woeful agreement was ratified just an hour ago.

"That's the end of that entry," Marc says.

Charlotte looks troubled. "This document, Marc. I've never seen it in any of the Staunton papers, and my father never said a word about it."

Marc glances at Cole. "Hang on a bit, Charlotte. The captain has more to say on that topic. The next entry is three years later."

August 6th, 1928 - HomePort

The past three years have been unmitigated hell. My wife grows more unendurably vindictive with each passing hour.

Save for those times when she leaves town, I have abandoned HomePort for the refuge of my work. When in the house, I spend most of my time up here in the tower. Our hellish contract remains fully in force, my reputation in tatters.

I was discreetly encouraged by the Lodge not to run for re-election. It seems they are happy to take my money, but concerned about appearances. And that in a secret society! My social options, not vast to begin with, are limited to Grubb and a manager from work. I can't even go to church without drawing stares and muted whispers.

I've kept my part of the bargain until yesterday, when on my impulse, Cookie and I brought Dorrie to visit her mother. Prudence is in New York, due to return within the week. It was inhuman that Annie could see her own child at least once. Cookie and I thought this best accomplished while the child was young enough not to understand, but old enough to travel. It was perhaps the most joyous day of my life, those few hours with my little girl. I spent the entire train ride watching her play with a doll I had given her to mark the occasion.

When I first explained to Annie who the child was, there was a flash of recognition, though only for the briefest of moments. I hope Annie understood her young one was loved and well cared for. I dare not bring Dorrie again. She'll soon be old enough to prattle of such a trip. Given the nature of Provincetown, the news would inevitably find its way to my wife, with dire consequences.

"This next bit is really rough," Marc says turning to Charlotte. "You need to tell us whether Lola can handle it."

October 30th, 1928 - HomePort

Prudence is even more irrational. I live on the edge of total disgrace, fearful of her outbursts and indiscretions, yet held hostage by her pervasive insistence she will ruin me if I leave.

Her hatred of Annie burns with a fierce flame I now firmly believe has its roots in some sort of mental disorder.

Moments ago, I witnessed the depth to which my wife is willing to stoop to humiliate me. Lola, I apologize for recounting what, by the time you read this, I pray you will have forgotten for years. Yet the accusations are so vile I must defend your memory of me, and so I am writing them down before a word is forgotten. Given the delicacy of the topic, this is the only way possible, so let me begin.

Wishing to view my sleeping daughter before I departed for the day, I approached her room early this morning, heard a voice, and stopped outside her door. As best I could ascertain, Lola had awakened to discover she had become a woman. Prudence slept in the next room and for once had answered her daughter's cries of alarm. As I listened, it became clear Prudence was in the midst of explaining the facts of life. After a time, she said the most horrible thing a mother could ever say to a daughter.

"Men are beasts who prey on women," she said, her voice dripping with venom. "You are now vulnerable to them and need to know men often abuse girls like you and then abandon them to ruin. That is the way of this world. There is little a woman can do once you fall into their clutches. Your father took advantage of me when I wasn't much older than you are now. This happened to Annie as well. Through her foolishness and naïveté, she fanned the flames of your father's lust and paid for it with her life.

You must stand guard against him and all men. They want only one thing, and once they have taken it, you too will end up like your beloved Annie. Be wary, Lola. Heed your mother's words and trust no man."

With this example of Prudence's vindictiveness, I find no need of any further recounting, and so I shall close.

Charlotte's eyes are wide. Her usual confidence seems shaken. "So this is why Lola's so afraid of everything. What a shitty thing to do to a child."

"Prudence can't have been in her right mind," Marc says. "I agree with you, Charlotte. It would be nearly impossible to hear that said, grow up in a house with all that hatred, and keep your bearings. When you think about it, Lola paints a picture of a happy childhood because she can't bear the truth, the poor old thing. Do you think she can deal with this?"

Charlotte seems to need a minute. "She can if it's presented right. As out of touch as she may seem, she's extremely pragmatic and incredibly strong. I think she'd accept the truth if we were at her side to soften the blow. This makes me want to get to the bottom of things even more. For her sake."

Cole says, "Then you better keep reading, Marc."

November 28th, 1928 - HomePort

It seems Prudence has gone for good. She left today in a great hurry, taking but few possessions for reasons I do not know. Even so, blessed peace and calm reign over the house for the first time in years. From what I can discern, she went to Boston for a doctor's appointment two days ago. Returning just yesterday, she gave instructions to have her things packed as quietly as possible and slipped out in the middle of the night. She left a note that simply said, "Bring the slut here if you wish. I am beyond caring and shan't ever return."

I have all the evidence I need for divorce based on desertion.

"But he never did," Charlotte says, clearly displaying her confusion. "Why not?"

Marc holds up his index finger. "Hang on just a bit longer. If what he says is true, this guy put his word above all else."

January 15th, 1929 - HomePort

My wife is the cruelest, most vindictive being ever to walk the earth. To avoid scandal, I need her consent to the separation agreement, but two months have passed, and I can't find a trace of her. I've sought out Agnes, who refuses to say a word. I couldn't even buy an answer from her. There's no record of Pru's death to be found. Grubb says the best I can do is to declare her a missing person and wait for seven years until she's pronounced dead.

Yesterday I tried to bring Annie back to HomePort. We set out from the farm in time for the afternoon train, but she grew more agitated with each passing mile. When she saw the depot, she grew so distraught her wailing and clutching made it impossible for us to board. There was no choice but to return to the farm. Once in sight of its familiar barns and silo, she immediately became her former, tranquil self.

Castleton and his wife strongly advised against another attempt, insisting that Annie was a creature of extreme habit. They feared the stress of changing her routine would incur more brain damage, and swore she was welcome to live out her days with them as a member of their family.

I fear Annie will never see Provincetown again. Last night, I dreamed she was with me in the tower. We surveyed the exquisite intersection of land, sea, and sky until morning's light restored me to a deep, dark loneliness devoid of all hope.

"That's the end of that entry," Marc says. "There's another one dated a couple of years later."

"Read it," Charlotte says, her eyes pensive. "I never knew any of this. I don't think Dad did either. If he had, I'm sure he would have told me when I took over."

Marc continues.

May 18th, 1931 - HomePort

Prudence was buried two days ago. It was only through a request from the undertaker to place her in the New Bedford plot that I learned my wife's fate. I stood in the shadows and saw her casket lowered into the earth with a feeling as close to satisfaction as a decent Christian might admit.

Her physician was the only mourner other than myself, if I might stretch the truth and describe myself in such a fashion. Plying him with questions and a bit of cash, I learned Prudence had hidden from the world for more than two years. She'd lived, if you can call it that, at an elderly aunt's ramshackle farm in Padanaram, in an old house too decrepit to generate even modest rental income. Learning the aunt had died earlier in the year, I forced entry to the farmhouse and secured Pru's diaries, my signed testament, and the photographs she had used to threaten me. I also retrieved Mother's diamonds, which rightfully belong to Lola now.

The diaries tell a tale of hatred, loathing, and wantonness I haven't courage to repeat verbatim. Suffice it to say, Pru felt she had to marry me to save her family. It appears she once had some affection toward me, but my long absence and Morrison's slavish attentions seems to have fostered a descent into lasciviousness that would best that of any sailor returning to port after years at sea.

I must confess I am somewhat saddened by my wife's constant disappointment in me. It seems she had high hopes of making the best of things when Lola was born. That final altercation with Mother seems to have convinced Prudence her sole use to me was to provide an heir. Surprisingly, she remains circumspect as to the identity of Lola's father. I guess I'll never know for certain, though in my heart I still claim that singular honor.

The birth of Annie's child seems to have unhinged Prudence. The few entries from that time forward are plots to keep Annie separated from our child and from me. It appears that Pru had one of Castleton's neighbors in her employ to make sure I kept my word. It's only by sheer luck Dorrie wasn't seen the day we took her to visit her mother.

I have just gotten off the phone with Pru's doctor who has confirmed he had treated her for the pox for years, even sending her to a specialist in Boston when it entered its latter phase. Apparently, she left HomePort to die alone like an old dog because the lesions were becoming visible, and she was too proud to let anyone, especially me, see them. The doctor speculates she took her own life when the discomfort grew too much. Fortunately, he's had the decency not to alert the authorities.

Much as I felt abused by my wife, I am now quite willing to bear partial responsibility for the mistakes and misassumptions that led her to such a dismal fate. I have no doubt she succumbed to madness. Her physician declared it quite likely, and it is the best explanation of her behavior these last few years. I should never have married her when she was so young and vulnerable and then left her to her own devices. I should have made her sail with me on the Andoria. I am not without culpability. This I see at last. While I loathe the thought of all Prudence has done over the years, I take some solace in the fact that her actions may not have been completely within her control.

All that remains of my late wife is the snare of scandal and gossip with which she has enmeshed me. After reading of the bitter life she has just departed, I hadn't the heart to use her own words against her. I've just returned from the beach where I have burnt the contract, the photographs, and the diaries, lest my resolve weaken. It is done. Her aspersions shall remain unchallenged for my lifetime. I accept this as my penance.

Charlotte shakes her head and reaches for Brad. "Damn. What a mess. Prudence could well have gone mad. The captain is right. She doesn't deserve the reputation that's come down through the years. I'm glad to see his remorse. It gives his story a bit more credibility."

Marc catches her attention. "Charlotte, there's another important entry. I won't take the time to read right now, but it's from December 29th, 1951. In it, the captain says he was going to have your father make changes to his will. I need to know if the captain set up any funds or made equal provisions for Dorrie, Annie, and Lola in late '51 or early '52. The trust should have added two beneficiaries back then."

"Well, I can answer that without looking it up. He never set up any major codicils other than the annuity for Dorrie. The last update to his will was in 1949 when he added a few bequests to household staff and employees of Staunton and Company. Lola fulfilled all the directives of his will to the letter. I'm confident she'd never have held back on any of his wishes had she known them, including giving Dorrie her fair share of the estate. What was the date of the journal entry again?"

"December 29th, 1951."

"Let me check one thing." Charlotte walks to her desk and turns on her laptop. "I can access the office files from here." After searching for a moment, she says, "He died three weeks later. So far as I know, he never did what he said. I'm sure my dad would have made any changes if he'd been asked. That's all I've got. Sorry, guys, I'd love to have something better for you."

"Don't worry," Marc says. "I've got an idea. If we can prove it without tipping off Lola, we'll have our answer." He smiles lovingly at Cole. "This is a job for Della. It'll get her mind off of things."

Charlotte studies the exchange, then suddenly beams at the two men. "Looks like I'm not the only one with big news in the romance department. It's about time, guys. About friggin' time."

The Fugitive

When Marc and Cole return to HomePort, the house is strangely silent. Marc gives Cole a kiss, then says, "I want to clear up some things with Helena. I'll be back in a bit."

Climbing the stairs to the Bates Motel, he knocks on her door. There's no answer. He lopes downstairs to the kitchen. There's no one there. Looking out the window, he sees Helena's pink, Hello Kitty bicycle, a sure indication she's not gone into town. Downstairs, he finds Lola seated in an old-fashioned rocker in the mistress's parlor. Her head is back, her eyes closed, her mouth open, and a sliver of drool hangs from her chin. Marc softly calls her name. She doesn't move. He gently touches her arm.

"Lola. Wake up."

Lola stirs and immediately brings her hand to her mouth. "Bad habit, sleeping during the daytime. I shouldn't give in to it. I get so run down these days, it's getting hard for me to go more than a few hours without forty winks."

"Lola, have you seen Helena? I can't find her anywhere, and her bike is still behind the house."

Lola sits up. Her eyes widen. "As a matter of fact, I haven't seen her all day. Why? What's wrong?"

"Nothing. I wanted to show her something. I'm sure she'll be back soon." Marc steps back into the hall, and, when out of Lola's hearing, begins to run. He finds Cole in the studio. "She's gone, Cole. Helena's gone."

Cole sets down his brush. "What do you mean, gone?"

"Looks like she took our getting together far harder than she led us to believe. I'm beginning to think she's left HomePort or worse."

"Doesn't Lola know where she is?"

"No."

"How about Dorrie?"

"Let's go see."

Dorrie has nothing to report, so the two men return to Marc's room.

"Helena must have left a note or something, Cole. Get the key to her apartment. Maybe she's just hiding in there."

Helena's apartment is eerily quiet with signs of a hasty departure. Marc spies an envelope with his name on it. He opens it as Cole draws closer.

"What does she say?"

Stricken, Marc sits down and reads aloud, "Until this moment I never understood how hard it was to lose something you never had. Take care of Lola for me. All my love, Helena."

Cole turns pale. "Shit! I should have been more considerate. I was just so focused on us. We gotta find her. There's not a minute to lose. C'mon." Cole races out the door and over to Marvin's apartment. He pounds loudly on the door. "Marvin. Wake up. It's Cole."

"Gimme a minute."

After a short wait, the door opens a crack and Marvin's bloodshot eyes appear, blinking rapidly in the light of day. His face is unshaven. He has on a torn t-shirt and a pair of ratty briefs. His stomach droops over them. His breath reeks.

"What is it?" he asks, a note of anxiety in his voice. "I didn't do nothing."

Cole seems unable to hide his impatience. "It's not you. It's Helena. Have you seen her today?"

"Not to speak to, but there was a lot of noise next door. So loud I got up to see what was going on. Just as I did, I saw her march down the stairs and get into a taxi. She looked weirder than usual, all dressed in black with a thick black veil over her face."

"What time was that?"

"Two hours ago."

"Did you see the driver?"

"No, but it was a Crazy Cab."

When Cole and Marc return to their room, Marc places a call. After a brief conversation, he hangs up. "Helena was dropped off at the bus station. Check the schedule."

"I don't need to. The only departure before now is the Boston Bus."

"She's got a couple of hours on us."

"Yeah but we can catch it. It stops everywhere."

The two men race down to Marc's car. He turns the key in the ignition. Nothing happens. Opening the hood, Cole swears.

"What is it?"

"This car isn't going anywhere."

"What do you mean?"

"No distributor cap. Just a note."

"Shit. What's it say?"

Cole reads,

"I love and yet forced to seem to hate,

I do, yet dare not say I ever meant,

I seem stark mute but inwardly do prate."

Marc shakes his head. "Good Christ."

"What?"

"That's just too fucking much, even for Helena."

"I don't get it," Cole says.

"It's a poem called *On Monsieur's Departure,* I read it to her once."

"Yeah, so?"

"It was written by Queen Elizabeth the first."

"You got to hand it to Helena. She sticks to her own kind."

"This is no time for jokes, Cole. She's got a history of attempted suicide."

"And you let me tease her like that? Damn it, Marc. You should have told me. Should we call the police?"

"No I've got a better idea. There's a Cape Air flight in an hour. Call a cab."

Bruce from Crazy Cab shows up in ten minutes. "You took Helena to the bus, right?" Marc asks.

"Yeah, about three hours ago."

"Describe every detail of what she was wearing."

"Well, she had on this long black veil, so I couldn't see her face, but she was dressed completely in black, full length skirt and black shoes. She looked like a Victorian widow."

"Did she take the Boston bus?"

"Yeah, she got right on after I dropped her off.'

"Get us to the airport!"

Planes, Boats, and Trains

Two seats are available on the twenty-minute flight to Boston. Thanks to the water taxi, Marc and Cole are staking out the Transportation Center a half hour before the Provincetown bus is due.

"What makes you think she'll still be on the bus?" Cole asks. "She could have gotten off at any stop along the way."

Marc takes a deep breath. "Bear with me, this is pretty out there, but the voices in my head say she's on the bus. Ever since I moved to HomePort, I've had these strange intuitions, as if spirits are trying to communicate. One presence seems to hang out in the tower and another in your studio."

Marc searches Cole's features. They seem to be registering not disbelief, but bewilderment. "You, too?" Cole asks. "I feel the one in the studio all the time. It's almost as if she critiques my work before my brush hits the canvas."

"Well, I'm glad you've made her acquaintance, because she and the guy upstairs turned my mind to mush the moment I realized Helena had run away. It's the captain and his mother, Laetitia, and they're both freaked out. It will destroy Lola if Helena leaves, and they know it."

"Why didn't you say something?"

Marc grins. "Why didn't you?"

"Same reason, no doubt. Afraid you'd have thought I was nuts. Hey, here comes the bus."

The two men duck behind a cement wall and watch the passengers disembark. Few emerge: a husband and wife with three small children, an elderly woman with two canes, two middle-aged nuns, three young students, and a tall man in army fatigues. No woman in black.

"She must have gotten off," Marc says.

"Or changed costume. We can't follow all of them. They're going to go their separate ways, but we shouldn't give up so easily."

"Hang on. Let's think. Where would Helena go?"

"New York," Cole says. "She'd be most apt to find work there this time of year."

"So she'd take a bus or a train, right?"

"Yeah, she's afraid to fly. Let's go see what buses are headed to New York."

"That's kind of tricky, Cole. Some of them load inside the station, some on the street. Let's split up and see where these folks go. Rule out anyone that leaves the Transportation Center. Let's call each other if we spot anything."

The family hails a cab. The students meander down the street. The man in fatigues strolls over to a waiting Bolt Bus. Cole follows him at a safe distance. The nuns walk past Marc's hiding place in animated conversation, their long rosary beads clacking as they pass.

Marc chooses the elderly woman and follows her halting progress into South Station. She orders a cup of tea and carries it to an empty table. Marc sits at the next table and studies her closely. It could be Helena underneath a masterful makeup job. He can't quite tell. The woman looks up at him with an inquiring glance but shows no sign of recognition. Marc glances at the queue on the platform, then quickly dials Cole. "Forget the guy. I've found her. Meet me inside South Station."

Cole is there in no time. Together they sidle out to the platform. The Acela to New York is due to depart, and a crowd has gathered behind two stanchions, waiting to board.

Marc points at the two nuns. "Do you see it?"

"See what? There's two of them. Nuns always travel in pairs. There's nothing unusual about them."

"You sure? Look again."

Cole bursts into laughter. "Oh, for God's sake. We've got her."

"Well, we still have to get her out of that crowd."

"Not a problem," Cole smirks. "Just follow my lead." He walks toward the nuns, who are slowly inching forward in the queue. When he reaches them, he quickly flashes his wallet. "Homeland Security. Please come with us, Sisters."

Marc moves closer, trying his best to impersonate an undercover agent. When everyone stops to stare, the taller of the two nuns looks oddly pleased.

"That's all right, officer. We'll go quietly." She holds out her hands for handcuffs, then says, "I didn't know you cared."

"We both do. Much more than you realize," Cole whispers, "That's the whole point. I'm so sorry Helena. I didn't know."

"Bless you, child," Helena says, turning to glare at Marc.

"Much as I'm sure you'd enjoy them, handcuffs won't be necessary, Sister," Marc interjects, much to the astonishment of the crowd. "Just come with us. We have a few questions for you."

Helena and her mysterious companion pick up their luggage, then docilely step between the two men. On closer inspection, the second nun betrays a faint application of mascara and the slightest trace of blush. The group walks back into the station in silence. Once inside, Helena removes her wimple and says, "I'm famished, how about a pizza?"

Marc and Cole exchange hooded glances. "Let's clear up a couple of things first, Sister Helena," Marc says. "Who's the novice? Sister Bertrille?"

Helena smirks. "Ricotta Gnocchi, Marc Nugent and Cole Hanson. Marc and Cole, Ricotta Gnocchi."

Cole chuckles. "Pretty slick, Helena. The last place I'd ever think to look for you was in a habit. How'd you set all this up on such short notice?"

"Well, I knew Ricotta was leaving for New York today. It was simple to have her bring the costumes with her when she got on the bus in Hyannis. After that, it was just a few trips to the restroom and voila!"

Marc grins as relief washes over him. "Not bad. Hey Sister Ricotta, next time you want to get closer to God, take the *Illusions II, the Drag Tour* sticker off your suitcase. It will make a hell of a difference. Your train's boarding, girl. You'd better run. Sister Helena will be returning to the convent with us."

Ricotta, twirling her beads like a stripper, sashays back to the train amidst astonished stares from the passengers.

Turning to Helena, Marc takes her arm. "And as for you, Mother Superior…. Do nuns ever hear confession?"

Sorry, Wrong Number

The plane ride back to Provincetown is polite but tense. Helena says little and retires immediately to her apartment as soon as they arrive. Back in their room, Cole lounges on the bed reading while Marc collects his things to take to the tower.

Mission: Impossible. Brandon.

Marc reaches for the phone but Cole wrests it from him and answers with a brusque greeting. "No, you can't talk to him, and you might as well give up trying." Cole's face clouds with anger. He snaps the phone shut and then turns it off.

"I don't need you to…." Seeing the look on Cole's face, Marc thinks better of confronting him.

"You don't need to put up with that fool," Cole says. "Let me take his calls for a bit. He'll get tired of talking to me and give up."

"You don't know him. Despite all Charlotte's done, I'm still worried he'll track me down. He left one of his worst rants yet on my voicemail yesterday. He was barely coherent, just mumbling the words 'user' and 'liar,' repeatedly. Then he said, 'I know where you are.'"

"What? Why didn't you tell me?"

"I can't tell if he was just trying to scare me or he really knows. I know I shouldn't, but I still feel I could have done more to help him. He gave me so much, and now he has so little. I know I didn't take it from him, but still…."

"Don't beat yourself up. We've been over and over this. You've already endured more than most."

"He may actually know where I am. I swear I saw him coming out of the Soup Kitchen yesterday, but I've been wrong so many times, I just can't be sure. I hit the gas and got a speeding ticket, but if it *was* him, I don't think he saw me."

"All the more reason for me to take the calls from now on. If he comes for you, he'll have to deal with me. He might as well know that in advance. Case closed."

Tea and Sympathy

Helena is late for tea and Marc is troubled. Making small talk with Cole and Lola, he can barely focus his thoughts. At last, Helena arrives dressed in a simple black dress, her only jewelry a single strand of luminous, *faux* pearls. In her right hand, she holds a small black clutch, in her left, a framed photograph.

Lola, seeming to sense her mood, touches her arm. "Sit down, dear. I hope all is well?"

"Yes, on the whole it is, though I confess to a touch of homesickness today."

Lola leans forward, appearing eager to learn something new. "I seldom hear you speak of your family, dear, for all I speak of mine."

"Well, as you can imagine, nobody has much to do with me."

"Ah, the petty behavior of the masses. Man's inhumanity to man. And even so, you miss them, don't you?"

"Well, one of them. My grandmother. I've told you about her before."

"Oh yes. I recall. Did she live with you, my dear?" Almost as an afterthought, Lola hands round the teacups.

"No, but not far away. I went to her house after school since Mom worked until six. I lived with Gandma toward the end of high school when things got messy at home."

Lola's eyes grow distant. "No greater love than a grandmother's. I remember mine."

"I've heard yours was amazing," Marc says.

"Oh my, yes," Lola replies. "Not your typical little old lady by any means. She died when I was ten, but even so, I have the fondest memories of her. How old was your grandmother when she died, Helena? I assume she has passed on?"

Helena crosses her legs and takes a delicate sip with her little finger extended. "Oh yes, indeed. She had a stroke, poor thing, at eighty. She lingered on for a couple of weeks only able to communicate with her eyes."

Lola seems rattled. "How strange. My father was just like that before he died."

"He was?" Helena's voice is soothing and encouraging, though she avoids looking at Marc or Cole. "How terrible for you. There's nothing worse than watching someone who is aware but unable to communicate. It's like their mind is imprisoned."

"Absolutely. Poor Father. For days after his stroke, all he did was make these strange sounds and look upward."

"Upward? That's odd. Do you know what he was trying to tell you?"

"No. I never could figure it out—something about me going to bed. They sent him home from the hospital saying he had a few weeks at best, and all he did was look up toward the roof and repeat the same unintelligible words. He was so agitated, he even cried, which I'd never seen him do before."

"Where did he have his stroke? At the office?"

"Charlotte's father had taken over the day to day by then. Father had his stroke right here in the house. He fell from the ladder to the tower. I always thought he felt poorly, tried to summon help, and the stroke hit before he could get all the way down."

"Such a shame," Helena sighs. "My grandmother had hers on the cellar stairs. I'll never forget coming home from school and finding her on the damp, cold floor."

Lola worries the pendant around her neck. "Oh, how horrible! Something like that never leaves you. I was in my bedroom upstairs when I heard the crash. I was the first to find him lying there, so cold and pale. I've never gotten over it."

"Did he try to speak when you found him?" Helena asks.

"Yes, though he was hardly able. He couldn't move his jaws, but I kept hearing him say the same words over and over again."

Helena leans forward in her most intimate and encouraging Barbara Walters' manner. "What were they exactly?"

"Well, I'm still not sure. What I heard didn't make any sense. It still doesn't. He kept saying something like, 'Don't wait up. Don't wait up.'"

Helena shudders. "Oh, that's just terrible. I still see Gandma moaning on that cold floor, nearly lifeless. I'll remember the day until I die."

Worried Helena is overdoing it, Marc raises his eyebrows in warning, but Lola's face is filled with empathy, her voice more gentle than usual. "When did it happen, dear?"

"Ten years ago, today."

"Oh, *now* I understand. It makes perfect sense why you're feeling depressed. I'm never myself on the 29th of December. In some ways, the day I found Father is worse than the day he died. It was the day he ceased to be what he always had been. Is that a picture of your grandmother? May I see?"

Helena passes her a photograph of a kindly woman in a purple wool suit. When Lola looks down at it, Cole and Marc share a silent high five. Helena glares at them.

"Oh, Helena, she's lovely," Lola says.

"Yes, she was." Helena pours another cup and drinks it in one gulp. "Ain't life a bitch, sometimes?"

Don't Wait Up

When the trio return to Marc's room, Helena plants herself, scowling, on the chaise. Her arms are tightly folded, her eyes aflame. "I can't believe all I do for you, Marc."

Marc interrupts what is about to be a severe dressing-down. "The 29th of December. The day he wrote the testament. It's all coming together. You were brilliant!"

"Lower your voice. Lola has ears like a cat." Despite her concern, Helena seems to soften a bit.

"Why did he keep saying, 'Don't wait up.'? No one understood then, and I still don't," Cole says, aiding Marc's deflection.

"Don't wait up." Marc pauses. "Don wait up… donwaitup…." Marc's ghostly visitor provides the answer. "Dumbwaiter! He was trying to tell her that the journal was in the dumbwaiter!"

Helena claps her hands, all petulance forgotten. "That's why he kept looking up toward the roof."

Marc, relieved to escape Helena's wrath, is overjoyed. "Of course. He wanted her to find the journal so he could change the will before it was too late. It all makes sense, and it clears Lola. She never knew!"

"And it makes me feel much better about the captain," Cole says in a subdued voice. "He tried everything to make amends before he died. Imagine how frustrated he must have felt having decided to do right and then being unable to do it. He ended up just like Annie, the poor bastard."

Sensations of intense joy overtake Mark as the captain signals his appreciation. His enthusiasm is contagious. Marc embraces Helena. "Della, you are really something. You made everything come together. Let's go out and celebrate with a nice big steak!"

"Not tonight, Perry," Helena replies, once again in perfect cadence. "There's something I have to do. It can't wait."

Never having seen her turn down a free meal before. Cole seems concerned. "What's that?"

"I need to call Gandma."

CHAPTER 11
ON THE ROAD AGAIN

October 11ᵗʰ, 2009 – The Tower, HomePort

When Cole gets back from wherever he insists on going by himself every day, we're going to try to locate the Castleton farm. The key is the old Cape Cod rail line. The farm had to be nearby. If Dorrie is right, and they crossed the Canal—which I'm quite sure they did—we're talking Rochester, Carver, Middleborough, Lakeville, the Bridgewaters, and that's about it. Dorrie's dream has been accurate so far, why wouldn't it be right about the rest?

A Field Trip

The Plymouth Registry is just opening when Cole and Marc arrive. A search of the directory unearths a Castleton property in Middleborough. The owner, Vendra Castleton, has sold a number of lots over the past thirty years.

Marc turns to Cole. "No doubt the farmland was sold off for development. The address is always the same on these deeds, though—2732 East Main Street. Maybe she kept the farmhouse."

They find East Main with no difficulty. When they reach number 2732, the likeness to Cole's paintings is uncanny, though the old farmhouse is an eyesore amid trimmed lawns and freshly-painted suburban houses. One barn has collapsed. The other tilts precariously. The silo is still standing, but only a single piece of its metal roof remains. The house is large, though rotted shades in the second story windows suggest much of it is no longer in use.

Cole strides to the front door. He taps a tarnished brass knocker in the shape of a whale, which sets hounds within baying. No one answers the door, though the dogs continue to howl.

The two men survey the property, finding signs of recent activity. A wheelbarrow leans against a tilting woodshed, and two scrawny hens peck the dirt behind a wire enclosure with fresh footprints leading to and from it.

"I don't think anyone's home. We came all this way for nothing," Cole says.

"Just a minute. I thought I heard something."

They walk to the side of the house and then back to the front door. The dogs continue to bark, but there are no other signs of life. Marc and Cole return to the car and start their trip back to Provincetown. Just before they reach the highway, they spy a walled cemetery across the street from a classic, Greek-revival church. On a hunch, Marc pulls over.

The headstones go back to the early 1700's. Under a tall oak, they finally find a large stone with the names and dates of Amos and Grace Castleton carved into it. Below them is the name Vendra.

"There's just a birth date beside her name. No date of death. And look at this." Cole scuffs the edges of a small rectangle beneath his feet. It's carved with a single name, *Annie*.

"Do you think it's *our* Annie?" Marc asks.

"Could be. We don't know if Amos and Grace had any other children, but Annie is on their side of the plot.

Marc nods in agreement. "Let's not give up so quickly. Something tells me Vendra is still living in that house. It's such a wreck, anyone else would have torn it down. She might have been hiding from us."

The two men break for lunch, then return to the farm. No one answers the door when Cole knocks. "Still no one. I guess we've hit a dead end," he says turning to leave.

Marc shakes his head, writes a brief note asking Vendra to call him about an important matter and slips it under the door. Then he walks toward a distant outbuilding where wood is stacked in long neat rows. He points to a shed where an elderly woman is sharpening an axe with a whetstone.

"Excuse me," Marc says.

The woman turns with a start. She's plain and heavy, in her late seventies or early eighties, dressed in tattered coveralls, a flannel shirt, and hunter's vest. Her white hair is cut in a mannish style, and she wears work boots. Her hands are callused, her skin mottled from years in the sun. Her face has several large wens, and one of her front teeth is missing. Her voice is none too welcoming.

"What do you want?"

"I'm sorry to disturb you. By any chance are you related to Amos and Grace Castleton?" Marc asks with all the courtesy he can muster.

"What the hell do you want with them?"

"We're trying to find out what happened to a woman named Andoria Machado. Do you know anything about her?"

"Machado, Machado? Name doesn't ring a bell."

"How about Staunton?"

"What about Staunton? Whatever can you want with Staunton?"

Marc grins at Cole. They've struck a nerve. "We're trying to find the family that cared for a woman from the late-twenties to the mid-fifties. She was called Annie, and the family was a great help to a Captain Staunton."

Marc smiles in an effort to put Vendra at ease. He's had the foresight to bring a picture of the captain and one of his journals. Vendra seems to recognize the picture but stares out at the ramshackle outbuildings for a moment before finally speaking.

"You seem like nice enough young fellas, but I'm afraid I can't help you. I don't recall ever seeing the man in the picture. It was a long time ago, but I'm sure I'd remember if I had. Now if you'll be excusing me, I've got to split some wood, cart it in, and fire up the cook stove."

A Losing Proposition

Dismayed, Marc and Cole start the long drive back to HomePort. Passing the cemetery, they turn onto the highway. After a few minutes, Marc ends their petulant silence. "She knows more than she's saying."

"Obviously. But she's not going to tell us."

"And without her, we're right back where we started. A random grave marker with a first name and no date is nowhere near enough proof for Lola."

It's just dusk when Cole and Marc reach Provincetown. The setting sun is a large red orb illuminating East Harbor. Passing the dunes, they pull up to the light at Conwell

Street. Looking casually at the driver in the car beside him, Marc quickly hides his face. "Shit!"

"What's wrong?"

"That's Brandon beside us. I don't think he's seen me yet, but he's sure to recognize my car. We've got to ditch him."

When the light turns, Marc rapidly accelerates. Brandon's Jeep shifts into the lane behind them, gradually gaining speed. Marc turns into the National Seashore. The two cars speed through the dunes. Marc skids through a stop sign cutting off a taxi returning from the airport. Its horn blares in indignation. He races through the Beech Forest, the trees just a blur in the corner of his eye. At one curve, Marc nearly loses control, barely avoiding a large tree close to the road. Looking in the rear view mirror, he sees Brandon is gaining on them.

Marc runs a red light onto Route Six, then heads toward Truro. Brandon follows. Marc passes the dunes before East Harbor, praying the perennial speed trap is manned. Just before the spot, Marc brakes. Brandon maintains his speed and draws up alongside. Marc pounds the steering wheel with his fist. '"Damn. The cops aren't there. They're always there except the one time I need them."

Brandon tries to run them off the road. Marc presses the pedal to the floor and the ancient Volvo springs past the Jeep, nicking its front bumper. East Harbor passes in a flash. Days' Cottages blur to a single, white line. The two cars race past High Head.

There's not a police car in sight, even when they pass the Truro Police Station. Near Truro Center, Marc darts between an oncoming delivery truck and a logy Prius festooned with bumper stickers, cutting off the Prius and careening onto the off-ramp. The Prius slams on its brakes and sounds its horn with an angry squawk. Brandon, braking rapidly, heads into a tailspin. He misses the exit and stalls in the opposite lane just as a Truro cruiser appears, its lights flashing.

Marc ducks into a parking lot, his white-knuckled hands still gripping the wheel. Once his heart has stopped pounding, he slowly drives to Cold Storage Beach and parks facing the ocean. Provincetown can be seen in the distance. The monument, the library, and the houses along the shore make the view seem quaint and picturesque. The idea that Brandon has been lurking amid such beauty and tranquility is more threatening to Marc than his near escape.

"I always knew he'd find me."

Cole pulls Marc close. "We'll figure out how to get rid of him. There's no way you're going through this alone. Let's take the back road home, find Helena, and plan our next move."

The Facts of Life

Helena is dusting the grandfather's clock. With one look, she sets down the feather duster and leads them into the mistress's parlor. After Cole's brief summary, she agrees to meet them in his studio once she's tended to Lola. In minutes, Helena is at the door with three glasses and not one, but two, bottles of wine on a silver tray. The effect on Marc is immediately reassuring, as if HomePort were an impregnable fortress, and he is now safe behind its walls.

Helena opens the first bottle and fills all three glasses to the brim. "Are you okay, Marc? What can I do?"

"I'm not sure there's much we can do, other than be prepared for the worst," Cole says. "Except for getting a ticket just now, Brandon has done nothing that might involve the police, unless you could pin the threatening calls on him, which would take time we can't afford. The best we can hope is that he'll be jailed for a day or two."

"Do you think you can reason with him, Marc?" Helena asks.

Marc stares at the portrait of Prudence Staunton. It may be the light or just his state of mind, but Prudence doesn't seem anywhere as innocent as the last time he saw her.

Cole answers before Marc even realizes Helena is speaking to him. "I've taken his calls and heard his voicemails. This guy is not firing on all cylinders."

"That limits our options a bit," Helena replies, "although I'd still like a shot at him to be absolutely certain he can't see reason. What do you think he'll do?"

Marc finally frees himself from his memories. "I've thought a lot about that over the past few months. He was a decent person until the drugs took over. After that, he pulled a knife on me, and I suspect he'd do it again. Even so, I'm more worried about him giving Lola a heart attack than what he might do to me."

Helena studies Marc closely. "You're right. Maybe you should get out of town for a while. Try to lead him away from her?"

"If you guys think I should, I will. I hate the thought of it, though. I don't want to be cowering from Brandon all my life."

"It would just be for a short while," Cole says. "Until he gets tired of looking for you and gives up."

"Yeah, but if he finds out I was here, he could start hounding Lola."

When Marc falters, Helena asserts herself. "Cole, Marc's right. Sometimes you just have to stand your ground. I've got a bit of experience with this sort of thing. Backing down doesn't ever do much good. We should be doing whatever we can to protect Marc, as well as Lola and Dorrie. We can't leave them to cope on their own. They were there for me in one of the worst times in my life. I'm not about to see either of them threatened by some tweaked-out son of a bitch."

Marc puts his head in his hands. "I'm getting a headache. Could we change the subject for a while?"

Cole nods. "Helena, you've said more than once that Lola and Dorrie were there for you. Tell us what happened."

"Sure. Those two old girls are my guardian angels." Helena settles back, a woman with a story to tell. "I used to live over near Bradford and Franklin Streets in a former guest house divided into tiny apartments. I'd have my coffee on the porch and see Dorrie walking up Bradford Street first thing every morning."

"On her way to Daryl's grave," Marc says.

Helena takes a heroic sip. "Exactly. To make a long story tolerable, I'll just say that after a while, she'd stop for a chat. There was one time I was really glad she did. I'll never forget. It was one of those August mornings where the windows have been open all night long, but it's still sweltering when you wake up. I'd been to the Crown and Anchor the night before, and this guy cruised me at Spiritus afterward. Fool that I was, I brought him home. I was wearing a sort of Barbarella outfit: a short green skirt with green gloves, green boots, long windswept hair, and enormous boobs. With that getup, anyone with half a brain cell would recognize a drag queen, so I figured he knew the score even if he was pretty drunk. Anyways, I brought him home, though a voice inside said, 'Don't do it.' He was pouring it on so strong, as if he really liked me. That always lowered my defenses. Me and Sally Fields."

Helena takes another lengthy sip while studying the two men for their reaction. "Things progressed to the point where he was working my equipment. And enjoying it a lot until he passed out, in case inquiring minds want to know." She smiles coyly, then her face hardens. "When I went to chat with Dorrie the next morning, my trick was still out cold. As we're talking on the sidewalk, he comes to, goes ballistic, and starts trashing my room. He even threw my gowns and wigs out the window. We got into a huge fight. I gave as good as I got, but things got pretty rough after a while. Dorrie rushed over to Tips for Tops'n and called the police. Marched right in during breakfast and demanded the phone. If she hadn't, I might have been killed.

"By the time the cops arrived, the asshole had broken three of my ribs and knocked out my two front teeth. As they carted him away, he started yelling that I'd robbed him. The police seemed to believe him, and I was scared shitless. Dorrie knew all the officers, and she let them have it. They acted like Cub Scouts by the time she was through. She told me she'd never let him hurt me again, and I believed her. She was so tiny, but yet so strong and righteous. I'll never, ever, forget how she protected me that day.

"An ambulance took me to Cape Cod Hospital. Next morning, as I'm sitting there feeling sorry for myself, doesn't Lola walk in. I'd heard stories about her—she'd been a recluse for years—but this was the first time I'd ever seen her in the flesh."

Cole leans forward, clearly recalling the day Lola found him on MacMillan wharf. "Did Dorrie tell her what happened to you?"

"No. Jimmy was in the ambulance with me. He told Dolores, and she told Lola, who had herself driven to the hospital to see how she could help. When I was discharged, she insisted I come to HomePort to recuperate. What's more, she paid for everything, including my dental implants. I've been here ever since."

Marc empties the first bottle, opens the second, and tops off Helena's glass. "What about the guy?"

"He turned out to be married with a house in Truro. Based on Dorrie's eyewitness account and, I suspect, some pressure from Lola, the police arrested him for assault. It caused quite a scandal—Truro macho guy versus P'Town drag queen. It was in the paper for weeks. I had to go to court and everything."

Helena describes how her lawyer recruited a panel of so-called "experts" from the Old Colony Tap to play "pick the drag queen" at the trial.

"The idea was that I'd have dressed less memorably if I were looking to rob someone. You should've seen the prosecutor," Helena says with a thin-lipped grin. "He went apoplectic with his objections, but my lawyer was able to convince the judge that these men had the necessary 'expertise.' She explained that they talked about and checked out women constantly, making them ideal witnesses. The judge, a woman who grew up in town and knew a thing or two, was finally convinced. Whenever my picture in that Barbarella outfit was on the screen, every one of them picked it. I was a star at last."

Helena's laugh falls flat. "Then my lawyer mixed in pictures of me in more sedate costumes with different wigs and subtle makeup. She added some pictures of other queens and straight women. Every time they picked the drag queen in the second round, it wasn't me. It was a cashier from the hardware store"

Helena downs her glass. "You know, that beating convinced me it's not all laughs out there. Straight people do awful things to gay people every day. I'm more protective of myself since I learned that lesson. I'll never let something like that happen to me or anyone else I care about."

"Gay people do awful things to gay people every day, too," Marc says quietly.

Helena hurries on, as if to distance herself from his remark. "I've learned there's no middle ground. You have to be yourself, not what you think will please someone else, no matter what the risk. And you should never settle for anyone, or anything. And you've got to have a strategy to protect yourself, which is exactly is needed to deal with Brandon."

Cole stares pointedly at Marc but says nothing.

"I fixed the bastard, though," Helena says, adopting a more assertive tone. "No one can treat me that way and get away with it. I got a ride to his waterfront mansion in my best Lilly Pulitzer, and had a little heart-to-heart with his rich-bitch wife. I told her how her husband came on to me and how he went at it once he got my outfit off. She pushed back hard, saying I was crazy. Even threatened to call the police and tell them I was blackmailing her. Finally, I said, 'Look, honey. It's no skin off my nose, but if he beat me up are you really sure he won't do the same to you one day?'

"With that, she broke down and told me she'd suspected for a long time he was a closet case. She was certain he'd been stepping out and putting her at risk for years. She had all the money and kept it in the divorce. Supposedly, he pulled some strings and ended up in the Merchant Marines. What he gets up to on the high seas these days, I can only imagine. Without Lola and Dorrie building me back up, I'm not sure I'd have survived."

Marc looks over at Cole who seems deep in thought. Then Helena stands and straightens her chair, her brown eyes ablaze with defiance. "So, gentlemen, let me make one thing perfectly clear. I'm taking all this very personally. That little prick isn't messing with *my* family and getting away with it. This is war."

CHAPTER 12
THE GENTLEMAN CALLER

Four days later, Lola summons Marc, Cole, and Helena to tea. An air of tension accompanies them into the parlor. Cole and Helena have scoured the streets of Provincetown looking for Brandon, with no success. They've even checked the Truro jail, but he seems to have vanished without a trace. They haven't told Lola, though she's grown increasingly concerned about their subdued mood and frequent absences.

They are hardly seated before she begins her inquisition. "What's gotten in to all of you? You'd think there'd been a death in the family. I've never seen such sour faces."

"It's not really something we can discuss," Marc says gently.

Lola takes a deep breath and sits upright in her chair as if bracing for battle. "Another 'personal issue' no one is supposed to care about, Marc? I thought we'd been down that road already."

Suddenly, the doorbell rings in short staccato bursts, followed by violent pounding. Helena jumps to her feet. She's wearing her Mrs. Danvers outfit. Her skirt rustles loudly as she runs to the door. "Lola, stay put with your head down. Marc, Cole, you guys hide. I'll deal with it."

Before Lola can say a word, Marc pulls Cole into the mistress's parlor where they can watch unobserved through its thick lace curtains. Helena positions herself in the front hall. She exchanges a quick glance with Cole who nods and pulls Marc close. Slowly, Helena opens both doors.

Brandon, painfully thin, sways as if he were on a boat in rough seas. His beard has several days' growth. His red hair looks as though it hasn't been washed for days. His loose-fitting clothes are wrinkled and dirty. He stares up at Helena with wide, crazed eyes.

"Where is he?"

Helena steps onto the porch, leaving one door slightly ajar. "Where is who?"

"Marc."

"Marc who?"

"You know who."

"Darling, this is beginning to sound like a bad knock-knock joke. Who is it that you want, sweetie?"

"Marc Nugent. And don't sweetie me."

Marc presses close to Cole, grateful for the comfort of his muscles, broad chest, and steady heartbeat.

"Marc Nugent," Helena says, as if trying to recall. "Hmm. I'm not sure I know anyone by that name. This is Miss Lola Staunton's residence."

"Don't bullshit me, whatever you are. I've been searching for him all week. I've driven up and down every street in town looking for his car. I finally found it in your driveway."

"Well, bully for you. There are only two problems. First, that's my car, and second, there's no person here by that name."

"Cut the shit, bitch. I know Marc's here. My friend told me he's been hiding in Provincetown since he ran out on me last fall, and I saw Marc driving that car a few days ago. You tell that good-for-nothing bastard to meet me in the Macho Bar at nine tonight, if he knows what's good for him. Tell him it's Brandon—Brandon Hammond—and if he doesn't show up, I'll come back and rip this place apart until I find him. He'll know I mean business."

Brandon's face is purple with rage. Marc starts to come to Helena's aid until Cole restrains him.

Helena is suddenly all sweetness and light. "Oh, Brandon Hammond, is it? Well, that's a horse of a different color. I've got something for you."

Brandon steps forward like a child expecting a present. "What?"

"This." The punch to his groin propels him down the stairs, onto the drive, and into a fetal position, where he lies moaning and rolling in the dirt, hands cupped between his legs.

After standing over him for a few minutes with her foot on his chest, Helena wipes her hands, clasps them over her head in triumph, climbs the stairs, and slams the door shut.

Not On My Watch

As Marc and Cole watch from the kitchen, Brandon limps to his car, then drives slowly past Dorrie's house. Once he's out of sight, the two men race to the parlor where Lola stands staring blankly at the fireplace. She's dreadfully pale, and the vein on the side of her head throbs violently. Helena stands beside her, her arms around her waist, a troubled look on her face.

"Just what was that all about? Is that young man who I think he is?" Lola asks, her voice faint and slightly slurred.

"Yes, Lola, that's Brandon," Marc replies. "Come sit down. Helena get her some tea."

Each man takes an arm and escorts Lola to her chair. Once seated she says, "Don't worry about me. It will pass. Marc, are *you* all right?"

Helena pours a cup for Lola, then places one in front of Marc who slumps on the sofa shaking violently. Cole wraps both arms around him as Helena massages his shoulders.

"Nasty piece of work," Lola says, her wide eyes never leaving Marc's face.

"That's for sure," Helena says. "And if he hasn't learned his lesson just now, there's more where that came from."

Cole's face is a storm cloud. "You're not alone, Helena. If I ever see that little shit again, he's going to wish he never came to town."

"How did he find you, Marc?" Lola asks, her hands still shaking though color is slowly returning to her face.

"There's only one way he could have known where Marc was," Cole answers when Marc doesn't respond. "Alan and Chuck must have told him once Charlotte's house changed hands. The bastards."

Helena studies Marc for a moment, then walks to the window and looks out. After a minute or two, she returns to where her friends sit rubbing Lola's frigid hands. "You both have to get out of here, right now," she says assertively, "before Brandon thinks better of it and returns. We've got to go on the offensive, and we need somewhere to prepare. I know just the place."

Marc, regaining focus and anxious to control his fate, starts to protest. "He's probably parked at the end of the driveway waiting for me to leave. He'll just follow me."

Helena's tone brooks no interference. "He's also doped up, malnourished, and weak as water. We're not putting Lola at risk, or Dorrie for that matter. We've got to lure him away from HomePort. I'm not going to just sit around and wait for a home invasion"

"But Helena—"

"No buts, Marc. We're leaving. That's final. You two cut through the woods and walk the beach until you get to West Vine Street, then go over to Charlotte's house. That's the last place Brandon would expect to find you. I'll take your car. He'll think you're hiding in it and follow me. I'll lose him out on Route Six like you did. Then I'll park the car in the School Street parking lot and meet you at Charlotte's."

Helena bends down so that her face is just inches from Lola's. "And you, Your Majesty, are going to do exactly what I say whether you like it or not. Lock the doors, stay in the library, don't turn on any lights, and don't let anyone in. I'm going to call Dolores and tell her to come over. I'll have Dorrie call the police if Brandon's car returns."

Lola nods and says nothing. Marc and Cole remain seated, staring at Helena in astonishment. "Get moving," she yells. "Right now! No back talk."

Cole and Marc answer as one. "Yes, Mommie Dearest."

Do You Come Here Often?

Marc feels like a complete idiot. Since they rendezvoused at Charlotte's house, Helena's dyed his hair black, covered him in peel-off tattoos, and glued a thick, black mustache to his upper lip. She's made him change into a leather vest and chaps she's gotten from God knows where and has hung a pair of handcuffs from his belt loop. His pointed leather boots add inches to his height while severely pinching his feet. He'd barely been able to walk from Napi's to the A-House in them.

It's after nine, and Brandon is still waiting for Marc to arrive, unaware he's standing directly in his line of sight. The Macho Bar is the one place in town where Helena would never fit in, no matter what she wore. Well aware of this, she's ordered Marc and Cole to go as her eyes and ears and wait for the arrival of one of Marvin's hustlers—part of a convoluted grand plan the two men still don't quite understand.

Brandon is a mess. His red hair is uncombed, and his clouded eyes lack focus. He stares into his drink, his thin lips pursed in an arrogant sneer. He makes no effort to talk with the other patrons, who seem to be giving him a wide berth. His hands twitch, and his breathing is shallow. Suddenly his features darken. He takes the toothpick from his drink, removes the olives, drops them in the glass, holds the pick in front of his face, then snaps it in two.

Even with Cole at his side, Marc feels panic. He stares at Brandon, then catches himself, looks away, then glances back again against his will. Closing his eyes, he recalls the violent scene in New York: the smell of Gun Oil, the leather chaps crumpled on the bed, and the katana pressing against his throat. When he surveys the bar again, for an instant the patrons seem to be waiting in line behind Brandon. Only Cole's reassuring presence keeps Marc from bolting.

At exactly nine twenty, a dark-skinned, handsome man neither Cole nor Marc has ever seen before swaggers into the bar. As he sits, every head but Brandon's turns to stare.

He's wearing a tight black t-shirt that accentuates his lithe swimmer's build, a pair of tight jeans that accommodate a tantalizing bulge that extends partway down his left thigh, and a black leather vest that frames his well-developed chest. His eyes are a deep, cornflower blue, his hair lustrous ebony.

Only when the man sits beside him does Brandon look up. After a quick appraisal, he turns back to his near-empty drink as if the vision next to him is not worth a second glance.

"Give me a Bud," the hunk says in a virile voice, "and whatever my friend here is drinking."

Marc's cell phone rings. He answers it with a guttural "Yeah," that doesn't quite ring true. As Cole seems to struggle to maintain his macho pose, the voice on the other end of the line is assertive and succinct.

"Marc. Helena. Don't say another word, just listen. I don't want Brandon recognizing your voice. Marvin's boy, Hal, should be there by now. He's going to put the make on Brandon and get him shit-faced. Then he'll take him to HomePort where I can keep him under wraps. If Hal needs help, you and Cole provide it. Remember, let Cole do all the talking. You should be able to stay at home tonight. I'll find you in the morning and let you know what happened."

The line goes dead.

When the bartender returns with a can of beer and a gin martini, the dark stranger places a friendly arm on Brandon's shoulder.

"You can call me Hal. Drowning your sorrows, bud?"

Brandon removes Hal's arm as if it were leprous. "Far from it. Just planning my next move."

"Next move for what?"

"Getting a bit of my own back."

"Someone mess with you?"

"Fuck, yeah—my ex. I took the prick in to live with me in my loft, put up with all this bullshit about being a writer, and listened to all his crap about love and monogamy. I gave him every goddamn thing I had, and when the money ran out, he walked out on me without even saying where he was going."

Hal reaches over and pats Brandon's hand, which is quickly withdrawn. Hal seems unfazed. "Tough break. How'd you track him here?"

Brandon explains how Alan and Chuck saw to it a mutual friend told him Marc's whereabouts.

"Interesting. So your boy bailed just like that?" Hal places his large hand on Brandon's leg. This time, it stays put.

"Yeah, took everything while things were good, then bolted. I'd been damn good to him, and almost believed he was interested in me, not just what I had. He certainly said it often enough, but it turned out to be bullshit. I was trying to figure a way to tell him my folks had lost all their money and that we'd have to move. Somehow, he found out before I got up the nerve. In no time at all, I lost my loft and ended up with nothing but my car. Then today some goddamn drag queen in a maid's uniform punched me in the nuts."

Brandon sounds so pathetic Marc struggles not to laugh aloud. *Some leather queen. More like leatherette.*

When the bartender favors Hal with a flirtatious wink, he keeps his focus on Brandon.

"Well, that's P'Town for ya—always the unexpected. Seriously, that's a lot to go through, though if your ex wanted to leave, he had the right, didn't he? Did you ever consider getting on with your life rather than being so hung up on him?"

Brandon slams his glass on the bar so hard his drink spills. "Nobody walks out on Brandon Hammond. I'm gonna teach that son of a bitch a lesson he'll never forget. By the time I'm done, he's gonna regret the day he was born."

Brandon's face is purple, and his hands twitch violently. Marc, appalled by what Brandon has become, skulks toward the stairs until Cole pulls him close. The bar grows quiet. Only Hal seems unfazed by the violent response.

"What time's he supposed to meet you?"

"He was supposed to be here at nine if he got the message from the wacko bitch that punched me." Brandon glares at the men beside him who have been unable to suppress their smiles. "He's got five more minutes. After that, I'm going after him and fuck her up, too."

"Where does he live?"

"Some big-assed house at the far end of Commercial Street."

"A big old house with a tower and a long driveway?"

"Yeah."

"I know the place. It takes a while to get here from way out there. How 'bout a drink to replace that one while you wait?"

"You buyin'?"

"Sure."

Hal smiles and signals the bartender, then returns his hand to its resting place, though higher up than before.

Brandon leans forward, breathing gin into Hal's face. "Hey, what's your name—Hal? I'm Brandon. Brandon Hammond. Anybody ever tell you you're hot?"

"I thought you'd never notice."

Show Me the Way to Go Home

When Brandon finally abandons his vigil, three more martinis have abetted the drugs he'd taken earlier. Though he can hardly walk, he blatantly propositions Hal with lewd suggestions that have the other patrons smirking into their drinks. To their surprise and palpable dismay, Hal phones a taxi, helps Brandon off the stool, and escorts him outside. Marc and Cole take their cue and follow at a distance.

"The Provincetown Inn," Hal says to the taxi driver before hailing the two men. "You guys headed that way? I could sure use a hand with my friend, here."

Cole says yes. Marc remains silent as they help Hal push Brandon onto the backseat. Cole and Hal get in on either side of him. Marc sits in front, staring straight ahead. Before the cab pulls from the curb, Brandon's head flops on Hal's shoulder.

"Twenty bucks each if you help get him up the hill," Hal says.

When they reach their destination, Hal and the driver drag Brandon out of the cab. When he slumps on the hood, each man takes an arm or leg for the long haul up the path. The cool night air does its work. Brandon is marginally conscious by the time they reach the balcony. When the men set him down, he gropes Hal, burying his face in his chest and sliding his hand inside his pants.

"You're in for a hell of a time tonight. Wait 'til you see the things I can do with this big boy. I'm gonna make him sing and dance, then I'll milk him dry and have you begging for more. You'd better cancel all your plans for the next twenty-four hours at least."

Everything that Marc once admired about Brandon has vanished. There's no trace of his charm, generosity, caustic humor, or intelligence. All that remains is an erotic intensity that, given his decrepit appearance, permeates the air with pathos.

When Brandon passes out yet again, Hal rolls his eyes at the taxi driver.

"He's not going to be up for much of anything, despite all he's promising," the driver says with a nervous laugh. "I'd be happy to fill in for him if you want to back a different stud."

Hal hands each of the men a twenty. "I appreciate the offer, but I'll take it from here, thanks. I'd love a rain check, though."

"Sure," the driver replies. "Anytime. Just say the word. Call Crazy Cab and ask for Bruce. I'll be there in five minutes flat."

Grinning at Marc and Cole, Hal throws Brandon over his shoulder and carries him into Marvin's apartment.

As Marc stands staring at the closed door, Cole pulls him into a tight embrace. "Brandon will be out of commission for the rest of the night, if not longer. You need a long hot shower to wash all that crap off you. I'll be happy to help. I suggest you cancel all your plans for the next twenty-four hours at least...."

CHAPTER 13
IS THAT ALL THERE IS?

Next morning, there's a minute's wakefulness before Marc remembers Brandon is in the Bates Motel. He reaches for Cole and caresses his cheek. Just as Cole takes him in his arms, the bedroom door flies open. Helena, hands on hips, is wearing her maid's outfit, complete with the purple handkerchief pinned to her right breast. Her orange wig is piled high in a monumental beehive that reduces Dolores' effort to the minor leagues.

"Plenty of time for that later. Get dressed, you two. You don't have a minute to lose. Meet me on the balcony ASAP!" She races back to the Bates Motel.

"What in the name of God was that?" Cole mumbles, still half asleep.

"Our fairy godmother. We better obey." Wiping sleep from their eyes, the lovers stumble into their clothes and meet Helena as instructed. She's holding a large silver tray laden with coffee, pastries, and mimosas.

"If you interrupted us for brunch with everything that's going on, I'll…." With a single glance from Helena, Marc's annoyance collapses.

"You know, Marc," Helena says, "it seems I've always got your back, but you never get mine. Let me be the lead bitch for once, and I'll make it well worth your while. You're gonna love this, trust me." Helena unlocks the door to Marvin's suite. Her hairdo is higher than the doorframe. She bends over, then charges inside holding the tray in one hand.

"What was it Ziegfeld said? 'Don't lower the headdress... raise the arch?'" Cole mumbles as they follow Helena into the apartment.

Helena sets the tray on a table by the door. "Rise and shine, cupcake! Momma's been hard at work all night on our video. It's gonna be a global sensation."

Brandon sprawls stark naked on a grimy sofa. His thin legs are splayed, his stomach a mound in an otherwise flat plane of pale, white flesh. When he sees Marc, he propels himself off the couch, stretches his puny arms full length and lunges.

"I'll kill you, you motherfucker. I'm gonna kill you."

Helena's ready. With a forceful shove, she sends Brandon careening on his back. He tries again, but Helena raises her hand in a karate pose and gives a piercing screech. Eyes wide with incredulity, Brandon cowers on the floor.

"Now, does everyone know everyone?" Helena asks in a saccharine voice. "Marc, you remember Brandon?"

"Yes." Even though Brandon is outnumbered, Marc feels his pulse quicken and his mouth go dry.

Helena continues her introductions. "Cole, I don't think you've had the pleasure, have you?"

"No, I don't believe I have."

Cole clenches his fist and steps forward until Marc grabs his arm and pulls him back.

Brandon sneers but stays where he is.

"Cole is Marc's partner, Brandon," Helena says. "As in person who honors, loves, and respects his mate, in case you are unclear on the concept." Then she makes a little gesture as if she were introducing guests at a cocktail party.

"Cole, Brandon, Brandon, Cole."

Brandon rages, but doesn't move.

Marc's thoughts are everywhere at once. *I couldn't be in better company if anything happens. Even so, I can't figure how we can get Brandon to back off. He doesn't care what he does. Now he's found me, he'll be stalking me for years, a half-wasted, murderous shadow. I can't live like that.*

Helena turns to Brandon. "And you, dear. How 'bout a little coffee, big stuff?"

She hands him a cup. He stands, quickly downs it, then places the cup on the table with a dazed expression. "Please have a mimosa, darlings," Helena says to Cole and Marc in her best Kitty Carlisle impersonation. "And do sit down. The main event is about to start."

"Where's Hal?" Brandon asks as he sits on the sofa.

Helena puts her index finger to her bottom lip and smiles demurely.

"Hal? Hal who? I'm not sure I recall anyone named Hal, darling. It's such a butch name I'd certainly remember it. I'll bet he's quite the hunk. Are you sure you didn't dream him up? Anyways, let's get this show on the road. Brandon, I understand you came here looking for Marc."

Brandon mumbles something unintelligible and stares belligerently.

"Please speak up, darling. I want to be sure we all understand each other. And you came to Provincetown to see Marc because?"

"That's between Marc and me, bitch."

Helena plants a stiletto heel so close to Brandon's crotch that Marc and Cole wince. "Let's try again, Brandon, cupcake. You came to Provincetown to see Marc because?"

"Because he fuckin' ruined my life, and I'm going to mess him up."

Helena lifts her leg over Brandon's head, spins around on one foot, grabs him by the neck, and twists his head back. "You're going to do what?"

"Ow, you're hurting me!"

"Repeat after me. I'm not going to hurt Marc."

"I'm not going to hurt Marc."

"Not now. Not ever."

"Not now. Not ever."

"I'm going to be a good boy, sit back, and watch my global video debut. It's high time I was on camera instead of behind it."

"I'm going to…. What the fuck?"

Helena releases him, tosses him a blanket, and picks up a remote from a nearby table. An image of Brandon, stark naked and aroused, appears on the enormous wide-screen TV. The resolution is perfect. Every detail shows.

"Hurry up, man," Brandon calls as the camera pans the room. "Where are you Hal, you hot stud. Let's get down to business."

Brandon's eyes are heavy, his words slurred. His right wrist hangs limply in front of his sunken chest. His wasted neck makes his head seem enormous. In contrast, his upright sex is diminished by a tangle of pubic hair that makes him look like a eunuch. Far from erotic and enticing, his effete pose, pursed lips, and brittle impatience make him look petulant and inconsequential.

Marc smiles to himself. *About as intimidating as a French Poodle.*

"Let's get this show on the road! It's party time!" Brandon says.

As the camera zooms in on his face, the tinny sound of a tinny piano wafts from the bedroom, and a famous voice recalls the day her house caught fire.

Brandon pivots wildly, searching for the voice as Helena sashays into view wearing a short blonde wig covered by a silver turban. A strapless evening gown of silver lamé barely disguises pendulous breasts that hang almost to her knees. Her eyes are dark with mascara. Costume jewelry cover her wrists and fingers. Carrying one of Lola's canes, she hobbles across the screen mimicking Peggy Lee in a final, grotesque, near-death performance.

As Helena dodders in front of him, Brandon tries to stand but falls back on the couch. His erection, besieged by cold, liquor, and the bizarre vision before him, beats a hasty, unequivocal retreat.

"Is that all there is?" Helena lip-syncs as she totters through Peggy's well-worn routine. Reaching the second chorus, Helena extricates a large, fake, magnifying glass from her décolletage. Focusing it on Brandon's crotch, she nods vehemently when Peggy suggests it might be a better idea to keep dancing.

Canned guffaws overwhelm the music. Helena mugs for the camera as Brandon stares blankly. When Peggy sings of something being missing, Helena points to his crotch, frowns, then raises both hands and looks petulantly up at the ceiling.

From their seats, Cole and Marc erupt in hysterical laughter. Brandon gapes as if living his worst nightmare. Part of Marc wants to turn off the video and try to reason with him, but the memory of cold steel lays that thought to rest. Instead, he places his faith in Helena, praying she'll know when she's made her point.

The bawdy, on-screen antics continue as Helena, with double entendre and suggestive glances, skewers the naked Brandon. When Peggy speculates on her final disappointment, Helena holds her forefinger and thumb an inch apart, shakes her head in exaggerated dismay, then rolls her eyes like Theda Bara.

By now, Cole and Marc are laughing so hard they can barely breathe. Brandon remains coiled under the blanket while Helena stands beside him, ready to pounce. It's clear she's hit a nerve. Brandon's hostility is slowly giving way to mortification.

The performance ends to wild applause and shouts of "Brava diva, Brava." Helena curtsies and bows, blowing kisses to an imaginary audience. Eventually, she signals for silence.

"I'd like to thank my supporting actor," she says in a breathless, star-struck voice. "Ladies and Gentlemen! Brandon Hammond, the well-known pornographer from Chelsea, New York City, in his on-screen debut! Give him a hand!"

She points to Brandon who, by this time, has passed out and is snoring loudly. The camera zooms in on his drooling mouth. As it pans the length of his torso, the dubbed-in audience responds with hooting and catcalls. Helena calls for silence a second time. When the camera reaches just the right spot, she arches her eyebrows. "Even though it was a bit part, he gave it all he had." There's one last close-up of the snoring Brandon before the audience bursts into applause and the screen fades to black.

"You bitch!" Brandon leaps off the couch only to be tripped by Helena's right foot and tossed into a chair like a pillow. Then she holds a clenched fist to his face. "Cole, be a darling? Go into the bedroom and get the laptop on the bureau? Now, Brandon, listen *very* carefully," Helena says when Cole returns with the computer. "The video you just saw is all ready to email to your parents, Alan, Chuck, and forty or so of what pass for your friends these days. I've also got an Xtube posting ready to load back in my apartment."

Brandon looks as though he might have a stroke. "How do you know my family and friends?"

"Thanks for reminding me, darling. Here's your iPHONE. I just *love* the leather case. It's so butch." Helena tosses it on the couch. "Now, Cole. If this jackass makes one more move other than to leave here and never come back, hit the send button. I'll be sure you have the video and email addresses for insurance should you ever need them in the future."

Cole mans his post, star-struck. "You got it, Helena. Did I ever tell you I adore you?"

Catching Helena's eye, Marc mouths the words, "I love you."

Helena drops out of character for just a moment, wipes her eyes and then, with what seems a tremendous force of will, focuses back on the task at hand. She turns to Brandon, who lies huddled in near shock, taking his chin in his hand. She begins to speak in the tone and mannerisms of Nurse Ratched.

"Now, Brandon, sweetie, I want this to be perfectly clear. No more threats. It's over. Marc has left you, and you just have to suck it up and deal. You will leave town today without any more nonsense. Never to return. Right?"

"Right." The single word is a whisper, but is so potent with resignation and humiliation Marc believes him at once.

Helena smiles sweetly. "Oh, that's marvelous, darling. Get dressed, sweetie, and I'll call you a cab."

So Long, Dearie

Cole and Marc stand outside the kitchen window as Helena brays farewell from the balcony, waving her purple handkerchief as if departing on the *Queen Mary*. She's insisted on staying near the computer until Brandon's taxi leaves. When his cab arrives, she cackles and yells down to him, "What an unexpected pleasure! It's so kind of you to visit me in my loneliness."

"I wondered when she'd get around to that one," Cole whispers. "We've seen everybody but the Wicked Witch of the West these last few months. With that beehive, she doesn't even need a pointed hat."

Brandon surveys the vision on the balcony, shakes his head as if it were all a bad dream, then slides meekly into the cab. He looks so downtrodden and defeated Marc almost feels sorry for him.

"All clear," Helena shouts, waving her handkerchief in exaggerated triumph as the cab rumbles down the hill. "The battle is won!" She grabs the railing, stretches one leg out and leans back, a victorious World War II pinup girl with hair like a Navy torpedo.

"Helena," Marc yells back. "You were brilliant! Where on earth did you find a video studio to edit that amazing performance overnight?"

Helena crosses her arms and shakes her head. "I respectfully refuse to answer on the grounds that I might incriminate someone else. I will share a beauty secret, however."

"Dare I ask?" Marc whispers to Cole.

"Sure, go ahead. She deserves her moment in the sun."

"Is it the hair, Helena? Looks like you've finally conquered Mount Everest."

"Why, thank you for noticing, darling. I think of it more like defying gravity. I like that term. Someone should write a song with that name. In any case, you'll never believe my secret."

"I'm sure I can't begin to imagine."

"Well it was driving me crazy, so I finally pried out of Dolores how she does it. You'll never guess."

"No, I'm sure I couldn't begin to—"

"Shellac."

"What?"

"I've been saving it as a surprise for a special occasion. If this isn't one, I don't know what is. Anyhow, I got Dolores tipsy on Vinho Verde, and she finally told me. That beehive isn't her real hair. She's as bald as a baby's bottom. I should have realized ages ago it couldn't be real. But then, I was never all that good in physics."

"Well congratulations on another fashion triumph," Marc says. "No doubt hairdressers around the globe will welcome the trend you've revived, though I worry about the environmentalists. But seriously, how did you ever pull off that video?"

Helena crosses her arms again and slowly moves a finger across her lips.

"Were you born yesterday or what, Marc?" Cole asks, shaking his head. "Nearly everyone in town knows Marvin services men by appointment, tapes the sessions, and sells access to them on his website. What do you think the traffic at night is all about?" Cole is clearly enjoying himself. "He sets up a piece of plywood in the vestibule, then opens his door when someone shows up for a session. The light you keep asking about are the camera lights shining through the unoccupied glory hole. Some detective you turned out to be, Sherlock."

Marc recalls the scores of men he's seen leaving the balcony over the past months. "What would Lola say if she knew?"

Lola's imperious tones ring out from the window behind them like the voice of doom. "She'd say she is not the Mayflower Madam, and HomePort is not, nor ever shall be, a house of ill repute. Please tell Marvin for me that he has twenty-four hours to pack his wagon and get the hell out of Dodge. Helena will write him a substantial check for his troubles."

CHAPTER 14
TO TELL THE TRUTH

That night, in the midst of foreplay, Cole lights a joint. What Marc anticipated as an intimate victory celebration is immediately done in by his insecurity. "Do you already need something turn you on besides me?"

Cole freezes. "C'mon Marc. It's nothing like that. Things are good. Real good. I don't need a joint to show you some love."

Marc wraps his arms around himself and starts to rock back and forth. Tears fill his eyes when Cole attempts to pull him close. "Is this a letdown from all Brandon's shit or something else I need to know about?"

The effort fails. Marc remains rigid and unyielding. At last he speaks. "I'm not sure what it's about. I just know the idea you might need something to make love to me has ruined the moment."

"I don't *need* anything to make love to you. I thought I'd made that perfectly clear by now. I just figured we could chill together a bit after all of today's craziness. That's not what this is about. It's the same old issue, isn't it?"

"Well, no, I guess, yes. Well, maybe."

"Okay, out with it."

"This is probably stupid, but I feel something's coming between us."

Cole's face darkens. "You've made enough hints these last few weeks to make *Page Six*. I just can't figure what it is you think could come between us. This is the last thing I'd expect now that Brandon's out of the picture. You know there's nobody else."

"I do, it's just that there's a big part of you that I still don't know. Take today, for instance."

"What about today?"

"After Brandon left, you just disappeared."

"That's not true. I spent a lot of time trying to explain to Lola how Helena got rid of Brandon. That was surreal!"

Marc smiles, recalling how delicately they had all tried to explain why "Is That All There Is?" was just the right song to vanquish the fierce and intimidating man who'd scared Lola out of her wits. Cole grins as well, and some of the tension between them dissipates.

"But then you disappeared," Marc says. "When I got back from picking up the mail, you were gone and weren't back until midafternoon."

"You know I need alone time now and then. I was so freaked out by the whole scene with Brandon and all the disruption of the last few days, I just needed some 'me' time to get my act back together."

Marc knows that he's making too much of things, but he can't seem to control himself. "When you go off by yourself, I feel I'm not enough for you. Sometimes I think you're like a lone wolf out in the woods, beholding to nothing and no one."

Cole's green eyes probe Marc's with an intensity that nearly frightens him. "Do you really want me beholding to you, Marc? Do you want me focused exclusively on you the way Brandon was?"

"No. I don't mean beholding. I mean…."

Marc folds further in on himself as Cole places an arm around him and whispers, "I know I can be a pain in the ass sometimes. I've always been a loner. For years, I figured love was never going to happen for me—that I'd been denied it because of who or what I was. I'd have a trick now and then to take the pressure off, but wouldn't let anyone get close because I never trusted them to stay.

"Since I came to HomePort, I've been working hard to change that. It started the day I met Lola, after I burnt my paintings. I figured, why not? I can care for this strange old woman, be her caretaker. Might as well, because I doubt life will offer much more than that. I became a part of this crazy joint we call home, and something happened. I began to care about Lola, not *for* her, but *about* her. I began to care how Helena got through her wacked-out days. I recognized the frightened person underneath who yearned for love almost as much as I did, and gradually I changed from a caretaker to a caregiver. It felt good, this caring. I wanted more. Then you came along.

"When you put the studio together for me, and Lola told me she'd saved my paintings, I finally understood the toll resentment and suspicion take on a person's psyche. I saw what I'd done to myself and decided I had to take a chance on loving you. When you free yourself from baggage like that, love becomes possible. It *can* grow imperceptibly, just the way the captain's love for Annie did. I know, because that's what happened to me. I've been on my own for so long, being part of a couple doesn't come easy. You have no idea how hard I'm trying, Marc. I'm giving it everything I can."

Marc smiles up at Cole. "I just worry sometimes everything that's happened to us just raises the odds we won't go the distance."

"Well, that's a charming thought. Does that mean the honeymoon's officially over?"

"Cole, don't make fun of me...."

"You don't get it, do you?"

"Get what?"

"All you're missing by being so much in your head. Everything that's happened to us will help us better appreciate what we have, if you'd only let it."

"Huh?"

"C'mon, you stick-in-the-mud," Cole says with a grin. "We're going for a little ride."

Cole rummages the bedside table and stuffs something in his pocket. "Give me the keys."

"I thought you didn't drive."

"I haven't for a long time, but give me the keys."

Marc, taking one look at Cole, surrenders them immediately.

Sometimes, Life's a Beach

The two men descend the stairs in silence. Cole starts the car, struggles with the stick shift for a moment, then heads down the driveway. Turning right towards the Province Lands, the car bucks and jolts its way to Herring Cove. Once there, Cole drives to the far end of the parking lot.

"Okay, get out."

Marc does as he's told.

"Now strip!"

"What?"

"Strip and throw your clothes in the car."

As Marc stands beside him in a near state of shock, Cole steps out of his clothes then dives into the ocean. When he surfaces some twenty feet out, he yells to Marc. "Are you coming or what?"

His face radiant, Marc quickly strips and follows. The two men splash and caress, twirling each other's bodies in the refreshing water. They race along the shoreline at one with the waves. Finally, without having said a word, they float on their backs, holding hands, staring at the stars above, the bodies barely visible in the enveloping darkness. At last, they swim to shore.

"There are towels in the trunk, right?"

"Yes," Marc replies.

"Okay, I'll get them. You stay here." When Cole returns, the two men towel each other off, then sit cross-legged facing each other.

Marc takes Cole's hand. "That was a religious experience. This is what you do every day out here, right?"

"Yup. Nothing clears my head and helps me focus like a good swim and some quality time with Mother Nature."

"This is where I saw you that very first day."

"I know. I came on to you, remember?"

"Is that why you didn't bring me here? Were you too embarrassed?"

Cole laughs. "Hell no. I'm not going to apologize for being attracted to you. You never asked why I come out here, you just moped around and made dumb hints, so I let you wonder."

"I didn't want to intrude. We all need a little quiet time now and then."

"We do? That's news to me. I thought we had to stand guard over each other twenty-four seven and be so deep in each other's shit that we were completely codependent by our first anniversary."

"Cole, I've been a fucking idiot."

Cole's wide smile permeates the darkness. "Perhaps just a little bit, babe. Get this through your head, though. I'm not a lone wolf, but I do need time to bring things into perspective. Then I can be there for you whenever we're together. We're built differently, you and me. You're a handful in your own right, to say nothing of Helena and the rest of the crowd. I just have to recharge my batteries sometimes. That's all it is, all it's ever been, and all it will ever be."

"I'm sorry. I love you so much, I guess a bit of Brandon's behavior rubbed off on me."

"Don't worry, just knock it off. I'll make a deal with you. You want to swim with me each morning, you come right along. Something tells me you'll give up by mid-October, but you're welcome any time. Just don't get pissed if I don't say anything while we're out here."

"Not every day, Cole. But I'd like to know I could."

"You dope. When are you ever going to realize all you have to do is ask?"

"I'm sorry. My drama ruined everything. What can I ever do to make it up to you?" Marc asks reaching between Cole's legs.

Cole rummages in his pocket, stands, and lights the joint. Marc, shifting to his knees, grins up at him, holds out his hand, takes a long toke, then slowly exhales. "I'll bet you ten bucks I'll have you howling in five minutes, Mr. Wolf...."

What's Right is Right

The following morning when Cole sets out for his swim, Marc maintains his usual routine up in the tower. He'd debated whether to tag along but decides to respect Cole's need for private time and stay home. Marc is slightly sheepish as he recalls his tantrum the night before. Then, grinning, he takes a ten-dollar bill from his pocket and tacks it to his billboard.

Marc's cell phone interrupts his reverie. Not recognizing the number, he ignores the call. Instead, he closes his eyes and imagines Cole swimming from Herring Cove to Hatches Harbor, his strong arms pulling him forward, his lithe body parting the waves. Then Marc turns to his writing. It's nearly noon before he checks his voicemail.

"Mr. Nugent, This is Vendra Castleton calling," a terse voice announces. "I found your note the day after you left it. I've been thinking a lot about your visit. I wasn't straight with you, and it's been bothering me so much I can hardly sleep. If you're willing to come back to the farm, I promise you'll get the truth. Just call and let me know when you're coming."

When Cole returns, the two men waste little time. Within the hour, they are en route to the Castleton farm. Vendra's waiting for them by the front door in the same tattered overalls and flannel shirt she'd worn when they first met her. She beckons them into the house where they're immediately surrounded by five baying basset hounds.

"Shut up. Shut up, for Chrissake," she says, swatting halfheartedly at the dogs with a newspaper. "Just walk past and don't pay them any mind. They'll settle down after a spell." She holds out her hand. "Let's start all over again, gents. Vendra Castleton, daughter of Amos and Grace Castleton."

Marc and Cole follow her into a dark, low-ceilinged living room where she motions for them to sit on a tattered sofa. She sits in a Morris chair for a minute, deep in thought. Her jaw works a bit. She palms a pipe, stuffs it with tobacco, and lights up. Taking a long, satisfying drag, she starts to speak.

"First I want to apologize. I wasn't straight with you fellas, and it's been preying on my conscience in strange ways ever since. Yes, I knew the captain. What's more, Annie lived with us for years. She was like a ghost, more dead than alive except when the captain came on Thursdays. She was a family secret. I'd never said a word to anyone about her, and when you showed up out of the blue like that, I couldn't think what to say.

"After you left the other day, I got to believing there had to be more to the story than I remembered. I rummaged around the house and found some things. If I didn't know better, I'd say there was someone or something leading me to them. I don't know what made me go upstairs and look in Mother's room. I haven't been up there in years, but I found this tucked away in a little tin box at the bottom of her wardrobe."

Vendra shows them a small diary with gilt-edged pages. "Reading this, I got Ma's perspective on all that happened with Annie; how she tried to kill herself, how they nursed her back to health, and how my aunt Carrie went to live in Provincetown to care for the child."

Vendra looks sheepishly at the two men as if apologizing for her deception. "Once I understood what really happened, I started having these strange dreams. I'd see 'Auntie' as I called Annie, in her room. She'd kneel down to pray, and when she finished, she'd take another book, open it, takes something out, open it, look inside for a minute, kiss it, put it back, and blow out the lamp. I don't know if I ever actually saw her do this, but the dream kept repeating itself, sometimes more than once a night. I *never* remember my dreams, but I remembered this one all day long.

"That book began to drive me crazy. I knew I'd seen it somewhere, but for the life of me, I couldn't figure where. I've spent the last few days going from room to room like a lunatic, trying to see if I could find it in this dump. Yesterday I did, in an old reticule up in the attic. Ma must have put it up there. As you can tell, I don't have much use for such things."

Vendra produces a beaded drawstring purse and removes a small green book embossed with the words *Key of Heaven,* its interior carved out to fit a delicate gold box. Removing and opening the box, Vendra retrieves a gold locket on a delicate chain. Inside is a photograph of the captain and Annie. She seems to be in her forties, the captain in his sixties. They gaze at each other with undeniable affection.

"We've got it," Marc says smiling at Cole. "We've got everything we need."

"Annie's daughter, Dorrie, is one of my dearest friends," Marc says, fighting back tears. "People in town swear the captain drowned Annie as a young girl. Seeing her alive at this age as well as the visible love between them will mean so much to Dorrie. What else can you tell us?"

"Well I suppose the best way is to start from the beginning," Vendra says. She takes another tug on her pipe, settles back, and begins.

Vendra's Story

"Annie boarded with us for years. She had a room behind the kitchen. Pale, she was, with beautiful dark hair and lovely clear skin, though as I recall, her features were quite plain. Once I read the book, I always thought she looked like Jane Eyre.

"Annie dressed in old-fashioned clothing and never said a word. I think she was mute or next thing to it. She was always going to the window, parting the curtain and looking out, as if she was waiting for somebody. Ma would take her by the hand and try to distract her. I remember Ma saying at the time, 'Annie dear, the captain's not expected today. Today is not his day.'"

Vendra describes how the captain came to visit each week. Confirming the details in his journal, she tells how he sat with Annie for hours without saying a word. "She was always different when he came to visit. More outside her shell. When he wasn't around, she'd stare off into space as if she could see somethin' nobody else could. But for that short time he visited each week, she seemed to be more with us, though she still didn't ever speak.

"One Thursday, the captain wasn't at the station. Well, that set off a ruckus, I'll tell you. Pa was gone the very next morning. Didn't say a word, just up and gone. That weren't like him, because he was always around the farm, tending this and that. I woke up, and Ma was out milking the cows. Then the chickens got out. It was bedlam, a blasted mess around this place the whole day he was away. Ma even got run over by a heifer.

"Pa got back late that night and went right into the parlor with Ma. Didn't even put the mare in her stall, just left her at the hitching post—something he'd never do. After a while, they sent me to fetch Annie. When I brought her to them, they told me to get upstairs. I didn't, though. I listened at the door. I couldn't hear what Pa said, but I heard the poor woman wail at whatever it was. I'd never heard her do more than sort of moan or grunt when she tried to make herself understood. This was such mournful, pathetic sound. It wasn't speaking, more like an animal in pain. It made me sick to hear it."

"About three weeks later, Pa was sitting in the office, reading the paper as he did most nights. I heard him yell, 'Mother, git in here, right away.' Ma came running and then there was a lot of whispering I couldn't make out. I did hear her say, 'Do we tell her?' and Pa saying, 'I just don't know, Grace. I just don't know if we should. After the way she took him being sick, it'll kill her.' He just kept saying that.

"I have a hunch what was in the paper. When I was searching the house, I found this in Ma's desk. It's from around the time I remember," Vendra says, opening the drop leaf of a carved oak desk and reaching for a manila file. "You can have it, if you want."

Marc eyes a yellowed clipping with the heading *Cape Philanthropist Dead at 81*. Beside the caption is the same photograph of her father Lola keeps by her bed.

The two men study the obituary in silence. "What happened to Annie after that?" Marc asks.

"Annie didn't last but a couple of years. I don't think they ever told her he was dead, because she just stood by the window waiting for him from that day on. Soon after, she grew hard to handle. She'd steal my doll and cradle it for days at time. She'd often leave the room if someone else entered, afraid they'd try to take the doll away. Pa finally bought me a new one because Annie was always taking mine.

"She gave my parents a tough time those last two years. She ran away five or six times. Every time they found her waiting at the train station, five miles from here. The last time she took off, the poor thing got a cold that turned to pneumonia. She'd no will to fight it, and before long, she just sort of wasted away.

"She's buried over in the cemetery across from the Green. There's a simple stone in the family plot that says 'Annie.' No last name, though. We always considered her one of us, and I guess my folks thought it best to bury her the way we knew her. I can show it to you if you want."

"That's all right," Cole says, gently. "We found it last time."

Marc leans forward in his chair. "I hope I don't sound impertinent. I heard what you said about Annie never being spoken of, but that's not much of a reason to keep all this from us. There's something else, isn't there?"

Vendra takes another long drag on her pipe. "I was afraid you'd catch on. Well, I've made up my mind to come clean, and that's just what I'm going to do. Every week, the captain gave Ma money for caring for Annie and to buy clothing, groceries and such. There was also a specific allowance for Annie's own needs and wants. It was five dollars a week, which was a lot of money back then. The problem was Annie would never spend it. She never went anywhere, she ate like a bird, and Ma made all her clothes. So Ma put it in the bank in trust for Annie's daughter. I know this because Ma left specific instructions in her will that I should try to find the child. But I never did. By the time Ma died, I needed the money.

"Five dollars a week adds up. Ma left the money alone, interest adding to interest. The account was in her and my name, though I never knew about it until she passed. Annie died first, then Pa a few years later. Ma got senile, though she lived on to her late nineties, and then there was just me. After Pa died, we couldn't work the farm, so I started selling land piece by piece over the years. Things got so bad I started using Annie's money to pay the taxes so I could stay on. I never felt right about it, so when you both just sort of showed up, the only thing I could think of was getting rid of you as quick as I could."

"The captain left his daughter an annuity. I don't think she's going to mind," Marc says. "What she wants most is to know was what happened to her mother."

"Well, I was brought up better than to take something that isn't mine. You tell her for me, I was at my wits end and would have lost my home without her money. And give her this. It's rightfully hers."

Cole accepts the locket, then holds out his hand in farewell. "We sure will."

The two men take their leave of Vendra. Reaching the cemetery, Marc stops the car. He and Cole walk back to the small, rectangular stone. Marc bends down to touch it. "Somehow seeing this and knowing who's buried here makes the horror of what happened back then so real. Poor Annie. Such a wasted life."

"She's not the only one. Poor Captain Staunton. So sad to be so courageous yet so afraid of what others might think."

Marc looks up with a start, recognizing in those words the man he had nearly become.

It's About Time

At the stroke of four the next day, Helena answers a knock on the parlor door. Charlotte, Cole, and Dorrie file in. Marc takes up the rear, the journal secreted behind his back.

"Greetings, my dears, how lovely to see all of you," Lola says from her seat at the tea table. Suddenly, she spies Dorrie. "What's *she* doing here?"

Dorrie sits defiantly down on the swan couch, reaches for a scone, and eying Lola takes a big bite.

"Marc, what is the meaning of this?" Lola demands.

As Dorrie sits chewing, her eyes twinkling with glee, Marc takes a deep breath. "Lola, I've asked the family here because there is something important we have to tell you."

"That woman is *not* family."

Charlotte takes Lola's hand. "I tell you what. You listen to what Marc has to say and then tell us if you feel the same way. He's going to read what your father wrote just before he had his stroke and fell from the tower stairs."

As Lola stares in astonishment, Marc opens the captain's journal and begins to read aloud.

December 29ᵗʰ, 1951 - HomePort

So many years have passed, yet these words are still difficult to write. Even so, I must, for a sense of the end of things has overtaken me these past few days. Before I am called to whatever fate awaits me, my daughter, Aloisa, and her sister, Andoria, must know the truth.

Once the legal provisions I am planning and this testament are complete, my earthly work is done. I shall leave this journal with the others, under lock and key, with instructions for my children to read it upon my death. Coward that I am, this written confession must suffice.

Annie remains part child, part woman—kind, gentle, and simple in mind—to this very day. Now past sixty, she has the same innocence and grace as when we first met. According to the Castletons, she still saves a special smile just for me.

For more than a quarter-century, I have traveled nearly two hundred miles each week to sit in silence with her for a few short hours. When they discontinued passenger rail service, I rode the freight train. Given it loaded near the plant, it was easy enough to negotiate for the engineers to accommodate me in the cab. A few extra dollars and a word to their supervisors saw to total discretion. In the afternoon, I'd make my way to Yarmouth, spend the night with an old friend, and ride the morning freight back to town.

I've hardly missed a week's visit with my beloved in all that time. She always seems to recognize me, though she has never regained her use of language. Ours is a communion of knowing on a different plane. I sense the same quiet comfort I felt when first we recognized our mutual affection, and I find more solace in a single hour with her than in all the years of my accursed marriage.

Castleton and his wife have been kind beyond all expectation. Their daughter, Vendra, named for another Staunton ship, has come to love Annie, whom she has known from birth as "Auntie." They play together as Lola and Dorrie once did, disparate in age, united by isolation. The irony is not lost on me that a child was provided where fate had robbed Annie of her own. I see God's mercy in that.

Castleton's sister in-law, the much-loved Cookie, saw Dorrie through to womanhood and died of cancer just two years after achieving that goal. She approached the task with rare dedication, raising my daughter as her own, encouraging her to be loyal, courageous, and generous of heart. Cookie was mother, teacher, mentor, and friend to the young girl who, by constant proximity, absorbed her self-sufficiency, strong values, and fierce sense of justice. I cannot overstate my gratitude to the woman who forfeited twenty years of her life to raise a child I was forbidden to acknowledge. Cookie gave all that I could not, saying all the while that Dorrie brought meaning to her widowed existence.

Once again, I write another litany of cowardice and deceit. This time, I blame no one but myself, which makes my task even more difficult. Certain there is little time left, I have finally resolved to overcome the forces set in motion by my wife's hatefulness. The pall that hovers over the next generation must be cast aside. Enough prevarication. Let me begin.

For much of their youth and young adulthood, my two children, Lola and Dorrie, were fast friends. In our isolated world back then, there was little distinction between friendship and kinship. Not knowing they might be sisters, the two women bonded as such, spending countless hours in heartfelt companionship. The fact they loved each other without need of a shared name was a source of great comfort to me. Yet, in a single day, that bond was severed like the parting of an anchor chain. Whether they discovered my shame or succumbed to rumor, I was afraid to ask, but some immutable wedge was driven between them. Their estrangement grieves me more than I can say, and I fervently wish they will reconcile after reading this missive.

I should have broken my silence years ago, but the weight of my pain is such I have lived this last quarter century by staving off all emotion, lest I lose the will to carry on. I hid behind a facade of gruffness and distance, knowing of the scandal that tarnished my good name, while sworn to endure it in silence. That is why I kept you, Dorrie, at a distance. I could not look at you without seeing my beloved Annie, particularly as you grew to womanhood. Many were the times I watched you lovingly from the tower, only to find within the hour I was crossing Commercial Street to avoid you.

Marc studies Dorrie closely. Her eyes are closed. Her breath comes in short gasps. He is consumed by joy that he has provided what she's searched for all her life. Dorrie seems to sense his thoughts. She opens her eyes, smiles, then makes a subtle gesture as if saying "get on with it." Marc gets on with it.

As I watch the sun set over the bay for what may well be the last time, I realize mine has been a life of cowardice in the realm of personal relationships. While undaunted by whale or wave, I have trembled at the thought of admitting my flawed humanity to two young women. As my life force sets like the red orb before me, I realize what a staggering loss of meaning and fulfillment this fear has engendered.

When I saw Annie yesterday for what I am certain was the last time, I begged her forgiveness for having ruined her life. She put her hand over her heart and smiled as if to contradict everything I had said. Love, contentment, and trust radiated from her as if from some greater, all-knowing source. Either she has forgiven me long ago, or her soul has transcended to that better place where forgiveness is a matter of course.

Annie is as sweet and pure, simple and trusting, as she was when I first realized my great passion for her. I could not have helped but love her with every fiber of my being. Our love is the mainstay of my dismal existence, and I go to my maker certain of the rightness of it.

Even so, the litany of my failings assaults my brain like a jackhammer. I was a cad to keep Annie from our child. I made an orphan of Dorrie, though I, her father, lived but yards away. As Death seeks me out, all too late I see my actions for what they were: unconscionable, cowardly, and destructive to those I loved most. Given the enormity of my crimes, I expect neither forgiveness nor salvation. Even so, there are steps I can take before departing this world that may bring some small comfort to those whom I have wronged.

Dearest Lola, I trust you with all my heart to do what is right. Aloysius Grubb took the Staunton secrets with him to his grave. With my passing, you and your sister will be the only ones who know the truth and the only ones who matter. Please, for the sake of the man I strived to be if only in my aspirations, please see these wishes are executed.

Marc studies Lola. She seems to stare across the room as if reliving all sorts of memories. Dorrie is also watching her closely, anxiety clouding her features. Marc glances quizzically at Charlotte, as if to ask whether he should continue. She nods her head, as does Helena, her brown eyes filled with concern. He returns to the journal entry.

Tomorrow I shall set up a fund with Grubb Junior to ensure that the weekly payments for Annie's sustenance continue beyond my death. My devoted first mate and his family shall not want for anything in this life. I shall leave them one hundred thousand for their loyalty. Young Grubb will add a codicil to my will placing Dorrie, Lola, and Annie under the direct protection of the HomePort Trust, which he shall oversee. The prior arrangements I made for Dorrie's welfare are simply not enough. She is a Staunton and should inherit as such. Grubb shall see that all is made right, of that I am certain. He is as loyal and trustworthy as his father.

With those tasks resolved, I shall go to my fate in peace. Bring on the demons of retribution. I am steeled and ready for them. No hell could be greater than the one I have endured in this miserable life. May God have mercy on my undeserving soul.

Marc sets down the journal and looks at Lola, then Dorrie. "The captain signed and dated this, and from what we can tell, put it in a compartment at the bottom of the dumbwaiter, started down the ladder, and had his stroke."

Lola brings her hand to her throat, clutching her necklace so hard that a red line wells up on her neck. Dorrie watches intently as if willing her to be strong. Cole gives Annie's locket to Lola whose hands are shaking so badly Helena has to open it for her. Lola stares at the photographs inside.

"I've been living in a fantasy world," she says at last. "I've held this mausoleum together for six decades to honor a family that isn't mine. What a wasted life. There, I've finally said it out loud. Lord knows, I've told myself the same thing so many times before." She looks so bereft everyone in the room remains silent. At last, Dorrie speaks in a soft, loving voice so out of character Marc has to look twice to be certain who is talking.

"Now you see here, Lola, dear. It ain't no way like you just said. You've given love and support to people that needed it most. You've made your own family right out of your own life. That ain't no waste, not by a long shot. There's not one in a million that could do that. Most people would just sit around feeling sorry for themselves. None of these folks, including me, would have hung around this mausoleum as you call it, for a hot second if it weren't for you. Yes, you treated me like shit for nearly sixty years, but I never stopped loving you, Sister. Not for one instant. And now I understand why, so the past don't matter no more."

"But we'll never know if we are sisters or not," Lola says, barely getting the words out. "Even Father wasn't certain. He never made those changes to his will. You have to believe me, Dorrie. I'd have done what he wanted. I've always felt I wasn't entitled to all of this, even if there's no way to prove it now."

Cole looks around the room and then speaks in a somber voice. "Oh yes there is. A simple DNA test will tell."

"And resolve issues around the estate that might otherwise take years of litigation," Charlotte adds in a whisper.

Lola and Dorrie's eyes meet. Everyone else holds their breath until Dorrie bangs her fist on the tea table. "Now wait just a goddamn moment. That money is Lola's. I've got all I'll ever need from the annuity the captain—I mean, my father—left me. I got a house paid for free and clear, and most important, I have all of you. There's not a goddamn thing in the world I want except to make up for the time Lola and I lost, and maybe a little something more to calm my nerves."

She holds out her cup to Lola who pours the whiskey with hands shaking so badly that Charlotte leans over to steady them. Then Dorrie points at Lola. "And you—you've got this big old place running like clockwork. Charlotte's makin' money hand over fist. The gang here takes care of the house for you. What are we talkin' 'bout at our age? It ain't like we're gonna throw our caps over the windmill. Let's just take whatever time God will give us to get back to the way we used to be. What's DNA gonna tell us that we don't already know in our hearts? Cole and Marc aren't your sons, but you love them as if they was. You love Charlotte like a daughter. Helena's not your daugh...." Dorrie pauses for a moment, a perplexed look on her face, her momentum stalled by the unexpected territory in which she finds herself. "Let me try again. Helena's not your son, neither, but you love her, I mean him—"

"Like a daughter," Helena interrupts, bringing a much-needed laugh.

Dorrie blushes slightly, though her dark eyes remain focused on Lola. "Whatever. What I'm tryin' to say is that we've all made family of each other. A better goddamn family than most, if you ask me." She folds her arms in smug determination as Lola searches the room for reassurance. One by one, everyone else slowly nods in agreement.

Lola rises from her chair, totters to the couch where Dorrie is sitting, throws her arms around her, and kisses her on the lips. "Sister," is the sole word Lola can muster before her tears start to fall on Dorrie's upturned face.

Grave Doings

HomePort enters a golden age. The house once filled with yearning now brims with warmth, affection, and good humor. Dorrie spends every day with her sister, reminiscing and helping her to prepare the Staunton papers for the Historical Society. The two women often laugh without cause when others are present, as if enjoying some compelling, private joke.

After a few weeks, Cole and Marc swap living arrangements with Dorrie, who moves into the big house to be near Lola. The men quickly establish a comfortable routine of work in the tower and studio in the morning, a long walk with Frida in the afternoon, tea with Lola, Helena, and Dorrie at four, and dinner a deux save Saturday night, when the family gathers at HomePort and talks until the wee hours.

Marc often wakes before Cole and lies silent, awed by his presence, recalling the choices and events that brought them together. From the worst moments of his prior life has come a new life overflowing with contentment. The thought humbles him beyond his capacity to do it justice, reinforcing his commitment to give Cole the time and space he needs.

Lola arranges for the captain and his beloved Annie to be reunited in HomePort's cemetery. Shortly thereafter, Daryl is brought to his new resting place beside a monument inscribed with both Lola and Dorrie's names. It's as if the two women are assembling loved ones within HomePort's bounds as some sort of provision for the afterlife.

Trial by Jury

Cole, Charlotte, and Marc huddle at the Bookstore Restaurant in Wellfleet, drinking mulled cider to warm themselves. An hour earlier, the judge in the trial of Grubb vs. Thetford and Conner had issued his verdict in Charlotte's favor.

"Hal's testimony was compelling," Cole says to Charlotte. "I'm glad you took Helena's advice and advertised to find him. It really strengthened our case."

"Yes. Fortunately, he read my ad in the *Banner*. It's so strange he happened to be in the Macho Bar with a pocket recorder, but I guess a lot of reporters carry one in case a story develops. Hearing Brandon describe Alan and Chuck's breach of intent on that tape seems to have had a huge impact on the judge. I wish Hal hadn't left so quickly. I wanted to ask him to come with us, but I guess he had to make a deadline."

Cole seems keen to change the subject. "Speaking of Brandon, what do you think will happen since he didn't appear in court?"

"He's in contempt, and the judge seems inclined to follow through with a sentence. I've asked my attorney to propose court-supervised rehabilitation. Brandon's a mess. I tried to see him in New York before we served his subpoena, but I couldn't get past his door. He's staying in a flophouse. By the look of things, he's one step away from living on the street."

Marc winces at the thought.

CHAPTER 15
A LIFE WELL SPENT

As if determined to make up for lost time, Lola hires an army of caterers for a spectacular New Year's Eve celebration. By the time Marc and Cole arrive, HomePort, lavishly decorated by a battalion of local florists, is ablaze with light and festivity. At ten that evening, thirty honored guests sit down at the massive dining table that has not served such a gathering for more than eighty years.

Lola sits at the captain's place at the head of the table, Dorrie at the far end, in Prudence's seat. Everyone is there: Dolores, Helena in a magnificent gown with train, Charlotte and Brad, as well as many friends from town. Dolores' son, Jimmy, stuns the assembled guests. Clean-shaven, his jet-black hair trimmed, and his ample frame tucked into a rented tuxedo, he seems more a suave South American gigolo than a ubiquitous handyman. The transformation is so profound Marc has to look twice. Catching his eye, Dolores seems ready to burst with maternal pride.

Minutes before midnight, Lola signals the waiters to serve champagne, rises from the table, and holds her glass high. "My dears, this is the last of the Joseph Perrier my father set down. I can think of no better company with whom to share it. I'd like to ask you to join in something that would please him immensely. Would you all be so kind as to rise and drink a toast to his beloved daughter who at long last takes her rightful place at HomePort. To my dear sister, Andoria!"

Those not in the know stare at each other in mute surprise. Dolores' mouth gapes. Marc savors a moment of triumph. His detective work has successfully eluded her able reconnaissance. Recovering quickly, the assembled friends stand and cheer, "To Andoria!"

Marc sips the champagne cautiously, assuming it will be decades past its prime. He's stunned to find it magnificent. Suddenly he hears the captain's voice.

You don't think I'd allow bad champagne at a time like this? This moment deserves the very best. I've been protecting that vintage for decades for just this moment, you fool.

Marc chuckles to himself. He's grown accustomed to such commentary within the bounds of HomePort.

Dorrie stands, smiles as if embarrassed, then fends off further attention with a wave of both hands.

Jimmy, none the worse for several glasses of wine, yells, "Speech!"

Dorrie seems to stand a bit taller. She smiles shyly, her eyes bright. "As a matter of fact there *is* somethin' I want to say," she begins, as the guests around the table grow silent. "First, everybody but Lola, please sit down. Sister, you stay put."

Lola begins to protest, but Helena, seated to her left, leans over, takes her hand, and whispers. To Marc's surprise, Lola does just as Dorrie asks. When the expectant guests are seated, Dorrie raises her glass.

"New Year's is about new beginnin's, and we've certainly seen a lot of them 'round this joint lately. We're finally together as a family after all these long, empty years, with new friends and old. This here's a moment to remember, folks. I ask you all to stop for a moment and think where you'd be without the kindness and caring of my dear sister."

Lola makes a dismissive gesture as if to silence Dorrie, who thumbs her nose in return. "No way, Lola, you won't get your way this time. There's some things that just gotta be said. Whether you want it to or not, it's time for the truth to come out."

For a second, Lola's face loses color and her knuckles whiten. Dorrie seems not to notice.

Marc urgently whispers to Cole, "Is Dorrie off her rocker? She's not going to tell them about Lola's real father, is she? People don't need to know the whole truth. What Lola just said was enough."

When Cole rolls his eyes, Marc turns his attention back to Dorrie who takes a deep breath and continues, her voice somber.

"I want you to look around, Sister, at all these people. You've touched the lives of every one of 'em—and more— in ways that made all the difference. When people were sick and couldn't pay their bills, you made it look like the doctor forgot to send them. When kids needed money for college, you saw to it they got a Staunton scholarship. When folks built a theater, you paid for the roof anonymously. When whales were tangled or dolphins stranded, you funded their rescue. I could go on and on, and you know it.

"Everyone in this room knows Provincetown's always been a special place. Some would even say magical. What they don't know is all you've done to keep it that way. You've thrown Staunton money around like hayseeds while holed up in your fancy parlor, always making sure no one knew for certain what you were up to. Without you, folks would never have found love, nor their true reason for livin'.

"You're always talking about the Staunton legacy. Well, Sister, I'm here to tell you you've lived up to it in every sense of the word. I may have just learned I'm a Staunton, but I've always known you're the best of the lot."

Staring Dorrie in the eye, Lola raises her glass in one hand as her other clenches the table for support. Then she looks from one friend to another with pride and the slightest trace of self-consciousness. Her lips work as if she's about to say something in reply, then she shakes her head, straightens her shoulders, and, with a self-deprecating smile and a toss of her head, drains her glass.

Time stands still. Lola's white hair shines like a halo in the candlelight. Her diamond pendant flashes with fire in the light from the chandelier. As the group applauds, she casts a gracious glance around the room and then, with dignity befitting a monarch, bows her head in acknowledgment.

Seated to her right, Marc sees a single tear trickle down her cheek as the grandfather's clock strikes midnight.

All Good Things…

Two days later, Marc is summoned from his house to the mistress's parlor early in the morning. He finds Dorrie and Lola in animated conversation. Dorrie stands as soon as he enters the room.

"Marc, go get your car. We gotta sneak Lola out of here and get her to Boston, right away."

"What do you mean, sneak?"

"Well, the only way I can get this stubborn old goat to see a specialist is if there's no fuss. I know that much for sure. I made an appointment at Mass General a week ago. I just told her 'bout it, and she says she's not goin'."

"I'm not following you." Marc feels his stomach constrict. He looks rapidly away from Lola.

"I'm afraid you're in the midst of a *teedjous* family battle, Marc," Lola says with a wan smile. "I've known for some time I have a severe heart condition. Dorrie has wanted to shanghai me off to Boston for treatment from the moment I told her about it."

It's clear from Dorrie's tone she's retracing old ground. "Why the hell not? It's not like you can't afford it."

Lola seems to be enjoying the confrontation. "My dear sister. As I've told you a hundred times, I refuse to leave HomePort under any circumstances. We all have to die sometime. I've been hanging on for the holidays, and New Year's was such a great swan song I'm perfectly ready to go."

Dorrie scowls. "Can you talk some sense into her, Marc? She's as stubborn as can be. There might be somethin' they can do for her in Boston."

"Yes, they could medicate me so I don't know who I am, stick me full of needles, and strap monitors on me. That's no way to live, like a vegetable. Not for me, thank you very much."

"Marc, I'm hopin' she'll listen to you."

"I'm not sure I should be weighing in on this, but I do have a couple of questions. Lola, do you have any pain?"

"None."

"Any symptoms?"

"A little shortness of breath if I walk too fast, but nothing that gets in my way."

"Are you satisfied with your life? Any unfinished business?"

"I'm completely satisfied. Now that Dorrie and I have patched things up and said what needed to be said, there's no unfinished business."

"What does your doctor say will happen?"

"A massive, fatal heart attack. He says it's inevitable."

"Or one that leaves you with one foot in the grave and one out. No way to live or die," Dorrie mutters.

"What do *you* want Lola?" Marc asks.

"To be *compos mentis* for whatever time I have left and die in my own bed. I want my sister and the rest of my family around me. I've had quantity of life. I want quality, now. I want to live until I die, no in-between. At this point, I'd trade one last hour with all of you for a year of medically-sustained limitations."

Dorrie's dudgeon is gradually melting into misty-eyed resignation. "Done in by my own devices. You two! Damn you both! I give up!"

Lola smiles in triumph. "Now, Marc, not a word to anyone but Cole. I don't want any special treatment. I'm counting on the two of you to be ready when the time comes. In the meantime, I don't want Helena overdoing it. She'd have me in traction before I could get a word in edgewise."

Dorrie shakes her head. "Once again, high-and-mighty Lola Staunton gets what she wants. Bridge or rummy, you spoiled old coot?"

"Cribbage."

All too familiar with the squabbling that will continue for most of the day, Marc takes this as his cue to leave.

* * * *

January 23rd, 2011 – Dorrie's House

Death came gently for Lola—dear, wonderful, crotchety Lola—at home in her own bed, just as she wished. There were no advance symptoms, just the long-anticipated heart attack, only three weeks after her New Year's triumph.

Dorrie is so attuned to HomePort and all of us, she must be psychic. She says she heard something in the middle of the night—as if the house let out a great moan. She went to check on Lola, found her unconscious, and called to say we should come. By the time Cole, Helena, and I got there, Lola was barely breathing. Dorrie was cradling Lola's head in her hands, whispering not to be afraid. As we gathered beside the bed, Charlotte arrived. As if she'd been waiting for her, Lola looked up at us with the most beautiful, loving eyes, smiled contentedly, and it was over.

At that moment, I had an amazing vision, as if Lola's essence ascended right in front of me. Not to heaven in the traditional sense, but into a body of spirits stretching back in time. I sensed many of them had a profound love for HomePort and each other. I know it sounds crazy, but I'll stand by what I saw. It's as though the forces that haunt this place let me see behind the curtain so I'd know Lola's spirit lived on amongst them. We never proved whether she was the captain's daughter, she and Dorrie never wanted to know, but it was immediately clear these spirits considered her a Staunton. Dorrie was right. Lola was the best of the lot.

The cadre of spirits greeted her with a depth of love that struck me dumb. I somehow understood they'd been watching over her for her entire life. For the first time, I saw the captain. Tall, stern, and quite the hunk! He embraced Lola as the others crowded around her. I know this sounds nuts, but I swear he smiled at me. Lola looked back to see what he was smiling at and then waved at me. She looked so happy and seemed to want me to know she'd come home. I saw Lettie take her hand, then they all faded away in a gentle light.

This happened in an instant that felt like an hour. No one else in the room seemed to notice, although Cole told me later that he saw the strangest look of contentment on my face. He said I seemed so peaceful he worried I'd taken leave of my senses.

I'm totally convinced now that what I saw in the journal and on the moors that night wasn't just in my head. Somehow, knowing that for certain changes everything, and just in time to reassure the others that Lola is at peace in a better kind of existence.

Now I know all this, I can deal with her passing. After all, she was more than ready to go. But it's still the end of a great legacy. Aloisa Davis Staunton, Mistress of HomePort, Lady of the Manor, Mother of us all. Dead at ninety-six. I'm so glad I knew you, Lola. Thank you for taking a chance on me. It changed everything.

* * * *

Three days pass before Charlotte feels up to her designated duties. When the family finally assembles for the reading of Lola's will, Dorrie is conspicuously absent. Charlotte shrugs when Marc asks where she is. "Dorrie said to say she's already read it, and it's old news. She's in the kitchen, making squid stew for dinner. She told Dolores to take the night off to prevent her from snooping."

There are few surprises. The Morrison portrait is donated to the Art Center with the strict proviso it never be seen in the HomePort mansion again. Cole is instructed to deliver the painting whenever he no longer needs its inspiration. Other than some gifts to charity, provisions for Jimmy and Dolores, and a generous bequest to Vendra Castleton, Lola has left the HomePort Trust intact, with Dorrie replacing her as its sole beneficiary.

When Charlotte is finished, Helena produces champagne and four glasses. "Lola used to joke this would be her epitaph if she hit the right age. Far as I'm concerned, she came close enough, so I'd like to read it anyways. It's from the gravestone of a woman named Rebecca Freeland who died in 1741 in Nottingham, England, and it goes like this, 'She drank good ale, good punch, and wine—and lived to the age of ninety-nine.' Helena raises her glass. "Here's to Lola. Safe travels, my dear, safe travels. Say hi to Bette, Mae, and the other gals for me. Don't you worry darling, I'll see to it HomePort is cared for."

* * * *

A few days later, Dorrie, now Mistress of HomePort, moves her bedroom to the captain's study. She continues the ritual of tea at four beginning with a toast to Cole's stunning portrait of Lola that dominates the ornate room from the very spot where the Morrison had once hung. She's seated in her swan chair, wearing her pointed glasses and all her jewelry. Beside her is a half-empty teacup. Her lips are pursed as though she's about to tell a joke or make a caustic remark. Cole's rendering displays a captivating combination of warmth, wit, strength, determination, and perhaps most compellingly, love and contentment. Hers is the face of a woman who lived life on her own terms. Studying the portrait, Marc reflects with pride that Cole's mastery has captured Lola's many contradictions.

Cole and Marc deliver the Morrison portrait to the Art Association the very next day. Cole has no further need for an in-house critic. His works are selling well. At long last, the portrait of Prudence Staunton, executed in the early days of her ill-fated marriage, leaves HomePort for good. From that day forth, Marc swears he can see the captain and his beloved Annie in the tower at sunset, arms entwined, staring contentedly over the bay.

CHAPTER 16
SOME ENCHANTED
EVENING

In October, Helena emcees the Fantasia Fair Follies, a joyous cabaret, part of the annual transgender conference. Cole, Dorrie, and Marc go to the Crown and Anchor to see the show, a first for all of them.

Helena enters from above in a giant bubble, passing over the audience like Glinda the Good Witch from *The Wizard of Oz*. Reaching the stage, she takes a large safety pin from her bra and pops the bubble. Suddenly she's covered in plastic wrap, struggling comically to get out, cursing, tearing, and tottering back and forth. Finally extricating herself, she looks less like Glinda than a deranged Margo Channing. Her makeup is smudged, her hair in disarray.

She seems startled to see an audience. "Oh shit! The Crown," she says in a blowsy manner, as if having had one too many cocktails. "I was headed to Paris for fashion week and had to ditch. It was such a bumpy ride, and I simply could not figure how to fasten my seat belt. I should have known not to book a no-frills flight."

A handsome, shirtless young man in tuxedo pants, a bow tie, and suspenders, pushes a drink cart onstage.

Helena reaches for an enormous martini. "Oh well," she says, ogling the young man, "I guess there's no place like home." She raises the giant glass in a toast, takes a large swig, smacks her lips, shades her eyes, and peers into the crowd. "So what's going on here? Miss America? Or is it Fantasia Fair Follies?"

The crowd roars, "Follies."

Helena responds with a hand to her ear. "Follies? Oh, I just *adore* Follies. I'm so glad I dropped in. I love you gals! And so does all of Provincetown!"

The audience cheers, applauds, and stomps their feet until Helena signals for silence. "Seriously, now. I understand we have some real talent here tonight, and I know I'm keeping them. But there are few things I'd like to say from the heart. First to the performers. Ladies, have a ball tonight. You can't lose! We're mad about you already, darlings!" Helena blows a kiss backstage. "I certainly sympathize with what it takes to pull all this off: makeup, heels, girdles, and those damn pantyhose! The price we girls pay for beauty. And the effort it takes to maintain standards these days. Where has all the glamour gone? And style? And grace?"

As Helena drags a well-manicured hand across her brow, Marc and Cole nudge each other, then beam with pride.

Helena runs her fingers through her hair in half-hearted attempt to tidy it. "Then there are the hazards for stylish women in just getting about this town. Why just the other day, I was walking down Carver Street on my way to brunch at Bubala's. I don't feel dressed unless I'm wearing my stilettos, and that day was no exception. Full-figured girls like me—and I see quite a few of us in the audience tonight—have to be *verrry* careful on that hill. You know the one I mean, ladies. Gravity *will* take its toll.

"I stumbled a bit, right at the top, and it was off to the races. Mind you, I didn't fall but just kept tottering down the hill, across Commercial Street and into Café Heaven. Folks who saw me said it looked like a downhill event at the Winter Olympics. Fortunately, I landed in an empty chair beside two startled queens. I had a nice brunch, and I don't think they minded all that much once they got over the shock of my arrival. Contrary to what you bitches may have heard, I *did* offer to pay the tip."

Helena takes another exaggerated sip from her drink. "I guess what I'm *trying* to say is that it's tough out there, even in flats. Just think, though. If it weren't for dames like us, it would be simply *ghaaastly*. We *have* to watch out for one another and try to bring as much beauty as we can into this cold, cruel world. I'm sure you'll agree the ladies you're going to see tonight do just that. They're beautiful, both inside and out.

"Enough of me for now. I'll be back later with a couple of songs. How 'bout a hand for these wonderful performers? Let's bring 'em on in style with a good old-fashioned P'Town welcome."

Helena finishes her drink and exits to a prolonged standing ovation.

You Just Never Know

After the performance, Marc waits while Helena changes. Then they set out to join Dorrie and Cole at The Mews. Braving the damp fall winds in high heels, a strapless evening gown, and mink stole, Helena is so elated she covers several blocks of Commercial Street without seeming to notice the chill.

Reaching the Governor Bradford, she makes a quick appearance at drag karaoke, waves to the fishermen in the Old Colony, then heads to the Lobster Pot to work the room. At each detour, Marc waits patiently on the sidelines, knowing Helena wants to prolong a well-deserved triumph. At last, they reach the Mews and join their friends at a downstairs table.

"You were incredible," Dorrie gushes. "The way you kept the show movin', and your own routines! I loved that Ethel Merman bit. And your Peggy Lee! You oughta be on Broadway!"

Helena quickly downs Cole's glass of water, then winks at Marc. "Peggy's always held a special place in my heart. I got the idea from a review of her Broadway show. One critic wrote, 'She was so laid back, she was laid out.' It was good to get back out there again, but I have to say, those girls tonight deserve all the credit. Just think of the courage it took for them to get up on that stage."

Marc is quick to agree. "You said it. I sit by myself at a desk and fret about putting words on a page. Compared to them, I feel like a wimp. What they did took real balls."

Helena replies with a mischievous grin. "That's for sure, darling, and don't forget their balls are tucked up inside and taped down."

Cole chokes with laughter. "I guess that explains why there were no equestrian acts."

A swarthy man with a full black beard approaches, nervously shifting from foot to foot in front of their table. Marc had noticed him following them on Commercial Street and had almost confronted him out of fear for Helena's safety. The man is in his late thirties, over six-four with weather-beaten skin and dark, smoldering eyes. A tweed sports coat spans his broad shoulders as though its seams might part at any moment.

"May I help you?" Marc's voice has a strong warning in it. Even so, the man steps closer and catches Helena's eye.

"Excuse me, ma'am?"

"Yes?" Helena says, sounding apprehensive. "I've seen you before. You were watching me from the wings."

"Yes. Yes, I was," the nervous man replies, his face suddenly alight with pleasure. "I hope you don't mind, but I just had to tell you how impressed I was. You're quite the star. We don't get many like you in this neck of the woods."

"You can damn well say that again," Dorrie mumbles into her Brandy Alexander.

"Why thank you," Helena purrs, as Marc casts an admonishing glance her way. "Wasn't the show marvelous? Were you one of the performers? I'm terribly sorry. Things were so hectic backstage, I'm afraid I didn't notice."

"No ma'am, I just helped out with set changes. My cousin works at the Crown, and he asked me to give him a hand. Besides, I'm not sure I'd look good in those fancy gowns."

Helena smiles seductively. "Well you're not doing badly with what you're wearing."

"I'm not usually this dressed up. They asked me to wear a sport coat because it was on stage and such." He catches himself rambling and actually blushes.

Helena immediately comes to his rescue. "A man after my own heart. I've always appreciated the minimalist look in menswear. As far as I'm concerned, anything more than a smile is overdressed."

Marc kicks Helena's foot. She avoids his glare and smiles graciously at the man. "Do you have time to join us? These are my dear friends, Cole, Dorrie, and my chaperone, Marcus."

The man seems stunned by his good fortune. "I'd be honored, if you're sure I'm not intruding...."

"Oh, I'm sure. Trust me, I'm sure. Have a seat. Oh my, I don't know your name."

"It's Butch, Ma'am."

"Of course. Of course it is. I should have known." Helena seems ready to float out of the room at any moment, bubble or no bubble.

"Well my real name's Arthur, but folks have always called me Butch."

"I can't begin to imagine why. You'll have to tell me sometime." Helena sounds just like Marilyn Monroe singing, "Happy Birthday, Mr. President."

Marc leans over to Cole and whispers, "I give up. I've done all I can to warn her."

"Glad to hear it. He's as sweet as can be."

Dorrie adds, "And way out of his league, the poor bastard."

Butch pulls up a chair. "I work on the Maggie G. down at the wharf. She's a dragger."

"He should be right at home with Helena, then," Dorrie says in a stage whisper. "The way she's carrying on, she'll be draggin' him outta here in five minutes. She's sure got big ones, even if they *are* taped down. He's in for one hell of a surprise when he unwraps that package."

CHAPTER 17
A HAPPY DEATH

Marc wakes with a start at three in the morning. It's his turn to sleep in Dorrie's room, and his first thought is that she's roaming again. Tiptoeing to her bed, he studies her frail body in the dim moonlight. She's so thin her bones show. Her face is a disconcerting shade of gray. Her gradual decline over the past year has prepared him for her passing in some ways, but he still struggles with her inevitable departure. He draws close to listen. Dorrie's breaths are shallow, but one still follows another.

"Marc, get yourself to your own bed and get some rest. I don't need nobody watchin' me sleep, goddamn it." She's lucid for the first time in months, and Marc is overjoyed.

"C'mon Dorrie, try to remember. We've talked about this. Sometimes you're a bit fuzzy, and you don't know where you are. We agreed that someone would stay with you in case you woke up and were...."

"Out of it? Go ahead, say it. That's what you mean, ain't it?"

"Well, yes."

"We gotta face the goddamn facts, Marc. It's my time. You wouldn't believe the folks I've seen while I'm outta my head. I'm ready to go. They're waitin' for me."

Marc shudders. *But I'm not ready for you to go.*

As if reading his mind, Dorrie props herself on one elbow and takes him to task. "Now see here, Marcus Nugent. If you think I'm leaving you guys, you've got another thought comin'. I'm gonna haunt this place 'til you're sick of me, and even then you won't be able to get rid of me."

Marc takes her hand, recalling when they first met at the Purple Feather. She'd been so feisty, stealing his hot chocolate and calling him a "runnah." Her hand seems even smaller than when she'd first offered it that day.

Memories assail him: their weekly Scrabble matches, her stories of the "old days" in Provincetown, her faithful tending of the Staunton cemetery—a task Marc had taken on a year ago when she was found disoriented in Pilgrims' Park. Despite that episode, she'd adamantly refused to give up her daily visits. Marc had accompanied her every day from then on, weather permitting, sitting beside her on a wooden bench that Cole had built for her. He'd listen to her reminisce, learning even more about life at HomePort when she was young. He'd sometimes sense the other spirits congregating around her. Nothing definite, just a sense of warmth and contentment, as if they were preparing to welcome her.

When Dorrie was confined to a wheelchair, he wheeled her to the same spot. When she grew too weak for that, she begged him to continue the ritual without her, which he had, sometimes sensing the captain's grateful presence, other times Lettie's cautious approbation. There'd been no sign of Lola.

Dorrie looks up at him from the bed, her face radiant. "I'm between two worlds, Marc. I'm glad you guys are watchin' out for me in this one, don't get me wrong. But don't blame me for wantin' to leave it. My body is old and worn out. My mind don't work as it should. I've done all I want to do in this lifetime thanks to you and the others. Especially you, though. You made all the difference."

Marc feels a catch in his throat. "No Dorrie, you did that for me. You cared for me when I had no one else in the world to turn to. I never understood what you saw in me."

Dorrie stares up at him, her dark eyes shining. "Marc, I knew from the moment we met you was one in a million underneath all that fear and hurt. I'm damn proud of what you've become—as proud as I've been of anyone in my life. You've tended me and Lola as if we were your own kin. We're both so grateful for that, and we love you like the son we never had. It's your turn now, Marc. Your turn to live. Trust me. Use some of that love and carin' on yourself. Live, love, and laugh. Don't waste a single second of your days on earth. Be what you want to be, do what you want to do, and don't doubt yourself when I'm gone. Promise?"

"Promise," Marc answers, breaking into tears.

Dorrie smiles with such peace and certainty that calm and acceptance slowly descend upon him, though he still wishes for even more time with her. Despite their private moments at the cemetery, these last years have focused primarily on the HomePort family.

Dorrie responds as if reading his thoughts. "Now, no more of this weepin' and shit. I'm glad to have been here, but I'm also damn glad to go. I always knew you'd be here to take over when they come for me." She pauses for a moment as a quizzical look crosses her face. "And, goddamn it, I was right." She gasps, as if hit by a sudden shock. Her head falls back on the pillow, her breathing labored and sporadic.

Marc sprints to Helena's room. Pounding on the door, he yells frantically, "Helena, I think this is it. Call Charlotte and Cole. Dorrie's dying. I'm going back down to her."

Within a matter of minutes, Helena and Cole reach Dorrie's bedside. The body before them seems so unfamiliar, a mere shell that her powerful will has already departed. Dorrie's breathing grows slower and more labored as time passes. Helena sobs uncontrollably, leaning on Charlotte for support once she arrives. Cole stands behind Marc with arms wrapped around him, strong and calm except for gasps of breath that press his chest into his partner's back.

Shortly after sunrise, Dorrie regains consciousness. She looks around for Marc. Finding him, she smiles and says, "Thanks for being my friend." Then she turns to the others. "My family," is all she can muster before another spasm shakes her, and her eyes lose their focus.

That afternoon, Helena is adjusting the pillows when she sees Dorrie's lips move. Helena gestures for everyone to come close. As they do, Dorrie's face lights up in a wide smile. "Mother! Father! Daryl," she says in a loud voice, youthful, joyous, and certain. Then, "Sister!" And she breathes her last.

* * * *

January 8ᵗʰ, 2013 - The Tower, HomePort

She's gone. I still can't believe it. Dorrie's gone. She died on her birthday, having just turned eighty-eight a few hours before. She left so quietly. I expected her to cuss, swear, and fight death to the final round. Instead, she said her farewells and bowed out like a lady.

Cole is devastated. I'm doing everything I can to support him through horrific grief. He told me in bed last night that Dorrie and Lola made up for much of what he lost when his own family died. It's hell for him to lose a second set of parents. He'll be all right in time, though. I'll take good care of "The Man I Love."

Truth told, despite all I know of Lola's passing, I still feel as though someone cut my heart out. Dorrie knew from birth what her father learned far too late, and in so many ways, she taught me those lessons. I was always stronger for her faith in me. Then, of course, she was responsible for bringing Cole and me together. Now she expects me to carry on for her.

I'll do my best, dahlin'.

* * * *

At Dorrie's insistence, there are no calling hours, just a simple burial service in the Staunton plot. She's laid to rest between Daryl and Lola on a glorious winter day that bestows bright sun and the slightest anticipation of summer. Her mother's locket is clasped in her hands.

Marc presides, asking his friends to share impromptu remarks. Helena speaks of how Dorrie had saved her from the homophobic attacker. Butch shares for the first time that Dorrie had interviewed him the day he moved into Marvin's apartment. She'd brought a homemade apple pie, questioned him for nearly an hour and finally said, "I can rest easy now. All my kids are truly loved."

Recounting this, Butch breaks down. Helena steps forward to comfort him, placing her arms around him and resting his head on her shoulder. Others follow with similar tales of Dorrie's intuition and her gruff-but-loving nature. When it's Marc's turn, he asks Cole to stand with him behind the open grave. His back to the bay, Marc retrieves a piece of paper from his pocket. Then clearing his throat, he reads the eulogy he's written—the first of his writings ever to be read in public.

An orphan for most of life, Dorrie Machado gathered around her a family of her own making; as incongruous a crew as this town has ever seen. She loved us as her own kin, and all the more for our differences. With a face carved by salt and sunlight, and a diminutive frame that seemed stunted by fierce winds, she possessed a heart as strong as all those elements. Both intuitive and generous, Dorrie was at one with all that is right and just. This woman—daughter, sister, friend—gave unstintingly of her love. And we were all so much the better for her gift.

Now we grapple with our loss, though I am confident, loving us as she did, she is with us still. She swore she would be, and I've learned over the years she's always right. I picture her in the welcoming arms of her celestial family, others from this amazing place who've waited to be reunited with for her for so very long. We haven't lost Dorrie. We are merely sharing her love with them now, and trust me, there's more than enough to go around.

She's shown me enough love to last a lifetime, but now she's freed from the constraints of great age, I know she'll keep right on loving. I see Dorrie in all things. I feel her passion in the wind, see her joy in the morning sunrise, and sense her wisdom in the stars. She lives on in my hopes for my better self, and most of all, in the eyes of the man who just last night agreed to marry me. By caring so much for Cole and me as individuals, she brought us together and changed everything. So most of all, I see Dorrie in our dreams fulfilled.

Dorrie Machado, friend and kindred spirit—gentle guardian of this special place—rest easy and savor peace at last. Your love lives on in your children, whom you taught so very well, and in the legacy you leave behind.

In an improvised moment, Marc shares his final conversation with Dorrie, then asks his friends, including Dolores, Lydia, and Bea, to bear witness to his promise and help him live up to it.

He closes with a quote from Leonardo da Vinci: "As a well-spent day brings happy sleep, so a life well-spent brings happy death."

Where There's a Will There's a Way

After Dorrie's service, Charlotte instructs the family to return to HomePort for tea. The house seems vast, vacant, and ponderous, as if all life has drained from it. Marc searches for the energy he often feels from the old place, but as though in deep mourning, HomePort has nothing to say. He paces the hall lost in thought, sometimes smiling, sometimes wistful, until Helena escorts him to the parlor.

When the friends are seated, Cole unveils a portrait of Dorrie he has hung beside Lola's. The two paintings complement each other, highlighting likenesses of age and alacrity while capturing the unique and lovable quirkiness of the two women. They are both seated in swan chairs, having tea. Somehow, Cole has made the paintings seem like Lola and Dorrie are actually in the room.

Dorrie's companion portrait plays on her forthright nature. Her eyes shine with mirth, as if she's just delivered a caustic remark and is assessing its impact. Lola seems about to respond, and it's clear that Dorrie, leaning slightly forward in her chair with a teacup in her hand, is already contemplating her next move. The two women seem quite aware of an audience, as they so often were in those final days together.

Staring at the two portraits, Marc can almost hear their voices. Cole's works are so true to life, it's hard for the assembled friends to view them. Clearly, he'd painted both portraits at the same time and spent a great deal of time getting them just right. There's an uncharacteristic silence as each person in the room grapples with the finality of it all. It's the end of an era, what more can be said?

Charlotte takes a last gulp of her tea. It's real this time, not the usual distilled fare. She's taking no chances with her pregnancy. Then she steps in front of the portraits.

"This is tough for me, guys, so let's get it over with as quickly as possible," she sighs. "Individual bequests will be distributed at a later date, per Lola and Dorrie's instructions. They asked I read their final intentions as to the disposition of HomePort immediately after Dorrie's service, since that affects us all. They had Hart and Chandler handle everything. I felt being involved was a conflict of interest, so I know as much as you do at this point."

Charlotte unseals the envelope, and begins to read:

I, Andoria Machado, of Provincetown, do make this, my final will and testament, with a free hand. This document encompasses as well the final intentions of my beloved sister, Aloisa Davis Staunton, as agreed by us in the certain knowledge she would predecease me.

It is our intent to dispose of various items and funds too numerous to mention here in a manner suiting our temperament and long-held beliefs. As codicils to this document, instructions and bequests shall be delivered to recipients or discovered by same within the house and grounds of the HomePort estate. These notices shall be embossed with a seal identical to the one on this document, and are meant by us to have the same legal standing.

"So that was the big joke. A scavenger hunt," Marc whispers to Cole, who immediately hushes him.

Charlotte reads on, describing the creation of memorial museum to house Laetitia's paintings and provide a permanent home for the struggling historical society. Another bequest founds an artist and writers colony at HomePort. The colony has a mandate to support aspiring young individuals lacking the resources to pursue a career in the arts. The individuals selected, in addition to need and proven talent, must demonstrate the potential to embrace life without fear, show respect for all humanity, and find inspiration in diversity.

The group is informed that Cole, Marc, and Charlotte have been designated principal trustees of the colony. A handpicked board made up of like-minded community members will award HomePort fellowships to applicants vetted by an executive director. There are specific instructions that the director introduce HomePort's traditions to the fellows on their first day of residence.

"Why isn't Helena on the board?" Cole asks.

Charlotte ignores him and continues to read.

For services previously rendered, we gratefully bequeath the sum of forty million dollars to Harold Blithe. In addition, should he agree to accept the position, we appoint said Harold Blithe as the first full-time, resident, Executive Director of the HomePort colony. The position is his for life. A salary of one hundred thousand dollars per annum, along with a retirement program of equal value and life-long tenancy in the main house, is hereby bestowed upon the position. All HomePort traditions, most especially teatime, are to be scrupulously maintained under

*the aegis of said director, who is charged to care for HomePort
as if it were his own.*

Charlotte sets down the will

"Who the hell is Harold Blithe?" Cole asks.

"It's Hal, the fellow who testified at my trial," Charlotte
says, "but I don't understand why they left him all that
money and gave him that job."

Marc agrees. "I always thought Helena would care for
HomePort, as she always has. It seems cruel to cut her out
and leave everything to a perfect stranger, especially letting
Hal live there for the rest of his life when she should be the
one to stay on."

Through all this, Helena has been silent. When Marc
finally searches her face for a reaction, she bursts into
raucous laughter, as if she's pulled off the caper of a lifetime.
"Darling, I may be perfect, but I'm no stranger, let me tell
you. I've got forty million dollars, a good man, a job, and a
mansion for the rest of my life. More than a girl could ever
hope for in this two-bit town. Nothing cruel about any of
it, so far as I'm concerned."

Marc's jaw drops. "You're Hal?"

Cole jumps in, equally incredulous. "Who got Brandon
into Marvin's room?"

"And testified at my trial?" Charlotte shrieks.

Helena nods and smiles sweetly. "You had no idea?
Fabulous! I know you've never seen me out of drag but
really, my dears…." For a moment, she sounds just like
Lola. "Who else could have pulled it off? And, darlings, if
you tell anyone my legal name, you'll not live to repeat it.
I *hate* the name Harold. It's *sooo* gay, and as for Blithe, it's
simply *tooo* Noel Coward."

"Just a minute, Helena," Marc says. "There's no way you could be Hal. You called me at the Macho Bar when he was sitting with Brandon just ten feet away."

Helena seems more pleased by her subterfuge than her inheritance. "I did, and I didn't. Marvin dialed you on my cell phone and played a recording. Remember how I told you not to say anything? It wasn't just so Brandon wouldn't recognize you. It was so you couldn't ask me any questions."

Cole roars with laughter. "Well I'll be damned. Hal the hustler. Who ever thought you were such a stud?"

"Only those that needed to, sweetie," Helena replies with a lascivious grin, "though God knows, you both had your chance. Dorrie was in on the plan to get rid of Brandon. She and I both knew it would only work if he didn't recognize the man in drag who'd decked him earlier that day. The only way to be absolutely sure was to change my skin tone. This may be more detail than you want to hear, darlings, but Dorrie helped me with the spray-on tan. We had to go all the way, in case he got too frisky. *That* was a trip. I'll never forget that episode as long as I live. God love the old girl, she just got down to business without even blinking an eye."

Marc thinks back to the night Butch and Helena met. Until now, he'd never understood Dorrie's remark about the surprise in store for Butch. Marc looks at Cole in astonishment, obviously thinking the same thing, then they both struggle to contain their mirth.

"You know," Helena continues, "other than Dorrie, Butch is the only other person who knows what I really look like. The only man I've ever felt comfortable enough with to be myself. Wait 'til I tell him I can buy him a new fishing boat. A red one, I think. With a wet bar and a hot tub."

Lola and Dorrie's prank has hit its mark. After basking in her friends' incredulity for a while longer, Helena breaks the silence with characteristic flair, taking a silver tray with a bottle of champagne and three glasses from behind a bust of Shakespeare. "Darlings, before Lola died, she and Dorrie asked if I'd be willing to carry on the HomePort traditions and run the colony. When I said yes, they swore me to secrecy. That's when Dorrie told me she wanted champagne after her will was read, and I promised her we'd have it. I can't dig up a suitable toast, and I'm damned if I can find the right words after all this."

As Helena pops the cork and fills the glasses, Charlotte raises her teacup and signals for silence. "Actually, Dorrie never told me about their plans, but she made me promise to read these words as a toast. She wouldn't explain it, and I'll be damned if I understand the friggin' thing. For all I know, she might have been out of her tree when she wrote it. Anyways, here goes."

"Stop your weeping
And dry your eyes.
I'll say au revoir,
But not goodbye.
Get off your asses,
Then raise your glasses.
And drink a toast
To the geese that don't fly."

CHAPTER 18
FOR SHE'S A JOLLY GOOD FELLOW

It's the first ever "Welcome Tea" for HomePort fellows. The months since Dorrie's death have been consumed by evaluations, renovations, new construction, and faculty recruitment. Now the fellows are milling about in the front parlor with awed and confused looks on their young faces.

Helena stands in the hall, discussing last-minute details with the catering staff. She's dressed in a short blonde wig, a navy blue pantsuit with matching jacket, a white blouse, black pumps, and the pear-shaped, ten-carat diamond pendant with matching two-carat earrings.

Lola's breathtaking gems had appeared in Helena's jewelry box just the night before. With them was a note signed by Lola and Dorrie that read, "These diamonds are meant to be worn by the mistress of HomePort. That means you, Madame Director."

There are still bequests or hidden gifts like this popping up, as Lola and Dorrie's pranks continue from beyond the grave. Marc recently found a gold fountain pen inscribed with his name in the glove compartment of his car. He suspects Dolores, who inherited Dorrie's legacy from the captain, of planting bequests as part of some sort of postmortem conspiracy. He pictures her skulking about the grounds in a perfect disguise: dark glasses and a trench coat, her bald head covered by a slouch hat. Marc has chosen not to confront her. It's simply too wonderful to think of the gifts as coming from the dear old friends he still misses so much.

The grandfather's clock strikes four. Helena crosses the parlor to a podium between the portraits of Lola and Dorrie, and the guests meander to their seats. Once quiet descends on the room, Helena taps the microphone and begins to speak.

"Good afternoon trustees, members of the faculty, honored guests, ladies and gentlemen, and, most importantly, the first-ever HomePort fellows. On behalf of our late founders and the board of trustees, it is my profound pleasure to welcome the fellows to their one-year, all-expense-paid residency at the HomePort Colony. This is not your typical artist colony."

There are wide grins and some soft snickers.

"In fact, you could say it isn't typical of any colony in the solar system." Helena pauses for a moment, smiling broadly to reassure her audience she's in on the joke. "Sunday tea is a tradition of more than one hundred fifty years in this house, and, under the terms of your stipend, it is the sole obligation you have while in residence. The staff is circulating now to serve tea in honor of our founders. One word of caution about this long-held, HomePort tradition. If you are cautious about what you drink, choose the herbal. Now, before we acknowledge our benefactresses, are there any questions?"

The audience whispers for a moment before a young woman from the writer's program stands up. "I'm terribly sorry, Ms.," the young student pauses, seeming unsure how to address the poised professional woman at the podium.

Helena responds in an encouraging tone, "Handbasket,"

"Umm, yes. Ms. Handbasket."

"Call me Helena, dear."

"Uh… Helena," the student replies, as muffled laughter ripples through the room. "I think I speak for most of us when I say that now we're here we're even more confused about the intent of this program. Don't get me wrong, we're grateful for our stipends and accommodations, but some of us are still struggling to understand how the HomePort experience will help us achieve our artistic goals." Others nod as the student continues. "I've just completed an MFA program. Compared to that, HomePort seems more like a resort than an artist's colony. It looks as though we can do whatever we want, and you'll pay for it. What's that all about? I mean, how can that possibly help us become better artists and writers?"

Helena smiles and nods. "Thank you for your candor, Ms.…?" As she waits for an answer, the audience shuffles uncomfortably in their seats.

The young woman replies with an embarrassed stammer, "Hurtig—Jill Hurtig."

"Well, Jill, I am so grateful for your question, for it goes right to the heart of HomePort's mandate. Our founders," Helena says, pointing to the portraits of Lola and Dorrie, "left the bulk of their fortune to enhance the breadth, diversity, and meaning of the creative life. As self-taught women from a simpler age, they firmly believed experience to be the greatest of all teachers. Over the years, Provincetown has fostered a deep respect for the individual, offering and honoring seclusion or community as one saw fit. This unique town, to say nothing of HomePort's splendid isolation, had a marked impact on our founders' belief that one must, as they often said, chart one's own course. Despite difficult circumstances that might have fostered self-absorption and indifference, both women continued to learn and grow by doing just that.

"In the tradition of Provincetown's close-knit community, they shared what they learned. Dorrie Staunton was steadfast in her love and support for those cast aside by an uncaring world. Lola Staunton took active, if clandestine, interest in untold numbers of young artists and writers, providing the funds to fend off day-to-day intrusions and encourage the mystic forces that foster creativity.

"Perhaps HomePort's remote location was an incubator for these firmly held beliefs. Whatever the reason, the two sisters grew convinced that life experiences and the time to reflect upon them were the missing ingredients in today's creative endeavors. Their fervent wish is that you choose whatever you need to further your artistic growth without concern for time or money.

"Inspiration has many sources: the beauty of nature, the hard-edged realities of today's uncertain world, or liberating travel in a foreign land, to name but a few. Introspection, freedom, and most of all, time for oneself are what these activities have in common. You've already demonstrated your talent and craft; use the gift of this year to nurture your spirit and do whatever you need to develop your unique artistic voice."

Helena points to the portraits a second time. "Some of us in this room were mentored by these two incredible women. I speak for them as well when I say your time here is an opportunity that will bear fruit for the rest of your days. Ensuring you have all you need is a sacred trust. As your director, I pledge to do everything in my power to help you find that special place inside from which great art comes.

"Our review committee read more than three thousand applications to select the thirty of you who join us today. We're confident you have what it takes to move to the next level as creative, innovative artists. We believe you have the drive and determination to make best use of our offerings, and wouldn't have invited you here if we weren't certain. So relax, settle in, and let HomePort—and Provincetown— work their magic. Any further questions?"

There is absolute silence. Several heads nod. Cole and Marc look at each other with surprise. "Who knew?" Marc whispers.

Cole grins with pride. "Lola and Dorrie, that's for damn sure. None of us could have given a better answer than that. I wasn't sure Helena could pull all this off, but I am now."

Helena raises her cup and turning yet again toward the two portraits that stare down at her as if in approval. "Then, I give you our founders."

Charlotte, Cole, and Marc, seated in the front row, stand and raise their cups. Their faces are taut, their bodies tense, as they try to contain powerful emotions. With Helena's explanation of Lola and Dorrie's vision, the work is done. The rest of the audience rises, seeming to sense a poignant moment they only partially comprehend.

"To Lola Staunton and Dorrie Machado Staunton," Helena says, raising her cup and downing her tea in a single gulp.

Some in the audience follow suit. The sounds of choking and laughter fill the room as the guests realize what they're drinking. Lola's gag works as well as it had the very first time Marc came to tea. The fellows and trustees turn to each other with wide smiles as all pretense flees the room.

The party is off to a great start under Lola and Dorrie's benevolent gaze. Helena steps down from the podium and is immediately surrounded by eager, questioning fellows.

CHAPTER 19
STAUNTON'S LOOKOUT

August 31ˢᵗ, 2014 - Logan Airport

Back in the States at last after an amazing honeymoon. Cape Air willing, we'll be home in an hour. I can't wait to see how the house turned out. I still can't believe that Lola and Dorrie left us part of the grounds and the money to build our own home. How did they ever know how much we wanted to stay on? God I still miss those two old gals.

I can't wait to see how Charlotte's twins have grown. Those two girls have stolen my heart, just as their namesakes before them. I couldn't take the diapers and feeding full time, but I'm surprised how much I missed the little tykes. Who'd have thought?

* * * *

Charlotte is peering out from an upstairs window as the taxi turns into the drive. Frida, who had been stretched out in the sun, spies the two men and bounds toward them. In no time, she reaches Cole. As he bends down to pat her, she plants her paws on his shoulders and licks his face. After a moment, Marc receives a similar greeting.

"Welcome back! I've missed you guys," Charlotte shouts, drawing near. "It figures you two queens would come home to a brand new house, just like the friggin' Berwinds in Newport." She throws her arms around Marc and Cole who stare in pride at the building nestled amidst beech trees atop the highest ground on the HomePort estate.

"A honeymoon around the world while I'm up all night changing diapers," Charlotte says with mock severity. "My *au pair* left me in the lurch and ran off to Sophia with a Bulgarian waiter. It's another three weeks before the new one arrives. I'm warning you now, don't mess with me. I'm down to my last nerve."

It's immediately clear Charlotte hasn't hit her stride as a fulltime mother. Her impeccable fashion sense has given way to a more utilitarian wardrobe: a pair of jeans with a slight tear at the knee, a sweatshirt emblazoned with *Bear Week 2010,* and, most telling of all, plain, white sneakers. Her eyes look tired, but she radiates the same energy as always. There's a trace of spit-up on her left shoulder.

"How was Bora Bora? As romantic as they say? And not even a friggin' postcard from there? Surely you sex-crazed maniacs could have taken a breather to write one postcard."

She pouts for a moment before prattling on, sounding more than slightly envious of their freedom. "The house is amazing. I hadn't seen the finished product until last week. Helena and Butch kept it under wraps until it was furnished. Butch did an astounding job overseeing the work, and wait until you see Helena's décor! And the views!"

Marc is unable to hide his satisfaction with what he's already seen. "Well, the studio and garage were complete before we moved out of Dorrie's house so it could be renovated. Cole wouldn't even schedule his classes in Paris until his studio was completed. When he said he'd take care of everything, he really meant it. I haven't seen anything until now, though I did get a written promise from Helena not to do it in 'early brothel.'"

Cole chimes in. "Thank God for e-mail and Skype. I'd have been a wreck if I couldn't see the progress. Ever since I worked with my uncle, I've always wanted to design my own home." As Cole stares up at his creation, his eyes grow moist.

Marc puts an arm around him, then turns to Charlotte. "How are things with the Staunton, or should I say Grubb holdings in New York?"

"I've renamed it the HomePort Block. I can't believe they left that gold mine to me, on friggin' Madison Avenue, no less. But I have some other important news."

"What?" Marc asks.

"It's Brandon."

"What about Brandon?"

"Well, I've been keeping this quiet in case things turned out badly, but he showed up in my office about a month ago."

Cole's features darken. "What did *he* want?"

"To say thank you," Charlotte replies with the slightest trace of amusement.

"For what?" By now, Cole has clenched his fists.

"For using the money Alan and Chuck forfeited to pay for his rehab. The judge ordered court-supervised rehabilitation, and I used the money from the settlement to see to it Brandon got the best care possible."

Marc's jaw drops. "You did what?"

Charlotte seems quite pleased with herself. "And I hope you don't mind. I told him about your marriage. He sends you his sincere best wishes."

Marc feels an overwhelming sense of relief. "I'll be damned."

Helena, who has just arrived crossed the driveway from HomePort, taps her foot with impatience. "Okay, my turn. Did Brandon have any message for me? I suppose not."

Marc hums, "Is That All There Is?"

Helena grins, then punches him in the shoulder. "Welcome home, darlings. Get over here. Momma's missed her boys."

Marc and Cole are smothered in an all-encompassing hug. After a moment to catch up on each other's news, the four friends link arms and walk to greet Butch, Brad, and the twins. Frida leads the way to Marc and Cole's new home, frequently turning back to be certain they are following her.

Once inside, the tour begins. The house, a spacious contemporary whose large sunlit rooms are filled with exquisite art and furnishings, seems to have a special connection with its surroundings. The mottled light filtering through the beech trees makes the structure seem as if it had been there for years.

The tour culminates in Marc's third floor study, with its panoramic views of the harbor, Cape Cod Bay, and the Atlantic. Entering the room, he's astonished to see the captain's desk in front of a large picture window.

Helena seems to enjoy the stunned look on his face. "It's yours for life. I made a request of myself as executive director and agreed to a loan."

Marc runs his hand over the back of a carved chair, then surveys the elegant space with its oak bookcases and comfortable furniture. A larger replica of the interior of HomePort's tower, the room has the same qualities of isolation and separation as the original. The varnished wood, brass fittings, and mounted telescope invoke the impression of a ship at sea.

Paintings Cole has secretly produced to augment the stunning views bring cozy warmth to the space. There's one of Lola and Dorrie seated beside each other in the study. Somehow, Cole has captured the loving look Marc often saw when he spoke with them alone. The captain's journals are in a bookcase behind them, each of the twenty volumes delicately numbered in gold. On another wall is a portrait similar to the one Marc had once destroyed. He moves close to the painting and studies it in detail.

"What's this, Cole?" he asks.

The new portrait is larger than the original. Marc's features are less idealized, though they bear the same thoughtful, confident gaze. The background is that of the new room, not the tower at HomePort. Marc tries to imagine how Cole could have envisioned it before the room was built, for he must have painted the portrait before they left on their honeymoon.

"Do you know this guy?" Cole asks, with a trace of anxiety in his voice.

"Yeah, I do. He seems more real to me than the other one."

"Did you ever think you've grown into his shoes? I used the damaged painting as a study for this one, and I don't see that many changes."

"I see lots of similarities. But there's something different I just can't put my finger on. I'm more comfortable with this one for some reason."

Cole smiles his crooked grin and leaves it at that.

Beguiled by anticipation and memory, Marc steps onto the ample deck that encircles the room. He stares across to HomePort. It seems strange to be looking down at its tower from the place where he is to write from now on. *If I can. Now the captain's desk is here. Talk about extra pressure. All this space created and decorated just for me to write in, and I don't know if I even—*

Then he hears a familiar voice utter a single word: *"Bullshit."* Marc smiles at Dorrie's presence, shakes his head, wipes away a tear, and continues to survey the grounds, this time with pride.

The colony is bursting with activity. Two faculty members descend from the Bates Motel in animated conversation. At Dorrie's former home, four bicycles lean against a new, split-rail fence while a group sits at a picnic table in the backyard, manuscripts spread in front of them. Near Commercial Street, the foundation for the Staunton Memorial Museum rises from the ground.

Marc sees signs of Helena's stewardship everywhere. HomePort has never looked better, or more alive. The estate, with its studios secreted in the woods, restored gardens, and nature trails, buzzes with creative energy. Marc spots a young man editing a manuscript on the balcony in front of Marvin's old apartment and feels a twinge of competition. Even with all that Marc has been given, that process is still the same—with every word he writes, he's putting himself on the line. He silently salutes a comrade-in-arms and wishes the young man well.

There's a lot to be excited about, Marc tells himself, trying to overcome a tinge of melancholy. *Yet the HomePort I knew is slipping away. It belongs to the world now and can never again be the magical place it once was for me: a place of sanctuary, mystery, and second chances. HomePort is no longer a home, it's an institution, and will never, ever, be the same. I can't feel it anymore.*

Cole strolls onto the deck. He studies Marc for a few minutes as he stands staring moodily at HomePort's tower.

"I'll be right back," Cole says, lightly kissing Marc's cheek. Marc watches as Cole takes Charlotte by the arm and escorts her onto the deck.

"Now, Charlotte," Cole says with urgency. "Now. This is the right time."

Charlotte studies Marc's face, then nods and walks inside to speak with Helena. When Charlotte whispers in her ear, Helena nods as well.

"Brad, Butch, you guys take care of Lola and Dorrie. They've been fed and should be ready for a nap," Charlotte says in a tone that leaves no room for contradiction. "Come with us, Marc. Right now."

Marc smiles at the hapless look on Butch's face. It's clear the kids are not ready for a nap, but there's no arguing with Charlotte. Butch reaches down and picks up young Dorrie. She begins to scream. When young Lola starts to wail as well, Brad steps in to calm her. Marc accelerates his gait, feeling only slightly sleazy for making a clean getaway.

Voices from the Past

Cole, Charlotte, Helena, and Marc pass a group of fellows playing volleyball, then climb the granite steps to HomePort's front porch. When Marc and Cole study their new home from that vantage point, it blends so well into the landscape it can barely be seen.

Once inside the mansion, the friends enter the parlor to pay homage to Lola and Dorrie. After a few minutes of silent contemplation, the group ambles down the hall, past the grandfather's clock to the captain's study. As Helena stops to speak to a student writing in the mistress's parlor, Charlotte unlocks the door to the room where Lola and Dorrie both breathed their last.

The bed and wardrobe are gone. A replacement for the captain's desk stands in place of the original. The paintings spared Cole's wrath are hanging where they were when Lola first spoke of them. Cole and Charlotte watch closely as Marc, recalling all that happened in this room, reacquaints himself with its contents. He pauses by the bookcase, where all twenty of the captain's journals still sit on their shelf.

"I thought the Historical Society was going to take these. Why haven't they come for them? Are they waiting for the museum to be finished? Does anyone know?"

"Yes," Charlotte says softly, "I do. Days after Dorrie died, I got a strongly worded codicil stating that they could not leave the house until a specific, unnamed task was completed. On the anniversary of Lola's death, I received a bequest detailing the task with a charge to all of us but you, Marc. We were to inform you of your duties whenever we saw fit, but only after your new home was built. We've all just consulted, and we think now is the perfect time."

Helena steps through the doorway at that moment, her brown eyes brimming. "Marc, I think Lola and Dorrie knew when HomePort transitioned from a home to an artists' colony, it would be bittersweet for all of us. The presents and bequests were delivered over time in order to keep us focused. Those two gals sure knew what they were doing, giving us little projects and incentives to keep us energized.

"There's one final task, though. You are the only person who can possibly take it on. It was so important to Lola and

Dorrie that the captain's journals are not allowed to leave this room until you complete it."

Charlotte approaches the desk, takes a small key from a secret compartment, opens the bookcase, and extracts the twentieth journal. She hands it to Cole.

"This is their final bequest," Cole says, handing his husband the volume. "I don't have to tell you how much it means to the old girls. They'll do that for themselves."

Marc opens the gilt-edged book. On the first page, in Lola's spidery hand, he reads,

Dearest Marc,

Since you came to HomePort, you've shown such love for the place and done so many kind things for me that I can never adequately express my gratitude. Already owing you so much, I have one last favor to ask as the days of the Stauntons draw to a close. You once spoke of writing about my family. The story of your days at HomePort is a far more fitting remembrance than any Staunton biography. This is the story—the story of my real family—that I wish you to tell, for you are the only one who can.

If you are reading this, the Staunton legacy is complete. If you decide to take on the project, please humor me, Marc, and use this, Father's last journal, to write it. I love the idea of you rounding out the set, and who knows, someday the whole oeuvre might be published.

Finish my father's work, dear boy. Tell the world of our family—the one we created out of love and kindness. Tell the true story, not the fantasy I sustained for so long until you took the blinders from my eyes. I rely on you to make an honest woman of me, Marc. For my sake and in the name of truth, spare no gory detail. Share our story with the world and accomplish all my fabrications failed to do. I know you are capable, and pray you will use your gifts to redeem the Staunton name.

With my eternal love,

Lola

P.S. Would you consider calling your new home "Staunton's Lookout?" It only seems fitting, and I'd be so honored.

Cole, Helena, and Charlotte watch Marc closely as he struggles with what he's just read. From beyond the grave, he's received a request to do something that has eluded him for years. He sighs, turning inward, feeling a sense of inadequacy he thought he'd outgrown.

Cole takes the journal from his hand. "Marc, it's a request, not a command. You don't have to do it. The worst that will happen is that the journals will stay here in the house."

"Lola just suggested it. You don't have to decide right away," Helena adds. "Although I do think there's a story to be told. It only seems right that everything that has happened here not just fade away into history. But far be it for me to insist. Why don't you see what Dorrie has to say?"

Helena hands him a letter written in Dorrie's unmistakable scrawl:

Dear Marc,

You know me. I always have to have the last word. Lola helped me with some of the language but trust me, the thoughts are all mine.

First, thanks for being my friend, and for all you did to bring me happiness in my final years. I had a good last act thanks to you and the rest of the gang.

Second, enjoy your new home. You were always meant to be there. I saw that in my mind's eye the day you first shook my hand. HomePort knew the day you moved in that you'd build a home of your own here and be the next generation to live here in this magical spot. I felt the old place welcome you like no other

Third, fill your new home with beauty, love, friendship, and family. Make it the new HomePort, Marc, where Helena, Charlotte, and their loved ones can gather as a family as we all did for those last, wonderful months. After all, as you know better than most, a house just ain't a home until there's love in it. You can feel the difference. If kids come along, be sure to tell them of their two grandmothers who lovingly watch over them and their dads every single day.

And one more thing. Trust Cole, always. He knows you so well and loves you so much. He's always wanted you to reach your full potential, even way back when he was just realizing his feelings for you. He once told me about your getting hung up on first sentences, wondering if there was a way he could help you get past it. That's when I first knew for sure just how much he cared.

When Lola came up with the idea you should write our story, I knew you'd fart around for years over a perfect beginning or get so bent out of shape you'd do jack shit. (Lola says I should use more ladylike language, but why start at this late date? This way you're sure to know exactly what I mean.) Anyways, I knew if I were still around you'd be at my kitchen table night after night bitching and moaning about how you weren't making any progress on the book. Even though I'm gone, I have something to say about that. Does that come as any great surprise?

Listen to me, Marc. Whatever you do is up to you. All I'm asking is that before you decide you can't do this, you think about just how lonely and adrift we all were until we found each other. Think of someone like yourself growing up out in the sticks who just might need to learn that love comes in all different flavors, that friendship can span decades, and that a place like Provincetown can be a refuge when the rest of the world remains ignorant and cruel.

Who better than you to tell them from your own experience? It wouldn't be a bad thing for you to sort through everything that happened since you moved here. I bet by writing things down, you'd find out a few things about yourself that you never realized. To me, that seems damn good reason enough to write a book.

I could never tell the whole story, but I know you can, so I decided to whip up an opener to tempt you—to get the ball rolling, you might say. Here it is. "You never really know a place unless you live there." It's nothing profound, but you can go anywhere from there.

I was blessed to live my entire life in a town others merely dream of visiting. It's taken me a lifetime to figure it all out, but I can finally say I know the place at last. I just couldn't have been me anywhere else. Nor could you. I think that applies to most of us who were born here, and so many others over the centuries who found Provincetown when they needed it most. The place grabbed hold of their hearts. I know that happened to you. I saw it.

Try not to get hung up like you usually do, Marc. You've got your first sentence. The rest is up to you. Don't second-guess yourself. Just sit your ass down and write the goddamn book. If you decide not to, that's okay, too. But if you give it a try, I promise I'll be looking over your shoulder whenever you hit a rough spot.

With eternal love from your ever-grateful friend,
Dorrie Machado Staunton

CHAPTER 20
THE TWENTIETH JOURNAL

September 1, 2014 – Staunton's Lookout

You never really know a place unless you live there. Until last night, Provincetown was a state of mind—a place that spoke to my heart....

THE END

ACKNOWLEDGEMENTS

Special thanks to my wise and steadfast agent, Malaga Baldi, my publisher Ethan Day, my editor Jerry Wheeler, my gifted illustrator, Madeline Sorel, creative wizard Adrian Nicholas and all the other dedicated folks at Wilde City Press. I am also deeply indebted to James Carson, Maggie Cadman, and Cheri Johnson for their wisdom and encouragement.

To "The Nepenthe Crew"—Ed and Colin—thanks for your patience, endurance, and unfaltering support through uncharted waters. To Mother, Gram, and Dad, you are as much a part of this story as you are of me. To my amazing sister, Vee, what is there to say but, "Wouldn't it be a dull world…."

To my early P'Town readers, Marge and Elaine, Bob and Jeff, Liz, Nancy, Kerry, Roger, and most especially Tim, I offer my heartfelt thanks for your time and insight. To Bill, Bob and Maria, Tony, Terese, David, Janice, and Eli, I thank you for the pep talks, the dinners, the drinks, and most of all, the laughs.

To the wonderful, wacky, denizens of Provincetown—especially the dearly departed Ellie, Bea, Jean, and Kathleen—I am honored to have shared this unique bit of sand with you. When I found P'Town, I found home.

And last but far from least, to Jayne, who saved my life, "Thanks, Dahlin'. I had the steak…."

TRADEMARK ACKNOWLEDGEMENT

The author acknowledges the trademark status and trademark owners of the following places and items mentioned in this work of fiction:

Michelin – Michelin North America

Fortnum & Mason – Fortnum & Mason, PLC

Citicorp – Citicorp Corporation

Champagne Joseph Perrier – La Maison Joseph Perrier

Jeep Wrangler – Chrysler Group, LLC

CSI: Crime Scene Investigation – CBS Broadcasting Co.

iPhone – Apple, Inc.

Queen Mary – City of Long Beach Municipal Corporation

Vinho Verde – Comissao de Viticultura Da Regiao dos Vinhos Verdes Associacao

Page Six – NYP Holdings

The Wizard of Oz – Turner Entertainment Co.

A.C. BURCH

A.C. Burch spent his early summers on Cape Cod and since then, the sand has never left his shoes. His first visit to Provincetown sparked a romance with the town and forged a love of the sea that continues to this day. A.C. trained as a classical musician, but his passion for the arts extends to photography, the art scene in Provincetown and Miami, and, of course, the written word. His literary icons run the gamut from Jane Austen to Agatha Christie by way of Walter Mosely and Patrick Dennis.

Since 1987, A.C. has lived in Provincetown—since 1997, in an old house with views of Provincetown Harbor. He frequently channels "Little Edie" Beale in moments of domestic desperation and can sometimes be seen gardening with the same level of success. When not splitting wood for his vintage wood stove, A.C. splits his time between Provincetown and South Beach.